COMPULSION

Also by Shaun Hutson

SLUGS
SPAWN
EREBUS
SHADOWS
BREEDING GROUND
DEATH DAY
RELICS
VICTIMS
ASSASSIN
NEMESIS
RENEGADES
CAPTIVES
HEATHEN
DEADHEAD
WHITE GHOST
LUCY'S CHILD
STOLEN ANGELS
KNIFE EDGE
PURITY
WARHOL'S PROPHECY
EXIT WOUNDS

SHAUN HUTSON

COMPULSION

MACMILLAN

First published 2001 by Macmillan
an imprint of Macmillan Publishers Ltd
25 Eccleston Place, London SW1W 9NF
Basingstoke and Oxford
Associated companies throughout the world
www.macmillan.com

ISBN 0 333 73723 7

3 5 7 9 8 6 4

A CIP catalogue record for this book is available from
the British Library.

Typeset by SetSystems Ltd, Saffron Walden, Essex
Printed and bound in Great Britain by
Mackays of Chatham plc, Chatham, Kent

This book is dedicated to
Graeme Sayer and Callum Hughes

With thanks

ACKNOWLEDGEMENTS

IT'S THAT TIME again, when I thank a wide ranging, unconnected group of people and places for some kind of support, help, encouragement or drugs (oops, sorry, didn't mean that to slip out . . .) received during the writing of this latest novel.

Anyway, if you're in this list you'll probably know why but, in case you've forgotten why you're in it then read on.

Many thanks to my agent, Sara Fisher for her skill, expertise and ability to handle even the most fragile egos. She's just not too good when she's stepping off tube trains . . .

Continued thanks to everyone at my publisher's, especially Peter Lavery. Also to Matt Smith.

I don't usually give him a line on his own but my accountant, Mr Peter Nichols, deserves one. I'd give him a bloody knighthood if I could . . . Cheers, Pete.

Special thanks also to Jack Taylor, Tom Sharp, Barbara Grant, Karen (yes, look, you're mentioned . . .) and Jim at the Clydesdale bank in Piccadilly.

Thanks also to Lesley Tebbs, Lewis Bloch and Stephen Luckman.

My usual nods towards Dee, Zena, Nicky, Jo, Terri, Becky and Rachel. Thanks also to Janette for sorting out our computer.

Special thanks to Sanctuary Music. Rod Smallwood who frightened *me* to death with a phone call. To Polly Polglase. To Carol and Val. To my ever elusive, cheese-making, pig-breeding collossus of a friend, Wally Grove. Also to Steve, Dave, Adrian, Bruce, Janick and Nicko. As great as ever.

ACKNOWLEDGEMENTS

Many thanks to James Whale and Ash.

Many, many thanks to Martin 'gooner' Phillips for organising a football match I'm sure none of us will ever forget (my bloody legs still ache . . .). I think we all turned back the clock that afternoon, mate.

Special thanks to Hailey Owen. Christ knows where you are H, but wherever it is, I'm sure you're talking . . . See you soon. Many thanks also to Tori at Centurion card.

Thanks once more to Ted and Molly.

Indirect thanks, as ever, to Sam Peckinpah. Also to Bill Hicks. Both sadly missed.

Thank you to Nike football boots, even if it is just to remind me that I'm not nineteen anymore. I would have got that return pass then, honest . . . And also to Konami for inventing the best footie game ever to grace a Playstation. Mental blocks get eased *that* way nowadays.

As ever, thank you to the Rhiga Royal Hotel in New York and to Margaret in Lindy's in Times Square. We shall return.

A quick thanks to Cineworld in Milton Keynes where I now seem to spend most of my waking hours. Look, sixteen screens what the hell can I do?

Huge thanks to Liverpool Football Club and all those in the Paisley Lounge. Steve 'househusband' (and bloody student) Lucas and Paul 'just aim for the AA van' Garner. Also thanks to Aaron Reynolds, when he's not on holiday, and to Simon Whitfield who's had me in more headlocks in a season than I care to remember. I'll send you a receipt. Cheers to all of you.

I'm now, at long last, the proud and confused owner of a PC which means people can now annoy me via e-mail as well as phone and fax. However, for those of you who are computer literate (to me that means being able to switch the bloody thing on . . .) you will find, thanks to the incredible efforts of Graeme Sayer and Callum Hughes, a quite superb web site dedicated to all things Hutson. I read it every now and then to find out what I'm doing.

ACKNOWLEDGEMENTS

Check out *www.shaunhutson.com*

It's official and they've done a brilliant job on it. Thanks fellas.

The last few thank yous go to my mum and dad. I wish there was an adequate way of thanking them for everything they've done and continue to do but there isn't.

The same goes for my wife, Belinda. She organizes me, sorts out my financial stuff, calms me down and generally tolerates the kind of behaviour that would have had Mother Theresa looking for a pick-axe handle . . . What the hell, the only thing she *doesn't* do is write the books . . . I *am* because she *is*. Keep your *eye* on that Mazda, babe, because you won't get your *hands* on it . . . (unless it's tax deductible).

Finally, as ever, the other girl in my life. The apprentice cinema addict, trainee rock music junkie, fledgeling Liverpool fan and fully paid up member of the GLADIATOR appreciation society. My beautiful, wonderful, daughter. One day, all of this will be for you.

The last thank you is for you lot. My readers. Without you there would really be very little point to any of this. For your continued support I humbly thank you.

Let's go.

Shaun Hutson

Though this may be play to you, 'tis death to us.

Sir Roger L'Estrange

1

THEY MOVED EASILY in the darkness.

Three shapes: shadows within shadow, portions of the umbra that had taken on life and detached themselves from the blanket of night wrapped tightly around them.

Every so often the cutting edge of a torch beam would slice open the gloom, illuminating an object inside the house, sometimes lighting one of the three faces.

When the beam pinpointed their features, they looked like phantoms. Fugitives from an unwanted dream.

Two of them ravaged the ground floor of the house, stuffing cassettes into a bin bag.

Manic Street Preachers. Blur. Oasis.

The usual shit.

Simply Red – a foot crushed it contemptuously.

Videos were snatched from a shelf: *End of Days. Fight Club. The Blair Witch Project. 8mm.*

They all went into the bag.

Titanic – crushed underfoot.

The third figure ventured up the narrow staircase to the bedrooms.

Three doors. All closed.

The dark shape crossed the landing and pushed the first one open.

Beyond was a small room.

Posters on the wall: Boyzone. Steps. B*witched.

As talented as the paper they were grinning out from, the figure mused.

There was a large stuffed dog on the bed. The figure crossed to it and shook it, then tossed it aside.

Drawers were checked, skirts and T-shirts pulled out, scattered across the room.

Leggings, jeans, socks and knickers were also hurled aside with the other belongings.

There were some earrings on the dressing table.

Worthless.

The figure moved to the next room; it was slightly larger.

More posters. Above the bed was one of Manchester United.

The figure hawked loudly and spat on the picture. Thick sputum trickled down the faces of David Beckham and Roy Keane.

Cunts.

A small CD player was pushed into the black bag. It was joined by a Dreamcast console. Better pickings here.

On to the last room. There were lots of books – all swept onto the floor and trodden underfoot.

More drawers wrenched open, more clothes hurled around. The figure hesitated, then picked up a pair of knickers. Soft, white cotton. Fingers trailed over the gusset.

Nothing else worth having.

The shape stood on the bed, unzipped grubby combat trousers and urinated onto the duvet.

Downstairs, the other two were waiting.

All three of them left the same way they had entered; through a small window in the kitchen at the rear of the house. There were pieces of broken glass on the window sill, inside and out.

They made their way towards the bottom of the garden, swallowed up by the welcoming night.

It was an easy climb over the fence into the field.

They walked unhurriedly through the tall grass, dragging the dustbin bag.

Behind them, the house remained silent.

2

Carl Thompson drew gently on the cigarette, then blew out a stream of bluish-grey smoke. It mingled with the steadily swelling cloud already hanging in the flat.

The smell helped to mask the odour of damp that permeated the air inside the abandoned dwelling.

'Give us a light,' Graham Brown murmured, leaning closer to his companion.

Thompson complied and Brown sucked heavily on the Super-king.

At fourteen, Brown was two years Thompson's junior. Dressed in a dark blue Reebok jacket, combats and a pair of Nike trainers, he sat cross-legged on the bare floor of the flat like some kind of emaciated Buddha.

His skin had already suffered the first onslaught of pubescent acne; spots clustered on his cheeks, chin and forehead like a virulent rash. The redness was a marked contrast to the pallor of his flesh. Here and there hardened crusts of blood had formed, the result of Brown's insistence on picking the heads from the most troublesome of the blemishes.

Opposite him, Donna Freeman was glancing through the contents of the plastic bin bags they had filled during the burglary.

She was the same age as Brown. Dishwater blonde. Eyes sunken into the sockets. Red rimmed, as if someone had sketched around the orbs with a blood-stained pencil.

Her bulky clothes disguised the still-forming contours of her body.

She scratched at the crook of one arm.

Donna took a drag on the Silk Cut and regarded the haul disinterestedly.

Dressed in a black Tommy Hilfiger sweatshirt and dark grey fleece, she seemed to blend into the gloom. Tight black jeans hugged her legs, tucked into dark brown Caterpillar boots. The toes were scuffed and the leather looked as if it hadn't tasted polish for several months.

'Not much, is it?' she observed.

Thompson shrugged. 'Thirty quids' worth,' he said flatly, running a hand through his tousled hair. He then replaced the Nike baseball cap, toying with the brim.

Like his companions, he was dressed in designer clothes, all of which looked as if they were in dire need of a wash.

His face seemed to have escaped the worst ravages of overactive sebacious glands. No spots. No pock-marks. His skin, yet to feel the touch of a razor, was smooth. His eyes were dark, but alert.

He picked at some mud stuck to the sole of his Air Jordans. As it came free he rolled it between his fingers and tossed it in the direction of the far wall.

There were other things there, covered by sheets of clear polythene: portable TVs; video recorders; a DVD player and some discs; three computers; Playstations; Dreamcast consoles.

You name it, they had it.

Only Thompson, Donna and Brown had access to the flat. If anything went missing, each knew who was responsible. They decided what was sold – who to and for how much.

Final word went to Thompson.

A mark of respect.

Of seniority.

Of fear?

'Tenner each, then?' Brown asked, getting to his feet, the knickers slipping from his pocket.

Thompson nodded.

'I'm going home,' Brown told them.

'Don't forget your trophy.' Donna smiled, holding the knickers up.

'Cunt,' he grunted and snatched them from her. Then added, turning to Thompson again: 'Call me tomorrow, yeah?'

Thompson nodded and pulled open his jacket, tapping the mobile phone clipped to his belt.

Brown pulled open the door.

'Enjoy yourself, Graham,' Donna called. She made a fist of her right hand and shook it up and down.

'Why don't you do it for me, cunt?'

'I haven't got two minutes to spare.'

He slammed the door behind him. They heard his footsteps on the stone stairs.

'You going home?' Donna asked.

'Soon,' Thompson told her.

'See you tomorrow.'

He nodded, looking past her towards the piles of stolen goods.

Donna hesitated. 'Will your dad be home?' she asked.

'Who cares?' Thompson murmured, grinding out his cigarette on the floor.

She waited a moment longer, then walked out, leaving him alone.

He glanced at his watch: 12.47 a.m.

It was less than ten minutes walk to his home.

He decided to wait a little longer.

Perhaps the bastard would be asleep when he got in.

Perhaps.

3

GRAHAM BROWN LET himself in, paused a second in the hallway, then closed the front door.

From the sitting room he could hear the sound of the TV. Someone was still up.

He wandered into the small living room, almost tripping over a large doll that had most of its hair missing.

One half-open eye fixed him in a glassy stare.

Brown kicked at the object irritably.

Slumped in one armchair was his father, snoring loudly.

On the sofa, his mother lay with a thick cardigan on her feet to ward off the chill. The gas fire had been broken for as long as he could remember.

Brown crossed to his father and looked down at the sleeping man: his mouth was open wide, his head lolled back.

The remote for the TV was still clasped in one of his large hands.

As Brown prized it free, he saw that there were a couple of grazes on the knuckles of the man's right hand.

He flicked channels.

Fuck all on. Never was.

He glanced at his mother.

There was a red mark beneath her left eye, already beginning to turn a livid purple.

He saw several spots of blood on her lower lip.

Brown looked at his parents indifferently for a moment, then passed into the kitchen.

Plates were stacked both on the kitchen table and the draining board. Some had been washed, others still bore the remains of food.

The grey water in the washing-up bowl was freezing cold.

A mug handle protruded from the reeking liquid.

He took a glass from a cupboard and poured himself some milk from the fridge. It tasted slightly sour and he checked the date stamp on the carton.

'Cunt,' he hissed.

He drank it anyway, then left the dirty glass in the sink.

As he made his way back through the living room he paused and picked up the remote once more. He eased the volume up several notches, then tossed the device away and went upstairs.

The door of his sisters' room was open.

One of the girls was asleep on the top bunk, dreaming the dreams of any other nine year old. The eight year old was sitting on the floor undressing a Barbie that had one arm missing.

She looked up at him as he passed, heading towards his parents' room.

He found his mother's handbag on her bedside table.

Brown undid it swiftly and pulled out her purse, peering inside: a couple of used scratchcards; an old and useless lottery ticket; two fives and a ten.

He grinned and took the tenner, tucking it into his pocket. Then he replaced the purse and headed for his bedroom.

As he undressed he could still hear the sound of the TV blaring away downstairs.

He pulled the knickers from his pocket, sniffing at the gusset.

He slid them beneath his pillow.

4

She had no idea how long the baby had been crying.

Half an hour?

Longer?

Donna lay on her bed in a T-shirt, puffing away at the cigarette, the cacophony rattling inside her ears.

She took a drag on her cigarette. With her other hand she pulled gently at the small silver nose-ring in her right nostril.

It could be linked, if she wished, to any of the five earrings in her left ear or the three in her right.

She slid her hand up beneath her T-shirt and touched the ring in her navel. It still felt tender and would do for another few days. She had to remember to keep turning the ring in case the flesh healed around it.

'Shut the fucking kid up, will you?'

The voice tore through the darkness.

Her father.

'*You* shut him up.'

Her mother.

'Fuck sake! What's wrong with him?'

'He probably wants feeding.'

'Then fucking *feed* him!'

'You go and do his bottle, then, you lazy cunt. I've had him all day.'

The baby was still crying.

'Fucking change him too, he stinks. That's probably what he's crying about.'

'*You* fucking stink, you bastard.'

There was a new sound.

A hollow banging on the wall.

'That's that old cunt next door,' her father rasped. 'He's woken her up now.'

More banging on the wall.

'Fuck off, you old bitch!' her father roared.

He banged back.

She heard movement on the landing.

'Just get the bottle!' her mother bellowed.

More hollow banging from next door.

'I'll fucking kill that old cunt, I'm telling you,' he snarled.

She heard his heavy footfalls on the stairs, heard him blundering around in the kitchen.

In the next room, the baby was still crying.

The banging on the wall continued.

Donna swung herself off the bed and crossed to the wardrobe. One of the panels was cracked. The wood looked rotten.

The lock was new.

She had put it there herself.

She retrieved the key from her bedside table and unlocked it, rummaging among the boots, shoes and trainers there.

She finally took out a small box wrapped in a piece of velvet. Oblivious to the noises all around, she opened it and reached inside.

Her hand was steady as she held the hypodermic needle up for inspection.

The rest of the stuff was inside the box. The blackened, twisted spoon. The length of rubber tubing.

And the gear itself.

She put down the needle for a moment and fastened the tubing tightly around the top of her arm.

As she extended the limb she saw the heavy bruising inside its crook. Several track marks had already scabbed over.

There were two or three more between the toes of her left foot.

She pulled hard on the rubber tubing, simultaneously slapping at her arm to raise the veins.

They pulsed like tumescent worms beneath her pale flesh.

'Fucking shut it!' screamed her mother from the next room.

The banging on the wall came again.

The baby continued to cry.

Donna reached for the needle.

5

CARL THOMPSON DIDN'T recognise the woman; then again, there had been so many of them, why should he?

He rarely asked their names.

What difference did it make?

Since his mother had walked out when he was six, there had always been women around the house. Sometimes for months at a time, sometimes just for the odd night here and there.

They never stayed.

Just came and went, dropped from a never-ending conveyor belt.

A cunt conveyor belt.

There was obviously something about his father that women found attractive, but Thompson was fucked if *he* knew what it was.

Blondes. Brunettes. Redheads.

All colours. All kinds.

One had stayed for a month. Moved in with most of her stuff. She'd cooked and cleaned for them both

(*what was her name?*)

until his father had tired of her.

She'd packed her clothes again and moved out.

Alice? Alison?

He sucked on his cigarette and gazed at the contorted face of the woman in his father's bedroom.

He had a clear view of the entire room through the hole he'd chiselled in the wall.

Both she and his father were naked, sheathed in sweat. The woman's dark hair was hanging down in matted strands like serpents' tails. She was gripping the duvet with both hands as Thompson's father held tightly to her hips and slammed his penis into her.

Every now and then she would look over her shoulder at him.

At the veins bulging in his neck and temples.

At the clenched teeth.

Words were exchanged, but Thompson couldn't hear them properly. They communicated mainly by grunts and sighs that obviously meant something to *them*.

The woman was gritting her teeth now, her back arched. She reached back between her own legs with one hand and began to stroke her clitoris.

Thompson studied her features. She was in her mid-twenties. The make-up around her eyes was smudged and most of her lipstick was gone. He could see some of it on the duvet.

She was broad on the hips. There were stretch marks on her tits and thighs.

Thompson heard her suck in a racking breath.

Saw his father redouble his exertions.

Thompson himself felt his erection pressing uncomfortably against the inside of his jogging bottoms and he slipped them off.

He slid his fingers around his erection and began to move his fist slowly up and down.

The woman was saying something, but Thompson couldn't make out the words.

He synchronized his own rhythm to that of his father's powerful stokes.

The woman allowed her head to drop forward onto the bed, her body shuddering.

Thompson continued to work his throbbing stiffness, his eye pressed tightly to the hole in the wall.

His own breathing was harsh now.

He saw that his father was smiling.

12

It looked as if he was gazing straight at the hole in the wall.

Perhaps he *was*, Thompson mused.

Who cared?

Then the overwhelming feeling of pleasure wiped all other thoughts from his mind.

He saw the woman shudder in the last throes of her orgasm.

Fucking bitch.

He reached for a tissue.

6

VERONICA PORTER BROUGHT the Fiesta to a halt behind her husband's Peugeot and switched off the engine.

She yawned, catching a glimpse of her reflection in the rear view mirror. She suddenly peered more closely, inspecting the lines around her eyes.

Six months away from her thirty-first birthday and she was looking for crows' feet. She managed a smile, then swung herself out of the car and locked it.

The street lamp directly outside the house was on the blink again. It buzzed like an angry wasp, the sodium glare occasionally fading, then glowing even more brilliantly for a moment before settling into its usual sickly hue.

She had wondered about reporting the fault to the council, but had finally thought better of it. She had lived in Kempston all her life and the inadequacies of successive councils were all too familiar.

Kempston was about thirty miles north of London. Politely termed an 'overspill' town, it had, during the past ten years, become more of a dumping ground for all and sundry.

With its estates of 1950s houses and flats, it was depressingly similar throughout its length and breadth. There had been the inevitable encroachment of Barrett homes in the early seventies and more modern houses had been erected for those who opted for the millstone of a mortgage. But for the most part, Kempston's council residents dwelt in the same kind of accommodation their parents had known.

Of course, there was central heating now. Double glazing. Wall and loft insulation. Even fitted dishwashers and washing machines. But no matter how many examples of modern convenience were crammed inside, the houses themselves belonged to a more sedate age.

Ronni was a good example of this. She and her husband had well-paid jobs and enjoyed most of life's comforts. But she felt as if she somehow belonged on the estate. Her father still lived less than half a mile away in the house where she had been born.

The close proximity to London made Kempston ideal commuter country and prices of private houses had risen accordingly during the last ten years. But the town was predominantly a council-house haven.

Naturally, many had heeded the Tory mantra in the eighties and chosen to buy their council houses (there were enough two-up-two-downs with fake brick cladding to attest to that). But the majority of the people on the Waybridge Estate – and all the other estates in Kempston – desired nothing more than a roof over their heads and cared little whether that roof was owned by the council or ransomed by a building society.

Ronni made her way down the short path to the front door and let herself in as quietly as she could.

She took off her coat, then inspected her reflection in the hall mirror.

The image that gazed back at her had shoulder-length brown hair, and high cheekbones. A black polo neck and tight charcoal-grey trousers hugged her slim frame.

She paused and slipped off her shoes, glancing up the stairs, listening for any sounds.

When she heard none, she pushed open the living-room door and stepped inside.

Andrew Porter looked up from his book and managed a smile.

'I thought you'd be in bed by now,' Ronni said, surprised to see him.

He closed the book, pushing the piece of torn newspaper he

used for a bookmark between the pages. 'If you'd have phoned to say you were going to be so late, I *would* have been,' he told her.

She wasn't slow to catch the edge in his tone. 'All right, Andy, I'm sorry. Is that what you want to hear?'

'That'll have to do, won't it?' He got to his feet. 'Do you want a cup of tea?' he wanted to know.

'I'd love one.'

He wandered through into the kitchen and Ronni heard the sound of running water.

She sat on the sofa, drew her legs up beneath her and gently massaged her aching feet.

'What happened?' he called out from the other room.

'Mr Fuller had an accident. Cut his hand. It needed stitches. I took him to the hospital.'

'Why you?'

'Because I was there, Andy.'

'You're *always* there.'

'Oh, come on, don't start that again. We all work late when it's our turn.'

'You did your late shift last week,' he reminded her.

'Alison had to leave early today. I said I'd cover for her.'

'They use you there, Ronni.'

'Andy, it's my job. As supervisor there's more responsibility, you know that.'

'Then get some more staff in. How many people does it take to look after nine old bastards anyway?'

She eyed him irritably as he returned from the kitchen with her tea.

'*You'll* be old one day, Andy,' Ronni told him. 'You might be grateful for a place like Shelby House.'

'I'd rather top myself than end up in an old people's home. Sitting around waiting to die.'

'It's not like that. Some of them are only in their sixties. They're there because they want to be. They pay for their own upkeep.'

'Good for them.' He turned towards the door.

'Where are you going?'

'To bed. I'm on earlies this week, in case you'd forgotten.'

'I'll be up in a minute.'

He didn't answer, merely closed the door and climbed the stairs. She heard his footfalls, then the creaking of floorboards as he crossed into their bedroom.

Ronni exhaled wearily.

She glanced at the TV and its meaningless images, then she leant across and switched it off.

On top of the set was a gilt-framed photo.

Herself and Andy on their wedding day twelve years ago, smiling joyfully at each other with love in their eyes.

She wondered where those smiles had gone.

She wondered where that *love* had gone.

The two people in that photo were strangers to her now.

Ronni tried to remember when she'd first realized she no longer loved this man she'd married.

7

RONNI UNDRESSED QUICKLY and slipped into bed.

As she pulled the duvet around her she glanced across at the motionless form of her husband. He had rolled onto his side, his back to her.

She studied the outline of his body in the darkness. She could hear his low breathing, but she knew that he was still awake.

Perhaps she should tell him she no longer loved him.

With what purpose?

She ran a hand through her hair.

What was he going to do? Get up there and then, pack his bags and leave?

She wasn't even sure that was what she wanted.

Twelve years was a long time. They'd shared a lot of memories, more good than bad.

She wondered *why* she no longer loved him. It was a question that had plagued her for some time now.

What had stopped her loving him? Was it one incontrovertible moment? One act? One blinding flash of realization?

No.

It had been a gradual erosion of feelings. She didn't blame Andy. He hadn't begun behaving differently. He hadn't cheated on her

(as far as she knew).

He hadn't started hitting her. But something between them had died and she knew that – whatever it was – emotional resuscitation was out of the question.

She wondered if *he* felt the same. Was he as tired of *her* as she was of *him*? Was he, even at this moment, thinking identical thoughts?

Better not ask. You might not like the answer.

And, if he was . . . what then?

If he left, she would be alone.

Six months away from her thirty-first birthday and alone. Granted she was an attractive woman; there would probably be no shortage of companions. But was that what she wanted?

Face it. You're scared. You don't want him anymore but you're terrified of life without him.

She reached out a hand to touch his shoulder, then pulled it back slightly.

'Are you asleep?' she asked softly.

'Yes,' he murmured.

She smiled.

'Whatever it is, Ronni, can it wait until tomorrow?' he asked, still lying on his side.

'I'm calling in to see my dad tomorrow,' she said.

'Say hello from me.'

'You should come with me. You've always got on with him.'

'He's a good bloke.'

'I'm going to try and talk him into moving out of the house.'

'To where?' Andy asked wearily. He rolled onto his back. 'He's lived in that house all his life, Ronni. He's happy there.'

'He hasn't been happy since my mum died. She's been dead for two years and he still can't get over it. He told me he still cries some nights when he thinks about her.'

'What do you expect? They were married for forty-odd years. She meant everything to him.'

'I'd like him where I can keep an eye on him.'

'You visit him every day.'

'I'm going to try and get him a place at Shelby House.'

'And how the hell is he going to afford it? What do they charge there? Six hundred quid a week?'

'He's got some savings. He'd be able to afford it.'

'And what if he doesn't *want* to move?'

She had no answer.

'Just leave him alone, Ronni. He'll be fine.' Andy rolled back onto his side. 'Now, please go to sleep, will you? I'll be shattered in the morning.'

Within minutes she heard his low breathing settle into a more rhythmic pattern.

'Andy,' she whispered.

No answer.

Ronni lay on her back, thoughts tumbling through her mind. Sleep came slowly, almost reluctantly, but she finally drifted off into welcome oblivion.

Somewhere in the next street, the sound of a car alarm filled the night air.

8

THE NOISE INSIDE the classroom was getting louder.

Graham Brown sat back on his wooden seat, balanced on the two back legs, his shoulders resting against the rear wall.

Around him, the other thirty-five children either watched the board, chatted, scribbled in their books, or gazed blankly into space.

Brown had his eyes fixed firmly on the woman at the front of the classroom.

She was young. Early twenties. Barely out of college.

Fresh meat.

A 'relief teacher' he'd heard someone call her.

He smiled.

Miss Sinclair.

Short brown hair. Dark blue blouse. Black skirt. Pretty.

He ran his gaze up and down her slender legs as she wrote, the marker scratching across the board.

She was either determined to ignore the noise in the room or she was reluctant to turn and face the increasingly rowdy class.

Brown thought he knew which was more likely.

'Settle down now,' she called as she continued to write.

It was some shit about the war; about Hitler gassing Jews.

He took his eyes away from the board momentarily to look at his companion, who was busily copying what the young teacher wrote down.

'Fuck are you doing?' Brown sneered.

Clive Skinner nodded in the direction of the board. 'She's going to test us on it,' he said, brushing a strand of hair away from his face.

'So fucking what?' Brown grunted. He continued to rock backwards and forwards on his seat. 'I wouldn't mind testing *her*,' he said finally.

Skinner chuckled. 'What on?' he wanted to know.

'On my fucking knob.'

Several of the other boys sitting nearby laughed loudly.

Miss Sinclair finally turned to face the class. 'All right, settle down now,' she said, her voice cracking.

The noise barely abated.

She stood staring at the assembled throng.

Brown saw her swallow – he could see the uncertainty in her eyes.

'The names I've written here are all the names of Nazi death camps,' she said, gesturing behind her.

AUSCHWITZ

BUCHENWALD

TREBLINKA

BELSEN

'Of course there were many more,' she continued. 'But it was in places like these that prisoners were murdered in their millions.'

'Are they like the places in *Schindler's List*?' someone close to the front asked.

Miss Sinclair nodded. 'That's right,' she said, relieved that at least one of the class seemed to understand what she was talking about. 'Although the camp in *Schindler's List* was Plaszow. That was a forced-labour camp.'

'Why did Hitler kill the Jews, miss?' someone else wanted to know.

'Because he thought they were cunts,' Brown shouted.

There was a chorus of giggles and gasps from the others in the class.

'Who said that?' Miss Sinclair demanded, looking around.

Brown put his hand up.

'Come here,' she snapped, using her most authoritative tone.

Brown remained balanced on the back legs of his chair. 'He *did* think they were cunts, didn't he?' he persisted.

Miss Sinclair licked her lips and exhaled wearily. 'I told you to come here,' she repeated, raising her voice slightly.

'I'm busy.'

More laughter.

She took a step towards him.

Brown grinned at the advancing teacher.

She was no more than two feet away from him when he allowed his chair to tip forward.

It landed with a loud thump.

'I won't tolerate that kind of language in the classroom,' she said.

Brown held her gaze. 'What language?' he sneered. 'Cunt?'

'Go to the headmaster's room now.'

He didn't move.

'I'm not going to tell you again,' she said through clenched teeth.

'Fuck off.'

He saw the colour drain from her cheeks.

'You get to the headmaster now,' she repeated, her voice catching.

'Make me.'

All heads had turned towards the back of the room.

Towards the confrontation.

Brown sat immobile. 'What can you do?' he challenged. 'You know you're not allowed to put your fucking hand on me. It's assault. And if you do, I'll fucking kill you.'

For interminable seconds the two of them glared at each other.

The teacher finally leaned closer. 'If you won't go to the head, then *I'll* go and fetch him,' she said, turning away.

She was at the door when Brown stood up.

'Miss Sinclair?' he shouted. 'I've got something for you.'

She turned.

As she did she saw that his flies were open.

His penis jutted from the gap in his trousers.

He closed his hand around it and grinned.

She slammed the door as she left, the jeers and laughter ringing in her ears.

9

RONNI HANDED HER father the mug of tea, then sat down opposite him.

James Connor smiled appreciatively and touched her hand as he accepted the drink. 'Any chance of one of those biscuits you brought?' he said, winking.

'One, Dad,' she said, mock reproach in her tone. 'You've got to watch your cholesterol.'

'One's not going to hurt, is it? Anyway, last time I went to see the doctor he said it was all right. Nothing to worry about.'

'I know, I was with you.'

'Then pass the biscuits.' He grinned.

'That doesn't mean you can start eating what you like again.' She pushed the digestives across the table towards him, watching as he took one and nibbled it.

'Your mum used to go on at me about it too,' he said quietly.

Ronni nodded almost imperceptibly.

'She made sure I ate the right things,' he continued, rubbing his wedding ring with one thumb as he spoke, turning it on his thin finger. 'You're just like her, you know.'

When he looked into her eyes, she saw the sadness in his.

'I miss her too, Dad,' Ronni said softly. She reached out and touched her father's hand.

'It doesn't seem like two years,' he muttered. 'I still expect to see her sitting in her chair doing one of those bloody jigsaws she was always doing.'

Ronni saw a solitary tear roll down his cheek.

He wiped it away almost angrily.

'They say time is a great healer, don't they?' he snapped. 'Well, they lied. I still miss her as much now as the day she died.'

He touched his wedding ring.

Another tear.

Ronni got to her feet and hugged him tightly.

'Thank God I've got you, eh?' her father said.

'You should leave here, Dad. Move,' she offered.

'I lived in this house for more than forty years with your mother. You were born here. I don't *want* to live anywhere else.'

'But perhaps that's the problem. Perhaps there are too many memories here.'

'So where am I supposed to go? Do I come and live with you? How would Andy like that?'

'He wouldn't mind.'

Her father raised an eyebrow questioningly.

'If we had the room, Dad . . .' She allowed the sentence to trail off.

'Look, Ronni, I'm seventy-three,' he reminded her. 'I'm too old to be moving.'

'You shouldn't be on your own, Dad.'

'I can look after myself. I appreciate you coming in every day, but you don't *have* to.'

'I just like to make sure you're OK. If you need anything, I—'

'I can walk down the shops. It's ten minutes, that's all.'

'How's your leg?'

He turned away from the table slightly and massaged his right leg. 'It's a bastard, if you want the truth,' he told her. 'But it doesn't stop me getting around.'

'Do you get any help from the neighbours?'

'They're never there. Out working every hour God sends.'

'But if you fell or something . . .' she persisted. 'And it's not just that. This area worries me too. There's so much crime, Dad.'

He held up a hand to silence her. 'Ronni, stop it. I'm fine and just because a few kids have been getting out of hand it's no reason for me to move. This is Kempston, not New York.'

They sat in silence for a moment. Ronni sipped her tea.

'Anyway, you live on the same estate,' he continued. 'Why aren't *you* thinking about moving if you're so worried about the crime?'

'We're less vulnerable.'

'Because you're younger? Don't kid yourself.' He reached for another biscuit as silence descended once again. 'Perhaps you *should* be thinking about moving,' he said quietly. 'I might not want my grandchildren living around here. If I ever get any.' He looked at her with a gleam in his eyes.

'Dad, the time isn't right for Andy and I to have kids,' she said wearily.

You see, I'm not even sure I want to be with him anymore, let alone have his kids.

'If you don't get a move on, I won't live to see them.' He grinned.

'Don't say that.'

'Seventy-three and counting,' he reminded her, tapping his chest.

'We're not ready for kids,' Ronni said, avoiding his gaze. 'And *you* should have more important things on your mind than grandchildren.'

Ronni sipped at her tea. Her father turned his wedding ring gently on his finger.

'There are places at Shelby House . . .' Ronni said finally.

'No,' he told her flatly.

'Why not?'

'I can't afford it for one thing, and for another I'm not finishing my life in an old people's home.'

'Dad—'

He cut her short. 'No, Ronni,' he insisted. 'I'm staying here and that's it.'

'Is that you putting your foot down?'

'As hard as I can.' He smiled.

She finished her tea and got to her feet, crossing the small kitchen to rinse the mug under the tap.

As she did so she noticed he'd sneaked another biscuit from the packet.

'I saw that,' she said, grinning.

'Go to work, you,' he told her. 'And stop worrying.'

She kissed him on the top of the head and pulled on her coat.

'I'll be in again tomorrow, Dad.'

'I'll be here.'

He got to his feet and followed her to the front door, where he stood and watched as she walked down the short path, waving until she was out of sight. Then he closed the door behind her.

The silence inside the house enveloped him once more.

10

THE CLUSTER OF shops that served the Waybridge Estate was small.

There was a grocer's shop. Next to it was a small newsagent's and tobacconist's that actually sold fifteen different types of loose tobacco for the more discerning smoker.

There was a fish and chip shop, a launderette, a hairdresser's (bearing the name 'Cutz R Uz'), an off-licence, a small supermarket and, for reasons that no one had ever worked out, a shop that sold sporting trophies.

The puzzle to estate residents was not so much *why* the shop was there, but how it had managed to remain open for so long. And yet it had stood, like most of the others, for more than ten years. It sold bicycles and the most elementary of car spares too, along with a peculiar assortment of ironmongery. But sporting trophies remained its most immediately noticeable commodity. The window was full of them.

Trophies for darts. Football. Fishing. Bowls.

If there had been a competition for thickest nasal hair they would have had a trophy for it.

They supplied most of the local schools with their shields and trophies for sports days; at least in those schools that still upheld competition to be a good thing and not a psychological handicap to those athletically less gifted.

The newsagent's also contained a tiny post office. Giros could be cashed. Food stamps could be collected.

There were a couple of public phones, one of which had been ripped from its housing, and a postbox on the central concourse.

Carl Thompson sat on one of the wooden benches beside the phone that worked and took a drag on his cigarette.

He glanced at each of the shops in turn – at those who frequented them.

It was almost one p.m. The fish and chip shop in particular was busy with lunchtime customers.

There were also a number of kids from the local school milling around the concourse, clearly visible in their dark blue uniforms.

Young women pushed prams or pushchairs. One dragged a screaming toddler by the arm.

An older woman pulled a tartan

(*why were they always tartan?*)

shopping trolley behind her while she gripped the lead of a small dog in her free hand.

Two men talked animatedly outside the entrance to the newsagent's.

'Where are they?'

Thompson heard the words, but didn't speak. He merely sucked on his cigarette, watching the smoke rise from the glowing tip.

Beside him, Tina Craven chewed away at fingernails already bitten to the quick.

She was gazing in the direction of the off-licence.

'I wish they'd get a move on,' she said, still picking at her ravaged fingertips.

Thompson looked briefly at her.

Thirteen years old. Long brown hair that looked as if it hadn't been combed for days. Her eyes were narrow, giving her the appearance of a perpetual squint, something not helped by the large amount of mascara she wore. It seemed to have been applied so heavily the sheer weight of the make-up prevented her from fully parting her eyelids. She had one small whitehead on her forehead. Thompson gazed at it as if transfixed by the glare of a third eye.

There was a sudden flurry of activity nearby.

Shouts. Raised voices.

Both Thompson and Tina turned to see two small boys running from the off-licence.

Neither was older than eleven.

They were both carrying bottles of liquor.

Two cycles had been propped against a wall nearby and, as Thompson watched, the boys leapt onto the waiting bikes, stuck the bottles into rucksacks hanging off the handlebars and began peddling furiously.

The two bikes sped away just as a man came hurtling from the off-licence, shaking his fist at the two young thieves. He picked up a discarded can and hurled it, the metal ricocheting off a low wall. The lager inside trickled away through a crack in the pavement.

'You little bastards!' he roared.

The cyclists were already on the road, peddling away up the hill, past the small petrol station on their right.

One looked back and jabbed a 'V' sign in the direction of the shouting man.

Other eyes turned to watch the action.

The two men outside the newsagent's stood motionless for a moment.

The old woman with the shopping trolley and the dog peered in the direction of the fleeing boys.

Two teenage mothers broke off their conversation long enough to look round at the furious off-licence owner.

Then it was all over.

The moment passed.

Conversations continued.

'Come on,' said Thompson, getting to his feet.

'I hope they got vodka and not gin again,' Tina said as she followed him. 'I hate fucking gin.'

11

Shelby House Residential Home. The blue sign at the bottom of the drive displayed the words with pride.

No hint of the words 'old people's home'. They belonged to less enlightened days. No one who worked or resided there ever referred to the building as such.

The gravel drive was flanked on either side by cedar trees. Beyond were carefully manicured lawns, cut by a private firm, who visited once a week to trim the grass and tend the flower beds.

The drive itself curved slightly as it left the road until finally coming to a halt before the building itself.

Here there were parking spaces for up to twenty cars, but there were rarely more than two parked there at any one time.

Shelby House was a red-brick edifice, built in the early sixties and remarkably well maintained. The exterior paintwork was given a fresh coat once every two years. Only odd patches of green mould on the brickwork gave any indication as to the age of the property.

The well-kept gardens were enclosed by a high, wire fence and more trees, giving a feeling of peaceful solitude and isolation despite the fact that Shelby House stood more or less on the periphery of the Waybridge Estate. Some houses backed onto the rear gardens, but, for the most part, they were hidden from the view of the residents by high privet hedges and more fencing.

There was a patio area to the rear where residents could sit out in the summer. A number of bird tables, constructed by one of the residents, were dotted around the rear lawns and several nesting boxes, built by the same resident, had been bolted to the walls of the building. Wrens and blue tits regularly made homes in them.

The building itself was two storeys and contained eleven single and two double rooms, three of the singles being on the ground floor for the benefit of wheelchair-bound residents.

A small lift could be used by those not able to cope with the stairs.

Also on the ground floor was a pharmacy that dispensed the necessary medication to those residents who needed it. It was situated next to the large day room that looked out over the rear gardens and also contained a television set.

One of the single rooms had been temporarily transformed into a reading room, due to a temporary shortage of residents, but staff had found that its most common use was as a smoking room. A practice frowned upon, but tolerated.

Meals were served either in the rooms or, more often than not, taken in the small canteen, also on the ground floor.

There were staff quarters on the first floor. They were some-what spartan, but comfortable enough for the worker on the night shift.

At least one carer was present on the premises throughout the night in case of emergencies.

Spare mattresses, bed linen, pillows and chairs were stored in a large, well-lit cellar that could be accessed both by stairs and also by the lift that carried residents from floor to floor.

Nine residents lived in Shelby House, cared for by three permanent staff and visited once a week by a physiotherapist and, once a month, by a chiropodist.

For those who still had family, visiting times were flexible although the majority of visitors came at weekends.

The day-to-day cleaning of the home was carried out by the staff themselves, often helped by the residents, who appreciated the relative luxury of their surroundings and also the selfless dedication of those who cared for them.

The home was owned by a private corporation, who, as long as they were making a profit, saw no need to interfere in the running of the place. It hadn't featured in any media exposés either so they were more than happy and satisfied their investment was safe.

The atmosphere was one of fulfilment and happiness, for both staff and residents.

The sparrows and starlings that fed from the bird tables in the grounds accepted the bacon rinds, the peanuts and whatever other scraps they were given gratefully.

On the roof of Shelby House, several crows were perched.

Black eyes fixed on the smaller birds.

Watching.

Waiting.

12

'KILL THE CUNT.'

The words were said through clenched teeth.

Four shots were fired; one struck the body. Another the head.

The third missed.

The fourth blasted the head to atoms.

'Yes!' howled Liam Harper, watching as the zombie toppled backwards.

He hit the 'Pause' button of *Resident Evil 3* and reached for the bottle of vodka close to him.

Terry Mackenzie snatched up the handset and restarted the game.

'Don't lose any of my lives,' Harper warned, prodding his companion with the toe of his Adidas trainer.

'The Dreamcast one's better anyway. The picture's really good,' Mackenzie said, avoiding a swipe from a meat-cleaver and shooting a zombie in the face.

'The graphics, you mean,' Harper chided.

'Whatever.'

Carl Thompson glanced at the two eleven year olds as they sat just a foot or two from the TV screen, the flickering images reflected in their eyes.

Tina Craven, seated on the sofa beside him, swigged from the other bottle of vodka.

'Are we going to sit around here all day watching *them?*' she wanted to know, nodding in the direction of the two younger boys.

'Shut up, you slag,' called Harper and Mackenzie and they both laughed loudly.

Tina pulled a cushion from behind her and hurled it at them.

Thompson took a drag on his cigarette.

'Carl, I said—'

'I heard you,' Thompson interrupted. 'What do you *want* to do?'

She moved closer to him and ran one hand over his thigh and up towards his groin.

He grinned and pushed her away.

'I bet you wouldn't say no if it was Donna, would you?' she rasped.

Thompson got to his feet and wandered out of the room.

'You never complained before,' she reminded him.

She waited a moment, then got to her feet and followed him through into his bedroom.

'Where's Donna anyway?' she asked, chewing a stubby finger. 'I thought she'd have been here.'

'She's back at school,' Thompson told her.

'I thought she got expelled.'

'Just suspended for a week.'

'*I* got expelled.' Tina beamed.

Thompson reached beneath his bed, ferreting about for something Tina couldn't see.

'What time does your dad get home?' she asked.

'It all depends. Five or six. Sometimes he goes straight out after work.'

'Are *we* going out or what?' she demanded.

Thompson ignored her and continued with his search.

Tina sat on the bed, looking down at Thompson, who was still fumbling about.

She lay on it, glancing around at the posters blu-tacked to the walls: Alicia Silverstone. Sarah Michelle Gellar. A film poster for *The Matrix*.

The one above the bed had come loose at the bottom.

She reached up to re-attach it and the whole thing came away. Andrea Corr flopped across her.

'Leave it!' snapped Thompson.

'I was just trying to put it back for you.' She saw the hole in the wall. 'What's that?' She grinned, kneeling up and squinting through it. She found she could see straight into the next room. 'Is that your dad's bedroom?' she wanted to know, eye still pressed to the hole.

She heard the loud click behind her and turned.

Tina stifled a scream as she saw the barrel of the .22 air rifle aimed at her face.

Thompson grinned and lowered the gun slowly. 'Put the poster back,' he said, watching as she pressed the shiny paper back into position.

He broke the barrel and took a slug from his pocket, running one thumb over the pointed end before pushing it into the gun and snapping it shut.

Tina kicked out angrily at him as he stepped away from her.

'Come on,' Thompson said, brandishing the gun in one hand. 'You wanted to go out, didn't you?'

13

Jonathan Lynch shook his head wearily as he sifted through the file before him.

It was quiet inside his room, just the occasional ringing of the phone from his secretary's outer office cutting through the silence.

The headmaster of Howard Road Secondary School was a distinguished-looking man in his mid-forties. The touches of grey at his temples added to the overall appearance of a man in a position of responsibility, but sometimes troubled by the magnitude of it.

Opposite him, Graham Brown picked at the head of a spot and gazed aimlessly around.

He knew this room well.

Knew its paintings; its slightly worn grey carpet.

He should do. He'd been inside it often enough.

'You know why you're here, don't you?' Lynch said, finally.

'Miss Sinclair reported me, sir,' Brown told him, sniffing loudly.

'And you know *why* she reported you?'

Brown nodded.

'Foul and abusive language,' Lynch said, keeping his voice as even as possible. 'Lewd conduct.' He tapped the file before him. 'That goes with all the other instances I have here of similar behaviour during the last two years. Do you want me to read them out or can you remember them?'

Brown didn't answer.

'As well as being reported for using foul and abusive language more times than I'd care to repeat,' the headmaster began, 'there's also a catalogue of absenteeism. Truancy. Fighting. Threatening behaviour, against other pupils *and* members of staff. Shall I go on?'

Brown shrugged.

'No need is there?' Lynch said, closing the file.

The phone rang in the outer office.

'What are you trying to do, Graham? Get yourself expelled? Is that what you want?'

Brown didn't answer. He seemed more concerned with pulling the scab from another spot.

'Educationally, these are the most important years of your life, but that doesn't seem to bother you,' Lynch continued. 'These are the years that will equip you for work.'

Brown snorted disdainfully.

'Have I said something amusing?' Lynch wanted to know.

'What work? What work is there for people like me around here, sir? My old man can't even get a fucking job.'

'*Language!*' rasped Lynch.

'What do you want me to do, sir?'

'Try working, like your classmates. Do as you're told.'

'And that's going to get me a job when I leave, is it?'

'It'll give you more of a chance.'

'I might as well leave now. Or you might as well expel me now. I'm not going to get a job *now*. I'm not going to get a job when I'm sixteen.'

'What do you *want* to do when you leave?'

'Earn good money.'

'And the only way to do that is to work hard while you're at school, get some qualifications and *find* the job you want when you leave.'

'The only ones who're going to get jobs are the fucking arse-lickers who do "A" levels, then go to college or university. They're the only ones the teachers are interested in anyway. None of them could give a toss what happens to me.'

'That's not true.'

'You know it is, sir. You never get the teachers' pets in here, do you? How many of them have you threatened with being expelled?'

'What about your parents? Do they take an interest in what you do at school?'

'They couldn't give a toss.'

'*You* can change that.'

'How?'

'Talk to them. Let *them* know what you want out of life.'

Brown sniggered. 'I'll get what I want, sir,' he said, grinning. 'And I don't care how.'

Lynch regarded him silently for a moment, his expression a mixture of rage and frustration. 'Well, I won't allow behaviour such as you exhibited this afternoon,' the Headmaster snapped. 'You may not be interested in learning but there are plenty in this school who are. One hour's detention for the next three days. You're lucky I'm not calling the Police. You could be on a charge for indecent exposure. Get out of here.'

Brown got to his feet. 'You can't do anything and neither can the police, sir,' he sneered. 'And you *know* that. You can't touch me and neither can they.'

'The only one who can change this situation is you, Graham,' Lynch told him.

'What if I don't *want* to change it, sir?' the youngster said. He held the headmaster's gaze for a moment, then slammed the door behind him.

14

'IT'S GOING TO RAIN,' said Colin Glazer, peering out of the window of the day room. He was watching the banks of scudding grey clouds moving ponderously across the heavens.

'They didn't forecast rain,' Harry Holland offered, not taking his eyes from the TV screen.

'They would have done if they'd seen these clouds.' Glazer smiled. He watched them for a moment longer, then returned to his seat, wincing slightly as he sat down in one of the high-backed chairs that formed a semi-circle around the television.

There was a quiz show about to start on Channel 4. Most of the residents of Shelby House sat and watched it every weekday afternoon. It was as much a part of their routine as breakfast, lunch and dinner.

For the rest of the day, they were left to their own devices, but the nine of them who lived permanently within the building usually joined together for the delights offered by the television.

Janice Holland flipped open the pad on her lap and tapped it with her biro. She had already written the names of each person gathered around the set.

Every day they waited for the show. Every day she drew a tick beneath the name of each of her companions who got a right answer. At the end of the week they proclaimed a winner, who then chose their own small prize.

She looked around at the expectant faces.

At her own husband, Harry, aged sixty-eight; dressed in a

blazer and with his shirt immaculately ironed, his blue tie fastened in a perfect knot.

He was still a handsome man.

Janice was two years younger.

Next to him sat Eva Cole. Seventy-four. She'd worked as a seamstress in her husband's business until his death ten years ago. She had no family. He'd left her the business – which she hadn't wanted – so she'd sold it, made a tidy sum and retired to Shelby House. She was a softly spoken woman with snow-white hair and joints swollen with arthritis.

Beside Eva sat George Errington. At eighty-one he was the oldest of the residents. A tall, awkward-looking man with large hands dappled by liver spots. He peered alternately over and through the thick glasses he wore, as if not sure of the best way to view the television.

Errington spent most of his time in the day room, the majority of that watching the television. He'd once been a cinema projectionist and there was little he didn't know about films, old or modern.

He chewed on the stem of his unlit pipe and peered over his glasses at Donald Tanner, seated to his right.

Tanner, at seventy-three, was a keen card player and always eager to engage anyone interested in some kind of game. From poker to bridge, he was alert, intuitive and, if the occasion called for it, not averse to cheating. Something the other residents looked on with amused acceptance.

Provided they weren't playing for money.

Then there was Barbara Eustace: seventy-one, wheelchair-bound and the most recent addition to the list of residents at Shelby House, she had family, but at the moment Janice was unsure whether Barbara's son was unable or unwilling to care for his mother. It was something she was determined to find out in the coming weeks.

The theme music to the quiz show began and the watching residents greeted it like an old friend.

'Jack's going to miss this,' George Errington observed.

'Where is he anyway?' Harry Holland wanted to know.

'He's probably building something,' Donald Tanner interjected. 'I saw him outside earlier.'

'If he stays out he's going to get soaked.' Colin Glazer, smiled, noticing the first drops of rain hitting the windows.

'First question coming up,' Janice Holland said, drawing everyone's attention back to the screen.

The quizmaster had just finished introducing the contestants and was shuffling his stack of questions as he turned to the first contestant.

'Who wrote the novel "Crime and Punishment"?'

'Dostoyevsky,' a new voice called. 'One for me, Janice. Tick it off.'

Jack Fuller chuckled and pulled up a chair, rubbing his hands together.

'We were just wondering where you were,' Harry Holland said.

'Shhh. Next question,' Janice said.

'What is a female fox called?'

Three voices called out 'vixen'.

'That was mine,' Donald Tanner insisted.

'Mine,' George Errington countered.

'I'll give all three of us a point,' Janice said, ticking away quickly.

The questions continued.

Outside, the rain began to fall more heavily.

15

Ronni Porter held up the small plastic bottle, then took two tablets from it.

'Two milligrams, Glyceril Trinitrate,' she said, dropping the medicine into a small plastic dish.

Alison Dean nodded and ticked the sheet of paper attached to her clipboard.

'And twenty milligrams of Prazosin,' Ronni continued.

That went into a separate container.

Alison nodded once more. 'That's it,' the younger woman said.

There were seven of the small plastic dishes on the tray, each containing at least one tablet or capsule. Drugs to treat everything from angina to piles.

Alison looked directly at Ronni, studying her features for a moment. 'And what are *you* having?' she wanted to know.

Ronni looked puzzled.

'Prozac?' Alison wondered. 'Valium?'

She smiled humourlessly.

'It's not *that* bad, Alison,' Ronni said, none too convincingly.

The younger woman raised an eyebrow questioningly.

'You're married, you know what it's like,' Ronni insisted.

'But the difference is, I *love* my husband,' Alison told her.

Ronni had no answer. She merely glanced briefly at her companion, aware of how oppressive the atmosphere inside the pharmacy had become.

Alison Dean was a year younger than Ronni; a slender, auburn-haired young woman with wide eyes and an easy smile. She had worked at Shelby House for the past five years and during that time the two women had become close friends. Ronni liked her companion's relaxed manner and the two women also sought each other's company *outside* work when they got the chance. Just shopping trips and the occasional night out at the local multiplex or wine bar in town, but it was better than nothing. However, Ronni felt that it was *she* who needed these rare respites from work and home more urgently. Any break in routine was appreciated.

'So what are you going to do?' Alison asked.

'I wish I knew.'

'What about kids?'

Ronni frowned.

'Sometimes, having a child can put a relationship back on track,' Alison insisted.

'The last thing I need now is a child.'

'Has Andy mentioned it?'

'Once or twice. I know he'd love kids but he's never put any pressure on me to have them.'

'Does he know how you feel?'

'What am I supposed to say to him, Alison? "Sorry, but I don't love you anymore so why don't we go our separate ways?"'

'Is that what you really want?'

'I think so.'

'You *think* so? I thought you were sure.'

'I'm not sure of anything anymore.'

'Have you thought about going to Relate?'

'Andy doesn't even know there's a problem between us. It might come as a bit of shock to him if I tell him I've booked us in for marriage guidance.'

'If he doesn't know there's a problem, then you should tell him, Ronni. It's not fair on *him*.'

'I know. I've thought about that too. There isn't much I haven't thought about. I think all the time. It's just the *doing* I can't get around to.'

'Is there anyone else?' Alison asked quietly.

'Do you mean am I having an affair?' Ronni laughed bitterly. 'I wish I was, it would make things easier. I wish Andy was. That would solve *all* my problems, wouldn't it? I could throw him out with a clear conscience then.'

'Who else knows how you feel?'

'Just you. I can't tell my dad, can I? He's got enough to worry about.'

'How is he?'

'Up and down. Some days I go to see him and he seems fine. Others, it's as if he's made no progress at all.'

'It's bound to take time for him to get over it.'

'I wish I could be closer to him.'

'You go in every day, Ronni. What more can you do?'

'I want him here at Shelby House.' She tapped the worktop.

'And you think that would help him?'

'It'd help *me*,' she said, defiantly. 'I don't want to lose him, Alison.'

'It takes time to get over a death, you know that.'

'I've walked into that house some days and found him sitting in my mum's chair, holding her picture and sobbing.' She lowered her gaze. 'I'm scared he's never going to get over her death, Alison. He says life's not worth living without her. I think he *wants* to die. I'm not going to let that happen.'

16

ALL FOUR WHEELS were missing from the car.

Carl Thompson smiled as he saw the rusted Corsa standing uselessly on the tarmac outside the nearest garage.

He watched as Harper and Mackenzie ran ahead, hurtling endlessly round the stricken vehicle like Red Indians circling a wagon train. Harper stopped long enough to lash out with one foot and shatter what remained of a headlight. He and Mackenzie shouted in triumph and continued careering around the Corsa.

Tina Craven took a drag on her cigarette and pulled the collar of her Kangol jacket up around her neck.

'Why couldn't we have stayed at your place?' she wanted to know, glancing up at the sky.

The rain was still falling, but the initial downpour had been replaced by a mournful drizzle that covered the desolate landscape like a damp gauze. It swayed and undulated with each gust of wind.

'You said you wanted to do something,' Thompson reminded her.

'Getting fucking soaked wasn't what I was thinking of,' she muttered.

Harper and Mackenzie had stopped their relentless circling of the Corsa and were now inspecting the car more closely.

The driver's side door was missing. Seats had been slashed. The foam interior protruded like viscera from a bad stomach wound.

Wing mirrors had been torn off. The front and rear wind-screens had been smashed in. Not a scrap of glass remained in the front. There were some deep gouges in the bodywork. When Harper lifted the bonnet, the engine beneath was rusted. Parts had been torn out. Most of them lay scattered across the ground around the vehicle.

'Who uses these?' Tina asked, nodding in the direction of the garages.

There were two rows of them. Twelve in each.

Every door was painted a different colour.

Every handle was rusted.

Each door was dented or covered in a variety of graffiti.

'They're for the flats over there,' Thompson informed her. He gestured towards the blocks of fifteen-storey council dwellings that pushed upwards into the sodden sky about half a mile from where they stood. 'Nobody leaves their car here anymore. Not if they've got any fucking sense.'

Harper clambered behind the broken steering wheel and began making engine noises.

Mackenzie walked to each of the garage doors and kicked them hard.

The metallic clang reverberated in the air with each impact.

'So where are they?' Mackenzie wanted to know.

'Where are what?' Tina enquired.

'The rats.' Mackenzie grinned. 'Carl said there were rats up here.'

'Some as big as dogs, they reckon,' Thompson elaborated.

Tina shuddered. 'Well, why are *we* hanging around here if there are fucking rats here?' she said, looking nervously around.

Thompson raised the air rifle and grinned.

'Will that kill them, Carl?' Harper asked.

Thompson nodded. 'A .177 or a fucking BB just bounces off them,' he said. 'But this'll do the job.'

'You're going to shoot rats?' Tina grunted wearily.

'No.' Mackenzie sniggered. 'We're going to shoot *you*.'

He pressed one index finger to her face and shouted, 'Bang!'

'Fuck off,' she rasped, striking at him, but missing.

'There are nests up here,' Thompson continued, swinging the rifle up to his shoulder and squinting along the sight.

He squeezed the trigger.

There was a loud crack and the pellet slammed into one of the garage doors. It blasted away some peeling paint and left a dent large enough to get the end of a little finger into.

Mackenzie and Harper scurried across to the door and inspected the damage.

Thompson took another pellet from his pocket and reloaded.

He raised the rifle once again and fired.

The pellet missed Harper's head by inches.

It smacked into the metal door of the garage and dropped to the ground.

Mackenzie stooped and retrieved the flattened piece of lead.

'Fucking watch it, Carl,' Harper shouted, his heart thudding a little faster as he saw Thompson push another of the pointed pellets into the weapon. 'You could have hit me. *Cunt.*' He whispered the last word under his breath.

Tina laughed loudly. 'Let *me* have a go,' she said, reaching for the rifle.

'Fuck off,' Thompson said, flatly. 'You *would* fucking shoot him.'

'It wouldn't kill him, would it?'

'If you hit him in the eye. Or from any closer you could.'

Mackenzie and Harper hurried back to join Thompson and Tina. Harper picked up a piece of wood and began banging the garage doors. 'The noise might drive them out,' he said.

'We need some food or something,' Mackenzie insisted. 'Like bait.'

He dug in the pocket of his jacket and found a half-eaten bag of crisps. Some of these he scattered on the floor.

Tina laughed.

'We'll go *into* the garages,' Thompson announced. 'Hunt the fuckers down.'

Tina looked apprehensively at him. 'I'm not going in there if there are rats inside,' she said, her voice wavering.

'Then go home,' Thompson told her.

He drove his booted foot at the lock on the closest of the metal doors and shattered it with ease, then dug his hand under the door and pulled.

There was a loud screech and the garage yawned open like a huge mouth.

Thompson looked at the others. 'Come on,' he said flatly.

17

Ronni knocked lightly on the door and waited.

No answer.

She knocked again.

When there was no answer the third time she let herself in.

Janice Holland was sitting on the edge of the bed clutching at her chest with one hand.

'Janice,' Ronni murmured and crossed to the older woman, sliding one comforting arm around her shoulder.

'I'm all right, love,' Janice said, her face pale and sheathed in perspiration. 'Just a twinge.' She attempted a smile.

'Do you want me to get Harry?'

'No, don't worry him. He fusses too much as it is.' She tried to swallow, then pointed a shaking finger in the direction of the bedside table. 'Could you fetch me one of my tablets, please?' Janice asked.

Ronni retrieved the glycerine and watched as the older woman took one, popping it beneath her tongue.

Ronni then crossed to the small sink and spun the cold tap, filling a beaker with water. She passed it to Janice, who sipped gratefully at it.

'Don't tell Harry,' she said softly. 'He's got enough on his mind.'

'Are you sure you don't want me to get the doctor?' Ronni persisted.

Janice shook her head. 'No fuss,' she said. 'I'm fine now. As fit as a butcher's dog, as we say in Yorkshire.' This time she smiled broadly.

Ronni sat down next to her once again and held her hand. 'What happened?' she wanted to know.

'I just came back from the day room to fetch my glasses. When I got here I felt a little faint.'

'You should have pressed the alarm button. One of us would have come straight away.'

'No need to fuss.'

'It's not fussing, Janice. It's what we're here for.'

Janice squeezed her hand tightly.

'Do you want to lay down for a while?' Ronni continued.

'No, I'm fine now. I suppose I've got my mother to thank for this. Angina's hereditary isn't it?'

'I don't know.' Ronni smiled. 'You'd have to ask an expert.'

'My father worked in a hospital, you know. Halifax General. He was a porter. I don't even know if it's still there now. We used to live about a mile away. I remember the night my mother had the heart attack that killed her. He carried her all the way from our house to the hospital. She was dead before he got there.'

Ronni felt her hand being squeezed more tightly.

'My father carrying her and me and my three brothers following like little lost sheep,' Janice continued. 'I was only nine. The youngest. I can still remember his face when the doctor told him she was dead. I'd never seen him cry before.'

Ronni listened silently.

'She was only sixty-three,' said Janice. 'Younger than I am now.'

'What happened to the family?'

'We were sent to live with members of the family. I was sent to my aunt's in Nottingham. That was where I met Harry.'

'Do you keep in touch with your family?'

'No. Two of my brothers died in the war. The other one emigrated to Canada. I've just got Harry now.'

'Well, you make sure you keep him and you look after yourself.

We can't have anything happening to you with this anniversary coming up. How many years is it?'

'Forty-six. All good ones. Harry's got something planned but he won't tell me what it is. Do *you* know, love?'

'I've been sworn to secrecy, Janice.' Ronni chuckled. She studied the older woman's face for a moment longer, then got to her feet. 'Are you sure you're all right?' she asked.

Janice nodded. 'I'll just sit for a minute,' she said. 'Tell Harry I can't find my glasses if he asks where I am. He worries too much. You know what men are like.'

Ronni nodded.

Some of them.

She slipped quietly from the room.

18

'FUCKING HELL, IT stinks in here.' Liam Harper waved his hand in front of his face as if to dispel the cloying stench that enveloped him.

The inside of the long-deserted garage reeked of damp, neglect and something more pungent.

Terry Mackenzie kicked at a pile of old newspapers close by, watching as they toppled over.

Headlines about the Falklands War.

Margaret Thatcher.

Pictures of triumphant troops returning home.

Ancient history to him.

There were some empty, rusted cans of motor oil. A few tins of paint.

He kicked those over too, the crash reverberating inside the hollow shell of the garage.

The floor was several inches deep in dust, the motes swirling through the already rancid air as they were disturbed.

Thompson walked slowly through the derelict surroundings, scanning the gloom.

No sign of rats in here.

'Let's try another one,' he said and his companions rushed past him.

He heard them hammering away at the lock of the next garage.

'This is stupid,' Tina protested as he walked past her, unimpressed by her complaint.

The second garage yielded a similar harvest of desolation.

A battered old manual typewriter.

Some scratched and broken MFI units.

Even an old cassette player.

Harper picked it up and threw it against one of the walls, shouting loudly when it shattered.

Thompson walked to the back of the garage and peered at the rear wall.

No nests here.

Or in the third or the fourth garage.

It took a blow from a half-brick to finally shatter the padlock on the fifth door. Thompson stepped inside.

The smell was vile; like stale urine, but more cloying.

Rain water had seeped beneath the door and spread through the layers of dust.

He saw other marks in the carpet of filth.

Tiny tracks.

There was a metal toolbox propped on an old Formica-topped table.

Mackenzie opened it.

There were several screwdrivers in it. Two hammers. A Stanley knife with a rusty blade and hundreds of nails of all lengths.

Mackenzie pocketed the Stanley knife.

The rust that came off on his fingers looked like dried blood.

'Look.' Harper chuckled.

He was pulling at a pile of old pornographic magazines tucked away in one corner of the garage. Mackenzie took one from him and the two of them flicked quickly through the stiffened pages. Occasionally one of them would hold up the centrefold.

Harper rubbed his index finger over the breasts of one of the girls and giggled. 'This is your mum, isn't it, Tina?' he called.

'Fuck off,' she sneered, taking a drag of her cigarette.

Thompson lifted the air rifle to his shoulder.

There was movement at the rear of the garage.

Something small and sleek moved quickly from one corner.

He saw a tail.

He fired.

The pellet smacked into the wall and the rat darted back the way it had come.

Thompson reloaded and fired again.

He saw two baleful eyes sparkle in the dull light.

The eyes vanished.

'Did you hit it?' Mackenzie wanted to know.

Thompson shook his head.

More movement.

He still had the rifle pressed to his shoulder.

The rat scurried across his sights and he squeezed the trigger.

The pellet drilled into its thin body and it squealed, trying to drag itself along on the remains of a back leg that had been blown off at the hip.

Mackenzie ran to the toolbox and snatched one of the hammers from it.

He moved close to the rat.

It opened its mouth defiantly to show its long front teeth.

He smashed its skull with the hammer.

'There's probably more of them around here,' Thompson said, stepping out into the light.

It was then that he saw the cat.

A tortoiseshell, it was sitting about twenty feet away watching, apparently unconcerned by the noise and raised voices. Even when Thompson pointed the rifle at it, the creature didn't move.

He shot it in the right hind leg.

The cat hissed and leapt several feet into the air.

Thompson reloaded with incredible speed and fired again.

The second pellet hit it in the side, punctured the fur and knocked the wind from the animal.

It turned to run, but Thompson was after it.

Mackenzie and Harper joined the chase, Mackenzie hurling the hammer and missing by feet. The tool slammed into one of the garage doors with a deafening clang.

Thompson saw the cat dragging its injured back leg. Saw the blood.

He shot it in the other hind leg and it sprawled on the wet ground, scratching at the wounds.

It was a young animal. Barely a year old. Not very large.

He picked it up by its collar and looked at it.

The cat hissed and tried to scratch him.

Thompson held it at arm's length as he carried it back towards one of the open garages.

'Fuck the rats.' He grinned.

'What are you going to do?' Tina wanted to know, a mixture of curiosity and excitement in her voice.

'You'll see,' Thompson told her, his smile spreading.

19

THE VINYL SPARKLED as Colin Glazer wiped the soft cloth over it. He turned the record in his hand, careful not to touch the playing surface, then gently lowered it onto the turntable and placed the stylus carefully on the edge.

As the music filled the room he wandered over to his chair and reached for the book beside his bed. He winced as he felt the familiar gnawings of arthritic pain in his knees and lower back. They receded as he settled himself and flipped open the book.

He'd read it before, just as he'd read most of the volumes that filled the shelves on three sides of his room. The non-fiction was usually read at least twice. Sometimes even the novels.

Despite the size of his collection, the subject matter was fairly limited.

Military history. Crime. True crime.

There was a well-thumbed paperback copy of Truman Capote's *In Cold Blood* on the bedside table. He'd managed to pick it up at a car boot sale for 10p, along with some old Raymond Chandler novels and a yellowed copy of a Conan Doyle anthology bearing the legend '⅙' on the front.

Dorothy L. Sayers. Dashiell Hammett. Edgar Allan Poe. Ruth Rendell.

All vied for space on Glazer's packed shelves.

Fiction rubbed jackets with books about Charles Manson. The Moors Murderers. The Yorkshire Ripper. Jeffrey Dahmer. Neville Heath.

Despite the mutterings of some of his fellow residents about his morbid tastes in literature, Glazer found, more often than not, that he had become something of a lending library. Barely a day passed without one of his companions browsing the collection and leaving with a volume of one kind or another.

Glazer made a mental note to ask Eva Cole what she'd thought of the book she'd borrowed from him about Ruth Ellis. Eva, to Glazer's fascination, had been visiting friends in Hampstead at the time Ellis had shot and killed her lover in April 1955.

He looked up as the door opened, smiling when he saw Ronni standing there.

'I heard the music,' she told him. 'So I knew you were in here.'

'I bet you don't know what it is, do you?' Glazer grinned.

Ronni shook her head.

'Bunny Berrigan,' he told her. "I Can't Get Started With You". Harry Holland asked me if I could play it at his anniversary party. He says it's one of Janice's favourites. He picked out a few more he'd like me to play too.'

'You're the DJ, are you, Colin?' She smiled.

'I don't mind. I've always loved music. Listening to it. Dancing to it. Playing it.'

'You used to be in a band, didn't you?'

'In the fifties.'

'What did you play?'

'Drums and guitar. I learned the piano, too. I never wanted to do it professionally, but we used to play in pubs at the weekends. They'd give us free beer for the night. The girls used to like us too.' He winked exaggeratedly and Ronni smiled.

She crossed to the turntable and looked down at the vinyl. 'It's a good job you got your record player fixed,' she murmured.

'Jack had a look at it for me. He's a bit of a mechanical wizard is our Mr Fuller.'

'My dad's still got some '78s at home, but he's got nothing to play them on,' Ronni mused, looking at the other records beside the turntable. 'You can't get stack systems with turntables that play '78s anymore.'

'My grandkids have never even *seen* a record, let alone a '78. It's all CDs and tapes now, isn't it? They always laugh at me when they come.' His tone darkened slightly. 'Not that they come very often.'

Ronni turned to look at the older man and saw the sadness in his eyes.

'They hardly know me, Ronni,' he said quietly. 'I think that's the way my daughter *wants* it.'

'I'm sure it's not, Colin. I mean, she lives quite a way away, doesn't she?'

'She's got a car. Once a month wouldn't kill her.'

Ronni nodded almost imperceptibly.

'How often do you see *your* father?' he wanted to know.

'Every day, but that's different. He only lives half a mile away.'

'You still *see* him.'

But would I see him so often if mum was still alive.

'You never know, your daughter might even turn up this weekend,' Ronni offered.

'I won't hold my breath,' Glazer said flatly.

The record came to an end, and the needle stuck in the run-off grooves.

The constant clicking sounded like a mechanical heartbeat.

20

THOMPSON FOUND THAT by holding the cat at arms' length, he could avoid its claws.

The injured animal slashed at him every now and then, but a combination of shock and blood loss had reduced it to virtual helplessness.

He looked at its eyes, bulging in the sockets. Combined with the low mewling sounds it made, Thompson thought it seemed to be begging to be freed.

Tina lit another cigarette and followed him into the garage, her eyes fixed on the captive feline.

Harper and Mackenzie also stood close, looking alternately at the cat and Thompson.

Harper put the toe of his trainer into a puddle of blood that had dripped from the cat's wounds and smeared the crimson into the thick dust.

'Just let it go,' Tina said, feigning disinterest.

Thompson ignored her and reached into the toolbox as he passed. He pulled out the hammer and two rusted nails, each about four inches long.

With a sudden movement he slammed the cat against the rear wall of the garage. The impact stunned the already weakened creature and it hung limply in his grip.

Thompson moved with remarkable speed and precision.

He grabbed the cat's right forepaw in his left hand, slid a nail against the pad and brought the hammer down with tremendous force.

The nail pierced the pad and skewered the cat to the brick-work.

It squealed in agony and the pain seemed to galvanize it into action once more, but Thompson took another nail and repeated the procedure with its other paw.

Blood spurted from the pad, some of it splashing onto his sleeve, but he drove the nail home, his second blow missing and pulverizing one of the cat's toes.

It shrieked again and twisted madly, secured by the nails.

Its hind legs – rendered virtually useless by the air-gun slugs – pin-wheeled, but Thompson grabbed first the right, then the left.

'Let me have a go,' said Harper.

Thompson handed him the hammer and a couple of nails. 'Better do it quick,' the older lad said.

Harper pushed the point against the pad of the right hind leg and then struck as hard as he could with the hammer.

He missed and smashed a bone in the cat's leg. The strident shattering reverberated around the inside of the garage.

Thompson chuckled.

The flailing left hind paw caught Harper across the face, the claws gashing his skin just below his eye.

'Fucking bastard,' he snarled and struck again.

This time the hammer connected cleanly and the nail punc-tured flesh, but it merely protruded from the cat's paw.

He was forced to strike again to bury the steel prong in the brickwork behind.

He drove the fourth nail in and stepped back.

The cat was spreadeagled on the wall, held there by the rusty nails like some kind of badly mounted hunting trophy.

It was mewing softly, its eyes half closed.

The little bell on its collar tinkled every time its head moved.

There were spots of blood on the wall and floor.

Harper touched a hand to the scratches on his face and winced.

He reached into his pocket for the Stanley knife and jabbed it towards the cat's exposed belly, but Thompson grabbed his arm.

'Use the rifle,' he said quietly.

Harper picked up the weapon, broke it and pushed in a pellet.

'Not so close,' said Thompson, mockingly. 'Stand back there by the doorway.'

He and Mackenzie also retreated, watching as Harper raised the rifle to his shoulder.

'Aim for its eye,' Thompson told him.

21

Harper fired.

The pellet slammed into the wall six inches to the right of the cat.

A chorus of jeers greeted the miss.

Harper reloaded and fired again.

The second pellet tore off part of the cat's left ear.

It let out a renewed wail of pain and tried to struggle against the nails that held it steady.

Harper grinned.

'Come on,' Mackenzie snapped, grabbing at the gun. 'Give us a go.'

'One more go,' Harper hissed, shoving another pellet in. He snapped the barrel shut, pulled the stock into his shoulder and aimed.

The pellet powered into the cat's mouth and blasted away one of its upper canine teeth.

Blood filled its mouth and ran down its throat.

The noises it was making lessened in volume.

It was gurgling.

Mackenzie took the air rifle and aimed.

He missed the head, but drilled a pellet into the body.

He did the same with the second.

And the third.

'One hundred and *eighty*!' he shouted, waving the gun above his head.

'Fucking arsehole.' Thompson grinned, snatching the .22 from him. The older youth loaded it and handed it to Tina.

'Go on,' he said, presenting the weapon to her.

She shook her head.

'See if you can hit it,' Thompson persisted.

Tina took a final drag on her cigarette, then ground the butt beneath her trainers.

'Take the rifle,' Thompson urged.

She looked at the weapon. Then at the cat.

Then at Thompson.

'What do I do?' she said, a faint smile playing on her lips.

'I'll show you how to hold it,' he told her.

'Imagine it's a cock, you'll soon get the hang of it.' Harper sniggered.

'Fuck off,' Tina hissed, swinging the rifle around to face him.

Harper ran.

She grinned, then felt Thompson's hand on her shoulder, manoeuvring her back to face the cat.

'Look down the barrel,' he told her. 'Line the front sight up with the groove in the rear sight.' He was holding the weapon, his hand over hers. 'Now aim for its eye,' he told her, his mouth close to her ear.

She could see the glistening orb.

The cat's head was barely moving.

'Squeeze the trigger,' Thompson instructed. 'Don't jerk it. Just squeeze.'

She did as she was told.

The loud crack reverberated inside the garage.

The pellet struck the cat's collar and dented the little bell. It tinkled forlornly.

The cat meowed weakly. It was whining like a sick child now, the sound more or less constant; a discordant note that had no end.

'Good shot,' Thompson said, taking the gun from her and reloading.

'One more,' Tina pleaded and he allowed her to have the rifle again.

She raised it to her shoulder and sighted it.

Squeezed the trigger.

The pellet hit the cat in the right eye.

The projectile burst the bulging orb. Blood and clear liquid sprayed into the air.

Tina turned excitedly to Thompson, who was grinning.

Even Mackenzie and Harper managed some complimentary comments.

'Looks like you're the winner,' Thompson told her.

'Are you going to give me a prize?' Tina wanted to know.

Thompson took the gun from her and turned away from the garage.

'It's still alive,' Harper called.

'So what?' Thompson grinned. 'It's not going anywhere, is it?'

They were all laughing as they wandered off.

22

THERE WERE TWO others in the classroom with Graham Brown.

He recognized one.

An older boy, almost fifteen.

Gates or Bates or something.

Who fucking cared anyway?

The other one was a girl roughly the same age as Brown himself.

Tall. Brown hair. Thin face. Thick eyebrows.

He glanced across at her and grinned.

It looked as if someone had stuck two caterpillars above her eyes.

He kept expecting them to crawl away as she sat over the piece of paper, her biro scratching across it.

At the front of the class, reading, was Mr Albon.

Games master.

Ginger-haired little cunt.

He took most of the detentions. At least most that Brown had been present for.

Stocky. Red cheeked. Big nose.

Fucking big nose.

The clock on the wall above the door ticked loudly in the silence of the classroom.

How much longer?

Brown picked at a spot on his cheek.

He looked down at the sheet of paper before him: the school rules.

That was the standard punishment in detention. Copying out the school fucking rules.

He'd scribbled barely a dozen lines.

Fuck the rules.

Fuck the school.

Fuck Mr Albon.

The teacher had done his customary patrol of the room, hands clasped behind his back, but not a word had been uttered by any of the four residents of the room during the sixty minutes they had occupied it.

'All right,' Mr Albon said finally. 'Pack your stuff away and go.'

He checked his own watch against the wall clock, then watched as Brown and the other two stuffed their pens and pads hurriedly into their bags.

Sheets of paper were left on the desks for inspection.

'And I don't want to see *any* of you back here again, understood?' he called as they filed towards the door.

'Seeds on stony ground' was the phrase that sprung to mind.

'Flogging a dead horse' was another.

Brown barged out into the corridor, then strode for the main entrance beyond.

He stepped out into the playground.

On the school field beyond, a dozen or so boys were playing football.

Brown wondered about joining them, then decided against it.

His stomach rumbled protestingly.

He needed food.

He decided to call at the chip shop on the way home. It was better than the shit his mother cooked; that is when she could be bothered.

As he crossed the playground he noticed there was still a car parked in the area reserved for teachers' vehicles.

Brown knew that the silver grey Montego belonged to Albon.

He checked behind him and saw that the games master hadn't emerged from the building yet. Brown ran towards the car.

He hawked loudly, then spat on the windscreen.

With unerring accuracy he projected a second glutinous mass of mucus onto the driver's door handle.

The temptation was too great.

He pulled the bunch of keys from his pocket and raked them along one side of the car.

Chuckling, he ran off.

23

'DID SHE GO?' Barbara Eustace wanted to know.

Ronni nodded and picked up the dog, passing it to the older woman as if it were a child.

The Highland terrier licked at Barbara's face as she held it close to her and whispered lovingly in its floppy ear. 'Good girl,' she cooed. 'We don't want you making a mess inside, do we?'

The dog looked almost as old as its owner. The fur on its little face was greying around the muzzle and it moved with difficulty when walking.

One of the staff walked the dog twice a day for Barbara. It was hardly an unpleasant chore. Two hundred yards and the animal was fit to drop. Ronni had tried throwing sticks for it, but discovered it was quicker for her to fetch them herself.

It seemed to be in good health though and the other residents had no problem with its presence. Most of the time Barbara kept it in her room, where it slept in its small basket.

Otherwise, it trotted around as efficiently as its arthritic little legs would allow, following its wheelchair-bound owner and gratefully accepting any snacks offered to it by the other residents.

Ronni couldn't remember hearing it bark more than a dozen times since it had arrived with Barbara three months ago.

Then again, she reasoned, any sustained noise would probably cause the collapse of its little lungs.

Its red collar bore its name in silver letters:

MOLLY.

As Ronni pushed the wheelchair along the corridor she glanced at her watch.

Almost eight p.m.

She and Alison were due to finish their shift any time now.

And then?

She exhaled wearily.

Home?

'What's wrong, Veronica?' Barbara asked.

'You can call me Ronni, you know. Everyone else does.'

'You were christened Veronica, you should be *called* Veronica. I wouldn't expect you to call me Babs.'

Ronni chuckled. 'I wouldn't dream of calling you Babs,' she affirmed. They turned a corner, heading for Barbara's room. 'What makes you think there's something wrong, Barbara?' Ronni wanted to know.

'An educated guess. I'm quite perceptive when it comes to judging people's moods. I always have been.'

'Are you speaking as a former JP now?'

Barbara smiled.

'How long were you on the bench?' Ronni enquired.

'Fifteen years. I saw lots of people, Veronica. You get to know their moods the same way as you learn if someone's lying or not. It's instinct, I suppose.'

'Did you give up because of your accident?'

'Oh, heavens, no. I'd already been retired for more than ten years before the crash.'

'Did they ever find the other driver?'

'No. All I know is *he* can still walk. He was driving on the wrong side of the road. I swerved to avoid him, I barely touched *his* car. I was the one who ended up wrapped around a tree. He didn't even stop to see if I was dead or alive.'

They reached the door of Barbara's room and Ronni pushed it open. Barbara wheeled herself through, then lowered Molly down onto the floor.

The terrier waddled across to its basket and clambered in.

'Will you be OK now, Barbara?' Ronni asked.

The older woman nodded. 'I'll be fine,' she said. 'We *both* will.' She nodded in the direction of her dog.

'See you tomorrow, Barbara,' Ronni said and closed the door behind her.

As she headed back along the corridor she heard a car pulling up outside Shelby House.

Gazing through the nearest window, she watched as the driver climbed out.

24

GORDON FAULKNER SIPPED at his mug of tea and looked around the small staff room.

The walls were bare apart from a couple of watercolours painted by one of the residents. Faulkner focused on a crack in the magnolia wall and traced it with his gaze as if he were following the path of a vein across flesh.

'We should think about getting more staff for this place,' he said, glancing at Ronni.

'Why?' she wanted to know. 'Three of *us* to look after nine residents is plenty.'

'But there aren't three of us on these night shifts, are there?' Faulkner protested.

'When have any of us had any trouble?'

'I'd have thought this was a piece of cake for you after working at the hospital, Gordon,' Alison added.

Prior to his appointment at Shelby House, Faulkner had worked for five years as a porter at Kempston General Hospital. Mainly in A&E.

He'd handed in his notice the night after he'd helped wheel his nineteen-year-old nephew into surgery with multiple neck and facial wounds.

The product of a fight in a club.

The lad had died in his arms, his jugular vein severed by glass.

Faulkner's sister had taken her own life two months later.

He'd worked at Shelby House for the past eight years, joining the staff only days after his twenty-sixth birthday.

'Once the patients are in bed for the night, what the hell is there to do?' Ronni asked. 'I think the night shift's are peaceful. I quite enjoy them.'

'Then *you* do tonight,' Faulkner snapped.

'Who rattled your cage today?' Ronni enquired. 'You've been like a bear with a sore head ever since you got here.' She rinsed her own mug in the sink and set it down to drip-dry. 'At least you haven't got to take Molly for a walk,' she told him. 'I've already done it.'

'Did you have to stand and *watch* it have a crap so you could report back to Barbara?' he grunted.

'You'd better be a bit more cheerful with the residents, Gordon.' There was a severity in Ronni's tone that made him look warily at her.

'Miserable sod,' Alison offered, pulling on her coat.

'Wait a minute,' Ronni said, a slight smile touching her lips. 'I know why you don't want to work tonight. There's a match on TV, isn't there?'

Faulkner shrugged. 'I hadn't noticed,' he murmured.

'You bloody liar.' Ronni chuckled. She reached for the paper and flipped it open at the TV listings. 'Eight o'clock, ITV, Arsenal versus Spurs. Watch it in the day room. Most of the residents will be watching it anyway,' she insisted.

'No way. Don Tanner will want to bet on the game and Jack Fuller's a Spurs supporter,' Faulkner announced. 'If they beat us he'll *never* let it rest. I'll end up getting a load of stick *and* losing money.'

The two women laughed and headed for the door.

'Gordon,' Ronni said, pausing at the exit. 'Just keep your eye on Janice Holland, will you?' She told him about the incident that afternoon.

Faulkner nodded.

'She doesn't want Harry to know,' Ronni insisted.

'No problem. Go on then, home you go.'

He walked to the main exit with them, then waved them off, retreated inside and locked the large door.

Outside, it was colder than Ronni had realized. As she spoke her breath clouded in the air. 'Do you fancy a quick drink before I run you home?' she asked. 'We could nip down to the Horseshoes. It's only five minutes from here.'

Alison nodded. 'Not in any hurry to get home?' she murmured.

Ronni exhaled wearily.

'Just a quick one then,' Alison said.

They climbed into the Fiesta and Ronni started the engine.

The car moved away from Shelby House, the gravel crunching beneath the tyres.

25

THE THREE BARS inside the Horseshoes were busy for mid-week. Ronni was surprised at the amount of noise coming, in particular, from the public bar. As well as the customary backdrop of music from the jukebox and the constant crack of pool balls, there was also an unusually loud din of conversation filtering through.

Loud laughter was punctuated by shouts.

Ronni heard the sound of breaking glass.

She sipped at her Bacardi and Coke and glanced in the direction of the racket. 'It sounds as if someone's got something to celebrate,' she said quietly.

Alison nodded and lifted her own glass, the ice clinking against it as she drank.

'So, what would you do in my position, Alison?' Ronni wanted to know. 'You never did tell me.'

'I can't say, Ronni. Unless you're involved, it's difficult.'

'Would you leave Peter if you didn't love him anymore?'

'I don't know. I really don't.'

Ronni finished her drink and set the glass down.

The two women regarded each other silently for a moment, then Alison spoke again. 'Are you sure you don't love him anymore? It's not just that you don't fancy him anymore?'

'What's the difference?'

'Come on, Ronni, don't be naïve. Are you telling me the only blokes you've ever slept with in your life are ones you've been in love with?'

Ronni shook her head.

'Me neither,' Alison concurred. 'Even now, I see blokes I want to sleep with and I know Peter sees other women he fancies. It wouldn't be natural if we didn't. It doesn't mean we love each other any less.'

'You make yourself sound like a tart.'

'I'm being honest. Perhaps *you* should be too.'

'Meaning?'

'If you hated life with Andy so much you'd have moved out by now.'

'It's not that easy, Alison. We've been together for twelve years. Besides, I don't want to hurt him. I don't hate him. I don't hate living with him. I just don't love him anymore.'

'Then *tell* him. Be honest with him. The only one you're fooling is yourself. What do you think is going to happen? Do you think this is all going to change? You'll wake up one morning and you'll love him again? You'll be all over each other again like you were when you first met?'

'I'm not *that* naïve, Alison.'

'Isn't there anything Andy can do to help?'

'To make me start loving him again?' She shook her head.

'Then for Christ's sake put him out of his misery.'

Again the two women looked at each other for long moments, then Ronni got to her feet.

'I'm nipping to the loo before we go,' she said. 'I'll meet you outside.'

She made her way through to the public bar where the toilets were situated. As Ronni pushed the door open the noise hit her like a fist.

'. . . *Now we lay you down to rest, you're never gonna be more than second best . . .*' roared from the jukebox.

Ronni picked her way past the pool table where two youths were engaged in a game watched by half a dozen of their companions.

'. . . *roll the dice, don't think twice, we crush, crush, crush 'em . . .*'

77

Darts thudded into the board on the other side of the room.

The rest of the tables in the bar seemed to be occupied as well.

Sometimes couples. Sometimes clusters of people.

A man a couple of years younger than Ronni almost bumped into her as he emerged from the Gents still zipping his flies.

He smiled, running appraising eyes over her.

She sought the sanctuary of the Ladies.

It was mercifully quiet inside.

Ronni inspected her reflection in the cracked mirror that ran the length of the wall, aware of movement in one of the cubicles behind her.

The toilet flushed and a young woman dressed in a black top, short silver lycra skirt and expensive-looking high heels emerged.

With the benefit of her heavy make-up, Donna Freeman appeared much older than her fourteen years. Her dishwater-blonde hair had been washed and blow-dried, and she smelled strongly of designer perfume.

Ronni guessed it was Calvin Klein; whatever, it wasn't cheap.

She paused before the mirror and pulled a red lipstick from her handbag.

Ronni ran a hand through her own hair, aware that the girl knew she was being watched.

She applied the lipstick carefully, then dropped it back inside the handbag.

As she fluffed up her own hair she glanced at Ronni's reflection with something akin to disdain.

Then she turned and walked out.

Ronni turned to the first of the cubicles and pushed the door open. The cistern was cracked, the bowl full of stained paper.

She retreated into the cubicle Donna Freeman had used and slid the bolt.

As she sat down she noticed the piece of silver paper lying discarded beside the toilet.

Ronni could see that there were still flecks of white powder on it.

In the bar, the noise seemed to grow louder.

26

THE HOUSE WAS silent when she entered. Ronni closed the front door behind her and hung up her coat.

The red light was blinking on the answering machine and she pressed the 'Play' button.

It was Andy. He'd been offered some overtime. He wouldn't be home until late.

Good.

There was a loud beep as the message ended.

She moved through the house switching on lights, driving away the darkness.

She even switched on the TV.

The sound of voices filtered into the room.

It was a play or something. John Thaw was in it.

He seemed to be in everything.

Ronni glanced at the screen as she made her way back into the kitchen.

She boiled the kettle and made herself some tea.

As she sipped the hot liquid she leant against one of the worktops, gazing idly into space, the sound of the TV drifting through from the living room.

She looked across at the CD player perched on the microwave and wondered about switching that on too.

It was as if she couldn't bear to have a moment's silence.

Silence gives you time to think, doesn't it?

She jabbed the required button and the sound of the Corrs filled the room.

'. . . *What can I do to make you love me* . . .'

She almost smiled as she walked out of the kitchen and made her way through the living room, then upstairs to the bedroom.

Ronni changed into a pair of jeans and a big baggy sweater, then she sat on the end of the bed for a moment, facing the wardrobe.

There were two suitcases on top of it.

She took one down, wiped a thin layer of dust from the lid and flipped it open.

There were two old airline tickets inside.

She opened the first and inspected the date.

Five years ago. The last time they'd had a holiday.

A week in Corfu.

There were some photos too and Ronni reached for them.

Andy emerging from the sea.

A view from the hotel room.

Ronni in her bikini laying beside the pool.

And the two of them together on the beach, arms around each other.

(as if they were in love)

She remembered Andy asking a passer-by to take it.

Ronni dropped the photos and the tickets back into the case, then she pulled open a couple of drawers and took some clothes out.

She hastily folded a couple of T-shirts and placed them in the bottom of the case. She put a blouse next to them.

Some leggings. Knickers. A sweatshirt.

Ronni paused and looked down at the random selection of clothes in the case.

Go on then, finish the job.

She ran a hand through her hair, then closed the suitcase and lifted it back on top of the wardrobe.

For long moments she stood looking at it.

Why did you stop?

She wondered what she would have told Andy if he'd walked in then.

The truth, perhaps? He might have helped you pack.

Ronni sat down on the edge of the bed, head bowed.

She began to cry softly and the tears took her by surprise.

27

Jack Fuller knew he was going to die.

He'd been expecting it for the last three years and now he knew the time had finally arrived.

The only surprise was the way it would come.

He knelt in the heat, hands tied behind his back, the sun wringing perspiration from his body and baking his flesh.

Flesh that barely covered his bones. When he was standing upright he could count almost all of his ribs. There was so little skin and muscle covering his legs it seemed as if the limbs would shatter with each step he took.

And yet, like so many others like him, he lived out his daily existence in that condition.

Although perhaps to say that he lived was an overstatement. He and his comrades existed. No one lived anymore. Not in a world of brutality and sudden death like the one he had come to know so well.

Death was so frequent a visitor he felt he knew it like a relative, but never before had it come for him.

He had seen men die in their hundreds during the past three years.

Starvation.

Disease.

Brutality.

He had seen men cut their own throats with pieces of

jagged rock rather than exist another day in the conditions he knew.

Others had succumbed to the savagery of their captors: beaten to death with rifle butts for the smallest transgression; bayonetted repeatedly for the amusement of those who looked upon them as lower than animals.

Perhaps they had been the fortunate ones.

Daily, he saw men die from dysentery, typhoid, cholera, yellow fever and God-alone-knew how many other maladies.

Plagued at nights by mosquitoes, tormented during the day by insects, some could only lay helplessly and watch as the bloated flies fed on the pus that oozed from their leg ulcers.

And everywhere around the water was filled with leeches. They clung to a man until they had gorged themselves on his blood and then they dropped off, bloated and corpulent. Those who panicked and ripped the monstrous gastropods off were often left with the head embedded in their skin.

It had to burned out with a cigarette end.

The leeches carried disease too.

Everything in this godforsaken place carried disease and death with it.

For a handful of rice, men were worked to death.

And now, Jack Fuller knew that it was *his* time to die.

There were two others before him.

Both naked but for a small piece of cloth around their groins, as was Fuller.

They too were kneeling on the parched earth, the sun blistering their fragile forms.

He had no idea why they must also die.

All he knew was that in a couple of minutes it would be over.

And yet, despite the suffering, the hunger pangs that tore at his insides, the ulcers and the malaria, he wanted to live.

Some found death a welcome release from the hell that he knew as everyday existence; but in his eyes a man should value life above all things, and the thought of having it snatched away was intolerable.

But Jack Fuller knew he had no choice in the matter.

From his kneeling position he could see only the boots of the man who would end his life.

He heard words hissed in a language he now half understood.

Heard the sweep of the sword as it was pulled from the scabbard.

The first man had closed his eyes tightly.

His lips were moving soundlessly in prayer.

The sword flashed down.

The man's head was cleanly severed.

It rolled a few feet across the ground, propelled by a massive gout of blood from the stump of the neck.

The second man began to sob quietly.

Fuller could see his skeletal body quivering.

He heard words rasped at him.

Someone spat at the shaking man. Called him a coward.

Fuller saw the sword raised.

Heard the man's cries rising in volume.

Heard his entreaties.

Then the whoosh and the dull thud as the head was sliced effortlessly off.

Hot blood jetted into the air, some of it spattering Fuller and the realization hit him with even greater force.

He was next.

His legs were not bound.

Perhaps if he could get to his feet he could run.

Run as fast as his frail form would allow.

One of them might put a bullet in his back, but that didn't seem to matter now.

He looked across the ground and saw the two severed heads looking blankly back at him, eyes open like fish on a skillet.

He tried to rise, but the sole of a foot held him in place.

He prayed for help.

Prayed to a God who had looked down upon so much suffering for so long.

He opened his mouth to scream.

Please, God, I don't want to die.

Then the sword swung down.

28

He was screaming when he sat up in bed.

The residue of the nightmare was still painted vividly upon his mind and Jack Fuller could feel the sweat that sheathed his body. For interminable seconds he thought that the sweat was the product of the tropical heat.

Only gradually did he realize he was sitting in darkness.

In his room.

Safe.

His heart was thudding madly against his ribs – so hard it seemed it would shatter them.

He gripped the sides of the bed and looked around.

Jack Fuller didn't dare close his eyes in case the nightmare came flooding back.

Instead he stared around his room inside Shelby House.

He thought he was still screaming, but then realized the sound was only in his head.

He was awake.

It was over for another night.

He swung his legs over the side of the bed and placed them on the floor.

Contact with something tangible seemed to shock him back to reality and, at last, the nightmare began to recede somewhat.

Fuller dragged himself out of bed and stumbled across to the sink, where he spun the tap and drank some water, gulping it down like a man in a desert.

He gripped the porcelain with one hand to steady himself.

He was still standing there when the door opened.

'Jack.'

He turned slowly and saw Gordon Faulkner silhouetted there.

'Jack,' said the younger man. 'Are you OK?'

Fuller nodded, trying to control his breathing.

Faulkner stepped inside and closed the door behind him. He crossed to Fuller and put one hand on his shoulder. He could feel the older man quivering.

'Another nightmare?' Faulkner asked.

Fuller nodded. 'There was a time when I thought they'd stopped,' he said, his voice a feeble whisper.

'Do you want me to get you a sleeping pill?'

Fuller shook his head. 'I'll be fine now,' he insisted.

'Do you want to talk about it?'

'Again?'

'If you want to talk, I'll listen.'

'All part of the service.'

'That's right.'

Fuller drank some more water, then sat down on the edge of the bed.

'Same dream?' Faulkner wanted to know.

'They're always the same, Gordon. You know that.'

'About the camp?'

'The camp. The railway. The hospital. It never changes.' He smiled weakly. 'It happened over sixty years ago and yet it seems like yesterday. All of it.'

'Jack, after what you went through it's a wonder you're still sane.'

'I sometimes wonder if I am.'

'Where was it you were taken prisoner?'

'Singapore in 1941. I was seventeen.'

'You must have been terrified. *I* would have been.'

'We'd heard rumours about what the Japs did to prisoners. What they'd done to the Chinese back in '38. Cutting open pregnant women. Burying men up to their waists and setting dogs on them. Using people for bayonet practice. But we thought with us being Westerners, professional soldiers like them, we thought they might treat us differently.' He shook his head. 'Most of my platoon were dead within the first year,' he continued. 'Worked to death, starved or tortured.'

Faulkner reached out and touched the older man's arm.

'I read in papers that people say we should forget about it now,' Fuller continued. 'That what happened doesn't mean anything anymore. The politicians are the worst of the lot.' There was an edge to his voice. 'No one cares except those who went through it. I've tried forgetting about it, but then I think if I do that I'd betray the memory of all those men who died building that bloody railway. I don't *want* to forget any of the men those Japanese bastards murdered. And that's what it was. Murder. Pure and simple.' He swallowed hard and took another sip of water.

'You were a medical orderly, weren't you, Jack?'

Fuller nodded. 'The Japs were losing so many of us to disease they decided to set up a hospital at Chungkai in Northern Thailand,' he said quietly. 'Not that you could call it a bloody hospital. It was a collection of huts. We didn't have any supplies either. The Japanese guards used to come to us to be treated for things like VD and syphilis. We'd tell them what medical supplies we needed to help *them*, but they didn't realize it was stuff we wanted to help our own boys.' He managed a smile. 'We used needles made out of bamboo. We turned old cutlery into surgical instruments. We even used to spit into rotten bananas and the yeast that developed helped prevent Vitamin B deficiency. The blokes weren't too keen on taking *that*, but they knew it helped them.'

He afforded himself a brief grin. 'I was working there one day when they brought in this lad with tropical ulcers all over one leg. They'd been caused by bamboo shoots. Got infected. We knew the only way to save him was to remove the leg. He couldn't have been more than nineteen. A scouser. He kept on about how he didn't want to die so we told him we'd have to amputate.' Fuller was gazing ahead as if watching the incident being projected on the opposite wall. 'All we had to do it with was an old butcher's knife,' he murmured. 'I did it.' He suddenly looked directly into Faulkner's eyes and the younger man saw tears there. 'I took his leg off from the knee down,' Fuller continued almost apologetically. 'We didn't have any morphine. Two of the others held him down and I cut it off. I made him a cripple.'

'You saved his life, Jack,' Faulkner said, touching the older man's arm. 'What choice did you have?'

Fuller was silent for a moment. 'He was in the hospital for a week afterwards,' he said finally. 'We sent him out with an artificial leg we'd made from bamboo. I don't know if he survived the war. Probably not. The way they treated us, it's a wonder *anyone* got out alive.' He wiped a tear from the corner of one eye. 'We caught one of them when it was all over,' he said quietly. 'One of the guards. When news came through that the war was over, most of them just hopped it straight away. But we managed to capture this sergeant. He'd been a real bastard. He'd tortured men I knew, beaten them unconscious for no reason. It was as if, finally, after three years, we could get our own back on one of them. We tied him to a tree and took turns sticking slivers of bamboo into him. We even held up the wounded so *they* could do it. We *all* had a turn. And we all enjoyed it. It took him more than a day to die. I can still see him there now, screaming. The bastard. I know it's bad but we felt as if we were getting some kind of revenge.'

'After what you went through, Jack, I'd say you were entitled to some,' Faulkner mused.

'When you get treated like an animal for long enough, you start to behave like one. Everyone's got a breaking point. A point that they won't go beyond. There comes a time when you either fight back or just give up and die. I swore I'd never just give up. That's what I keep drumming into the others here.'

'Yeah, I've heard you.' Faulkner grinned. 'What hold have you got over the other residents, Jack?'

Fuller looked puzzled.

'I'm only kidding,' said the younger man. 'They look up to you here. They respect you. Probably because of what you've been through. I reckon *you* could run this place on your own.'

'Perhaps it's the military training.' Fuller smiled, wiping his cheeks again. 'It never leaves you, you know. The discipline. The self-belief. Is it so bad if others take it on board too?'

'No, it's not,' Faulkner told him. 'You sort them out, Jack,' he said, smiling.

The two men looked at each other for a moment longer.

'Are you going to be able to sleep now?' he wanted to know.

'I'll be fine,' Fuller said, pulling the covers over himself. 'Thanks for listening.'

'Goodnight,' Faulkner said quietly.

He closed the door of the room as he left.

Jack Fuller lay on his back staring at the ceiling.

Alone with his thoughts.

29

'THAT'S SHIT THAT IS.'

Liam Harper nudged Graham Brown and almost knocked the Catatonia CD from his hand.

'What do you fucking know?' the older lad snapped.

'The singer's all right, but the rest of them are cunts,' Harper persisted.

Brown ignored his younger companion and continued searching through the racks.

The HMV store in Kempston town centre was crowded with weekend shoppers. Music blaring from the speakers inside the building made it almost impossible to speak without raising your voice. At one end, the bank of screens was showing the latest Red Hot Chilli Peppers video. Brown glanced at it occasionally as he continued to sort through the racks.

Elsewhere in the shop, Carl Thompson, Donna Freeman and Tina Craven were moving amongst the bustling throng of shoppers.

Brown had no idea whether they were on the ground floor like himself and Harper or the first floor.

It didn't really matter at the moment.

He knew Terry Mackenzie was not too far away, playing on a Dreamcast machine set up in the games section of the store.

Brown glanced around and saw the security guard immediately.

Tall, dressed in a dark blue sweater and trousers.

Fat bastard.

As he watched he saw Tina Craven standing near the main doors, peering at the chart albums.

There was a young lad with her: Tony Morton. Barely ten years old, he wore a navy Kappa tracksuit top and Nike baseball cap.

Tina and the younger lad disappeared among the other shoppers and Brown returned to his browsing.

Finally, tiring of that, he made his way towards the escalators that would carry him up to the first floor.

There were TV screens all the way up and he peered at the images that were displaying a scene from 'The Beach.'

As he reached the top of the escalator he glanced around at the racks of DVDs and videos. There was a 'Two For the Price of One' sale on and the aisles were clogged with bargain hunters.

He looked across in the direction of the counter and saw Donna Freeman. She had two videos in her hand and was waiting patiently in a queue ahead of a young woman.

Behind the woman stood Carl Thompson.

The staff were run off their feet, Thompson noted with delight. They could barely cope with the flood of purchasers and enquiries.

The lines towards the tills moved slowly, but that suited Thompson.

The young woman in front of him was holding a *Friends* boxed set.

Yank shit.

She was also holding a blue American Express card in her free hand.

Ahead of her, Donna placed two videos on the counter and smiled at the harassed sales assistant. 'Do they do widescreen versions of these?' she asked, pushing the empty cases towards him.

'I'll have to check,' he said, hoping the possibility of waiting might put her off.

It didn't.

He moved to his computer and tapped in details.

Donna waited with apparent interest.

Behind her, the young woman tutted and glanced at her watch.

Thompson slid his hand into the pocket of his leather jacket.

He pulled out his mobile phone, one eye fixed on the American Express card held by the young woman in front of him.

The shining digits seemed to wink at him.

He pressed a corresponding key on his phone.

Just hold it there.

He had twelve of the fourteen digits.

The young woman lowered her hands.

Come on, you bitch. Show me the rest.

She moved the card to her other hand, one index finger over the first four numbers.

Thompson pressed in the last two then the expiry date.

Thanks a lot, Christine Williams.

He stepped out of the queue.

At the counter, the assistant informed Donna there were no widescreen versions of *Mystery Men* or *Stigmata*. Donna nodded and moved away from the counter leaving the cassette cases where they were.

The young woman with her boxed set of *Friends* moved forward gratefully.

Thompson was already heading for the 'Down' escalator.

When he reached the bottom he wandered out into the street.

Donna and Brown joined him.

Tony Morton and Tina followed moments later.

'Find the others,' Thompson said to the youngest of the group. 'We're going shopping.'

He looked at the readout on his mobile phone and grinned.

30

CARL THOMPSON LOOKED at the piece of paper before him.

At the American Express card number.

The expiry date.

The name of the owner.

All he needed.

'So now what?' asked Tina Craven.

'We phone a few shops,' Thompson said, sipping at his Coke. 'Make some purchases.'

'Like what?' Graham Brown wanted to know, picking the piece of dill pickle from his cheeseburger and dropping it onto the table.

'DVDs are popular,' Thompson said. 'If we call Currys, Argos and Comet, we can get one from each shop. Sell them for about a hundred each. We'll do the same with stack systems or TVs.'

Brown smiled and wiped tomato ketchup from his mouth. 'Yeah, those big fuck-off widescreen ones.' He grinned.

'*You'll* have to make the call,' Thompson told Donna Freeman. 'It's a woman's card. They'll expect to hear a woman's voice.'

She nodded and looked at the piece of paper with the relevant information scribbled on it.

'Aren't they going to want to see the card when the stuff's picked up?' Brown enquired.

Thompson shook his head. 'Donna can tell them she can't get into the shop, someone else is going to pick it up for her,' he said. 'They'll have all the details as soon as we phone the order through. They'll have checked the card. Found out it's all right. As long as they've got the name of the cardholder, the number and the expiry date they couldn't give a toss. What the fuck do *they* care who's picking the gear up? They'll already have been paid for it.'

'We could get them to deliver it.' Donna smiled, sipping her coffee.

'Good idea,' Thompson agreed. 'It'll save us lugging it back.' He pulled the mobile phone from his pocket and switched it on. 'I think I'll get a new one of *these* too.' He chuckled.

He called Directory Enquiries and got the numbers of the three electrical warehouses, scribbling them down on the piece of paper beneath the Amex number.

'Sorted,' he said, switching the phone off. 'Now all we've got to do is make our choice.'

He finished what was left in the Coke container and took a couple of chips from Tony Morton's share.

Morton sucked his milkshake, then took a bite of burger. He chewed noisily.

'What if that stupid bitch cancels her card before we can get what we want?' Brown demanded.

'Why should she?' Thompson wanted to know. 'It hasn't been stolen. The first *she'll* know about is when her monthly statement arrives and there's three grands' worth of electrical gear on it.'

The others around the table laughed. 'I wouldn't mind one of those fucking DVDs myself,' Brown said.

Thompson held out his hand. 'To you, eighty quid,' he said.

'Fuck off,' sneered Brown.

'Come on, finish that and let's go and check out what we're buying,' Thompson said, getting to his feet.

'You mean, what Christine Williams is buying.' Donna smiled.

Once again, they all laughed.

Others seated in the Burger King glanced briefly at the raucous group of youngsters gathered around the table.

Thompson met each stare, his face impassive.

Donna picked up the piece of paper and glanced at the fourteen-digit number.

'That'll do nicely.' She chuckled.

They filed out of the Burger King, leaving wrappers and the remains of unwanted food spread across the table.

The first stop was Comet.

31

Andy Porter lifted the last of the shopping bags into the boot of the car, then slammed it shut.

'Christ,' he muttered, rubbing his aching hands together. 'You'd think we were feeding a bloody army.'

Ronni smiled and slid into the passenger seat. 'Some of it's Dad's too,' she reminded him.

'Make sure you get the money off him.' Andy grinned.

The car park of their local Tesco was full. Vehicles prowled slowly back and forth along the lines of stationary cars waiting for the first gap to appear, ready to speed into it as soon as they could. They reminded Ronni of sharks patrolling bloodied seas, looking for stray survivors.

Andy clambered behind the wheel and started the engine. As soon as his reverse lights lit up, two cars sped forward, indicators blinking.

'Jesus, let me get out, will you,' Andy murmured, trying to manoeuvre the Peugeot through the waiting cars.

Both tried to move into the vacated space simultaneously.

Ronni looked round as she heard the blaring of hooters.

'Every man for himself.' Andy chuckled.

He drove slowly, watching for other shoppers emerging suddenly from behind parked cars pushing bulging shopping trolleys.

'You can drop me off at Dad's,' Ronni told him. 'I'll walk back after I've seen to him.'

'Don't be stupid. I'll come in with you. I haven't seen him for a while anyway.'

'I didn't think you wanted to.'

'You never asked.'

'He'll be pleased.' She reached across and touched Andy's thigh briefly.

He smiled, but didn't take his eyes off the mazelike aisles running between the lines of parked cars.

An Astra suddenly reversed out and Andy hit the brakes.

'*Dickhead!*' he rasped.

The Astra raced away at a ridiculously high speed and a Primera hurriedly shot into the space.

'Are you sure you couldn't get the night off?' Andy wanted to know.

'Don't start that again,' she said, wearily.

'Start what? I just asked.'

'It's my turn to do the late shift.'

'It's *always* your bloody turn.'

'I've finished early three days this week, you know that.'

'And I've been on lates all week. I feel like I haven't seen you at all recently.'

'It's not *my* fault.'

'It never is.'

'Why don't *you* take some time off to fit in with *my* shifts, if you're that bothered about us being together?'

He didn't answer.

'What would we do if we *were* off together, Andy?' Ronni said scathingly. 'Go out for a meal? Go to the pictures? No. We'd sit in front of the telly all night in silence.'

He turned a corner.

The figure appeared in front of the car as if it had stepped from thin air.

Andy hit the brakes so hard they were both slammed hard against their seat belts.

'Shit,' snarled Andy, glaring at the vision before him.

Carl Thompson looked down at the front bumper of the Peugeot.

It was inches from his leg.

'Look where you're going,' Andy called, winding down the window.

'Fuck you.'

The voice came from beside the car.

From Graham Brown.

'You could have run him over.'

Ronni heard a third voice.

Tina Craven was standing beside Thompson, staring in at them.

'You didn't look,' Andy snapped.

Thompson remained where he was, his gaze moving slowly from Ronni to Andy, then back again.

'You were going too fast,' Brown offered.

'Just get out the way,' Andy said irritably.

Thompson didn't move.

There was a loud thud on the rear windscreen.

Ronni turned in her seat to see Liam Harper standing there.

She felt her heart thudding hard against her ribs.

He too was watching them.

'Are you *going* to move?' Andy insisted.

Thompson was like a statue.

Andy reached for the door handle.

'Andy, don't,' Ronni said, shooting out a hand to hold him back.

'They're kids for Christ's sake,' he snapped, preparing to push open the door.

Another figure appeared close to the side of the car.

A young woman.

Dishwater-blonde hair pulled back into a ponytail. Heavy make-up. Padded leather jacket.

Ronni was sure there was something familiar about the girl. She caught a whiff of scent through the open window that sparked a memory in her.

The girl was chewing, and staring in at Ronni.

'Stay in the car, Andy,' Ronni said quietly.

'Either you move or I'll fucking drive over you, you little shit,' Andy called.

Still Thompson remained motionless.

Andy stepped on the accelerator and the engine roared.

Thompson moved aside.

'Thanks,' Andy said sardonically.

As the Peugeot moved past, they both heard the grating sound of metal on metal.

Thompson and the others were suddenly running, disappearing through the rows of parked cars towards the shops beyond.

Andy was out of the car instantly.

He walked around to the passenger side of the car.

There were two large scratches running from the wing to the door handle.

The paint had been shaved off; the metal badly gouged.

'Little bastards,' snarled Andy. 'Look at that.' He gestured angrily at the damage, then peered in the direction of the fleeing youngsters.

They had been swallowed up by the hordes of shoppers.

Ronni stepped out of the car and also inspected the wounds on the bodywork.

'Fucking kids,' Andy hissed.

From behind a Range Rover, hidden from their view, Carl Thompson watched.

32

RONNI SIPPED HER tea and gazed out of the front window of her father's house.

He was standing beside the red Peugeot speaking to Andy. She couldn't hear what they were saying, but every now and then she saw her husband gesticulating angrily. More than once he pointed to the savage marks made on the car's bodywork.

The television was on, the sound turned down to a whisper. It was bowls; hardly the most raucous of games at the best of times.

Her father had played for his work's team when she was younger.

Her mother too.

He still had her woods upstairs.

Along with all her clothes and other belongings.

Nothing had been touched since she'd died.

Ronni glanced at her parents' wedding photo on the coffee table beside the TV.

There must be a dozen pictures of her mother around the room, some discoloured by the passage of time.

In every one she was smiling.

Ronni reached out and touched the nearest one, tracing the curve of the smile with one index finger.

Outside, her father shook his head once again as he looked at the damage done to the Peugeot.

'Little bastards,' Andy hissed. 'I should have chased them.'

'It's probably a good job you *didn't* get out, Andy.'

'I think I can handle a bunch of kids, Jim.'

'What do you think they used on it?' the older man mused, touching the deep gouges.

'A bloody can-opener by the look of it. Keys or coins wouldn't have done that much damage.'

'Will you be able to claim it back off your insurance?'

Andy nodded.

'Kids these days . . .' James Connor said, allowing the sentence to trail off.

'I knew you were going to say that, Jim.' Andy grinned.

'Well, it's true. They don't respect anything. If *I'd* done something like that when I was fifteen, my *father* would have sorted me out.'

'Things are different now, Jim. The parents don't even know where the bloody kids are half the time and the ones who do don't care.'

'Have you and Ronni thought anymore about kids?'

'Ask Ronni.'

'I have. Now I'm asking *you*.'

'I'd like them, but Ronni doesn't seem too keen. Perhaps *you* can talk her round, Jim.' He patted his father-in-law on the shoulder as they turned and headed back towards the house.

'She stopped listening to *me* a long time ago, Andy.'

Both men laughed.

When they entered the house, Ronni was in the kitchen rinsing her mug under the tap.

'I've put all your shopping away, Dad,' she said.

'I could have done that,' he assured her.

'I know you could, but it's done now. I'll call in again tomorrow.'

'I've told you before, Ronni, you don't have to call every single day.'

'And I've told *you* it's no trouble.'

Connor looked at Andy. 'See, I told you.' He shrugged.

Andy grinned.

'Have you two been talking about me?' Ronni smiled.

'We've got more important things to discuss, haven't we, Jim?' Andy chided.

Connor nodded.

Ronni kissed her father and he stood at the door until they both climbed into the car and drove off.

The sitting room seemed so silent again.

James Connor reached for the TV remote and raised the volume, driving the solitude away.

He sat in his chair, gently turning the wedding band on his finger, occasionally glancing at the photos of his wife that smiled back at him.

Outside, the first droplets of rain began to fall.

33

At first, Donna Freeman didn't hear the banging on the bedroom door.

She stretched beneath the sheets, the earphones of the Sony Discman firmly wedged in place.

Only when the Sheryl Crow album finished did she finally detect the sound.

She heard her name being called.

'What is it?' she said irritably, reaching for the other CDs beside the bed.

'It's twelve o'clock in the afternoon.'

The voice belonged to her father.

So?

'Donna?' he persisted.

'Yeah, right.'

'Get up. It's twelve—'

'. . . o'clock in the afternoon. Yeah, you already said that once.'

'Give your mum a hand with the Sunday dinner,' her father ordered.

She heard the baby crying downstairs.

'I don't *want* any dinner,' Donna called back.

'Come on, you can't lay in there all fucking day.'

'I'm up,' she lied.

She heard the door handle rattling. Saw it turning.

'Unlock the door.'

'Why?'

'You don't need a lock on it, anyway. Come on, get up.'

'Yeah, I'm coming.'

'Donna?'

'Yes,' she called back angrily. 'I'll be down in a minute.'

There was silence for a moment, then she heard her father's footfalls on the stairs.

She reached for another CD, slipped it into the Discman and jammed the earpieces back into place.

Liam Harper waited at the end of the short path that led to the yellow-painted front door.

It always looked to him as if someone had smeared the wood with a coating of pus.

He grinned to himself at his own analogy and continued to gaze at the door.

Terry Mackenzie emerged a moment later, slammed the pus-coloured door behind him and hauled his bike from the overgrown grass of the front garden.

He joined Harper and the two of them rode down the path to the end of the street.

Tony Morton was waiting there for them.

'Your dad will be here soon,' Claire Brown said, watching as her son pulled on the Levi jacket.

'So?' Graham Brown grunted, heading for the door.

'He said he'd take you and your sister to the pictures this afternoon.'

'Let him take her, then. I couldn't give a fuck.'

Claire Brown gritted her teeth. 'Do you have to use that language, Graham?' she hissed.

'Tell him I didn't want to go. It'll only be some kids' film anyway.'

'He can hardly take you to see *Scream 3*, can he? Neither of you are old enough. He can't afford much with him being out of work. You should be grateful. Anyway, your sister likes the pictures.'

'Then let her go with *him*. But *I'm* not going.'

'Give him a chance, Graham.'

'Me? You were the one who fucking threw him out because he was always hitting you.'

'I didn't throw him out.'

'Then how come he doesn't live here anymore?'

'Your dad and I agreed to separate, you know that.'

'He still comes back here anytime he wants. He spent the night earlier in the week, didn't he? He comes back here, gets what he wants, then fucks off again. He couldn't give a fuck about us anyway. He didn't even when he *lived* here.'

'That's not true.'

'Isn't it? When he comes home he always beats the shit out of you and you're still stupid enough to let him in. I'll tell you something else: do you know why the only place he ever takes us is the fucking pictures? It's because for two hours he doesn't have to talk to us. He doesn't know what to talk to us *about*.' He held his mother's gaze. 'Once a month he turns up here and expects us to act like his little family again. Fuck him.'

Claire Brown reached out to stop her son as he opened the front door, then she stopped and held up both hands as if in surrender.

The door slammed behind him.

Tina Craven prodded her food disinterestedly and gazed blankly at the TV screen.

Elsewhere in the small living room, her two younger brothers, her mother and her father were also watching the flickering images. The two giggling boys, however, seemed more intent on jabbing their elbows into each other, each trying to knock the other's plate from his lap.

One of them pushed against her.

Tina shoved him back and he bumped into the other boy almost spilling his food onto the floor.

'Watch what you're doing,' her mother snapped.

'He started it,' the younger boy protested, licking gravy from his thumb.

Tina put her plate on the coffee table and sat back on the sofa.

'Aren't you hungry?' her mother wanted to know.

Tina shook her head.

'Take your plate out,' her father added. 'You can start the washing up.'

She got to her feet, picked up the plate and padded through into the kitchen.

'And put the kettle on too,' called her father.

Tina raised two fingers in the direction of the living room.

She hated Sundays.

Same routine.

Same shit. Different day.

She filled the kettle, then spun both taps and squirted Fairy Liquid into the sink.

She looked up at the wall clock.

She'd wait another hour.

The pound coins landed on the kitchen table with a thud. Carl Thompson watched them roll around, then looked at his father.

Ross Thompson was pulling on a leather jacket.

It smelled new.

He dug in the pocket and found another coin that he tossed amongst the others. 'Get yourself some fish and chips or something,' he told his son.

'What time will you be back?' Thompson wanted to know.

His father shrugged. 'We're going out for a meal later,' he said. 'I don't know.'

Thompson gathered the money and dropped it into his own pocket.

'Anything else you need?' his father asked.

Not from you.

Thompson shook his head.

'See you then,' the older man said and retreated from the room.

Thompson heard the door close behind him.

'Give her one from me,' he murmured.

He waited a moment, then reached for his mobile phone.

34

'YOU'RE SPYING AGAIN.'

The voice behind her made Ronni jump.

She turned to see George Errington standing behind her. He grinned and squeezed past her, heading for a chair in the day room.

'You scared me, George,' Ronni told him, smiling.

'That's because you were miles away,' he told her, opening the paper and scanning the headlines. 'Busy with your spying.'

'What do you mean?' she asked with mock indignation.

'You do it every Sunday. Every time someone comes to visit one of us.' He nodded towards the far side of the day room where Barbara Eustace sat in her wheelchair facing a smartly dressed man in his thirties. Molly sat on a chair beside her, curled up like a child's toy. The dog looked as if it was asleep, but every so often it would shuffle around, getting more comfortable.

'I'm not spying on *anyone*, George,' Ronni repeated. 'I'm just curious.'

'If you say so. If that's what you want to call it.'

'And what would you call it?' He tapped his nose and grinned.

'I was just watching Barbara and her son talking,' Ronni confessed.

'If I was her I wouldn't let him come within ten yards of me.'

'Why not?'

'His own mother and he can't even be bothered to look after

109

her. It was him who wanted her here. He even paid for her to come.'

'How do you know?'

'Janice Holland was talking to her last week. Barbara told her everything. He's some big shot in the City. Rolling in it. But Barbara's a bit of an inconvenience to him.' Errington raised his eyebrows. 'He doesn't want her around when he's entertaining his clients and his colleagues. So he paid to put her in here.'

Ronni looked on silently.

'That's kids for you,' Errington continued. 'I'm pleased *I* never had any.'

'You were married though, weren't you, George?'

'Twice.' He adjusted his glasses and peered over them at Ronni. 'Married twice. Divorced twice.' He smiled.

'And no kids?'

He shook his head.

'Have you got any family anywhere? Brothers or sisters?'

Again he shook his head. 'You could say I'm the last of the line, Ronni. I think that goes for most of us in here.'

'I saw somebody with Jack earlier.'

'His son's here today. He arrived about an hour ago. He's taken Jack out for a pint. He's a good lad. He comes once in a while.'

'I didn't know Jack had been married.'

'He wasn't. He met some girl . . .' Errington allowed the sentence to trail off as he shrugged his shoulders. 'They lived together, just never married.' He adjusted his glasses on the bridge of his nose.

'Colin's got family, hasn't he?'

'He never hears from them. I don't think any of them live locally. The rest of us are on our own.'

'You're not on your own as long as you're here, George.' She squeezed his shoulder.

'Is there anything else you want to know or can I get on with my paper?' He smiled.

'Sorry to have disturbed you,' she said indignantly.

As she turned away she glanced once more towards the far side of the day room.

Barbara Eustace sat motionless in her wheelchair as her son continued to speak.

35

'How CAN HE do that to her?' Ronni said reproachfully, sipping at her tea.

She and Alison Dean were seated in the staff kitchen on opposite sides of the small, Formica-topped table.

'Try seeing it from *his* point of view, Ronni,' Alison offered.

'Do you agree with it, then? Would you stick *your* parents in a home rather than look after them yourself?'

'We're not talking about me.'

'I don't know how he can live with himself.'

'We don't know all the details, Ronni. Barbara's probably better off here. At least she gets twenty-four-hour care if she needs it. Anyway, you're always talking about getting your dad to move here so you're in no position to slag off Barbara's son.'

'That's different.'

'Why?'

'Because I haven't got the time or money to give him the attention he needs in his own house. Barbara's son has.'

'You don't know that.'

'According to George Errington he's rolling in it.'

'George probably doesn't know all the details either. You know what he's like.'

Ronni sipped at her tea, then dunked a digestive in the steaming liquid. 'So, what *would* you do if one of your parents couldn't look after themselves?' she asked finally. 'Would you try to take care of them? Get them to move in with you?'

'Ronni, you can't answer a question like that until it happens.'

'Hypothetically.'

Alison shrugged. 'If I couldn't look after them myself, and we could afford it, I'd be happy to see them here, at Shelby House.'

Ronni nodded almost imperceptibly.

'You know how well the residents here are treated, Ronni. And most of them are here out of choice. Their *own* choice.'

'If we had the room, I'd still like my dad living at home with me.'

'He's probably happier where he is.'

'That's what *he* always says.'

'Then why don't you believe him? It might be the same in Barbara's case. She's probably happier here than if she was living with her son.'

Ronni gazed at the soggy biscuit for a second before pushing the remains into her mouth.

'You make it sound as if you feel guilty because you're not with your dad twenty-four hours a day,' Alison offered.

'I've got nothing to feel guilty about,' Ronni said a little too hastily.

'I didn't say you had. No one could have done more for him since your mum died.'

'I worry about him, Alison, that's all. I don't know what I'd do if anything happened to him.'

Alison reached across the table and squeezed Ronni's hand. 'He'll be fine,' she said softly.

Ronni nodded and brushed her brown hair away from her face.

Alison got to her feet, crossing to the sink to rinse her cup. 'Don't worry.' She smiled and made her way out of the small kitchen.

Ronni heard her footfalls echoing away up the corridor.

36

THE IMPACT OF his fist against the other boy's jawbone sent jarring pain up Graham Brown's arm. But the discomfort was forgotten as he struck again, this time opening a cut on his opponent's eyebrow.

Blood began to run freely from the wound and the sight of the crimson fluid seemed to galvanize Brown to even greater efforts.

He held the boy in a headlock and slammed his fist repeatedly into his face, droplets of blood now flying in all directions.

Some of it spattered those watching.

Brown felt sudden excruciating pain from his right leg.

He shouted angrily, but the pain seemed to intensify.

The skin of his inner thigh was being pinched so hard it felt as if someone had clamped a vice on it.

He let go of his opponent and pushed him away.

The other boy – his face already cut in half a dozen places – spat blood and ran at Brown, who was still rubbing at his throbbing thigh.

They collided and crashed into the wall of the school gymnasium.

Brown's head snapped backwards and cracked hard against the brickwork, momentarily stunning him.

His opponent wasn't slow to react and drove his left foot into Brown's groin so hard he felt it connect with the pubic bone.

Brown shrieked and clutched at his injured genitals, the breath suddenly torn from him.

All around him shouts of encouragement rang in his ears.

'Fucking kill him!'

'Rip his fucking head off!'

All good advice.

Others in the playground were gathered, engrossed, around the contest.

The two contestants faced each other with expressions of fury.

'You're fucking dead,' Brown hissed, rubbing his testicles.

'Come on then,' snarled his opponent.

They ran at each other.

The collision was greeted by a great cheer from the watching hordes.

Brown managed to drive his forehead into the face of his opponent, the impact staggering him too.

But the other boy came off worse.

His nose was pulped by the impact.

Blood gushed from the smashed appendage. It soaked into the front of his ripped shirt and dripped onto his mud-grimed shoes.

He teetered uncertainly for a moment, his head spinning. Then he wiped one palm across his bloodied nose and brought the hand away smeared with crimson.

'Teachers!' someone shouted and a number of the onlookers darted away from the conflict.

Others stayed to see the outcome.

Two teachers were rushing across the playground towards the mêlée.

Others in the playground stepped aside to allow them through. Some even followed.

Brown reached into his trouser pocket and pulled something free.

There was a *swish-click* as he pushed the blade release button on the flick-knife.

'Come on then, cunt,' he hissed and swiped at the other boy, who took several steps back.

'Do him!' someone shouted helpfully.

Brown struck out again. He caught the boy across the ear with the point of the blade: the lobe was cut cleanly through and fresh blood spurted into the air.

The teachers were pushing through the watching masses now.

Brown saw them both.

Miss Sinclair and Mr Albon.

Ginger cunt.

He lashed out once more, but his wild stroke missed the other boy.

Albon grabbed the youth's ripped shirt and hauled him aside.

The blade cut through the teacher's free hand; carved through his palm from the base of his thumb to his little finger.

There was a sound like ripping material and blood jetted from the deep wound. It arced into the air and sprayed Miss Sinclair's white blouse.

She screamed.

Albon shouted in pain and struck Brown hard across the back of the head with his split hand, the impact bringing renewed pain.

'You little bastard!' he yelled, his eyes bulging as he looked at the deep gash that was pumping blood so freely.

Brown sprawled on the floor, the knife skidding from his grip.

Miss Sinclair had turned pale. Her gaze moved alternately from her own blood-spattered blouse to the gaping wound in her colleague's hand. She felt her stomach contract and thought she was going to be sick.

The watching crowd dispersed rapidly.

'Get help!' Albon shouted, his words ringing in the air and directed, it seemed, at no one in particular.

Brown hauled himself up onto his knees, one hand feeling tentatively at the back of his head where Albon had struck him.

The teacher's blood had matted his hair.

As he looked at the games master he smiled.

37

'WHAT DO YOU mean there's nothing you can do?' Brian Albon's voice echoed around the office, a note of incredulity in it. 'The little bastard cut my hand open with a flick-knife,' he rasped, pushing the heavily bandaged appendage towards the headmaster.

Jonathan Lynch sighed. 'I know what happened,' he breathed.

'Then why the hell don't you do something about it?'

'It isn't as easy as that, Brian, and you know it.'

'It's assault. What could be easier than that?'

'The boy's fourteen.'

'I don't care if he's six. He pulled a flick-knife on me and he used it. There were witnesses.'

Albon gestured towards Amy Sinclair, who was sitting in one of the leather chairs opposite the desk, her cardigan fastened over her blood-stained blouse.

She was cradling a mug of tea in her shaking hands.

'And you struck him,' Lynch said quietly.

'Yes, I did. If I hadn't he'd probably have killed me.'

'You struck a fourteen-year-old boy. A boy in your charge.'

'For Christ's sake!' wailed Albon helplessly. He turned away from the headmaster despairingly.

'Brian, I don't have to tell you the rules,' Lynch persisted. 'You can't do that. You cannot strike a child, no matter what the provocation.'

Albon planted his hands on his hips and bowed his head. 'This is insane,' he murmured. 'I'm standing here defending my own actions when a kid cut me with a flick-knife in the playground of the school where I've taught for the last ten years.'

'That's the way it is now. You know that.'

'And what if he'd gone for Amy with the knife, Jonathan?' Albon wanted to know, turning back to face the senior teacher. 'He could have killed her. What would you have done then?'

'I'm aware of the situation,' Lynch told the games master. 'I'm also aware of the possible ramifications.'

'For who?'

'For you *and* for the school.'

'Have you called the police?'

Lynch shook his head.

'Why not?'

'There's nothing the police can do. The boy is too young. They can't bring any charges against him.'

'Possession of an illegal weapon,' Albon hissed, raising his index finger. 'Then using it. Assault. That's three charges for a start.'

'I'm not involving the police.'

'For the sake of the school?' Albon chided. 'Are you afraid of damaging its reputation, Jonathan? A reputation that's already been dragged through the mud by kids like Graham Brown. The boy is out of control.'

Lynch met and held his gaze.

'If you let this go then things will get worse ... if that's possible,' Albon muttered. 'Someone will be seriously hurt. It might be a child. It might be a teacher. It might even be you.'

'So what do you suggest I do with Brown?'

'I would have thought that was fairly obvious. Expel him.'

'There aren't enough grounds for dismissal.'

'What do you call that?' Albon demanded, again raising his gashed hand.

'It isn't that simple. I'd have to go before the school governors. There are procedures that have to be followed before a child can be expelled. There will have to be a formal internal inquiry into what happened today.'

'Good. The sooner the better. Because every day Graham Brown is here, he's a danger to the other children *and* members of staff. And, I'll tell you now, Jonathan, I don't want him in any of my classes.'

'You won't have to worry about that, Brian,' Lynch said wearily. 'I'm suspending you on full pay until this inquiry is concluded.'

Albon gazed incredulously at his superior.

'Brown is threatening to bring assault charges against *you* for striking him.'

38

Stealing the car hadn't been a problem.

Carl Thompson had watched as the man had scrambled out of the Renault and hurried into the newsagent's.

Just a quick dash.

Putting on his lottery.

Getting some fags.

No need to lock the door, back in a minute or two.

Thompson smiled.

So fucking easy.

Some people never learned.

He'd already sorted through the collection of cassettes in the car and thrown out the ones he didn't like.

Now he sat behind the wheel of the stationary vehicle with Nirvana blasting from the speakers.

Smells Like Teen Spirit.

Smells like a fucking shotgun. 'Bye, Kurt.

Thompson smiled.

He'd parked the Renault on the edge of the Waybridge Estate at the end of a leafy avenue.

Neat little houses. Neat little gardens. Inhabited by people with neat little lives.

Thompson noted that there were alarms on most of the houses.

They must have something worth stealing.

He took another long drag on his cigarette.

It was gloomy inside the car; the street lights hadn't come on yet.

Beside him, Donna Freeman was hunched forward over a piece of silver foil she was balancing on her knees. An index finger was pressed to one nostril.

Thompson watched her as he puffed on his cigarette.

She sat back, wiping white granules from her nostrils.

'Better?' he asked.

She nodded.

'It always makes me horny,' she whispered.

'*Everything* makes you horny.'

'I wonder what the bloke who owns this car would say if he could see us now.'

Thompson grinned.

'He'd probably want to watch,' purred Donna.

'Watch what?'

Thompson felt her hand slide along his thigh to his groin. She began to stroke him firmly through the denim, sucking in a deep breath when she felt his penis begin to stiffen even more.

'He'd want to watch you fucking me,' she breathed, her own excitement growing.

'Is that what you want?'

'You know it is. It's what *you* want too.'

'And what would he see if he watched us?'

He moved to face her, their mouths meeting as she expertly undid his jeans and freed his erection, her hand building a steady rhythm on the solid flesh.

'He'd see your cock in my hand,' Donna gasped.

Thompson slid his hands beneath her top and found she wasn't wearing a bra. Her nipples were already hard and she groaned as he outlined them with his thumbs.

'What else would he see?' Thompson wanted to know, his own breath now ragged.

He pulled her skirt up and forced one hand between her thighs, his fingertips brushing the silky material there, forcing it into her warm cleft.

Thompson ground the material deep inside her slippery sex,

then finally slipped the digits inside the waistband, through her downy pubic hair and into the moistness beyond.

'He'd see how wet I was,' she continued.

She pulled Thompson's hand from between her legs and held it up, studying the glistening fluid on his fingertips. She pulled them towards her mouth and sucked gently, tasting herself.

Donna raised her buttocks as Thompson's eager hands tugged at her knickers, pulling them down her thighs. She kicked them off. He replaced his hand, pushing two fingers deep inside her. His thumb grazed her swollen clitoris.

'What else would he see?' he rasped, pulling her towards him, allowing her to straddle him.

'He'd see this,' she grunted, guiding his erection towards the liquescence between her legs.

Donna lowered herself slowly, feeling every inch of his stiff penis penetrate her.

'And what would *he* be doing if he was watching?' Thompson growled through gritted teeth.

'He'd be holding his cock in his hand,' she gasped as she moved up and down more quickly. 'Waiting for us to come. Waiting for you to come inside me.'

The windows were opaque with condensation now.

Donna gripped Thompson by the shoulders as she continued to move up and down, her own pleasure building by the second.

'Fuck,' she whimpered.

'What would he be doing now if he was watching?' Thompson rasped.

Her only answer was a series of deep racking breaths.

Thompson gripped her chin in one hand and turned her face so that she was looking directly into his eyes.

'Tell me,' he demanded, barely able to control himself.

She closed her eyes as the intensity of the feelings drew nearer their peak.

'*Tell* me,' he repeated, forcing her to look at him.

'He'd be coming too,' she panted, her body shaking uncontrollably. 'Shooting it all over me. Over my tits. Over my face.'

He held her chin. 'Don't close your eyes,' Thompson told her. 'Don't fucking close them.'

She tried to tip her head back as she felt the beginnings of the orgasm sweep through her, but he held her chin in his grip.

'Look straight into my fucking eyes,' he told her, pushing his face closer to hers.

She shuddered violently once, twice, then again as the climax spread through her.

Her eyes were open.

Gaping wide.

She felt his hot fluid filling her and he raised his hips, grunting as he reached his own climax.

Donna continued grinding herself into his lap, her eyes still wide. Fixed on his.

He released her chin, allowed her to slump forward onto his chest.

Both of them were gasping.

His penis softened slightly, then slipped from the liquid embrace of her cleft.

She climbed back onto the passenger seat and reached for her knickers, wiping some oily white fluid from the tops of her thighs.

'Leave them in the car,' Thompson told her.

Donna gently slid the silky knickers around her sensitive labia, displaying the ejaculate that stained them. She stuffed them into the glove compartment.

Thompson offered her a cigarette and she accepted. A few of the street lights flickered into life and they wiped away the condensation coating the windows, looking out at the surrounding buildings.

'What *is* that over there?' she asked, nodding towards the large blue sign opposite: SHELBY HOUSE RESIDENTIAL HOME.

'It's an old people's home,' he told her. 'I bet it stinks in there.

Like that joke: "What's forty feet long and smells of piss? The conga at an old people's home".'

They both laughed.

'My nan was in one,' Donna said finally. 'I *think* it was an old people's home. She went a bit funny before she died. Couldn't remember her name. That sort of thing.'

'I bet it wasn't *that* place,' Thompson said, nodding in the direction of Shelby House. 'I heard it costs a fucking fortune for the old bastards to live there.'

'So they've all got money.'

'They *must* have.'

He threw his cigarette butt out of the window, his eyes now fixed on the sign.

Donna looked at him, but he was still gazing at the entrance to the driveway.

'They must be fucking loaded,' he said softly.

39

THE KNIFE FELL into the sink with a clang.

Helen Kennedy muttered something to herself and retrieved it, wiping the blade on her apron. She pushed her glasses back on her nose and leant closer to the cake, sliding the blade into an un-iced portion of the top.

The cake was cooked to perfection.

She expertly covered the top with icing, then reached for the piping bag and began making white patterns around the edges and base of the confection.

'How's it going, Helen?'

The voice startled her and she looked around to see Ronni standing in the doorway of the kitchen.

'Nearly done now, dear,' Helen told her, gesturing towards the cake with an arthritic hand, the joints badly swollen. It was as if they had been inflated from within, the knuckles set to burst. Helen flexed her fingers as best she could and continued with her task.

She was a small woman, who wore such pale make-up it looked as though someone had dusted her face with talculm powder. There was a small scar on her throat; the site of a successful operation two years earlier to remove a tumour of the larynx. When she spoke it sounded as if she needed a hearty cough. Her voice was rasping, almost robotic, but the effect was countered by the softness of her features and the kindness in her eyes. They still retained a sparkle that belied her seventy years.

Ronni crossed to the older woman and peered at the expert piping on the cake. 'It looks great,' she said admiringly. 'I wish I could do that.'

'I could teach you,' Helen offered.

'I'm too heavy handed, Helen. I'd end up with more icing on *me* than the cake.'

'I made my own wedding cake, you know,' Helen continued, still piping. She was adding swirls around the top now. 'Three tiers.' She chuckled.

Ronni couldn't help but smile at the infectious sound.

'When we came to cut it,' Helen said, 'my husband, Bill, was so nervous, he slipped and knocked the lot off the table. My mother said it was bad luck, but we just laughed. I think she *hoped* it would be bad luck. She never wanted us to marry.'

'Why not?'

'She didn't like Bill. It didn't help that I was pregnant, of course. She blamed him for that too.'

'Well, Helen, I suppose he did have *something* to do with it.'

Both women laughed.

'It takes two to tango, dear.' Helen grinned, showing some slightly discoloured false teeth.

Ronni nodded and smiled. 'That's true,' she agreed. 'What did your mother say about your child when it was born?'

Helen was silent for a moment.

Ronni could see a darkness in her expression.

'I had a miscarriage,' the older woman told her softly.

'I'm sorry, Helen.'

'If he'd lived he would have been nearly fifty now.'

'How do you know it would have been a boy?'

'We didn't, but we always *wanted* a boy so we'd convinced ourselves that he would have been. We tried again over the years, but . . .' She allowed the sentence to trail off.

Ronni watched the older woman working on the cake. She thought about reaching out to touch her arm, to let her know she sympathized.

Helen put down the piping bag and wiped her hands on her apron. 'I'll let that dry, then I'll do the top,' she said. 'The party's tomorrow, isn't it?'

Ronni nodded. 'Harry's still trying to make sure Janice doesn't find out what's going on.' She grinned.

'He's done well. It's not easy keeping a secret in a place like this. Janice asked me the other day if I knew what was going on, but I said no.' She put a hand to her mouth. 'Mr Glazer collected money from all of us for their present. He said he was going into town today to fetch it.'

'He went with Donald earlier.'

'I hope Mr Tanner doesn't end up in the betting shop or they'll never get back. He does like a bet, doesn't he?'

'He certainly does, Helen,' Ronni agreed. 'Anyway, I'll leave you to it.'

'All right, dear,' Helen murmured, refilling the piping bag.

Ronni watched the older woman for a moment longer, amazed by those arthritic hands that moved with such grace and skill. Then, finally, she stepped back out of the kitchen and made her way towards the day room.

40

THE BUSES THAT ran from the estates to the centre of Kempston carried twenty people.

Twenty-five if some stood.

They were small, nippy little yellow vehicles with the word BUZZER emblazoned on the sides.

The journey to Shelby House usually took about fifteen minutes, dependent upon the number of stops the bus had to make.

Donald Tanner checked his watch.

Another five minutes. Another two stops.

He enjoyed his little trips to the betting shop in town

(*especially when he came back with winnings*)

but they tired him.

He wiped perspiration from his forehead and glanced around at the other occupants of the bus.

A man reading a folded newspaper.

A young woman with a small child that was constantly pulling at her sleeve despite her protestations. She finally silenced it with a handful of sweets.

A middle-aged woman, who was fluffing up her recently permed hair.

Carl Thompson sat at the back of the bus, one foot on the seat. He was puffing away on a cigarette, blowing smoke at the NO SMOKING sign.

Tina Craven sat in the seat in front, picking at one chewed fingernail.

The bus began to slow down as it approached another stop, where two other people waited. Both women. Both in their thirties. The first of them was already reaching into her handbag for her purse.

As the vehicle slid to a halt, Thompson nudged Tina in the back and nodded in the direction of the exit.

She got to her feet and wandered down the aisle, closely followed by Thompson.

The bus doors opened with a hiss and the first of the women stepped on.

Donald Tanner was about to smile a polite greeting when Tina suddenly bundled into the woman.

The impact knocked her down the two steps. She shouted in panic as she toppled backwards, slamming into her friend.

Tina pushed forward past her.

Thompson grabbed for the handbag, but missed.

Some loose change from her purse spilled across the floor of the bus.

The driver rose in his seat, trying to help the woman, who had fallen back onto the pavement.

Her handbag dropped inside the bus.

Donald Tanner snatched it up and held it to his chest.

Thompson spun round and glared at the older man, his eyes full of fury.

'Come on!' Tina shrieked, already running up the road, narrowly avoiding a wild swing from the second woman.

Thompson held Donald Tanner's gaze for a second longer, then sped off up the street behind her.

The bus driver was helping the first woman to her feet. She seemed more angry than hurt.

The man who'd been reading the folded paper had already begun to gather up the spilled change. Tanner held out her handbag as if he was presenting her with some hard-won trophy.

'Thank you,' she said, gripping his arm.

He smiled triumphantly.

The bus driver clambered back on board and patted him on the shoulder.

'Well done, mate,' said the man gathering up the change.

Tanner beamed.

A right bloody hero.

'You sure you're all right, love?' the driver asked the woman.

She nodded. 'Bloody kids,' she rasped.

The doors hissed, then clamped shut.

The bus moved off.

Home at last.

Donald Tanner turned and waved as the bus driver sounded his hooter and raised his hand.

The bus had dropped him right outside the driveway of Shelby House.

He'd be glad to get inside.

That was a bit too much excitement for one day.

He wondered if he should mention it to the others. Jack Fuller would be proud of him.

No. Keep it to yourself.

He began the trek down the tree-lined drive.

'Fucking old bastard,' hissed Carl Thompson as he watched. From the corner of the street he saw Tanner disappear into the drive-way.

'Let's go,' Tina protested.

Thompson pushed past her and jogged across the street, slowing his pace as he reached the end of the driveway.

He saw Tanner halfway down the drive, his back to him.

Tina joined him. 'What are you doing?' she wanted to know.

'Thinking,' Thompson hissed without looking at her. He hawked loudly, then spat after the disappearing figure of Donald Tanner.

COMPULSION

As he passed the sign that read SHELBY HOUSE RESIDENTIAL HOME he spat on that too.

'Old cunts,' he rasped.

'Just forget about it, Carl,' Tina urged.

Thompson said nothing.

41

THE DRIVE FROM his house to work took Gordon Faulkner less than twenty minutes; especially in the evenings.

He guided the Corsa along the roads that led to Shelby House, occasionally glancing to his left and right at the uniform rows of houses that flanked the thoroughfares.

Lights burned in the windows of most.

Sometimes he would see shapes moving against the glowing backdrops or curtains being drawn to shut out the darkness.

He wondered what was going on within the modest dwellings.

The nightly ritual of watching TV?

Kids doing their homework?

Dinners being eaten?

The day's work being discussed and dissected?

The normal, boring monotony of day-to-day living, basically.

He eased the volume on the cassette player down slightly and turned the car into the leafy avenue, surprised at how many of the street lights weren't working.

The shadows were thick here and he flicked the Corsa's headlights to full beam.

They picked out the sign ahead: SHELBY HOUSE RESIDENTIAL HOME.

Beside it were two kids.

Both boys.

Both in their early teens he guessed, but in the darkness it was difficult to tell.

He slowed down at the junction, then drove across and on towards the gravel drive that would lead him up to Shelby House.

The two boys both turned to face the oncoming Corsa.

As their faces were illuminated in the headlights' glare, Faulkner could see they were younger than he'd initially thought.

Ten. Eleven, maybe.

Both were on bikes.

One was resting against the blue sign.

Faulkner could see that he was using the tip of a screwdriver to scratch into the blue paint.

As he drew level with them he wound down his window. 'Excuse me,' he called. 'Would you mind not doing that, please?'

Liam Harper ignored him and continued to gouge the paint-work.

'I *said*, would you stop that,' Faulkner repeated, his tone more forceful.

'Why?' Harper grunted, without looking at him.

'Just pack it in, you're damaging private property.'

Harper hacked even more venomously at the sign.

Faulkner pushed open his door and prepared to clamber out of the car.

Harper stepped away from the sign. 'I've finished now.' He grinned.

Faulkner saw what was scrawled across the bottom of the sign.

'That's criminal damage,' Faulkner snarled. 'You could be reported for that.'

'So report me,' Harper sneered.

Faulkner glanced at the words gouged into the sign, then at the grinning youth.

Behind him he heard movement.

Terry Mackenzie rode his bike alongside the Corsa, allowing the handlebars to scrape against the paintwork.

'Get away from here,' Faulkner said angrily.

'Or what?'

The voice came from the darkness around the entrance to the driveway.

Carl Thompson stepped into view.

Beside him was Graham Brown.

To his right, Tina Craven and Donna Freeman.

Both the girls were smoking.

'This is private property,' Faulkner told him. 'You shouldn't be hanging around here.'

'We're not doing anything,' Thompson said.

'Just move, will you?' Faulkner persisted.

'And what if we don't *want* to move?' Tina asked.

'Then I'll call the police.'

'And tell them what?' Thompson demanded. 'That we were standing here? We'll be gone by the time they get here. If they even bother coming.'

Faulkner slid back behind the steering wheel.

Brown hawked loudly and spat. The glob of mucus hit the windscreen of the Corsa and Faulkner jumped out of the vehicle once more.

'You dirty little bastard!' he snapped, taking a step towards Brown.

The boy didn't move.

Faulkner hesitated, aware that the other youngsters were now all around him.

'It's a nice place for the old people to live,' Thompson told him quietly. 'We walked up the drive and had a look.'

'You had no right to do that. Keep away from here.'

'We were just looking,' Thompson said. 'You can't stop us doing that.'

'You shouldn't be on private property.'

'Fuck off,' Tina hissed. 'You can't stop us.'

'We'll see about that.'

'Go on, then,' Brown said challengingly.

Faulkner looked at each of them in turn, then slowly clambered back into the driving seat again. 'I don't want to see you around here again,' he called.

They parted to allow him through.

He guided the Corsa slowly along the tree-lined drive, tyres crunching on the gravel.

He flicked on the windscreen wipers and they brushed away the phlegm.

Faulkner shook his head disgustedly.

Up ahead, he could see the lights inside Shelby House.

Something struck his rear window with tremendous force.

He spun round to see a crack in the glass.

As he hauled himself from the vehicle yet again he saw the stone that had been hurled at the Corsa.

It was as big as his fist.

Right, that's it. No matter how many of the little bastards there are . . .

Faulkner ran to the end of the drive, his heart hammering against his ribs. His breath came in short, angry gasps.

There was no sign of the youths.

They'd vanished, as if swallowed by the darkness.

42

Ronni sat at the table in the staff room watching Gordon Faulkner. 'You'll have to take Barbara's dog out for a walk before it gets too late, Gordon,' she said. 'You know Barbara likes to get in bed early.'

Faulkner nodded. He was standing gazing out of the window into the darkness, hands dug deep into his pockets.

'George Errington was complaining about feeling dizzy earlier on,' she continued. 'I rang the doctor and told him. He said to give him an extra twenty milligrams of Prazosin before he goes to bed, just to stabilize his blood pressure. He said there was nothing to worry about though.'

Again Faulkner nodded, but didn't turn. He was scanning the grounds, the spotlights on the exterior of Shelby House forming pools of brilliant white where they pierced the gloom.

Nothing moving out there.

'Alison will be in about six tomorrow morning,' Ronni added. 'And, by the way, we're expecting a visit from the Queen around ten. I'm leaving here to become a lap dancer and Alison has set up her own brothel. We're using Shelby House until we can find somewhere else.'

Faulkner finally turned and looked at her, his face expressionless.

Ronni smiled. 'You were miles away,' she told him.

'Sorry,' he said, returning to his vigil.

'Something wrong?'

He shook his head.

'You don't want to talk about it?'

'There's nothing wrong, Ronni.'

'You've done nothing but stare out of that window since you arrived.'

'Everything's fine.'

Tell her about what happened in the driveway.

He drew in a weary breath.

Tell her what? Half a dozen kids got mouthy outside. Big deal.

Ronni got to her feet and reached for her coat, eyes still fixed on her companion.

Faulkner returned her gaze, smiling reassuringly.

At least tell her about the sign. She's going to spot it tomorrow anyway.

'I'd better take Barbara's little rat for a walk,' he said, thinking that he could take some paint out at the same time and do his best to cover up the damage to the sign.

'She's a lovely little thing.' Ronni chuckled.

'See you tomorrow.'

'Don't work too hard.'

He heard the staffroom door close behind her. Heard her footsteps echoing away along the corridor.

From where he was standing he could see her heading for her car.

He pressed his face to the glass and cupped his hands around his eyes, squinting once again, into the blackness.

The overhanging branches of trees rustled in the wind like skeletal fingers. Some of the longer ones scraped against the roof of Ronni's car as she climbed in.

Faulkner remained where he was until she started the engine and pulled away.

He was momentarily illuminated in her headlights as she turned the Fiesta and headed towards the drive.

She raised a hand.

He waved back.

Outside, the trees shook again.

The wind was growing stronger.

43

THEY ATE IN SILENCE; only the dull drone of the television in the corner of the room offered a counterpoint to the hush.

Ronni balanced her plate on a tray she'd rested across her knees.

Andy had pulled the coffee table towards him and was hunched over his food like a vulture over carrion.

'You could have had yours when you got in,' Ronni said, nodding in the direction of his meal.

'I thought I'd wait for you,' he told her, pushing a forkful of potato into his mouth.

She tried to think of some kind of smalltalk. Something to fill the void.

Smalltalk? With your own husband?

'Did you see about your car?' she said finally.

He nodded. 'It's going to need a new wing,' Andy told her. 'The little bastards did a real fucking job on it.'

Ronni sighed.

'I should have gone for that one,' Andy muttered.

'Which one?'

'The tall one. The oldest. The one with all the rabbit.'

'They were kids, Andy. What were you going to do? Beat him up?'

'It might not have been a bad idea.'

'There were six of them.'

'Kids, Ronni, that's all. They were hardly the fucking Wild Bunch, were they?'

'They could have had knives.'

He shrugged. 'Your dad's right,' he murmured. 'It *has* all changed.'

'What?'

'Life. Kids. Everything.'

'Things *do* change, Andy.'

Like falling out of love with the person you married.

She looked at him for a moment, then returned to her food. 'When was the last time you agreed with my dad about something?' she asked.

'I've always got on all right with him. Your mum too, when she was alive.'

Ronni nodded almost imperceptibly.

'He still misses her, doesn't he?' Andy said softly. 'He was talking about her the other day when we were round there.'

'He talks about her every day. I sometimes wonder if he'll *ever* get over it.'

'What about you, Ronni? Do *you* think about her?'

'Of course I do. She always used to understand what I was trying to say. If I had a problem she'd know without me even opening my mouth.'

'Have you got a problem now?'

Ronni glanced across at him.

Did he know what she was thinking?

'What makes you ask?'

'I'm your husband. You're supposed to tell me, aren't you? I thought that was what marriage was all about.'

She managed her most convincing fake smile.

'Is it work? Your dad?' he persisted.

'There's nothing, Andy.'

Tell him the truth. At least be honest with him. Now's your chance.

'You'd tell me if there was?'

'Of course I would,' she lied.

Tell him about the suitcase on top of the wardrobe with some of your clothes in.

She was aware that his gaze was still upon her.

She took a last bite of her food, then got to her feet, carrying the tray towards the kitchen.

Andy put out a hand and touched her arm.

She paused and looked down at him.

'I love you,' he said quietly.

She smiled back. 'I know,' she told him.

She slipped away from him into the kitchen.

The luminous green hands of the alarm clock showed 12.06 a.m.

Ronni felt Andy move next to her, heard his low breathing.

Then she felt his hand brush her thigh.

His fingers traced a pattern over the smooth skin, then moved higher, sliding beneath her long, baggy T-shirt.

He gently outlined the curve of her pelvis, his hand gliding across her belly, then downwards to the warmth between her legs.

Ronni parted them slightly, felt him move closer to her.

She felt his warm breath on her neck and shoulder.

He kissed her cheek.

'It's late,' she whispered, without turning over.

Too late.

She heard him sigh and felt him withdraw his hand reluctantly. 'Sorry,' he murmured almost apologetically.

She closed her eyes, but sleep was a long time coming.

44

Janice Holland knew she was going to cry. She gripped her husband's hand and rested her head on his shoulder.

Ronni nibbled at her sandwich and watched them, struck by the sheer joy on their faces at being together.

Envious?

Harry was grinning, as usual. He pulled Janice more tightly to him as they danced, the music swelling from the speakers.

Colin Glazer presided over the turntable with all the care of a surgeon at an operation. He cleaned the vinyl with a cloth and blew on the stylus before playing each disc. Like the other residents of Shelby House he watched as the Hollands danced.

Ronni smiled as the couple moved with a lightness and grace that belied their years.

The staff had moved the chairs in the day room away from the centre to leave a space and it was within that area that Harry and Janice now waltzed slowly to the strains of Bunny Berrigan.

Donald Tanner clicked his fingers rhythmically as he listened to the music.

Beside him, George Errington looked on with a slight smile on his face.

Barbara Eustace and Helen Kennedy were over by the table set up in a corner of the room. They were also watching the Hollands dance, but Helen couldn't resist an occasional sly look at the cake she had made to celebrate their anniversary. She was justifiably

141

pleased with her efforts. Every now and then she nudged Ronni and nodded towards it.

Ronni smiled.

Eva Cole wandered over to join them, her shock of white hair covered by a brightly coloured party hat.

She watched as Jack Fuller took a small sausage roll from the plate and popped it into his mouth, chewing slowly.

'They look so happy, don't they?' Eva observed.

Fuller nodded, then wiped crumbs from his lips. 'Could I have the next dance, please, Eva?' he said grandly.

Eva chuckled. 'It's been years since anyone asked me to dance, Jack,' she confessed.

'All the more reason to say yes, then,' Fuller told her.

'You make the most of it, Eva,' said Ronni. 'He might not ask again.'

'I'd be delighted,' Eva said.

'Forty-six years,' Helen murmured wistfully as she watched the dancing couple. 'It's a long time to be with the same person, isn't it? They're so lucky to have each other.'

Ronni ran a hand through her hair.

How lucky are you? What exactly are you expecting to find if you ever have the courage to leave Andy?

'You don't get *that* long for murder, do you?' Fuller grinned.

'Jack, you *are* terrible,' Helen said, laughing.

'How long were *you* married, Barbara?' Eva wanted to know.

'Twenty-three years,' she informed them. 'We were childhood sweethearts. Lived next door to each other. Went to the same school. He told me when we were eight that he was going to marry me.'

'How romantic,' Eva cooed.

'I read somewhere that the average marriage lasts ten years these days,' Fuller interjected.

A chorus of mutterings met his remark.

'The slightest hint of trouble and people split up,' Barbara said dismissively. 'They don't want to work at their marriages.'

Ronni said nothing.

'Not like *them*,' Helen added, nodding in the direction of the Hollands.

The music finally came to an end.

Harry Holland took a step back from his wife, then bowed his head and kissed her hand.

The watching residents clapped loudly.

Janice was dabbing at her eye corners with a small handkerchief. 'This has all been so lovely,' she said, glancing around at her companions. 'You're all very kind.'

'We had enough trouble keeping it a secret, Janice,' George Errington told her as he got to his feet.

'Speech,' called Donald Tanner.

'Yes, come on, Harry, say something,' Jack Fuller echoed.

Holland held up his hands and waited for the good-natured goading to end, then he slid his arm around Janice's shoulder and coughed theatrically. 'We'd both like to thank you all for everything,' he began. 'You've all made the day wonderful for us. Personally, I'd like to thank Janice for putting up with me for forty-six years. I doubt if any man could have been as happy as I have for so long. I'm just glad *I* was the one she agreed to marry.'

Janice wiped more tears away.

'I've actually written a little poem for you, my love,' Harry continued, fumbling in his jacket pocket.

Ronni looked on as he unfolded the small piece of paper and glanced at it before fixing his eyes on Janice.

'It's not exactly Wordsworth.' Harry grinned. 'But here goes:

> The life we share is special,
> The love we share is true,
> There's nothing else on earth I need,
> As long as I've got you.
> You've taught me just what love means,
> Through all our years together.
> Years, I pray, we'll always spend now and then for ever.
> Through good and bad and old and new,
> I thank the Lord that I've got you.

A renewed round of applause greeted the poem.

Janice took the paper from her husband, glanced at it, then embraced him.

'Come on, you two,' Helen called. 'Come and have some of your cake.'

'A bloody poet too, eh, Harry?' George Errington said, shaking hands with the other man.

They both grinned.

Ronni and Helen cut the cake and shared out the portions.

'One more thing before we all get stuck in,' Donald Tanner interjected.

Janice dabbed her eyes again.

'A little present from all of us,' Tanner announced. He produced a dark blue box from behind one of the tables and held it before Janice.

'You open it, Harry,' she said. 'I'm shaking.'

Holland took the box from Tanner and eased the lid off.

The clock inside was about eight inches tall. Waterford crystal.

'It's beautiful,' Janice said softly.

A shaft of light from the sinking sun arrowed through the room and bounced off the crystal. It was as if the clock itself was reflecting a rainbow as the light broke up into half a dozen different colours.

'Thank you,' Harry Holland echoed. 'Thank you very much. All of you.'

Ronni kissed them both.

The sound of Frank Sinatra began to fill the room. Fuller whispered something in Eva's ear and led her into the middle of the makeshift dance floor.

Almost unnoticed, Ronni slipped out of the day room, leaving the residents alone. As she made her way along the corridor she could hear the sounds of music and merriment behind her.

They seemed a thousand miles away.

45

THE OFFICE OVERLOOKED the small car park and well-manicured front lawn of Shelby House.

Ronni sat gazing out into the rapidly descending gloom. The sun had bled to death in the sky, staining the heavens crimson. The clouds looked like gauze bundles, saturated with the deep red of the sunset.

Birds returning to their nests were black arrowheads against the blazing backdrop.

With the evening came a chill, one that permeated Shelby House despite the central heating.

Ronni looked at the paperwork before her with a weary resignation: patient reports, to be submitted to their doctors; pharmaceutical orders; stocklists that determined how much and what kind of food was kept in the kitchen; financial reports . . .

Etc., etc.

Ronni could feel a headache gnawing at the base of her skull. She reached up and massaged her own neck, gently twisting her head this way and that. It did little to help and she fumbled in her handbag for a couple of Nurofen. She took them with the tea she'd left on one corner of the desk fifteen minutes ago. It was stone cold and she winced as she swallowed the tablets.

Again she looked down at the paperwork, telling herself it should be done before she went home.

From the direction of the day room she could still hear music. Glenn Miller, she guessed. Her father had been a big fan.

Outside, she heard the sound of tyres on gravel.

Ronni glanced at her watch.

Moments later, there was a tap on the office door and she turned to see Gordon Faulkner standing there.

'How did the party go?' he asked.

Ronni smiled. 'They're still at it by the sound of things,' she told him.

'So what are *you* doing in here?'

'My job,' she told him, tapping the paperwork.

'Excuse *me*.'

'Sorry, Gordon. I didn't mean to be sharp. I just thought I'd leave them to it, that's all.'

'Did Alison come in this afternoon? She said she was going to.'

'She popped in for an hour, had a couple of drinks and a piece of cake. Don't worry, we've saved you some.'

Faulkner smiled. 'Go on then, Ronni,' he told her. 'Go home. You look fit to drop, if you don't mind me saying.'

'I didn't sleep too well last night.'

'Andy keeping you awake?' He chuckled.

'You could say that,' she confessed, but the smile she managed never touched her eyes.

'Well, I'm going along to see how the party's going,' Faulkner told her.

'I'll come with you. Say goodnight to everyone,' she said.

They walked together from the office, along the corridor, past the pharmacy and the staff room towards the day room.

The sound of the Glenn Miller band had been replaced by Duke Ellington.

'This could go on all night.' Faulkner grinned.

Ronni was about to answer him when she heard the sound of shattering glass.

It took her only seconds to realize it came from outside.

146

46

As RONNI TURNED and headed for the main doors she heard another loud crash.

She quickened her pace, Faulkner close behind her.

She paused at the top of the short flight of steps leading to the main doors and scanned the darkened area in front of Shelby House, lit only by spotlights.

The beams cut through the gloom.

There was nothing moving.

'Oh, Christ, look,' murmured Faulkner. He was pointing in the direction of his and Ronni's cars.

As he prepared to take a step forward, Ronni held out a hand to restrain him.

Her own gaze was fixed on the vehicles, in particular Faulkner's Corsa.

Finally, together, they walked slowly down the steps and over to the cars, their feet crunching loudly on the gravel of the drive.

'Shit,' muttered Faulkner.

His front and rear windscreen had been smashed in. Pieces of glass had sprayed into the car and also over the driveway around the vehicle.

Both wing mirrors had been torn free and broken.

The front two tyres were slashed.

As he walked around he saw that the back ones were in a similar state.

The bodywork had suffered similar mutilation. There were

deep scratches along both sides of the vehicle and, as he drew nearer, he saw what looked like white mist rising from the bonnet. There was viscous liquid all over it, some dripping onto the driveway; as he leaned nearer he could still see the paintwork bubbling.

'Don't touch it,' Ronni hissed. She picked up a stick and prodded the blistered paint. The wood crackled and blackened as it made contact with the liquid on the bonnet. 'Acid,' she remarked, then moved to inspect her own car.

The driver's side window had been broken and both wing mirrors lay twisted on the ground.

There was a large crack across the windscreen, the branch that had been used to make it still lay across the bonnet. The glass had spiderwebbed around the point of impact, but otherwise it had remained intact, despite the ferocity of the onslaught.

She crouched and inspected her tyres, relieved to see that all four were still undamaged.

Faulkner was standing with his hands cupped over his mouth, barely able to believe the destruction visited upon his car.

Carved into the passenger door were two words:

FUCK OFF

He shook his head incredulously.

Ronni was already striding up the driveway.

'What are you doing?' Faulkner wanted to know.

'Whoever did this can't have got far,' she told him.

He ran after her and shot out a hand to hold her back. 'Ronni, for God's sake! Whoever did this could be watching us now,' he snapped.

The words hit her like a thunderbolt.

She scanned the trees and bushes that flanked the drive and grew all around the front lawn of Shelby House.

Were there indeed eyes upon them now?

She took a step backwards. 'Who'd want to do this?' she mused, still gazing at the windblown trees and bushes.

'Let's go back inside,' he said anxiously. He put out a hand to guide her towards the safety of Shelby House. He felt exposed out here in the darkened drive.

'We've got to call the police,' she insisted.

Faulkner was looking at his car again, still reeling from the savagery of the attack.

The acrid smell of seared metal and acid-scarred paint filled the air around the Corsa.

There were several large dents in the side panels of both cars.

Ronni's, however, at least looked driveable.

'We must have disturbed whoever did this,' she said. 'It looks as though they ran for it before they could finish with my car.'

'Well, they did a fucking good job on *mine*,' Faulkner rasped angrily. He followed Ronni back up the steps to the main doors.

She paused once more, squinting into the gloom. Trying to pick out any signs of movement in the blackness beyond the reach of the spotlights.

She could see nothing.

47

'WHAT THE HELL are you talking about? We've *got* to call the police.' Ronni stood in the office and fixed Faulkner in an unblinking stare.

'What's the point?' he demanded. 'Whoever did it is long gone now.'

'They can check for fingerprints.'

'And then what?'

'Gordon, someone used acid on your car, slashed your tyres and smashed most of your windows.'

'I saw what they did, Ronni.'

'This isn't just some passing idiot who keys a car. You don't know *who* might be responsible. They could do it again. What do you think would have happened if we'd have disturbed them earlier? They might have thrown acid at *us*.'

Faulkner didn't speak for a moment, merely sucked agitatedly on a cigarette. 'Look, I'm as pissed off about it as you,' he snapped at last. 'More if you like. At least you can still drive *your* car. But I don't think it's a good idea to get the police involved.'

'Why not?'

'Remember where we are, Ronni.'

'What are you talking about? Someone walked up the drive, found our cars and deliberately vandalized them and you don't want the police involved?'

'Think about it. If the police come swarming all over here looking for evidence, what effect is it going to have on the residents? They'll know someone came up the driveway. They'll know someone was in the grounds. How do you think they're going to react to that? We've got people in our care with heart conditions and high blood pressure. The last thing we need is one of them having a stroke or a fucking coronary because they're scared they might be next.'

'Why should they be?'

'I'm not saying they will. I'm just asking you to consider the possible effect bringing the police here might have on the residents.'

'What kind of person is capable of doing something like that? *Why* would they want to do it? Don't *you* want to know?'

'Fucking right I do,' he replied, thinking that he already had a fair idea. 'It's *my* car that's a bloody wreck. I just think there's *ways* of doing it.'

'Such as?'

'I'll call the RAC. Get them to take my car away. Once it's off the grounds, the police can analyse it as much as they like.'

Ronni held his gaze for long moments. Then she nodded almost imperceptibly. 'I suppose you're right,' she murmured. 'There's no point in making everyone else panic.'

Faulkner finished his cigarette and ground it out in the ashtray.

'What did you mean when you said the residents might be next?' Ronni wanted to know.

'If someone was prepared to trespass on private property to trash our cars, you don't know what else they might do.'

48

It was getting colder.

Ronni paused outside the main doors and pulled her coat more tightly around her. Her breath clouded in the air.

However, as she fumbled in her pocket for her keys, she wondered how much of her shivering was due to the plummeting temperatures and how much to what had already happened that evening.

Her own car and the savaged wreck of Faulkner's Corsa stood nearby.

Ronni peered into the gloom, watching for any signs of movement.

What do you expect to see?

She crossed to the Fiesta and quickly slipped behind the wheel, locking the door behind her.

As she sat looking out of the windscreen she inspected the cracks on the glass more carefully. They didn't obscure her view enough to affect her driving and she should be able to manage even without the wing mirror that had been torn away.

She wondered what Andy would have to say when he saw the damage. That was now *both* their cars vandalized.

She pushed the ignition key into place and prepared to turn it.

Something made her pause.

Don't turn it.

Ronni swallowed hard.

What if the car was wired?

She looked down at the key, her hand resting on the steering wheel.

What if there's a bomb under the bonnet? As soon as you turn the key . . .

Ronni suddenly felt angry with herself. There was no bomb under the bonnet.

If you're so sure, then start the fucking thing. Go on.

The damage had been done by some idiots who

(who were crazy enough to use acid on Faulkner's car)

got a kick out of damaging other people's property.

That was it.

So start the engine and drive off.

She gripped the wheel with both hands and looked out into the darkness again.

Were there eyes watching her even now?

The damage to her own car was minor.

Faulkner's was wrecked.

Had that been part of the plan? Lull you into a false sense of security?

Ronni exhaled deeply.

Start the engine.

This was vandalism, not terrorism. There was no bomb in her car.

Then reach down and turn that little key. Twist it in the ignition. Easy as that.

No bomb.

Her hand was shaking as it hovered over the ignition key.

Paranoid?

She rested her hand on the key.

Turn it.

Ronni switched on the lights, the beams cutting through the blackness.

Turn the fucking key if you're so sure everything's fine.

Her breath was coming in gasps. She felt angry with herself for allowing her mind to drag her along such a line of thought.

A bomb in her car?

Bloody ridiculous.

So start the engine.

Absolutely bloody ridiculous.

She turned the key, heart thudding madly against her ribs.

Too late now.

The engine started first time.

Ronni closed her eyes so tightly that white stars danced behind the lids.

There was no bomb.

She stuck the Fiesta in gear and guided it towards the driveway, the wheels crunching gravel beneath them.

As she drove she glanced to her left and right, into the trees and bushes that stood sentinel there.

Nothing moved except the branches, buffeted by the wind.

If anyone was watching from behind those branches, she didn't see them.

49

'SHE'S JUST COMING out now.' Liam Harper spoke quietly into the mobile phone, watching as the Fiesta turned out of the drive-way of Shelby House.

'Follow her,' Carl Thompson told him, his voice sounding curiously metallic on the other end of the line.

Harper dropped the mobile back into his coat pocket, then rode his bike out onto the road.

Terry Mackenzie followed.

'Don't get too close or she'll see us,' Harper instructed.

'We should have done *her* fucking tyres too,' Mackenzie observed.

'Next time.' Harper chuckled as the two boys rode on, never once letting the Fiesta slip from sight.

As Ronni drove, she could feel a cold draft coming through the crack in her windscreen. She turned up the heating slightly.

Tomorrow, before she arrived at work, she'd take the car into a local garage; get the windscreen and wing mirrors replaced and get them to check that nothing else had been tampered with.

Like brake cables. Weren't they sometimes cut?

Ronni afforded herself a smile. Maybe her paranoia *was* getting a little out of hand after all.

Nevertheless, as she drove, she couldn't help but wonder who had damaged the cars. And why?

She wondered if Faulkner had any enemies he hadn't told her

about. Perhaps that was why *his* car had been so comprehensively trashed while hers had just been knocked about a bit.

Surely, if the perpetrator of the damage had been so hellbent on destruction, it would have been a minor step to have slashed *her* tyres too?

Perhaps that was also why he didn't want the police called.

It might be something personal.

Something he didn't want to talk about.

She began to consider exactly how much she knew about Gordon Faulkner. He was thirty-six years old. Lived alone. Used to work at the local hospital as a porter. Had never been married.

That was it. The sum total of her knowledge about a man she worked with on an almost daily basis.

She had no idea what kind of friends or enemies he had.

One of them could quite easily have damaged his car.

But why hers too?

She slowed down as she approached a set of traffic lights stuck on red.

On the road behind, Liam Harper also slowed down. He allowed his bike to roll alongside the Fiesta and sat waiting.

Terry Mackenzie rode ahead on the pavement, bringing his own bike to a halt fifty or sixty yards further on.

Ronni glanced at the boy on the bike beside her.

He was staring distractedly at the lights, anxious for them to change. When they did he moved away first, then allowed Ronni to cruise past him again.

She turned a corner and sought the lamp post outside the house where she usually parked.

After what had happened outside Shelby House earlier that evening, she was glad that the street light was shining on the vehicle. It felt like a little extra security.

Harper swung himself off his bike as he watched her bring the Fiesta to a halt.

Ronni sat behind the wheel for a moment, then finally clambered out. From the back seat she took a small plastic bag full of shopping.

She locked each door in turn, then double-checked the boot was firmly shut. Only then did she begin digging in her handbag for the house keys.

She found them and made her way up the short path to the front door.

Harper watched her enter, then pulled the mobile from his pocket and jabbed out the required digits.

'She's just parked the car,' he said as soon as the phone was answered.

'Where?' Thompson asked.

Harper told him.

'All right,' Thompson muttered. 'You don't have to hang around.'

Mackenzie joined Harper and both of them stood looking across at the house.

'What are we going to do?' Harper wanted to know.

'*You're* not going to do anything,' Thompson told him. 'Just leave it. Are you sure about that fucking address?'

Harper repeated it. 'What are *you* going to do?' he enquired excitedly.

'I might pay her a little visit later tonight; maybe remind her old man not to get so mouthy. Who knows?'

'If she looks after those old cunts *she's* probably got money too,' Harper offered. 'I bet when one of them dies they leave their money to her.'

'I might find out later. Now just get away from there before someone sees you hanging around.'

The line went dead.

Harper pocketed his own mobile, then swung himself back onto his bike.

'Well?' Mackenzie wanted to know. 'What now? Do we finish the job on the car?'

'Not outside her own house, you prick,' Harper sneered. 'Not this time. Come on.'

The two of them rode off.

Ronni didn't stay long at her father's house.

She unpacked the few items of shopping she'd got for him and stored each in its place. Then she made sure there was nothing else he wanted.

There wasn't.

She didn't mention the incident with the vandalized cars.

No need.

James Connor rebuked her gently for fussing over him. Then he thanked her and told her she'd inherited her caring nature from her mother.

He told her he loved her.

As he always did.

She told him she'd call in again the following day.

Ronni kissed him at the door, then walked back to the Fiesta and drove off.

Ten minutes later, she was home.

It was 9.46 p.m.

50

THE NOISE THAT woke him sounded like a creaking board.

James Connor blinked hard and propped himself up on one elbow.

The sound came again.

He murmured under his breath and swung himself out of bed.

It *could* be a floorboard.

The house was still settling. Timbers contracting, that kind of thing.

As he wandered out of the bedroom he glanced at his watch: 1.32 a.m.

He'd been in bed for more than two hours now, but his sleep had been fitful. He hadn't enjoyed a good night's sleep since his wife's death. Tablets from the doctor, herbal remedies from the chemists; none seemed to have given him that peace he had always found so easily when she'd been alive.

As he pushed open the door of the bathroom he was beginning to wonder if the noise he'd heard had been the residue of a dream.

The tiles of the bathroom felt cold under his feet and he shivered as he stood and urinated as quickly as a suspect prostate would allow. He was about to flush the toilet when he heard the sound again.

From below him this time.

Radiators cooling down?

He moved out onto the landing and looked down into the black maw that was the staircase.

The street lights were out. There was little natural light seeping through the bevelled glass panel in the front door.

There was a thud from below.

Movement.

He sucked in a deep breath and placed one foot on the top step.

It creaked loudly and he cursed the sound.

For interminable seconds he stood motionless at the top of the stairs.

The house was again filled with silence.

Perhaps the noise had come from next door, he reasoned. They had small children. One of them could be mucking about. Sound could be deceptive in the dead of night. Its source wasn't always immediately obvious.

He moved onto the next step, straining his ears.

His vigilance was rewarded with more sounds.

Low, occasional hissing. Like conspiratorial whispering.

The sounds would come in short bursts, then the silence would return again like a cloak.

This time he was certain the noises were coming from downstairs.

Connor stepped back onto the landing, then crossed again into the bedroom. He reached beneath his bed and pulled out the cricket bat that lay there.

As he straightened up he glanced at one of the photos of his wife propped on the bedside table. She watched him as he moved towards the staircase, clutching the bat before him.

He paused once more at the top.

Again he heard the low hissing sound.

His heart was thudding hard against his ribs now.

There could be no mistake.

Someone was inside the house.

51

As CONNOR EDGED slowly down the narrow staircase he wondered if there were better, more sensible options.

Bang on a wall, attract attention from one of the neighbours?

Call the police?

Minor problem: the phone was in the living room.

He was halfway down now, enveloped by the deep umbra.

The sounds were clearer.

There was movement from the living room and the kitchen beyond.

He paused and swallowed hard. Perhaps he should just go back upstairs. Let them take what they wanted. He had nothing valuable. The most valuable thing he'd ever possessed was gone: his wife.

Go back upstairs and leave them to it. What are they going to get? A TV, a microwave and a video.

Nothing worth risking your neck for.

He stood motionless, considering the options.

His palms were sweaty around the handle of the cricket bat.

His heart was hammering against his ribs so hard he felt sure the intruders would hear him.

Intruders.

How many were there?

He drew in a shaking breath.

Go back upstairs and wait for them to finish.

It seemed the most sensible choice.

Whatever was taken could be claimed back off the house insurance.

And what if they came upstairs? What then?

Confrontation might be unavoidable.

Bang on the bloody wall. Get help from the neighbours.

And what if they didn't come? What if they just banged back? Shouted that he was disturbing the kids?

Connor gritted his teeth.

There were intruders in *his* house. Someone was on *his* property, trying to steal *his* belongings.

If Margaret had still been alive he wouldn't have thought twice about confronting these intruders.

There should only *ever* have been one option.

The bastards weren't going to get away with it.

He felt suddenly angry with himself for even *thinking* about hiding from them and that anger propelled him down the last few steps into the hall.

He stood there silently, ear close to the door that led into the sitting room.

The occasional flash of torchlight showed beneath it.

Thieving bastards.

He put one hand on the door handle and waited.

There was a light switch just inside the room. If he could reach that and slap it on, he could catch them by surprise.

They'd probably run for it. If they didn't he'd lay into them with the bat.

He sucked in a deep breath. Anger had replaced fear now.

How dare they enter his house.

Silence from inside the living room.

Perhaps they'd already slipped out.

He moved the door handle slightly.

Had they heard him? Were they waiting for him?

He heard that whispering once more.

Now. Do it now.

James Connor pushed the living-room door open and flapped

at the light switch with one hand. The other gripped the cricket bat.

'Right, you bastards,' he snarled, stepping into the room.

As he did, he realized he'd made a mistake.

52

THERE WERE TWO of them: one man, one woman.

Although, as he looked at them, he realized the terms were barely appropriate. One boy and one girl would have been more to the point.

In the split second he burst into the room to confront the intruders he could see that the would-be thieves were in their early teens.

Still thieves, though.

Time seemed to have frozen.

In the glaring light they stared at each other. Then Connor saw the devastation in the room.

Everything it was possible to smash had been smashed.

Every ornament. Every picture frame.

They'd all been shattered.

Furniture had been overturned.

The sofa and one of the chairs had been carved open. Stuffing and springs protruded like entrails from a gutted corpse.

The television had been tipped off its stand, the screen splintered. A small plume of white smoke rose from the back of the broken set.

As he stood there he felt a cold breeze blowing from the direction of the kitchen. There was a broken pane of glass in one of the windows. Doubtless how they'd gained entry.

Gained entry to *his* house.

He moved towards the boy with a speed that belied his years, swinging the bat around with tremendous power.

The youth raised an arm to protect his head and the wood smacked against his forearm with a dull crack.

Connor swung again, this time at the girl. She avoided the blow and backed off towards the kitchen.

'Go on, get out!' Connor shouted.

He turned on the boy once more, bringing the bat down again as he tried to sprint past him. It caught him across the shoulder blade and sent him sprawling.

'Get out of my house!' bellowed Connor, reinforced by his success against the intruders.

They were both making for the kitchen now, the boy rubbing his injured forearm.

The girl pushed him into the other room and stood defiantly before Connor, who raised the bat again.

As he swung she stepped back into the kitchen.

Connor followed.

They were both making for the back door now, anxious to be away from the savage blows.

Connor almost managed a smile.

Then he felt a crushing impact against the back of his head.

White-hot pain filled his skull and he dropped to his knees, the bat falling from his hands.

He realized the third intruder had stepped from behind the open kitchen door.

Connor had no idea what had been used to fell him.

It didn't really matter.

Carl Thompson gripped the length of piping in one hand and stood over the old man.

Graham Brown snatched up the cricket bat and hefted it before him.

Donna Freeman also took a step towards him.

Connor knew he had to get up, but something told him it would be impossible.

He was right.

Thompson hit him again, splitting the back of his head open.

Brown swung the bat and caught him across the side of the face with a blow that splintered one cheekbone.

Donna brought the spike heel of her ankle boot down onto his outstretched hand, spearing the appendage and shattering several small bones. She then drove a kick into his ribs.

Thompson too was kicking hard into Connor's stomach and sides.

The old man tried to pull himself into a foetal position, hands clasped over his head.

Brown hammered at those hands with the bat, breaking three fingers until Connor could protect himself no longer.

The bat connected with his skull and effortlessly split the skin.

Blood was spreading across the kitchen floor as the blows continued to rain down.

'Fucking old cunt,' Brown snarled, bringing the sole of his boot down hard on the old man's face.

His nose broke – fresh blood sprayed into the air.

Brown was jumping up and down, one foot always landing on the old man, ensuring that each impact caused the maximum damage.

Thompson concentrated on the ribs.

Old bones.

They broke easily.

Donna kicked at his arms and shoulders, the toes of her boots making red circular marks on Connor's flesh.

They seemed to be competing to see who could inflict the most pain; not one piece of skin was left unmarked, not one bone unbroken.

Connor was lying on his back, eyes half open.

Blood was running from both sides of his half-open mouth, mingling with the crimson fluid already pouring from the dozens of cuts disfiguring his face.

His dentures dropped down and Brown dug two fingers into

the blood-filled orifice to pull them free. He scooped them out onto the floor and crushed them beneath one foot.

Connor was gurgling, blood filling his throat.

'That's enough,' snapped Thompson. 'Leave him.'

'What about the rest of the house?' Brown wanted to know. 'What about that fucking bitch and her old man?'

'Fuck it. Who cares? If she's upstairs now she'll be calling the law anyway,' Thompson told him, pushing his companions towards the back door.

He was about to join them when he noticed Connor's wedding ring.

Old. Might even be antique. Worth a few bob to someone.

He knelt beside the motionless man and tried to slide the ring free.

It wouldn't budge.

He pulled harder; hard enough to dislocate the finger. It came free of the socket with a loud pop.

Still the ring wouldn't move.

Thompson spat on it, using his saliva as lubricant.

The ring came free at last and he pushed it into the pocket of his Levi's.

Then he walked towards the back door, stepped outside and gently closed it behind him.

Lights flickered on in the house next door.

53

She heard the phone on the second ring.

Ronni rolled over in bed. The shrill sound pierced the night, jolting her from sleep as if she'd been stuck with a cattle prod.

She was disorientated for a second and peered through bleary eyes at the digits of the radio alarm, which glowed blood-red in the blackness: 3.04 a.m.

The phone was still ringing.

Andy murmured something, half asleep.

She was already out of bed, pulling her housecoat around her, padding towards the landing.

The phone was in the hall.

She made her way down the stairs quickly.

3.04 a.m.

Thoughts tumbled through her mind.

Who the hell could be calling at this time of night?

Shelby House?

Her father?

She reached for the receiver.

'Hello?' she said, clearing her throat.

She didn't recognize the voice; it asked if she was Veronica Porter.

'Who is this?'

The voice asked if her father was James Connor.

'Can you tell me what this is about?'

Fear trailed icy fingers up and down the back of her neck.

Her father was in hospital.

'Oh, God, what happened?'

The voice told her he was in intensive care.

Ronni's hands began to shake uncontrollably.

'What's wrong?' she demanded.

The voice told her he'd been very badly

(*very badly*)

injured. She heard the word 'assault', but it didn't register.

Neither did the word 'attacked'.

But 'intensive care' lit up in her mind like neon on a wet night.

She dropped the phone, then hurriedly snatched it up again, tears forming in her eyes. Her head was spinning and, for precious seconds, she thought she was going to faint.

'Ronni.'

The voice came from the top of the stairs this time.

Andy was standing there looking down at her.

The voice on the phone said something else, something she didn't hear.

'I'll be there straight away,' she said into the mouthpiece, then slammed the phone down and ran up the stairs, her face drained of colour.

'What the fuck's going on?' Andy demanded as she swept past him.

'It's Dad,' she blurted, hurrying into the bedroom, snapping on the light and pulling on leggings and socks.

'What's wrong with him?' persisted her husband.

She took off her T-shirt, pulled on a sweater.

'He's been rushed to hospital,' she said, her voice cracking. 'He's in intensive care.'

Andy snatched up his jeans and struggled into them. 'Get my car keys from the kitchen table,' he urged. 'I'll drive.'

54

'THEY ALWAYS SMELL the same, don't they?' Andy got to his feet and fumbled in his jacket pocket for some loose change.

'What?'

'Hospitals. That smell. Whatever it is.'

Ronnie ran a hand through her hair.

'Do you want a drink?' he asked. 'I'll get us one out of the machine round the corner.'

She shook her head.

'Just a coffee or something?' he persisted.

'I don't want a bloody drink,' she snapped. 'I just want to know how my dad is.'

He nodded, paused a moment, then wandered off to feed coins into the vending machine.

Ronni waited until he'd disappeared around the corner, then got to her feet.

The silence inside the intensive care unit was almost palpable.

There was a light on at the nurses' station just down the corridor, but no sign of a nurse. The one who'd shown them to these seats had disappeared not long after they'd arrived. Ronni couldn't remember the name on the woman's badge.

Patricia something-or-other.

It wasn't important.

The only thing that mattered was her father.

She looked at her watch: 4.17 a.m.

They'd been at the hospital for more than an hour already and still no word.

He'd undergone surgery.

Extensive surgery.

That was all she knew.

All they could tell her.

She wished the nurse would return so she could ask her what was going on.

If there was any news.

If her father was dead.

Dead.

She tried to push the word from her mind, but it clung on like a hungry leech.

Dead.

Ronni shook her head. She sat down again, noticing that the lace of one of her trainers was undone.

She made no attempt to do it up.

Extensive surgery.

Those words stuck too.

Ronni kept her eyes fixed on the door of the room opposite, wondering when someone would emerge to speak to her.

And tell her what?

That they were so sorry that her father didn't make it?

He was too old, you see, there were complications. There sometimes was after EXTENSIVE SURGERY.

She got to her feet again, wiping her sweating palms on her leggings.

Footsteps.

Ronni turned and looked in the direction of the nurses' station. Perhaps the nurse had returned. She could find out at last what was going on.

Andy trudged around the corner carrying two plastic cups of steaming liquid.

'It's meant to be coffee,' he said, holding it out towards her and attempting a smile.

She merely shook her head.

'Ronni, please—' he began.

It was then that the door of the room opposite opened.

55

THE DOCTOR WAS in his early forties. His long white coat was open to reveal a blue shirt and dark grey trousers. He carried a clipboard that he hugged to his chest as if it was a small child.

Ronni immediately took a step towards him and he looked at her with professional detachment in his eyes.

'How's my father, Doctor?' she asked.

The doctor glanced at his clipboard and found her name in the box marked 'Next of Kin'. He managed a smile, but the shrug that accompanied it told Ronni the news wasn't good. 'I won't lie to you, Mrs Porter,' he said quietly. 'His injuries are bad.'

Andy stepped closer and slid an arm around her waist. He saw the name tag on the doctor's coat: John Greenwood.

'Tell me,' Ronni persisted.

'He was suffering from major cranial injuries when he was brought in,' Greenwood said. 'His skull was fractured in three places and there was bleeding inside his brain. The report from Neurology shows that bleeding has been stopped, but the extent of the trauma was very severe.'

Ronni thought she was going to faint.

Andy guided her back towards one of the chairs.

'He's in a coma,' Greenwood continued, sitting down beside her.

'Is he going to die?' Ronni asked, tears glistening on her cheeks.

'The next forty-eight hours are crucial,' said the doctor. 'If he gets through those with no further complications, then his chances may improve, but there was damage to other parts of his body too.' He turned pages on the clipboard. 'Three broken ribs. A hairline fracture of the jaw. There was also considerable damage to the kidneys and spleen. I'm sorry.'

'Can I see him?' she wanted to know.

Greenwood hesitated a moment, then nodded.

'Do you want me to come in with you?' Andy asked, but Ronni was already on her feet, heading for the door of the room opposite.

As she reached it, she paused. Then, with a shaking hand, she pushed it open and stepped inside.

There was a nurse in the room, checking on the contents of a drip attached to James Connor's arm. She turned and smiled at Ronni, not expecting the gesture to be reciprocated.

It wasn't.

Ronni gazed at the shape in the bed.

It didn't look like her father.

It wasn't just the swathes of bandages that covered the top of his head and most of his face, the drips and tubes that ran from both arms and both nostrils. He looked *smaller*, as if he'd shrunk.

She could hear the steady blip of an oscilloscope and the mechanical wheezing of a respirator.

They're keeping him alive. Just those machines.

The nurse nodded in the direction of a chair beside the bed and Ronni sat down.

The nurse excused herself and left Ronni alone with her father.

She looked at the battered, bandaged face. The swollen arms, discoloured by bruises and cuts. The finger splints that supported the broken digits.

'Oh, Dad,' she said, her voice cracking.

The oscilloscope continued its rhythmic beeping.

An accompaniment to her muted sobs.

56

Ronni had no idea how long she'd been sitting with her father.

Time seemed to have lost its meaning.

Minutes. Hours. She had no way of knowing.

She merely sat staring at his ravaged face, wanting – above all else – for his eyes to open. For him to look at her.

Ronni held one of his hands gently, careful not to dislodge the heavily strapped broken finger.

Not that it would have bothered him, would it?

He's in a coma, isn't he? You could stick pins in his eyes and he wouldn't feel it.

She dabbed at her eyes with a tissue.

Coma.

The word was right up there with 'malignant', 'terminal' and 'inoperable'. One of those you prayed you'd never hear.

Coma.

Some people came out of them in a matter of hours.

Some never came out of them at all.

She swallowed hard.

Would that be the next step? The next phone call? The next decision?

We need your permission to switch off the machines.

Ronni lowered her gaze and screwed her eyes tightly shut. She rested her head against her father's shoulder; only this time there was no comforting arm placed around her. No one to tell her everything was going to be fine.

175

That had always been her dad's job when she was growing up. She wondered if she would ever feel that comforting arm again. Ever lose herself in his embrace.

Ever feel that love that only a parent and child know.

She reached up and touched his cheek.

He felt so cold.

She pulled the sheet up slightly, then leaned forward and kissed him on that same cold cheek.

She didn't even hear the door open.

Andy stood silently in the entrance for a moment, then stepped into the room. He coughed theatrically, then took a couple of steps towards the bed. 'Ronni.'

She straightened up, but didn't turn to face him.

He glanced at the old man and shook his head. 'Oh, Christ, Ronni, I'm sorry,' Andy offered, rubbing a hand across his own mouth.

'You're not supposed to say that until he's dead,' she murmured.

'He'll be OK. He's a tough old sod.'

'Does he *look* as if he's going to be OK?' she demanded and Andy was surprised at the venom in her words.

'The doctor said all we can do now is wait.'

'Wait for him to die?'

He put out a hand to touch her shoulder, then withdrew it hesitantly.

'Do you believe in God, Andy?' she said, her back still to him.

The question took him by surprise. 'I suppose so, yes.'

'So do I. I prayed to Him to let Dad live. Do you think He heard me?'

'Ronni—'

'Do you think He *heard* me?' she snapped.

'I'm sure He did.'

She remained motionless beside the bed.

'Ronni, listen,' Andy continued, 'there's someone outside who wants to talk to you.'

'Who is it?'

'His name's Marsh. He's a policeman.'

57

Ronni thought the man's shirt needed ironing.

She almost smiled at the ridiculousness of the thought. It had no right to intrude upon the more solemn ideas spinning around inside her head.

And yet she could not shake it free: the white shirt that Detective Sergeant David Marsh wore was badly in need of ironing. Also, his top button was undone; his tie crooked.

He ran a hand through his short hair and smiled as she entered the room.

Doctor Greenwood had allowed them to use his office while he continued his rounds.

There was another man with Marsh; a uniformed constable who was holding his cap in one hand, tracing the outline of the polished peak. He sat on a plastic chair against the far wall, occasionally picking pieces of fluff from his dark blue sweater.

Andy was there too, sipping at a cup of coffee.

Ronni sat down beside him, wiping her nose with a tissue.

'Mrs Porter, I'm Detective Sergeant Marsh, this is PC Wharton.' He gestured towards the uniformed man. 'I'll try to get this over with as quickly as possible. I know you want to get back to your father.'

'It's all right,' Ronni muttered.

No rush. He's in a coma. He's not going anywhere.

'Your father was attacked in his home,' Marsh began. 'We think he may have disturbed some burglars.'

'Burglars?' Ronni said flatly. 'He had nothing worth stealing.'

'Well, *they* didn't know that until they broke in, did they?' Marsh continued. 'Our initial reports indicate there could have been two or three intruders, and the extent of your father's injuries would certainly seem to indicate he was attacked by more than one person.'

'Who called the ambulance?' she wanted to know.

'Neighbours heard a disturbance. One of them went to check and saw your father lying in his kitchen.'

'What do you expect *me* to tell you?' she said wearily.

'You'd called round earlier in the evening, hadn't you?' said Marsh.

She nodded. 'I go to see him every day.'

'The neighbours told us. Did you see anyone hanging around when you arrived or left?'

Ronni shook her head. 'It was dark,' she reminded him. 'I wasn't looking for possible burglars.'

'Did your father keep any money in the house?'

'No.'

'No antiques? No family heirlooms? Nothing of value?'

'No. I told you, he didn't have anything worth stealing.'

'Everything has a value to a thief, Mrs Porter. You'd be surprised – even the smallest thing can be sold for a couple of quid. TVs, videos, that kind of thing.'

'He had a TV and a video. Perhaps that's what they wanted.'

'The television and video were both smashed, not stolen. As far as we could tell, nothing was taken from his house.'

Ronni looked puzzled.

'The intruders broke in via a back window,' Marsh continued. 'That's consistent with a number of other burglaries that have happened on the Waybridge Estate during the past few months.'

'So have you got any idea who attacked my father?'

'Not at the moment. There were a few fingerprints found at the scene, though. It's better than nothing. If we can match those prints to anything in our files we'll have a chance of pinning this on someone.'

'A chance?'

'I won't lie to you, Mrs Porter – ' Marsh sighed ' – the likelihood of us catching the men who attacked your father is slim.'

Ronni nodded resignedly.

'We were wondering if you could perhaps come and have a look around your father's house and see if anything *was* taken,' the DS said almost apologetically. 'I know it's difficult for you, but you might see something we missed and—'

Ronni suddenly stood up.

Andy followed her as she hurried out into the corridor.

Marsh and the uniformed constable looked on in bewilderment.

She saw the nurse from earlier sitting at the nurses' station and crossed hurriedly to her. 'Were you here when my father was brought in?' she wanted to know. 'His name's James Connor.'

The nurse nodded.

'You keep a record of patients' belongings, don't you?' Ronni persisted. 'Can I see what he had with him when he was admitted?'

The nurse reached for a sheet of paper and handed it to Ronni.

She glanced at it, then hurried back up the corridor.

'Ronni, what the hell are you doing?' Andy asked, following her back into her father's room.

Marsh had emerged into the corridor by now.

'I knew there was something,' Ronni told him, stepping back out of the room again. 'When I first saw him it didn't register, but now I know.'

Marsh looked vague.

'Something *was* stolen from my father,' Ronni said. 'His wedding ring is gone.'

58

Ronni sat with her eyes fixed on her father's battered face.

Andy sat towards the bottom of the bed.

The silence was broken only by the noise of the respirator and the oscilloscope.

'You need a break, Ronni,' Andy finally said, leaning foward.

She ignored him.

'There's nothing you can do for him,' Andy continued.

'You want me to leave him alone here?'

'He *isn't* alone. He's got doctors and nurses to take care of him.'

She never shifted her gaze from her father's face. 'It might be as simple as that for you, Andy. It isn't for me. If you're sick of hanging around, then you go home.'

He exhaled wearily. 'What good is sitting here going to do?' he wanted to know.

'He might wake up. I want to be here when he does.'

If *he does*.

'That could take time.'

'I don't care how long it takes.'

Andy got to his feet, dug in his pocket for a cigarette, then remembered he couldn't light it anyway.

'Look, you've got to face it, Ronni,' he said softly. 'He could be in a coma for days.'

'Thanks for your concern, Andy.'

'I'm just being realistic. I'm just repeating what the doctor said.'

'So what do you want me to do?'

'Come home. If there's any change in his condition you know they'll phone you.'

'You mean if he dies?'

He sighed again. 'Ronni, he's not going to die.'

'How do you *know* that, Andy? The *doctors* don't even know.'

'Well, sitting here staring at him isn't going to help, is it?'

'Go home, Andy.'

'You can come back again later. You need some sleep. You're not going to be any good to your dad if you're ill too.'

'Take the car. I'll get a taxi home.'

He ran a hand exasperatedly through his hair.

The door opened and a nurse entered. She moved quickly and efficiently around the bed, checking machines, adjusting drips. She even pulled open James Connor's eyelids and shone a penlight into each eye. Her name badge proclaimed she was Dawn Atkins. Her blonde hair was tied in a ponytail that swept back and forth as she moved around the bed, occasionally stopping to mark the chart she held.

'Is he going to be all right?' Ronni asked.

'We don't know yet,' the nurse told her. She stopped and looked at Ronni, noting the dark smudges beneath her eyes.

'How long have you been here?'

'It feels like a long time,' Ronni confessed.

'I've just been telling her she should get some rest,' Andy interjected.

'Your husband's right,' the nurse said, touching Ronni's arm. 'He *is* your husband, isn't he? You can never be sure these days.' She smiled and Ronni returned the gesture.

The nurse was a year or two younger than Ronni, but she exuded an air of authority that was comforting.

'I don't want to leave him,' she insisted.

'Go home and rest. That's what your dad would want you to do, isn't it?'

Ronni nodded.

Andy was already at the door.

Ronni leant forward and kissed James Connor's cheek. 'I love you, Dad,' she whispered close to his ear.

Andy held the door open and she walked out.

'I told you it'd be best if we went home,' he said.

Ronni pulled her coat more tightly around her and walked purposefully down the corridor in the direction of the lifts.

As they emerged into the hospital car park, the first hint of daylight was beginning to force its way into the sky.

A cold wind whipped across the open space and Ronni shuddered as she slipped into the passenger seat.

They drove home in silence.

59

THE WRITING ON most of the envelopes was in biro.

All different colours.

Different hands.

Some was in pencil. One or two even in fountain pen.

The envelopes were not sealed.

They bore no stamps or postmarks.

As Gordon Faulkner stood looking at the mass of white rectangles scattered over the floor of Shelby House's main entrance, he realized that the mail had been pushed through by hand.

He picked the envelopes up slowly, counting them.

'Someone's popular today.'

The voice made him turn.

Donald Tanner was making his way down the hallway, nodding in the direction of the envelopes.

Faulkner didn't answer. He merely continued picking up the unmarked mail.

'Late anniversary cards for Harry and Janice?' Tanner wondered, bending to help Faulkner.

He too saw the scribbled words.

No names.

Just the address.

Not even that in some cases.

Just SHELBY HOUSE written, sometimes in capitals, but mostly in a variety of scripts and vivid colours.

Faulkner continued sifting through the letters he held.

Tanner also picked up a handful and began counting them. 'Twelve,' he announced finally.

'Twenty-six,' Faulkner said, looking at the wedge of paper he held. 'Bring them through to the office, will you, please, Don?'

'Who are they for?' Tanner pondered.

'More to the point, who are they *from?*'

The two men looked at the piles of envelopes for a moment longer, then Faulkner reached for one and opened it.

There was a single sheet of paper inside.

He unfolded it.

'Oh, Jesus,' he murmured, staring at the scrawl before him;

I HOPE You DIE OF CANCER

'What is it?' Tanner wanted to know.

Faulkner reached for another of the envelopes, opened it, took out the single sheet and read it.

Fucking old Bastards

Tanner also opened one of the envelopes and glanced at the sheet of paper inside.

get a Tumor you Fucking old Cunt

The colour drained visibly from his face.

'Just leave them, Don,' Faulkner told him, but already Tanner was ripping open another.

Roses are Red Violets are blue
you'll soon be dead and we'll piss on you

Faulkner opened two more.

DIE OF A HEART ATTACK CUNT

Tanner's hand was shaking as he read another.

You will ALL DIE SooN

Faulkner reached for the phone.

60

'YOU CAN'T GO into work today.'

Ronni fastened her blouse, then sat in front of the dressing-table mirror and began combing her hair. She could see Andy's reflection there, gazing at her as she forced the knots and tangles from her brown tresses.

'You told me I couldn't do anything for Dad, Andy,' she replied. 'I might as well go to work. It'll keep my mind occupied. Don't you think that's a good idea?'

He merely stood watching her. 'You're being bloody silly,' he said finally. 'I didn't tell you to go to work, I just said there—'

'Was nothing I could do for my dad. I know what you said.' She began applying eye-liner.

'You haven't slept,' he reminded her.

'What about you? Shouldn't you be getting ready for work too? After all, you haven't got anything to worry about, have you, Andy? He's my father, not yours.'

'Thanks a lot. I was just thinking about you.'

She put on a little lipstick.

There was a long silence, finally broken by Ronni. She turned to face her husband and when she spoke the edge had left her voice. 'I really think it's best for me, Andy,' she told him. 'If I'm at work I've got things to do. If I stay at home I'll just sit here worrying all day. Besides, there are people at work I can talk to if I want to.'

'What about me?' he demanded angrily. 'Why the hell can't you talk to *me*? I'll take the fucking day off to be with you.'

She got to her feet and crossed to him, touching his cheek with one hand.

'Don't shut me out, Ronni,' he said. 'Not now.'

She kissed him on the forehead and turned towards the bedroom door.

It was then that the phone rang.

Ronni felt her heart hammering against her ribs.

She bolted for the landing, then hurried down the stairs.

Please, God, don't let it be the hospital. Don't let him be dead.

She snatched up the receiver. 'Hello?'

She recognized the voice at the other end immediately.

Gordon Faulkner sounded uneasy.

At least it wasn't the hospital.

Her heart slowed its pounding a little.

'Ronni?' he said.

She didn't reply for several long moments as she calmed herself down.

'Ronni?' he repeated.

'I'm sorry, Gordon,' she murmured. 'Miles away. I thought you might be somebody else.'

'Is something wrong?' he wanted to know.

'Yes, there is, actually. I'll tell you when I get in.'

'Perhaps I should wait until you get here, then.'

'Have you got a problem there?'

'I don't know *what* we've got.'

'What are you talking about, Gordon?'

'Something's happened.'

'Like what?'

'It's easier if you see for yourself.'

'I'll be there in twenty minutes,' she told him and hung up.

Andy was standing at the top of the stairs.

'Something's happened at Shelby House,' she told him. 'I've got to go.'

'Can't they manage without you for once?'

'I'm the supervisor. It's my responsibility.'

'*Everything*'s your responsibility at that place.'

She was already reaching for her coat. 'We'll talk when I get home,' she told him, snatching up her handbag.

'No we won't,' Andy said quietly.

She closed the front door behind her.

Andy wandered back into the bedroom and watched her climb into the Fiesta, shaking his head at the shattered windscreen and dented bodywork. The engine sputtered protestingly a couple of times, then reluctantly started.

She drove off.

61

'THIRTY-EIGHT LETTERS.'

Ronni sat at the desk in the office at Shelby House, the open envelopes all around her. Sheets of paper bearing vitriolic statements lined up like accusations.

'It took someone a long time to do those,' Gordon Faulkner added.

Ronni glanced at another.

YOU WILL DIE SCREAMING

She shook her head. 'Who else has seen these?' she wanted to know.

Donald Tanner had been joined in the office by George Errington and Colin Glazer.

'Just us,' Errington told her.

'I don't want anyone else to know about them,' Ronni said. 'They could frighten some of the other residents.'

'They did a pretty good job on *me*,' Colin Glazer offered. 'Who'd do something like this?'

'Someone with plenty of time on their hands,' Ronni said, again surveying the expanse of letters.

'But why?' Tanner wanted to know.

Ronni had no answer for him.

'What do you want to do about it, Ronni?' Faulkner enquired.

'We should phone the police,' she murmured.

'I think we should tell the others,' George Errington said. 'They've got a right to know.'

Ronni shook her head. 'It'll only worry them, George,' she said wearily. 'Leave it for now. Just keep it to yourself.'

'And when the police turn up?' Glazer demanded. 'What do we say then?'

'Perhaps that's a good enough reason not to call them.'

'If someone was prepared to go to this amount of time and effort, who knows what they might do next?' Tanner interjected.

'Do you want the police here, Donald?' Ronni said challengingly. 'Do you want the other residents to know about these?' She gestured to the obscenities.

'I want *something* done,' Tanner said defiantly. 'This is sick.'

The door of the office opened and Alison Dean walked in. She looked at the five people crammed into the small office then at the piles of mail. 'What's going on?' she muttered.

'These were pushed through the door last night,' Faulkner told her, handing her two or three of the letters.

Alison scanned them.

'Thirty-eight of them to be exact,' Ronni added.

'My God,' murmured Alison. She handed the letters back to Faulkner. 'Are they all the same?'

'Same tone, yes.'

'Hate mail. Threats,' Glazer said.

'Could they have been meant for one person?' Alison mused.

'Someone's not going to send thirty-eight nasty letters to one person all at the same time, are they?' Errington snapped.

'So they were meant for all of us?' Tanner asked, his face pale.

'For the time being I say we wait,' Ronni offered.

'Until what?' Tanner rasped. 'Until one of the threats is carried out?'

'And if we call the police, what do we tell them?' Ronni demanded.

'Show them the letters,' Tanner insisted. 'They'll know what to do. They'll catch whoever sent them.'

Just like they're going to catch whoever put my father in a coma.

'And if they catch them, what will they do to them?' Glazer sneered. 'Nothing. They've got more important things to be worrying about than a few bloody letters sent to an old people's home.'

'Colin has a point,' Errington admitted.

'Leave the police out of it,' Glazer continued. 'I agree with what Ronni says. We shouldn't let the others know about this.'

'And what if it happens again?' Tanner wanted to know.

'Then we'll deal with it,' Ronni said flatly.

'What do we do with these?' asked Faulkner, picking up one of the letters.

'Burn them,' Ronni said, angrily screwing one into a ball.

A heavy silence descended upon the room and Ronni was aware that all eyes were trained on her.

'Well, I'm keeping some,' Tanner said finally. 'I want *something* to show the police if I have to.' He gathered five or six of the obscene notes and folded them up, sticking them into his pocket.

'We're all agreed then,' Ronni said. 'None of this leaves the room? It's between *us*.' She looked at each one of them in turn and they nodded. Tanner held her gaze, then finally he too agreed.

Errington and Glazer wandered out of the room. Tanner opened his mouth to say something, then decided against it and followed his companions.

'Jesus Christ,' murmured Gordon Faulkner. 'I hope you know what you're doing, Ronni. Not calling the police.'

'I'll take responsibility, Gordon,' she told him.

'Goes with the position, does it?'

She eyed him angrily. 'Your shift's over, isn't it?' she wanted to know.

He nodded.

'Then go home,' snapped Ronni venomously. She began gathering the letters into one large pile.

Faulkner frowned, then walked out of the room leaving the two women alone.

'Are you OK?' Alison asked, watching as Ronni snatched up each new piece of paper.

Ronni paused for a moment and sniffed. The knot of muscles at the side of her jaw pulsed.

Then the tears came.

Painful and unstoppable.

62

'WHY DIDN'T YOU say something earlier?' Alison Dean wanted to know. She sat close to Ronni, one arm around her shoulder.

Ronni was cradling a mug of tea in both hands and staring straight ahead. 'What was I supposed to say?' she said softly. '"Excuse me if I seem a bit down today, but my father was beaten unconscious last night. He's in a coma and no one's sure whether he'll live or not"?' She wiped more tears from her cheeks, surprised that she even had the capacity for further weeping. She wondered if it was possible for tear ducts to dry up. 'You should have seen him, Alison,' she murmured, still staring straight ahead. 'He looked so helpless.'

'And the police haven't got any idea who might have done it?'

Ronni shook her head. She reached into her handbag for a tissue, muttering under her breath when she realized she hadn't got one.

Alison handed her one from her pocket and Ronni dabbed at her eyes.

'If he'd been *here* it wouldn't have happened,' she said, angrily. 'I always said I wanted him here. If he had been . . .' She allowed the sentence to trail off.

'Instead of being beaten up, he'd have got one of these sick letters,' Alison reminded her.

Ronni sucked in a weary breath.

Alison was sifting through them, shaking her head every now

and then. 'I can't believe Gordon didn't see anyone push these through,' she said quietly. 'It must have taken some time.'

'Whoever did it, did it during the night, Alison, you can't blame Gordon for that. I'd just like to know why they were sent.'

'There's lots of sickos out there, Ronni, you know that.'

'But who gets a kick out of terrorizing old people? What's the point?'

Alison had no answer for her. She merely continued looking through the abusive notes.

'I don't think you should be alone here tonight,' Ronni said finally. 'You're doing the night shift, aren't you?'

Alison nodded.

'I'll stay here with you,' Ronni offered.

'I'll be fine. Besides, you've got more important things to think about.'

'I'm going to the hospital this afternoon. I'll come back here when I've seen my dad.'

'Ronni, there's no need.'

'Those letters – ' she nodded in the direction of the sheets ' – they probably *are* some kind of sick prank, but I don't think any of us should be alone until we find out for sure.'

'I *won't* be alone. The residents are here. I appreciate your concern, Ronni, but everything'll be fine.' She returned to Ronni and took the empty mug from her. 'What will Andy say if you stay here?'

'It doesn't matter what he says.'

'You look so tired,' Alison said softly. 'You should never have come in today.'

'It's just as well I did.'

'Well, you don't need to stay here *with* me tonight,' Alison continued.

'Yes I do,' Ronni protested. 'And I'm going to. For the next few days we'll *all* do the night shift in pairs. Just in case.'

Alison nodded and turned to leave the room.

Ronni waited until she reached the door, then called her name.

The other woman turned.

'Thanks,' Ronni said.

'For what?'

'Just thanks.'

Alison smiled and stepped out of the office.

Ronni was left alone.

She heard Alison's footsteps as they echoed away down the corridor.

Then she turned and picked up the first pile of letters.

63

BARBARA EUSTACE PULLED the blanket around her legs as a fresh gust of wind swept across the front of Shelby House. She shifted position in her wheelchair and manoeuvred herself closer to the end of the path. There was a concrete ramp there, but she decided to remain where she was.

Ronni made her way down the gentle slope from the path to the drive.

Helen Kennedy thought about following, but then decided against it.

Barbara's dog scuttled across the gravel drive and onto the lawn beyond. The little terrier hurried after its small rubber ball as fast as its stumpy legs would carry it.

Barbara looked on and smiled.

When she shivered slightly, Helen tucked the blanket more tightly around her.

Night was less than an hour away.

The wind shook the trees on either side of the drive. Ronni turned up the collar of her coat and glanced up at the darkening heavens. Thick banks of cloud were scudding in from the west, threatening more rain.

'Hurry up, Molly,' Barbara called, 'or we'll all be soaked.'

The little dog raised its head at the sound of its name, then trotted off across the lawn towards the thick privet hedge to retrieve its ball.

Ronni smiled as she watched it, then turned to see that Helen was guiding Barbara's wheelchair down the ramp. The two older women joined her.

'What's the news on your father, Veronica?' Barbara asked.

Ronni looked vacant for a moment.

'Alison told us what happened,' Helen elucidated. 'We're all very sorry.'

'She shouldn't have told you,' Ronni murmured, picking up the rubber ball and throwing it for the dog to chase.

'You shouldn't keep things like *that* to yourself,' Barbara observed. 'It does you no good to bottle them up.'

Ronni didn't answer. She merely dug her hands in the pockets of her coat and walked slowly.

Why the hell did Alison have to mention it?

Helen pushed Barbara along beside her.

'If there's anything we can do, Ronni . . .' Helen offered, but the sentence merely trailed off.

'I appreciate it, Helen. But there's nothing *anyone* can do except wait.'

'What did they say at the hospital this afternoon?' Barbara enquired.

'That he's stable. There's been no change.'

'I'll say a prayer for him tonight,' Barbara offered.

Ronni smiled gratefully and took the ball from Molly when the little dog trotted back to her. She handed it to the dog's owner.

Barbara threw it and the little terrier set off again.

'We heard about the letters too,' Helen said flatly.

'What letters?'

'The abusive ones,' Helen told her.

'Did Alison tell you about those too?' She sighed.

'No. Mr Errington did,' Barbara said.

'I asked him to keep it to himself.'

'We had a right to know, Veronica.'

'I didn't want you to worry. I didn't realize keeping secrets around here would be so difficult.'

'Do the police know?' Barbara continued.

Ronni shook her head.

'Are you going to tell them?'

'Not yet.'

Barbara was about to say something else when she heard barking.

'Molly,' she called.

The dog was standing facing the high privet hedge that enclosed the lawn area.

Its high-pitched bark arrowed through the growing gloom.

Ronni spun round in the direction of the sound.

'Molly!' Barbara called again. 'Come here.'

The dog continued barking, then suddenly hurried off through a gap in the privet.

'I'll get her,' Ronni said, setting off across the lawn.

She passed the discarded rubber ball.

The barking subsided into a low growl.

'Come on, Molly,' Ronni called as she drew nearer the hedge. She could hear the guttural sound more clearly now. 'Come on, you little sod,' she murmured under her breath, looking for a gap in the privet through which she could squeeze.

There was sudden movement behind the hedge.

The rustle of leaves and branches.

Then silence.

64

'MOLLY?'

Ronni picked her way along the hedge, still looking for a way through.

She called the dog's name again.

Only silence greeted the shout.

No growling.

No barking.

Nothing.

There was a break in the hedge about ten feet ahead of her and she found that she could just about edge her way between the branches. Stems of privet scratched at her face, but she slipped through and emerged on the far side.

There was no sign of the dog.

Another pathway ran to her left and right, but here the hedges and flowerbeds were not so neat.

Out of sight. Out of mind.

She made a mental note to have a word with the gardeners next time they came.

Ronni turned to her right and headed back in the direction she had last heard the growling.

Weeds grew thickly and the grass beyond the path was ankle high, festooned with thistles in places. The trees towered over her, their lower branches occasionally swiping at her when the wind buffetted them.

The path led to a paved area where some wooden garden

furniture had been placed to provide somewhere else for the residents to sit during the summer months. But the wood was cracked and warped. There was an arm missing from one of the chairs. The nails that had held it in place were rusted the colour of dried blood. A tall, thick hedge of rampant bramble surrounded the area like natural barbed wire.

'Molly!' she called again, moving on through the paved area, cursing when she caught her sleeve on a low-hanging branch. The thorn cut her skin and drew blood.

'Shit,' she muttered, sucking at the welling crimson fluid.

A crow, perched on one of the lower branches, squawked loudly. Its black eyes were fixed on her as she moved.

There was movement to her left.

Ronni spun round, but saw nothing.

She was aware of how dark it was becoming. She was forced to squint in the rapidly advancing dusk.

She wondered why her heart had begun to thump harder.

'Molly!' she snapped, her patience beginning to fray.

No barking.

No growling.

Then she heard a snuffling.

She stood still, gazing in the direction of the new sound.

A hedgehog?

No. It was too early in the day.

So what the hell was it? A stray cat? A rat?

The thought made her shudder.

It had to be Molly.

Didn't it?

This is bloody ridiculous. She can't have disappeared.

The dog wouldn't have run out onto the driveway, she reasoned. Even if it had, it would never reach the road beyond. The poor old thing would collapse from such a long trek.

Ronni turned back. She moved once more through the paved area with its warped garden furniture.

Then she heard the barking.

Ronni sighed relievedly and followed the strident noise.

She made it back to the path and hurried along towards a large oak tree that thrust upwards as if attempting to drag the clouds from the sky.

The barking subsided into growls.

'Molly!' she called.

The dog was at the base of the tree.

Ronni looked up and saw a squirrel. It was nibbling contentedly on something it held between its paws. That's what must have made the noise beyond the overgrown hedge, she told herself.

'Come on,' Ronni said, scooping the dog up into her arms. 'He's not doing *you* any harm, is he?'

Molly barked once, then licked Ronni's face. She grinned and headed back towards the gap in the privet.

As she reached it, the dog suddenly twisted in her grip and jumped to the ground.

It hurried back the way it had come, barking loudly once more.

'For Christ's sake, Molly,' Ronni hissed angrily.

She watched as the dog scuttled back towards the tree and began growling again, its head tilted upwards.

Ronni waited a moment

(*I should leave you there, you little bastard*)

then trudged off after Molly again.

The dog was barking incessantly now. It rushed backwards and forwards as fast as its little legs would allow, occasionally stopping to growl in the direction of the tree.

Ronni looked up. There was no sign of the squirrel.

'Come on,' she snapped and picked up the dog once more.

She didn't notice the two cigarette ends lying on the damp grass near the foot of the tree.

Not even the one that was still burning.

65

THE PAIN WAS unbearable. Jack Fuller had put up with the headache for most of the day but, finally, it had become intolerable.

He eased himself slowly off his bed, keeping his eyes closed until he was sitting upright. Then he stood up.

The dizziness hit him as hard as the wave of nausea.

He stood still for a moment longer, then took his first faltering steps towards the door of his room.

Down the corridor, he could hear the sound of the television blaring away in the day room. There was a subdued sound of chatter also coming from the room.

He leaned against the corridor wall as a fresh wave of pain enveloped him. He was still standing there when Alison Dean emerged from the day room.

Fuller tried to smile, but it came across as a grimace.

Alison hurried to his side.

'Bloody headache,' he told her. 'I haven't got any tablets in my room.'

'I'll get you something for it,' she told him. 'You go back to your room, Jack.'

'I'd rather come with you,' he said.

Together they walked to the end of the corridor and rode the lift to the first floor.

She offered him her hand as they stepped out, but he merely smiled and walked on slowly.

The rooms on the second floor were empty except for the single occupied by Donald Tanner and the double that housed Harry and Janice Holland. The other double on that floor served as staff quarters for whoever was doing the night shift.

The first floor was also home to the pharmacy and a second linen cupboard.

Alison fumbled in her pocket for the necessary key. 'It's cold up here,' she said, shivering.

There was a draught sweeping up and down the corridor. It made the hairs on the back of her neck rise.

Fuller was also shaking slightly. He rubbed his hands together gently and watched as Alison opened the door.

She slapped on lights and stepped into the pharmacy.

The walls were lined with shelves and every one of those shelves was stacked with pharmaceuticals; every kind of drug needed for the welfare of the Shelby House residents.

Alison found him 300mg of fenoprofen and disappeared into the staff quarters for a second, returning with a glass of water. 'They'll start to work soon, Jack,' she said as she handed them over, shivering again as she watched Fuller swallow the pills with the water, then wipe his mouth with the back of his hand.

Alison turned and realized that the draft was coming from inside the room. She crossed to the window and noticed that it was open a fraction.

'Who the hell left that open?' she mused, pushing it shut once more.

Fuller pointed at something on the window sill. 'Wait a minute,' he said and joined her beside the window.

There were several flecks of white paint on the sill.

Fuller pushed open the window and peered out.

The paint around the lock was scarred and scratched, the wood of the frame deeply gouged in places. Fuller ran his finger over the marks.

It was as if a tool of some kind had been used on it. From the outside.

66

Ronni glanced at her watch: 8.53 p.m.

She massaged the bridge of her nose between her thumb and forefinger for a moment, then closed the file before her.

Her mind hadn't been on her work anyway.

More than once during the evening she'd sat staring at the phone on the corner of the desk wondering if it would ring.

The hospital?

No news is good news and all that crap.

She wondered about ringing *them*. Just to see if there'd been any change in her father's condition from earlier in the day.

If there had been, they'd have let you know.

From downstairs, she could hear the sound of the television.

Ronni decided to join Alison and the residents. At least when she was surrounded by people it gave her less opportunity to brood.

She got to her feet.

It was as she rose she heard the noise.

A muted crack.

Like . . .

Like what?

She wasn't sure what it was.

She pushed the file back into the drawer.

The sound came again.

That same muted crack like . . . like something striking glass.

That was it. The sound was like an object hitting glass.

A small stone or something.

It came again.

This time she was sure the noise was close by.

She walked to the window and peered out into the darkness; nothing but the trees blowing in the strong wind.

Perhaps it was one of the branches scratching against the window.

Even though the trees are twenty yards away?

There were marks on the window.

No bigger than the tip of her little finger, but still noticable.

Holes in the glass, as if something pointed had been tapped hard against the pane.

Three marks.

Ronni wondered what the hell they were. She was convinced they hadn't been there when she'd begun working that evening.

She contemplated opening the window to get a better look, then thought better of it.

For long moments she stood there, silhouetted against the window, framed by the light from behind her.

She cupped her hands around her eyes. Still she could see nothing in the grounds but the wind-blown trees.

Something smacked into the glass, level with her right eye. It drilled into the window, creating another hole like the other three.

The impact almost made her scream.

She jumped back from the window, turning to switch off the light.

She felt suddenly exposed.

Her heart was thudding hard against her ribs.

Ronni backed out of the room, eyes fixed on the four cracks in the glass.

For what seemed like an eternity she stood motionless in the doorway.

Waiting for a fifth.

It never came.

She waited until her heart slowed its frantic beating, then closed the office door and headed downstairs.

As she made her way to the day room she sucked in several deep breaths, trying to compose herself.

Ronni swallowed hard as she walked into the day room and saw that the curtains had not yet been drawn.

They were gaping wide, spilling light from the room into the gloom outside.

Donald Tanner, Helen Kennedy, Colin Glazer and Janice Holland were sitting at a table close to one large window playing bridge.

Ronni crossed immediately to them and pulled the thick velvet curtains closed, glancing out into the night.

'Help me with these, will you, please, Alison?' she called, trying to make her tone as light as possible.

The other residents were sitting watching television.

Molly, laying close to Barbara Eustace's wheelchair, raised her head and watched as the two women set about their task.

The little dog barked once.

George Errington reached down and patted her. 'What's wrong with you, girl?' he wanted to know, peering over the top of his glasses.

The dog barked once more.

Ronni heard the sound and moved to the next set of curtains. She was aware of Alison's eyes upon her and when the two women locked stares, she merely shook her head gently.

Alison looked puzzled.

Molly was barking incessantly now, facing the window where Alison stood.

'What's wrong with her, Barbara?' Harry Holland asked.

Barbara Eustace patted her lap and called the dog's name.

The little terrier continued to bark.

Alison reached for the curtains, a bemused smile on her face.

As she did, the window exploded inwards.

67

FRAGMENTS OF GLASS sprayed into the room like crystal shrapnel. The sound of the shattering window was accompanied by a scream of pain and fear from Alison, who stumbled backwards, blood running from two cuts.

Ronni saw a stone the size of a man's fist bounce onto the floor in the centre of the room. She rushed towards the exposed window, the cold wind rushing through the shattered pane. Grabbing handfuls of velvet, she dragged the curtains shut, then turned her attention to Alison.

A piece of glass about six inches long had cut her cheek just below her right eye.

There was another gash on her left forearm, but apart from that she seemed uninjured.

The residents seated near the windows hurriedly moved away.

Others either struggled to their feet or remained rooted to the spot in shock.

Molly continued to bark madly.

Another window was shattered.

Helen Kennedy screamed this time.

'What's happening?' Alison gasped in terror, tears and blood mingling on her cheek.

Ronni folded a handkerchief and pressed it to the cut, forcing Alison to hold it there.

There was a third explosion of glass as another window pane was obliterated.

Colin Glazer opened a gap in the curtains in an attempt to see what was going on.

'For God's sake!' shouted Jack Fuller and pulled him away.

Seconds later a stone crashed through the glass and smacked into the far wall with enough power to dent it.

'Put all the lights out!' Ronni shouted.

Tanner and Fuller did as she instructed.

Harry Holland held his wife tightly in his arms.

Molly was barking even more frenziedly now.

Ronni rushed out into the corridor and headed for the pay-phone in the hallway.

Tanner followed, slapping at light switches as he did.

The ground floor was in virtual darkness now.

Ronni snatched the receiver from the cradle and dialled. She hit two nines, then dropped the phone and shielded her face as a lump of stone exploded through one of the glass panels of the main doors. Two more struck the thick wood and, somewhere behind her, another window was smashed. Broken glass erupted inwards, lumps of it breaking again when it hit the corridor floor.

Tanner shielded his head with both hands.

Jack Fuller suddenly emerged from the day room and hurried up the stairs as quickly as he could.

'Jack, stay where you are,' Ronni shouted, but the older man ignored her entreaties and made his way to the main landing.

'I think I can see them,' he called.

Ronni spun round. 'Get away from the window!' she bellowed.

The stone that hit the glass also struck Jack Fuller. It caught him on the temple, slicing open the soft flesh with ease.

He dropped to his knees.

Donald Tanner hurried to his companion's aid while Ronni snatched at the phone once more and tried to dial.

'I'm all right, Don,' Fuller insisted, rubbing at the cut with his fingers. He gazed at the blood there.

The voice at the other end of the line was asking which service Ronni required.

A window on the first floor was smashed.

'Police!' Ronni snapped.

She gave the address, then dropped the phone back onto the cradle.

In the day room, Molly was still barking.

Ronni could hear crying too.

One of the residents? Alison?

She hurried up the steps to join Tanner and Fuller on the landing.

'There,' Tanner said, pointing out into the gloom.

Ronni saw them.

Small dark figures.

'They look like kids,' Fuller observed.

Ronni nodded.

She saw one duck down and snatch up a large stone.

Saw it come hurtling towards the building.

It hit the stonework close to another window and bounced harmlessly off.

The one that followed it crashed through.

Then the figures were gone.

Swallowed by the darkness.

Ronni heard her own breathing, harsh in her throat.

Jack Fuller sat on the stairs with one hand clapped against his cut head. Blood was soaking into his handkerchief.

Donald Tanner squatted next to him, an arm around his shoulder.

In the day room, Molly had stopped barking.

Ronni walked slowly down the stairs, her footsteps echoing through the silence – a silence that was every bit as sudden as the furious cacophony that had preceded it.

'I think they've gone,' muttered Tanner.

Ronni walked slowly down the corridor towards the main doors, glass crunching beneath her feet.

Alison emerged from the day room in time to see her approach the shattered panel in the partition.

'Stay away from there,' she called.

But Ronni advanced a little nearer, her flesh puckering as cold air rushed into Shelby House through the jagged hole.

There was a torch in the small office close to the door and Ronni stepped inside and emerged with it, hefting the light like a club before her.

She switched it on and the beam cut through the darkness. Motes of dust swirled in the brightness as she advanced.

'Ronni.' Alison's plaintive cry echoed through the blackness. 'Don't go outside,' she implored.

Ronni raised a hand as if to silence her.

She shone the torch through the broken pane, sweeping it back and forth.

Nothing was moving.

The silence outside was almost palpable.

She unlocked the main doors and stepped out onto the stone steps beyond, still using the torch like a searchlight to probe the gloom.

The torch light glinted on something scattered around her feet.

Dozens of metal objects, smaller than her little fingernail.

She picked one up and rolled it between her thumb and forefinger.

It left an oily residue.

Ronni was still trying to figure out what it was when she heard the first of the sirens.

68

THE HAMMERING SEEMED deafening.

Ronni blew out her cheeks and looked in the direction of the two glaziers, who were placing boards over the smashed window in the main door.

'We'll go up to the main office,' she said finally. 'It's quieter there.'

Detective Sergeant David Marsh got to his feet and followed her along the corridor.

Broken glass had sprayed across the floor and he eased his way past Alison Dean, who was sweeping it up with the help of Helen Kennedy and Eva Cole.

Alison's cuts had been attended to by the same paramedics who were now gathered around Janice Holland. She was seated in one of the high-backed chairs in the day room, a portable ECG attached to her chest.

Her husband stood beside her.

Through the open door of another room, Marsh saw Jack Fuller seated on his bed, his head bandaged. He smiled thinly as the policeman passed.

Marsh followed Ronni up the stairs to the main office where she offered him a seat and closed the door.

The banging of the glaziers receded somewhat.

'Did anyone get a look at their faces?' Marsh said, flipping his notebook open to where he'd already scribbled a few notes.

Ronni shook her head. 'Mr Fuller saw them,' she said. 'So did

Mr Tanner, but none of us could make out their features. If you're asking for a description, I can't help you.' She drew hard on her cigarette. 'All I know is that they were kids,' she continued.

'How old?'

'I told you, I didn't see their faces.'

'I know that, but from their build? Boys? Girls?'

'Boys, I think. Probably about twelve or thirteen. I really don't know.'

'And the attack lasted for five or ten minutes?'

Again she nodded. 'It seemed like longer, but five or ten minutes would be about right.'

The DS dug in his pocket and pulled out three of the twisted pieces of metal Ronni had found on the porch. He dropped them onto the desktop.

'What are they?' she wanted to know.

'Airgun pellets from a .22 rifle,' he told her. 'We found seventeen of them lying outside the main doors. Five were embedded in the wood. That's what cracked your window.' He nodded towards the four holes in the glass behind her. 'You're lucky *that* didn't come in as well.'

'Oh God.' Ronni sighed, tilting her head backwards.

'Has there been any other trouble at Shelby House in the last few days?' Marsh wanted to know.

'Like what?'

'Weird phone calls. Vandalism. That kind of thing.'

Tell him about the letters.

Ronni ran a hand through her hair.

And what about the damage done to the cars? For Christ's sake tell him.

She pulled open the drawer of the desk and reached inside.

Marsh took the piece of paper from her and glanced at the words scrawled there.

fuck off and die of cancer

'There are thirty-seven more where that came from,' Ronni told him.

Marsh looked through the others she handed him. 'When did they arrive?'

'Yesterday.'

He glanced at the envelopes. 'All hand delivered,' the DS mused.

Ronni nodded.

'Do you think there could be a link with what happened tonight?' he asked.

'You're the policeman. *You* tell *me*.'

Marsh read more.

'Why would kids send letters like that?' Ronni murmured.

'For the same reason they put bricks through your windows tonight. It's a game to them.'

'A game?'

'I've seen it before, Mrs Porter. Me and every copper on the force has had to deal with kids like this at some stage of their career.'

'But they could have killed someone tonight.'

'It wouldn't have bothered them. You're lucky they only used stones and an airgun. It's not unusual for us to take knives, baseball bats or even crossbows off the little bastards. Excuse my French.' He managed a wan smile.

'So what can you do?'

'We can run fingerprint tests on the airgun slugs and these letters. If any of the perpetrators have been printed before they'll be in the files.'

'And then?'

'That's about it, I'm afraid, Mrs Porter. Even if we identify them, which is unlikely, chances are they'll be under age. If they are, there's nothing we can do.'

'What are you talking about? You've seen the damage they've done.'

'Yes I have, but that doesn't make any difference. They could have burned the place to the ground with you lot inside it. If they're under age there's not a thing we can do.'

Ronni looked at him incredulously.

'Offenders over fifteen, no problem,' Marsh told her. 'We can lock them up. But if they're younger than that, we're helpless. Ten per cent of all crime recorded in this country is committed by kids aged from ten to fourteen. The Met reckon that forty per cent of all street robberies and a third of all car thefts and burglaries in Greater London are done by kids in that age range. There's *nothing* we can do about it. And the kids know that too.'

'What about their parents?'

'Some don't know. Some don't care. You can't know where your kids are twenty-four hours a day, can you? On the other hand, some are as worried as we are, but they're just as helpless to stop them.'

Ronni stubbed out her cigarette and gazed at Marsh through the rising plume of smoke. 'But what if you catch them?' she wanted to know. 'There must be some kind of sentence that can be used against them.'

Marsh shrugged. 'The courts put them in council care, but they usually escape and reoffend,' the policeman said. 'There just aren't enough secure council homes to cope with them.' He brushed some fluff from his sleeve. 'There was a kid up in Yorkshire a few years ago who had a conviction record seventeen pages long. He was eleven. There's another one called Spiderboy. They reckon he'd stolen two hundred cars by the time he was fifteen. One of the little bastards even dressed up as a woman and managed to nick twenty-two charity boxes before he was caught. That was *after* he'd stolen a car and assaulted a police officer. He was twelve.'

Ronni shook her head slowly.

'With most juvenile crime, it follows the same pattern,' Marsh explained. 'They start with shoplifting and other petty stuff, then graduate to more serious crime like assault or doing robberies.'

'And what about the kids that attacked Shelby House tonight? What might *they* graduate to?'

'Your guess is as good as mine, Mrs Porter.'

'I've got nine residents and two staff under my supervision, Detective Sergeant. What the hell am I supposed to tell them? That I'm sorry, but the police can't help them?'

'We'll do our best. But if I told you we were going to catch them I'd be raising your hopes.'

'And even if you *do* then there's nothing you can do to them.'

'I know it's no consolation, but *I* find that just as frustrating. Me and every other copper in the country.'

Ronni exhaled wearily.

A heavy silence descended, finally broken by Marsh. 'Is there any news about your father?' he enquired.

'There's no change in his condition. Are you any nearer catching the people who attacked *him*?'

The DS wasn't slow to catch the edge in her tone. 'We're doing our best, Mrs Porter,' he said, holding her gaze. 'I wish we had the resources to catch *every* criminal.'

The DS got to his feet and wandered across to the cracked window in the office. He pressed his forefinger gently against each of the holes made by airgun pellets. 'This may well have been a one-off tonight,' Marsh said. 'They've probably had their fun here now. They'll move on to some other poor sod.'

'And what if they don't?'

Ronni's words hung unanswered in the air.

'Why here? Why Shelby House?' she continued, her voice low.

'You're a prime target.'

'What does that mean?'

'Old people. They can't fight back. These kids aren't looking for a fight, Mrs Porter. Like I said, it's a *game* to them.'

'But there are plenty of other places around here they could . . .' She allowed the sentence to trail off.

'It's a *new* game,' Marsh said flatly. 'Pure and simple. Don't look for any complex motive. You won't find one. They picked *you*. That's it. They'll stop when *they're* bored or when *we* catch them.'

'End of story?' she said sardonically.

'I can leave a couple of constables outside,' he told her. 'But only for tonight.'

'And that's it?'

'It's the best I can do, Mrs Porter. I'm sorry.'

She got up and held open the door of the office, allowing Marsh to leave. 'I'm sorry too,' she said flatly and closed the door behind him.

She heard his footsteps descending the stairs.

Ronni crossed to the window and peered out into the night.

When she ran a hand through her hair, she found she was shaking.

69

THE WOOD WAS nearly two inches thick. Ronni touched it gently with her fingertips, satisfied that nothing could penetrate.

Every broken window had been covered with it until the glaziers could return the following morning to replace the shattered glass.

Debris had been cleared from the corridors and rooms inside Shelby House.

The emergency services had long since left.

Those residents whose rooms had been damaged during the attack had been temporarily moved to other quarters within the building.

Everyone – not that they needed reminding – had been told to keep their curtains closed.

Ronni walked the downstairs corridors slowly, checking doors, occasionally peering into rooms when she saw lights shining beneath.

Jack Fuller was sitting in the chair beside his bed with a book cradled in his lap. He had a piece of gauze over his eye, held in place by two adhesive strips.

'How are you feeling, Jack?' Ronni asked.

'I'm OK,' he told her, smiling. 'I've seen worse.'

She nodded and closed the door as she moved back into the corridor.

George Errington, with the aid of two Mogadon, was sleeping soundly.

Barbara Eustace had also found the blissful oblivion of sleep. Molly lay curled in her basket close by her owner's bed. When Ronni glanced into the room, the little dog raised its head as if to inspect the intruder.

Colin Glazer was lying in bed with a pair of headphones on. He raised a hand in Ronni's direction when he saw her.

She continued her vigil, pausing for a moment beside one of the broken windows on the other side of the corridor.

Helen Kennedy and Donald Tanner both slept too.

Ronni made her way up the stairs, past another boarded window on the main landing.

There was a light burning in Eva Cole's room.

Ronni tapped gently on the door and walked in.

Eva was sitting on the edge of the bed crying softly.

She dabbed at her eyes with a handkerchief when she saw Ronni, as if ashamed of her tears.

Ronni crossed to her and slid a comforting arm around her shoulders. 'It's all right, Eva,' she said, wishing she could sound a little more convincing.

'Why would anyone do that?' the older woman whimpered. 'What have any of *us* ever done to deserve that kind of treatment?'

Ronni held her tightly.

'I heard some of the others talking,' Eva said. 'Mr Fuller said it was children.'

'No one knows for sure, Eva.'

'I've been here ever since my husband died. I've always been happy here. I don't want that to change.'

'It won't, I promise.' She wiped a tear from the older woman's cheek. 'Do you want something to help you sleep?'

Eva shook her head.

'You lay down now,' Ronni whispered. 'Try to sleep.'

Eva gripped her hand tightly for a second as she prepared to move away. 'You won't leave us, will you?' she wanted to know.

'Of course not,' Ronni told her. 'Goodnight, Eva.'

She pulled the door shut behind her.

'Another one who can't sleep?'

The voice startled her and she turned to see Harry Holland emerging from the room he shared with his wife.

'How's Janice now?' Ronni enquired.

'She's sleeping. The paramedics said she'd be fine. I was worried about the shock, what with her heart . . .' He allowed the sentence to trail off.

'Can't you sleep either, Harry?'

'I'll settle down when Janice is asleep. I'll sit with her until she drops off. I was just going downstairs to get one of the papers from the day room.'

Ronni nodded. 'If you need anything during the night, you call,' she told him.

Holland smiled and made his way downstairs.

Ronni pushed open the door of the room she shared with Alison Dean and leant against it for a moment.

'Oh, Christ.' She sighed. 'What a night.'

Alison was sitting on the bed wearing just a T-shirt and leggings. The cuts on her arm and face had been dressed.

'What did the police say?' Alison asked.

'Not much,' Ronni told her, slipping off her shoes and sitting on the chair next to the window. She looked out into the impenetrable darkness.

'What if they come back, Ronni?' Alison wanted to know.

'The police said they won't. Not tonight, anyway.'

'And what about tomorrow? And the night after?'

Ronni merely shook her head and continued to gaze out into the night. 'I wish I knew,' she whispered.

70

'WE'LL FIND HER, Barbara,' Ronni said, one hand on the arm of the wheelchair-bound resident. 'She can't have gone far.'

'She can't get through the fence,' Janice Holland added, pulling up a chair beside the older woman. 'She's probably just hiding somewhere.'

'She always comes when I call her,' Barbara insisted, gazing out across the lawn at the other residents of Shelby House, who were wandering about peering into bushes in search of the missing dog.

Ronni tried to remember the last time she'd seen the little Highland terrier. Jack Fuller had spent most of the afternoon throwing a ball for it to chase. After he'd sat down to eat his food, the dog had continued romping happily on its own, even occasionally wandering back towards its owner. Ronni herself had fed it two or three sandwiches.

'She'll be all right, love,' Janice insisted, holding Barbara's hand as Ronni finally wandered off to join the search.

She ran a hand through her hair, remembering the previous day when the terrier had scurried away into the overgrown area at the front of the building. Perhaps it was there now.

As she made her way around the side of Shelby House another thought struck her. One she was anxious to push to the back of her mind.

Could Molly have trotted up the driveway and out onto the road?

Across the road perhaps? Was she now roaming even further afield? Or had her little adventure been cut short by the wheels of a speeding car?

Ronni hardly dared think about it.

George Errington joined her. 'I don't know why she's worried,' he said, peering over the top of his thick glasses. 'The bloody dog's too well looked after to run away. It knows where it's well off.'

'Don't be rotten, George. Barbara's very attached to that dog. Haven't you ever had a pet?'

'I had a dog myself when I was a kid. Big old mongrel he was. We had to get rid of him, though. We lived next door to some old woman who kept cats.' Errington chuckled. 'My dog got in her garden one night and killed two of them.'

'What did you do?'

'My dad took him to the canal, put him in a sack and threw him in.'

Ronni looked horrified.

'We couldn't afford vets' bills to have him put down humanely,' Errington told her. 'I cried for two days when my dad told me what he'd done.'

'I'm not surprised. I just hope Molly hasn't run out into the road.'

'She won't have got that far.'

'I wish I was as confident as you, George. I'll check the driveway. You have a look over by the hedges.'

The two of them separated. Gravel crunched beneath Ronni's feet as she made her way slowly along the driveway, pausing to look behind the low bushes that flanked it. She wondered if the dog might have found somewhere secluded and simply fallen asleep. After all, it had enjoyed more exercise in one afternoon than it usually did in a month. It was probably exhausted.

She could see the fresh marks in the drive made by the wheels of the glaziers' van. They had left about half an hour ago. All the broken panes and splintered frames had been replaced.

She hoped Shelby House would not be needing their services again.

Ronni was practically to the end of the drive by now and she stood there silently for a moment, watching as several cars drove past. It wasn't a particularly busy road, but vehicles using it were prone to speed and, once again, she tried to push the image from her mind of Molly crossing that thoroughfare.

The screech of brakes. The sickening thud.

Don't even think about it.

She waited a moment, then turned and began trudging back down the drive towards Shelby House.

Away to her left there were sounds of movement in the bushes.

She paused, then stepped through a gap in the low hedge to investigate.

'Molly,' she called.

The sounds continued.

There was a narrow strip of grass, then more tall privet.

The sound was coming from the other side of the hedge and she looked for a way through.

'Molly,' she said again.

The privet formed an impenetrable green wall and Ronni decided the only way through was the one she had taken the previous day.

She turned the corner.

The figure loomed up at her.

Ronni almost screamed. 'Christ, George,' she said, her heart thudding against her ribs. 'Didn't you hear me calling?'

'Sorry,' Errington muttered.

'I heard a noise on the other side of the hedge,' she told him, swallowing hard.

'That was me. You should see the state of the bloody garden around there. All overgrown.'

'I *have* seen it. Any sign of Molly?'

He shook his head.

'We'll keep looking for a bit longer,' Ronni said, glancing up at the sky. Rain clouds were gathering. With them came the threat of darkness. The night was less than two hours away. 'She might have even wandered back inside while none of us were looking,' Ronni offered. 'She's probably lying in her basket in Barbara's room right now.'

Errington raised an eyebrow.

'All right, maybe not.' Ronni sighed. 'But let's check anyway.'

They made their way back down the drive towards Shelby House.

71

AT FIRST SHE thought the ringing of the alarm was part of her dream. Ronni tried to force her eyes open, but despite the fact that she'd managed barely four hours of fitful sleep, it still felt as if someone had sealed her lids with glue.

She sat up and silenced the electronic buzzing.

6.50 a.m.

Her back ached. Her neck ached. Every part of her seemed to have stiffened during the night. Doubtless due to the fact that she'd slept upright in a high-backed chair instead of crawling into bed.

She could remember sitting down in the chair, but the rest was a blur. She guessed she must have been so tired she didn't even make it as far as the bed.

Now she heard movement behind her and Alison also stirred, shielding her eyes from the sunlight that poured in through the window.

'Oh God,' she groaned, rolling onto her stomach.

'Rise and shine,' Ronni murmured, massaging the back of her neck with one hand.

'Where did you go last night?' Alison asked, her voice still thick with sleep.

'I couldn't sleep. I walked around. Sat in the day room for a while, then came back up here.'

'Did you sleep in the chair?'

'I must have just dropped off,' she said, stretching her arms, listening to the joints crack.

'Did anything happen during the night?' Alison said, a note of concern in her voice.

Ronni shook her head. 'Perhaps the police were right,' she murmured. 'Perhaps we've had the worst of it. If any damage was done I didn't hear it. There weren't any windows broken. I'd have heard.'

Alison swung herself out of bed and peered out of the window into the gardens that surrounded Shelby House. Some blackbirds were bouncing about on the lawn, digging in the soft earth for worms. Other than that, nothing moved.

'What about Molly?' Alison murmured.

Ronni could only shrug.

'I dread to think what Barbara'll be like if anything's happened to that bloody dog,' Alison continued.

Ronni began taking clothes from the pink and white sports bag she always brought when she was on night shift.

Alison padded towards the door. 'Mind if I use the bathroom first?' she said.

Ronni shook her head and heard her colleague making her way down the corridor.

She dressed quickly, then headed downstairs. As she reached the ground floor she heard some of the residents stirring. Some had trouble sleeping at the best of times, but after the attack on Shelby House, the sense of unease she herself had felt the previous night seemed to have communicated itself to most of those who dwelt within the building.

Ronni was relieved to see that there was nothing lying on the mat below the letterbox.

No more of those letters.

She walked to the end of the corridor and looked through one of the glass door panels into the driveway.

Ronni selected a key and unlocked the main doors.

She stepped out into the porch and almost tripped over the object there.

It only took her a second to realize what it was.

225

The dog bowl was yellow. It looked new.

There was something in it.

Ronni could smell the coppery odour of the blood.

She swallowed hard, wondering what she should do.

Don't touch it. It might have fingerprints on.

There were several red smudges around the rim.

She knew she couldn't let Barbara Eustace see it.

Ronni turned and glanced back towards the main doors.

As she did, she saw the paint.

Yellow. Red. Blue.

Letters a foot high had been sprayed all over the doors and several walls.

As Ronni read them she tried to swallow, but it felt as if someone had filled her throat with chalk.

FUCKING DIE

She shook her head.

OLD CUNTS

She finally turned and hurried back inside, locking the doors behind her.

In the main office, she reached for the phone.

72

DS David Marsh sipped at his coffee and glanced at the notes he'd scribbled on his pad. 'I'm sorry, Mrs Porter,' he remarked, apologetically. 'I don't know what else to say to you.'

'You could say this won't happen again,' Ronni snapped. 'You could tell me you've got some suspects in custody. You could tell me what the hell I'm supposed to say to my residents.'

'If I told you this won't happen again I'd probably be raising your hopes. If I said we had suspects in custody I'd be lying. As for what you tell your residents, I can't help you.'

'How about, "Don't worry everybody, the police will protect us"?'

'We're doing our best. I told you last time how difficult it is.'

'First the hate mail, then the attack and now this. And you say there's nothing you can do?'

'What do you *want* me to do, Mrs Porter?'

'Find the bastards who are doing this. Until you do, put a police guard on Shelby House.'

'I can't do that.'

'Why? People's lives could be in danger here.'

'I know that, and as I also told you before I'm as frustrated as you that we've caught no one yet.'

'They've killed the dog.'

'You don't *know* that. You said yourself it might just have run off.'

'What has to happen before you'll help us?'

'More than finding a dog's bowl full of blood on your porch. And I *am* trying to help.'

'Then give us some protection.'

'I *can't*,' he snapped. 'Look at it from *my* point of view. I've got nothing concrete to go on. Some obscene letters were pushed through the door. A few windows were broken. Graffiti's been sprayed on a couple of walls and a dog belonging to one of your residents is missing. That hardly merits a twenty-four-hour guard. I wish it did, but it doesn't.'

Ronni ran a hand through her hair.

'None of the fingerprints we took from the letters or the airgun pellets matched up with anything in our files,' Marsh continued. 'We haven't got a clue who's doing this or why. Like I said to you, it's just a game to them.' There was a heavy silence finally broken by the policeman.

'Do any of your residents have money or valuables on the premises that you know of?' he said.

Ronni shook her head.

'Why?'

'I wondered if robbery might be the motive.'

'How would those kids know if there was money in here or not?'

'It would be a reasonable assumption.'

'What do you mean? Old people don't trust banks, they keep their fortunes under their beds, that kind of thing?' Marsh wasn't slow to catch the disdain in her voice. 'It doesn't happen like that,' she snapped.

'There is *one* thing I could suggest,' he muttered.

'Anything.'

'You could try hiring some kind of private security firm if you want twenty-four-hour cover. I can give you some names—'

'Forget it,' she sneered, cutting him short. 'There's no way we could afford it. It looks like we'll have to take our chances, doesn't it?'

He got to his feet. 'How's your father?' he asked.

'There's no change. I don't suppose you've got any idea who attacked him *either*, have you?'

He caught the edge in her voice. 'No,' said the policeman flatly. 'But we're working on it. And we'll carry *on* working on it.'

'Very reassuring.'

He moved towards the office door. 'I'll see myself out,' he said quietly.

The DS almost collided with Alison Dean as he stepped out of the office. They exchanged brief smiles and he left.

'What did he say?' Alison wanted to know.

'Nothing worth hearing,' Ronni snapped. 'They can't give us protection.'

'Do they think the same people are responsible for the letters and the attacks?'

'They don't know.'

'I told the residents about the graffiti, like you said,' Alison informed her. 'I didn't mention the dog's bowl.'

'Thanks. I suppose we'd better see about cleaning that paint off the walls.'

Alison ran a hand through her hair. 'Ronni, it's probably the wrong time to say this,' she said falteringly. 'But I'm not sure how much more I can take.'

'Join the club.'

'No, you don't understand. I don't think I can stay. I was thinking of leaving.'

Ronni met her gaze, her eyes narrowing slightly. 'If that's what you want, Alison,' she said wearily.

'I'm scared, Ronni. I don't mind admitting it. Especially after what happened the other night and now this business with the graffiti and the blood and—'

'When do you want to leave?' Ronni snapped. 'Today? Tomorrow? You don't have to work your notice if that's what you're worried about.'

'Look, I don't want to walk out on you while things are like this, what with your father and that, but—'

'If you want to go, then go. And *this* has got nothing to do with my father.'

'I just said I'd been thinking about it. You'd still have Gordon to help look after the residents.'

'I won't stand in your way, Alison. But don't take *too* long deciding, will you?'

She got to her feet and headed for the office door. 'I've got things to do,' Ronni continued. 'We can't *all* run away, can we?'

And she was gone.

73

MOST OF THE paint came off with some hot water and a little turps.

Colin Glazer, Donald Tanner and Harry Holland did their best to help. By two in the afternoon, the walls were virtually pristine again.

Alison Dean stayed inside for most of the day. Ronni was grateful for that.

The other residents performed one more search of the grounds in their bid to find Molly, but Barbara Eustace's dog remained missing.

As the afternoon drew on, the tension inside Shelby House grew almost palpably.

By the time the residents had eaten their dinner and the sky was bruised with purple clouds, Ronni was aware of a feeling akin to collective dread spreading through the building like a virus.

When night finally coloured the sky, there was a nervous silence throughout Shelby House that she had never experienced before.

She moved from room to room drawing curtains, pausing each time to peer out into the blackness, not really knowing what she expected to see, but fearful all the same.

The residents were gathered in the day room watching the diet of nightly soaps that usually occupied them from seven to nine. But Ronni noticed that they were gazing at the screen with apparently little regard for what happened before them.

Minds elsewhere?

She could understand that.

Alison remained with them in the room and, again, Ronni was grateful. She herself retreated to the office upstairs and sat with a cup of coffee while she filled in the paperwork that needed doing. She may as well have been doing a crossword blindfold.

Mind elsewhere?

She crossed to the window and looked out.

Nothing moving.

Perhaps it was too early.

Perhaps they didn't come until the small hours when everyone was sleeping.

Or would it be different tonight?

She moved back to the desk and tried to continue with her work.

The knock on the door gave her an excuse to stop the pretence.

'Come in,' she called and turned to see Janice Holland standing there. She was smiling as usual.

'Sorry to disturb you, love,' she said.

'Please *do* disturb me, Janice.' Ronni grinned, offering the older woman a chair. 'Is anything wrong?'

'Nothing anyone can do anything about. We all know you're trying to help and we appreciate it. Whoever's been doing these things are evil. I was always brought up to respect other people's feelings. I don't think that's so important to people anymore, is it?'

'It won't go on for ever, Janice. What's been happening will stop.'

'Who's going to stop it?'

Ronni wished she had an answer.

'Harry said that the police couldn't do anything. Is that right?'

'They've got no suspects. They don't know *why* the attacks have started.'

'Do they know why Barbara's dog was taken?'

'They still say they're not sure that she was. She might have just run off.'

'You know that's not true, love. Molly would never run away. The poor little thing's like us. She's got nowhere to go. They *have* taken her, haven't they?'

Ronni sighed wearily. 'It looks like it, Janice, but don't say anything to Barbara will you? She's upset enough already.'

There was a long silence finally broken by the older woman. 'Is there any news about your dad?' she wanted to know.

Ronni shook her head. 'There's no change,' she murmured. 'He's no better.'

Janice reached out and touched her hand. 'And no worse either,' she said, a hint of mild rebuke in her voice.

Ronni managed a smile.

'I'll say a prayer for him tonight,' Janice told her.

'Thank you, Janice.'

The older woman got to her feet. 'I'm off to bed now,' she announced. 'Harry's still downstairs watching the television. At least I'll get the chance to read in peace for a while before he comes up.'

'Do you feel OK, Janice?'

'Just a bit tired, love. But then I think we all are, aren't we?' She made her way towards the office door and closed it gently behind her.

Ronni got to her feet and glanced out of the office window once again.

Still nothing moving in the grounds.

She hoped to God it stayed that way.

74

Normally, when she entered, Janice Holland would put the main light on. For once she hesitated, reluctant to illuminate the first floor room so brightly.

Instead, she crossed to her bedside table and switched on the lamp. It gave off a comfortingly dull yellow glow. More importantly, it made her feel less exposed. She closed the curtains quickly, not wanting to dwell before the windows any longer than she had to. Once the curtains were safely drawn she couldn't resist peeking between the swathes of material, straining her eyes to see into the darkness beyond.

The wind had been building gradually during the day and now she watched the branches of the trees shaking. Trembling as if they were afraid.

Janice knew how they felt.

She crossed to the small sink, spun the tap and filled the glass with water, then she took the bottle of Trinitrin from her cardigan pocket and slipped one under her tongue. She studied her own reflection in the mirror above the sink before washing the small tablet down with water.

Earlier in the day she had felt a little faint on more than one occasion, but hadn't mentioned it to Harry. He would only worry, she reasoned, and – considering the catalogue of incidents over the past few days – she wasn't surprised she felt a little under the weather. But the Trinitrin kept her on an even keel. She had little or no discomfort from the angina as long as she remembered to take the tablets.

Janice shivered, surprised at how cold it felt inside the room. She crossed to the radiator and found that it was on a high setting already. She bent down carefully and adjusted the thermostat, moving it to maximum. Harry would complain if it was cold when he came to bed. The chill played merry hell with his rheumatism.

She paused and looked at the Waterford crystal clock, running one finger over the perfect glass. It was a truly beautiful piece of work and she had given it pride of place in this room she and her husband now called home. They couldn't have wished for a finer gift from the other residents of Shelby House. It had certainly been an anniversary to remember. Janice felt sad that the happy memories of that wonderful day had been overshadowed by the events that had occurred since.

Nonetheless, she looked fondly at the clock once again before turning to the wardrobe to retrieve her nightdress.

She pulled the first door open. As usual, it squeaked loudly on its hinges. She made a mental note to get Harry to oil them.

She opened the other door.

The dead dog was hanging from a piece of electrical flex.

Janice recognized it as Molly immediately.

She tried to suck in a breath, but couldn't.

Her eyes were riveted to the body of the little terrier.

The flex had been fastened so tightly around its neck it had almost severed the head.

Molly's bloodied tongue lolled lifelessly from one corner of her mouth.

Both eyes had been gouged from their sockets. Only empty black craters choked with congealed blood remained.

The animal had also been eviscerated. Its stomach walls hung open like reeking, fleshy curtains. Remnants of its intestines bulged through the rent like corpulent worms.

And now the stench hit her. A wave of putrescent air that clogged in her nostrils and sent her reeling back.

Red-hot pain clutched at her chest, pain that seemed to force the breath from her. It tightened as surely as a screw until Janice felt as if someone was sitting on her sternum exerting more and more pressure.

White stars danced before her eyes and she felt as if she was falling.

She put out a hand to stop herself, but it was impossible.

Janice crashed into the table that supported the clock and the crystal timepiece went flying, shattering on the ground.

She hit the floor hard, the pain in her chest now intolerable.

Tears rolled from one eye and she tried to suck in enough breath for a scream. Any sound to alert someone.

She wanted Harry.

The body of Molly swayed gently back and forth in the wardrobe and Janice found her tortured gaze drawn to it.

She finally let out a strangled gasp.

As she lay there, she heard footsteps hurrying towards the room.

Then, there was only darkness.

75

RONNI HAD HEARD the noise as Janice Holland crashed into the table. Now she burst into the room and saw the older woman lying on the floor, eyes half open, a thin ribbon of mucus running from one corner of her mouth.

'Oh my God,' she gasped and immediately crossed to her.

As she did, she saw the gutted dog hanging in the wardrobe, the shattered clock and other ornaments scattered across the floor.

Images crowded in on her from all sides until her own head spun.

She grabbed Janice's wrist and felt for a pulse, digging her fingers almost savagely into the pliant skin.

If there was one there it was very weak.

Ronni pinched the older woman's nostrils shut and pressed her mouth to Janice's, trying to breathe her own life back into the woman.

After three breaths she pumped the frail chest; listened for a heartbeat, felt for a pulse, then repeated the actions.

And now she heard footsteps on the stairs.

Alison Dean reached the landing first and hurried into the room.

She screamed when she saw the remains of the dog, the sound reverberating inside the room.

'Phone an ambulance!' Ronni shouted. 'Quick!'

Alison stood transfixed, her stomach contracting as she gazed at the dead terrier displayed there.

'Alison.' Ronni repeated, still massaging Janice Holland's chest. 'Get the ambulance, now!'

Her companion nodded and reeled out of the room, bumping into Harry Holland and Jack Fuller, who were behind her.

Holland hurried inside, shaking his head when he saw his wife sprawled so helplessly on the floor. 'No,' he gasped and dropped to his knees beside her, clutching one of her hands. He watched as Ronni continued to work frantically at resuscitation.

Jack Fuller was staring at the dead dog.

Helen Kennedy appeared in the doorway and put a hand to her mouth as she saw what was happening.

Ronni tried again to find a pulse.

'Please, God, no,' whispered Harry Holland, kissing his wife's hand. He never took his gaze from her face.

Ronni could find no pulse.

'Don't go,' Holland begged, tears welling in his eyes. 'Janice, please don't go. Please.'

Jack Fuller was on his knees beside Ronni now. He also felt for a pulse, running his fingers over the sunken veins in Janice Holland's neck. He shook his head imperceptibly. 'She's gone, Harry,' he said softly.

'She can't be,' Holland wailed. He looked at Ronni, shaking his head imploringly. Then, he stooped forward and kissed Janice's forehead. 'My darling,' he whispered, his body shuddering. 'Don't go. I love you.'

Tears were coursing down Ronni's cheeks. She put an arm around Holland's shoulders and felt the agonized spasms racking his body as he continued to kneel beside his wife.

Helen Kennedy crossed herself.

Jack Fuller bowed his head and looked first at the shattered remnants of the crystal clock scattered across the floor, then at the dead dog.

He felt a cold breeze and wandered across to the window.

Paint had been scraped off the outside of the frame close to the lock.

In the distance, a siren blared.

76

No one slept that night.

Once the ambulance had taken Janice Holland away

(on Ronni's instructions, Harry had been accompanied by Alison Dean)

the remaining residents had gathered in the day room.

Ronni herself had told Barbara Eustace about her dead dog.

There had been more tears, as she'd expected.

Eva Cole now sat with the wheelchair-bound woman, holding her hand, occasionally squeezing her arm comfortingly.

Helen Kennedy sat with them, head bowed.

Colin Glazer and Donald Tanner wanted to bury Molly in the grounds of Shelby House, but Ronni refused to let them leave the building until morning.

'Aren't you going to call the police?' Eva wanted to know.

'What's the point?' snapped Jack Fuller. 'They won't do anything if they come, will they, Ronni?'

'They don't care about us, do they?' George Errington added, looking over his thick glasses.

'I don't know what they could do, George,' Ronni said.

'What they've done so far,' Donald Tanner spat. 'Nothing.' She wasn't slow to catch the vehemence in his tone. 'What's it going to take to make them do something?' Tanner continued. 'Janice is dead. Barbara's dog was butchered. Are you going to wait until one of *us* is strung up and cut open before you do anything?'

'Don't blame me, Donald,' Ronni protested. 'I agree with you. The police should be doing something. I've tried to get them to help us, but they won't.'

'Perhaps you haven't been trying hard *enough*,' snapped Fuller. '*You're* supposed to take care of us, aren't you? Doesn't that include making sure we're not subjected to things like this?'

'What do you expect me to do, Jack? What *can* I do? What could I have done to prevent *any* of what's happened in the last few days?'

Fuller merely shrugged.

'Why did they kill Molly?' Barbara Eustace asked plaintively.

'I wish I knew, Barbara,' Ronni said, softly.

'The bastards are laughing at us,' Errington hissed.

'Because they know there's nothing we can do to stop them,' Colin Glazer added.

'Us or the police,' Fuller offered.

'I asked the police for help,' Ronni said angrily. 'They refused.'

'Then ask them again,' countered Errington.

'They won't do anything,' Ronni protested.

'They don't care,' Glazer snapped. 'That's why.'

'Look, I'm as scared as the rest of you,' Ronni said, looking around at the array of faces before her. 'But I don't know what I can do.'

'I'm not *scared* of them,' Fuller asserted.

'*I* am,' Helen Kennedy offered.

'Then they've won. If we give in to them, that's it.'

'Jack, this isn't the army now,' Ronni told him. 'It isn't some battle of wills between us and whoever's doing this.'

'Then what is it?'

'The police think these are more than likely kids. It's some kind of sick game to them.'

'A game that involves slaughtering dogs and killing people,' rasped Tanner. 'You should know how we feel, Ronni. Look what happened to your father.'

'My father's got nothing to do with this,' she said dismissively.

'Any one of us could end up the same way as him. At least he's still alive. Janice is dead,' Errington said angrily.

Ronni met the older man's gaze and was surprised at the fury in his eyes.

'It isn't Ronni's fault,' Eva Cole interjected.

'Someone has to help us,' Errington snapped. 'The police won't. Why can't she?'

'If there was anything I could do, don't you think I'd have done it by now?' Ronni retorted. 'I'm doing my best. We all are.'

'Well, it isn't good enough,' Errington told her. 'Harry Holland's lost his wife. Try telling *him* you're doing your best when he gets back.'

'I wasn't to blame for what happened to Janice.'

'For God's sake, stop arguing,' Helen Kennedy said imploringly.

'Why do you think they hung Barbara's dog in the wardrobe?' Fuller wanted to know.

'To frighten us,' Eva Cole answered.

Fuller shook his head. 'They could have left the body anywhere. In the drive. On the lawn. They could have thrown it through a window. But they didn't and I know why. I know why they hung it in Janice's wardrobe. And so do you.' He jabbed an accusatory finger at Ronni.

She looked on expectantly. 'Jack, they did it to frighten us. Eva's right.'

'No,' Fuller rasped. 'They did it to prove they could get inside Shelby House.'

Silence greeted his remark.

Ronni swallowed hard. She wanted to disagree with him, tell him he was wrong, but something at the back of her mind wouldn't let her.

'You know I'm right,' Fuller persisted.

His words hung unchallenged in the air.

'Who'll they pick on next?' he demanded.

77

THE PHONE CALL came at 11.26 p.m.

Ronni reached wearily for the receiver and pressed it to her ear. Could it be news of her father? More pain?

'Hello, Ronni.'

She recognized Alison Dean's voice immediately.

'How's Harry?' Ronni wanted to know.

'The doctor here examined him. He said he's OK to come back to Shelby House. He's hardly spoken a word since we left Janice.'

'When will you be back?'

'I'm putting him in a taxi. He should be there in about half an hour, he—'

'You're doing *what?*' There was a long silence at the other end of the line. 'Alison,' Ronni snapped. 'What do you mean you're putting him in a taxi?'

'I can't come back there, Ronni. I'm sorry. I did warn you. I—'

Again Ronni cut her short. 'Fine,' she said flatly. 'Collect your stuff tomorrow. No, better still, I'll get Andy to drop it round your house. It might be better if we didn't see each other for a while.'

'Ronni, I'm sorry.'

'Forget it, Alison. I'll call Gordon. He can cover for you.'

'If there was any other way—'

'I said forget about it. I don't need you here.'

'Will you tell the residents why?'

'Why you're running out on them? Yes, I'll tell them. You're scared. Well, we're *all* scared, Alison, but you do what you have to do.'

She hung up. For long moments she kept her hand on the receiver, trying to control her emotions.

Anger, fear, disappointment: all of them whirled around inside her head.

She felt the same kind of helplessness she'd felt when she'd first walked into the Intensive Care unit and seen her father so beaten and battered.

She told herself she had to remain in control; the residents relied on her. She had to be strong for them. They were starting to look shell-shocked.

One or two of them had returned to their rooms. The others were still gathered in the day room.

Safety in numbers?

The remains of the little dog had been cut down and sealed in a black dustbin bag. They would bury it in the garden in the morning. Ronni had locked the door of the Hollands' room after tidying up as best she could. She had gathered the pieces of the shattered clock and put those in a smaller bag. Now she sat at the desk and prepared to dial Gordon Faulkner's number.

She needed someone else with her for the remainder of the night.

Just in case.

When he finally answered his phone she told him briefly what had happened.

He promised he'd be there within the hour.

Ronni placed the phone gently back on the cradle, then posted herself at the window of the office, gazing out into the gloom, trying to pick out the headlights of the taxi carrying Harry Holland. Or the single beam of the motorbike Faulkner now rode since his car had been trashed.

She watched for headlights.

Or whatever else might be moving around in the darkness.

Again she checked her watch, her hand shaking slightly.

The light of morning was a long way off.

78

SHE KNEW SHE should have gone home.

Gordon Faulkner had been telling her so all morning.

He had told her before he'd helped bury Molly's body in a shallow grave in the gardens of Shelby House, helped by Jack Fuller and Colin Glazer, watched by a weeping Barbara Eustace.

He'd told her again afterwards.

Finally, she'd succumbed to his entreaties.

Just for a few hours. Go home. Get some sleep.

She'd called a taxi and told the driver to take her home. As the vehicle pulled away, she promised Faulkner she'd be back by six that evening, despite his insistence he could manage without her help.

The driver had babbled on about something and nothing.

Ronni had barely heard a word.

Only as the cab turned into her street had she become animated.

She had leant forward between the two front seats and told the driver to keep going.

She didn't want to be dropped off here.

Could he take her on to the hospital?

She'd arrived fifteen minutes later.

Ronni rode the lift to the intensive care unit and approached the nurses' station. She recognized the uniformed woman who sat there scribbling notes on pieces of paper: it was the nurse who'd been on duty that night her father had been brought in.

Three days ago? Four? Time seemed to have lost its meaning.

Nurse Patricia Gallagher smiled efficiently at her.

'I came to see my father,' Ronni told her. 'Would that be possible?'

'It's Mrs Porter, isn't it?' said the nurse.

'You've got a good memory.'

'It goes with the job.'

'Has there been any change in his condition?'

Nurse Gallagher shook her head. 'The doctor's due to see him any time now,' she said. 'But you can sit with your father until he comes.'

Ronni smiled gratefully and entered the room where James Connor was.

For long moments, she stood with her back to the door, listening to the mechanical raspings and wheezings that filled the room. The insistent blip of the oscilloscope. The rhythmic thud of the ventilator.

The only things keeping him alive.

She crossed to the chair beside his bed and sat down, reaching out to touch his hand.

Was this how Harry Holland had felt the previous night? Watching the life of the one he loved slowly draining away?

Ronni reached out and plucked a stray eyelash from her father's cheek, feeling how cool his skin was.

'Dad,' she whispered.

The ventilator wheezed.

Some of the bruises had darkened, yellowed at the extremities. A few of the cuts had turned from red to purple as they scabbed over. Perhaps it was a sign that he was getting better. If his injuries were healing, then it must mean he was going to recover.

All he had to do was wake from the coma.

As ever, she was shaken by the savagery of the injuries he'd sustained.

Angered by the ferocity of the attack.

Infuriated by the knowledge that whoever had perpetrated it was still walking free.

Why did you come?

She wondered but could find no reasonable answer.

Was it because you saw Janice Holland die and you wanted to see that there was still a spark of life within your own flesh and blood?

She squeezed his hand more tightly, careful not to touch the tube that ran into a vein there.

That's why, isn't it?

Ronni got to her feet and leant over to kiss his cheek.

You've seen him now. You know he's still alive. There's nothing more you can do.

'See you soon, Dad,' she murmured.

She was gone before the doctor arrived.

79

'I WAS BEGINNING to wonder if you were ever coming home again.'

Ronni closed the front door behind her and looked up to see Andy heading down the stairs.

'How many nights is it you've stayed at that place?' he continued.

'Don't start, Andy, please,' she murmured. She hung up her coat and wandered through into the living room.

'Are you going back tonight?' he wanted to know.

She nodded.

'Jesus Christ, do you have to do *every* fucking thing there?' he snapped. 'Why can't the other staff pull their weight?'

'Gordon can't manage on his own and Alison's left.'

'I don't blame her. Perhaps you should leave too.'

'There are things happening . . .' She allowed the sentence to trail off.

'Like what? What's so bloody important you have to be there every single night? Some blokes wouldn't stand for it, you know. Some would put their foot down.'

'And say what, Andy? That I can't work there anymore? That I can't go in because *you* don't want me to? I *have* to be there. I'm the supervisor.'

He grabbed her arm. 'And *I'm* your fucking husband,' he rasped. 'Sometimes I think you forget that.'

She shook loose angrily. 'I couldn't ever forget that,' she replied. 'Even though I might want to.'

He followed her through into the kitchen. 'What's that supposed to mean?'

'Just leave it.' She began filling the kettle.

'No,' he told her. 'What do you mean? I think I've been pretty
good about this. In the last week or so you've spent all your time
either at work or at the hospital.'

'My father's in a coma, what do you expect me to do? Just
leave him there?'

'The hospital said they'd ring you if there was any news. You
don't have to *keep* going back.'

'You bastard,' she breathed.

'Well, what can you do? Sitting staring at him isn't going to
help, is it?'

'It helps *me*,' she snarled. 'If it was *your* parents you'd be there
every day, wouldn't you? That's always been the way hasn't it,
Andy?'

'I was never that close to my parents. You know that.'

'And you've never been able to understand why I was so close
to *mine*.'

They regarded each other silently for a moment.

*Go on. Tell him now. You've got the opportunity. Tell him it's
over between you. You've been looking for an excuse.*

'All right, your dad I can understand,' Andy said finally. 'But
why are you always at Shelby House? That *is* where you are, isn't it?'

Ronni sighed wearily. 'And where do *you* think I've been,
Andy? With another man?'

'No, but—'

'But what? Do you think I'm having an affair?'

'You couldn't blame me for thinking about it, could you?' he
told her.

'I wish it was as simple as that,' she murmured. 'Does that put
your mind at rest?'

He regarded her warily. 'So what's been happening?' he asked,
finally.

The kettle boiled and she poured water into the two mugs on

the draining board. 'Hate mail. Vandalism. The pet dog of one of the residents was killed. Cut up. Last night another resident died of a heart attack. The funeral's the day after tomorrow.'

'Who's doing it?'

She could only shrug.

'What do the police say?'

'They say they're helpless. No leads. No suspects.'

'And you're going back there tonight?'

'What do you expect me to do? Ignore it? I work there, Andy. I *care* about the people.'

'You could get hurt yourself.'

She sipped her tea.

'Is that why Alison left?' he demanded.

Ronni nodded.

'Then perhaps you should leave too,' Andy told her. 'It sounds like someone's trying to get at the residents, not you.'

'And I told you, I'm not turning my back on them.'

'If someone's having a go at *them*, not you, then keep out of it.'

'You haven't got a clue, have you?' Ronni sneered. She picked up her tea and headed back through the living room.

'I know why you're staying with them,' Andy said flatly. 'You think helping *them* will make it easier to cope with what happened to your dad.'

'Don't try your bloody cod psychology on me, Andy.'

'It's true, isn't it? You blamed yourself for what happened to your dad. You think that if you can help the old sods at Shelby House then that'll clear your conscience.'

She glared at him for a moment and he was surprised at the fury in her eyes. 'I'm going to have a bath before I go back,' she told him.

'Keep out of it, Ronni,' he said, following her to the bottom of the stairs. 'It's not your concern.'

She reached the landing.

'It's nothing to do with you,' he shouted.

She slammed the bathroom door behind her.

80

OF THE TWO cemeteries Kempston possessed, Fairview was the largest.

As Ronni gazed discreetly around her, she thought it already looked half full. Rows of headstones stood in perfectly straight lines, stretching away almost as far as the eye could see.

Behind, there was a large expanse of neatly mown, undisturbed ground. Over a slight rise, there was land that was still overgrown and in the process of being made suitable for the deceased of the ever-growing town to lie in. A small bulldozer stood unattended amidst the knee-high grass and weeds.

For bleak seconds, Ronni wondered which part of the cemetery her father would end up in. And, ultimately, herself.

The eight remaining residents of Shelby House stood silently around the grave of Janice Holland as the vicar spoke.

Ronni hardly seemed to hear his words. But she knew what he was saying. Speaking the litany that was the burial service. Saying phrases he must know by heart. Lines he'd repeated before a thousand grieving families. And would repeat before a thousand more.

The breeze that had been blowing when they had first arrived had grown in ferocity. The cellophane-wrapped bouquets lying beside the grave crackled like dried leaves beneath heavy feet.

There was one from each of the residents. A special one from Harry Holland, who now stood beside her, head bowed.

His hands were clasped in front of him.

Barbara Eustace had a blanket wrapped around her legs to shield her from the cold.

Helen Kennedy stood behind the wheelchair, occasionally dabbing at her eye corners with a tissue.

Eva Cole pulled up the collar of her coat, protecting herself against the chill breeze.

Colin Glazer, George Errington, Donald Tanner and Jack Fuller, all resplendent in freshly pressed suits, stood on the far side of the grave.

Jack Fuller was shivering slightly.

The vicar finally finished speaking and turned towards Harry Holland. He nodded and took a couple of faltering paces forward, bending to pick up some of the earth at the side of the grave.

For interminable seconds he stood, gazing down into the yawning hole.

Ronni was about to move to his aid when he threw the dirt in. It landed with a thud on the lid of the coffin. He turned and moved back to her side, wiping a tear from one cheek.

One by one, the other residents followed his example.

Helen Kennedy crossed herself as she stood at the graveside.

Ronni watched each of them perform the ritual; then she and Gordon Faulkner also added their tribute.

Harry waited until they had all finished, then returned to the grave again and dropped in one single red rose.

'Goodbye, my darling,' he whispered. 'Sleep tight. I'll see you soon.'

Ronni thanked the vicar, then took Holland's arm as he turned away, guiding him towards the gravel path nearby.

'They say it gets easier as time passes, don't they?' murmured Gordon Faulkner.

Jack Fuller continued to gaze at the grave. 'They lied,' he said bitterly.

The little group turned and made its way back towards the waiting minibus, Faulkner pushing Barbara Eustace in her wheelchair, ensuring that she was safely lifted into the back.

The other residents took their places inside the bus and waited for Faulkner to start the engine.

The drive back to Shelby House took less than forty minutes and most of it was completed in silence. Apart from a few coughs and sniffs, those seated within made little sound.

Harry Holland stared blankly out of the side window, occasionally wiping his eyes with his fingers.

Colin Glazer reached out and squeezed his arm comfortingly. He wished that he could tell Holland everything would be all right. He wished he had words to soothe the pain the other man must be feeling, but he knew he hadn't.

Faulkner swung the minibus into the driveway of Shelby House, muttering to himself when he saw the first spots of rain spatter the windscreen.

Ronni was thankful the imminent downpour had not come during the funeral itself.

Small mercies, eh?

As the minibus drew nearer the building, she was the first to see. 'Oh my God,' she whispered, a knot forming inside her stomach.

And now Faulkner was aware of what she was gaping at.

The letters, two or three feet high, were sprayed on the main doors and across the porch.

Harry Holland also saw them.

Soon, everyone inside the bus had.

ONE DOWN 8 TO GO

81

'Wʜᴀᴛ ᴅɪᴅ ᴛʜᴇʏ sᴀʏ?'

Ronni dropped the receiver back onto the cradle and sat back in her chair. 'That someone will come and have a look when they can find the time.' She exhaled angrily.

Gordon Faulkner shook his head. 'Why won't the police do anything?' he wanted to know.

'According to them, they prioritize emergency calls. Graffiti sprayed on walls obviously isn't very high on their list.'

'Even when it's a direct threat?'

She could only shrug. 'Is it a direct threat?' Ronni murmured. 'They know one of the residents is dead. That's it.'

'They're implying there'll be more.'

'They must have been watching for them to know about Janice. Watching last night. Watching the funeral today.' She got to her feet and crossed to the window. 'They're probably watching us right now.'

'Jack Fuller reckons they broke in.'

'How else would Molly's body have got inside the wardrobe?'

'But the Hollands' room is on the first floor. Someone would have heard them.'

Ronni didn't answer. 'The police say it's some kind of game,' she said finally. 'But surely there must be more to it than that? There's something here they want. There must be.'

'Money? Jewellery? Other valuables?'

'I don't know, Gordon,' she said wearily. 'That's what we've got to find out.'

There was a long silence, finally broken by Faulkner. 'What are you going to do about Alison?'

'Replace her. She won't come back. I'm not sure I *want* her back.'

'Who the hell's going to come and work here with all this shit going on?'

'That's *my* problem, not yours.'

'No, Ronni, you're wrong. It's *my* problem too. Because as long as there are just two of us working here then that's more responsibility.'

'Are you going to ask me for a pay rise, Gordon?' She smiled. 'Until we get someone else, it's just you and me.'

'Just the two of us in the firing line.'

'Listen, if you're not happy with the situation, *you* can leave too. I'm not holding a gun to your head to get you to stay.'

'I can understand why Alison left.'

'So when are *you* going?'

'I'm not.'

'Can I have that in writing,' she mused.

'So, if the police won't help us, we're on our own,' he said, and it sounded more like a statement than a question.

Ronni nodded. 'The detective in charge said this could all end as suddenly as it began.' She sighed. 'I wish I could believe that. If they broke in once, chances are they'll try again. If they *are* looking for something specific inside Shelby House, they'll keep trying until they get it.'

Faulkner nodded.

'First, we have to find out what's in here that they could want,' Ronni continued. 'We'll have to ask the residents if any of them have got anything of particular value. If they've got any money stashed here. That kind of thing.'

'But how the hell would those bastards outside know who's got what in *here*?'

She could only shake her head.

'Perhaps they don't. Perhaps they're just taking a chance. But it looks like they'll keep coming back – until they find something else to entertain them.'

'So, what do *we* do?'

'Stop them getting in.'

'That might be easier said than done.'

'You're right. But what else can we do?'

82

A NAIL GUN.

A selection of hammers.

A blowtorch.

Chisels and screwdrivers.

Several power drills.

Every one was immaculatley clean and in perfect working order.

Jack Fuller took them from the toolbox and laid them before him.

In the compartments within the box there were screws and nails of every length, suitable for any job Fuller chose to undertake.

'This lot should do it, Jack,' Gordon Faulkner mused, staring at the array of tools.

Fuller regarded each of them in turn. 'Where shall we start?' the older man wanted to know.

The timber had arrived less than twenty minutes earlier.

Stacked on a lorry bearing the legend PHILLIPS AND SONS, it had been unloaded by two youths in their late teens, who had gazed at the watching residents in bewilderment. Every thickness and type of wood they stocked seemed to have been ordered.

Ronni wrote the older man a cheque and pushed it into his hand. She assumed he was the PHILLIPS noted on the paintwork of the lorry.

The youths, more than likely, the SONS.

Colin Glazer, Harry Holland and Donald Tanner began moving the wood from the front of the building.

'My lads can help you with that,' Phillips said.

'We can manage,' Tanner told him flatly.

Phillips shrugged and climbed back into the cab of the truck. As he drove away he could already hear the sound of saws coming from behind him.

By mid-afternoon, they stopped.

The wood had been cut to the required lengths and, more to the point, tiredness was beginning to set in.

Ronni made tea and she and the residents sat around on the patio at the rear of Shelby House drinking it, enjoying the brief rest.

Few words were spoken.

Ronni paid particular attention to Harry Holland, but he seemed unusually chirpy considering the circumstances.

Jack Fuller finished his drink first and wandered off around the side of the building. He was joined moments later by George Errington.

'We'll cover all the windows on the ground floor,' Fuller said, wiping perspiration from his face.

'Not *all* of them,' Errington murmured. 'Leave the office as it is.'

Fuller looked at him, then at the designated window.

He understood.

Three wooden slats across every window. Each one four feet across and three inches thick.

Fuller supervised the erection of the makeshift bars.

Ronni pulled at them, wondering if they would be strong enough.

'If they want to get in badly enough, then they will,' Fuller said. 'But these might be enough to put them off.'

'I hope so, Jack,' she muttered.

The office window remained unprotected.

If she noticed, Ronni said nothing.

The work continued into late afternoon.

As the time ticked around to 4.45 p.m., the sky began to fill with clouds. Eva Cole thought she heard the first rumblings of thunder.

Fuller, Glazer and Gordon Faulkner finished the last few windows as quickly as they could, then retreated inside.

Dusk fell like a blanket within two hours.

By seven-thirty it would be dark.

83

THE RAIN THAT had been falling for the last hour or so had eased off to an irritating drizzle.

As Carl Thompson moved through the bushes, he displaced branches and water sprayed onto those behind him. There were some muttered complaints from Graham Brown and Tina Craven as they were drenched.

Thompson silenced their mutterings with a glance.

As he walked, he was constantly flicking his lighter on and off, the flame spearing up into the damp air like a miniature beacon.

'We should burn the whole fucking place down,' Brown offered. 'Let the old cunts fry.'

Liam Harper laughed loudly and, again, Thompson silenced him with a stare.

'We're not burning anything,' the older youth said finally. 'We don't have to.'

'So how are we going to see what the old bastards have got while they're still in there?' Donna Freeman wanted to know.

'They're shitting themselves. They'll probably just *give* us their stuff when we get in.'

'And it wasn't hard getting in last time, was it?' Brown chuckled. 'Even carrying that fucking dog.'

From their position in the bushes, the group looked at the looming edifice of Shelby House. There were lights burning in a number of the downstairs rooms as well as on the landing and in a couple of other places on the first floor.

'Just get on with it, will you?' Tina Craven complained. 'I'm soaked already. I don't know why you just didn't take whatever they had the last time you broke in.'

'Shut up, you slag,' Liam Harper hissed.

Tina spun round and swung a punch at him, but he ducked and scuttled away in the direction of the drive.

'This isn't just about money,' snapped Thompson. 'It's about teaching those old farts some fucking *respect*.'

Followed by Terry Mackenzie, Harper began to pick up some of the larger pieces of rock from the driveway.

Thompson watched them advancing towards the building.

'Go and help them, Tina,' he said.

'Why can't I come in with you and Donna? Help you look for the money?'

'I told you, this isn't about money,' Thompson snapped. 'Just move it.'

'Yeah, move it.' Brown grinned.

She sloped off to join the two boys in the driveway.

Thompson waited a moment longer then nudged Brown. Followed by Donna, they set off across the large open expanse of lawn, moving quickly and ducked low.

'What the fuck is that?' Brown said, pointing to the wooden slats that had been placed over every window.

'I don't think they want us to get in.' Thompson smiled.

The phone call came at just after nine that night.

In the office upstairs, Ronni picked up the receiver. 'Shelby House,' she said.

The caller wanted to speak to Veronica Porter.

'That's me,' she said, her heart thudding a little faster as she thought she recognized the voice.

The caller identified herself as Nurse Patricia Gallagher.

Oh, God, no. Not now.

Her father's condition had taken an unexpected turn for the worse.

'What's happened?' Ronni asked breathlessly.

The doctors had noted his blood pressure was rising alarmingly. They weren't sure why, but they feared it could cause a damaged blood vessel inside his brain to rupture. He was being kept under constant observation.

'I'll be there in twenty minutes,' Ronni said, her hand now shaking.

She pressed down hard on the cradle, then dialled a taxi.

'Please hurry,' she insisted. 'It's very urgent.'

Ronni snatched up her coat and handbag and made her way downstairs to tell Gordon Faulkner what was happening.

It was 9.07 p.m.

84

THEY WERE IN the shadows at the side of the building now, and all three of them slowed their pace.

Thompson could see Harper, Tina and Mackenzie outside the front of Shelby House, occasionally illuminated by the lights from inside.

'They better not start chucking those stones until we're inside,' Donna said, reaching into the pocket of her Kangol jacket.

'They know what to do,' Thompson assured her.

When she opened her hand, he could see a small round white tablet in the palm.

'Got any of those to spare?' Brown wanted to know.

'Twenty quid each,' she said, holding out her other hand.

'Fuck off.'

She swallowed the speed dry and grinned at him.

'Fucking druggie,' Brown grunted.

Thompson moved away from the squabbling pair and discovered an unlit room. He tugged on the first of the wooden slats and found it was well secured.

So was the next.

He moved on.

'I'll be fine on my own,' Faulkner insisted, practically pushing Ronni towards the main doors. 'Just go, Ronni.'

She unlocked the doors and stepped out onto the porch. The taxi was waiting, engine purring.

She hurried across and slid into the back seat.

Faulkner watched as it turned around and disappeared up the driveway, its tail-lights gradually swallowed by the gloom.

Then he prepared to lock the doors once more.

As he did so he saw something move in the bushes to his right.

Thompson finally came to the ground-floor office window, smiling when he saw none of the protective wooden bars sported by the others.

'They forgot one,' he called.

He squinted through the makeshift bars, trying to see into the office beyond. There was a bar of light showing beneath the door, but other than that, nothing.

'This is going to be a piece of piss,' Brown sneered, pulling a black bin bag from inside his coat.

Thompson fumbled on the ground for a piece of stone to break the window. Once that was done, it was merely a matter of reaching in, slipping the lock and pushing the window open.

As easy as that.

His two companions looked on as he finally closed his fist around a lump of jagged stone.

'There's someone out there.'

Gordon Faulkner was still peering myopically into the gloom, his eyes fixed on the bushes that grew thickly at one side of the driveway.

'Don't go out,' Donald Tanner urged.

'Look,' Faulkner insisted, pointing towards the waving bushes.

Tanner could see nothing. 'They can't get in, Gordon. Leave it.'

'If I can catch them on the grounds, then the police will *have* to do something,' he hissed angrily. 'The bastards have got away with this for too long.'

'You don't know how many there are,' Tanner warned.

'To hell with it.' He pushed the keys into Tanner's hand.

'Lock the door behind me.'

'I can't.'

'Do it.'

The older man hesitated for interminable seconds, then nodded.

As Faulkner moved down the stone steps from the porch he heard the key turn.

The bush was still moving.

Perhaps whoever was behind there hadn't seen him coming.

Right, you bastards.

He advanced across the drive.

85

To the rear of the building, Carl Thompson hefted the stone before him, then struck the glass hard.

Crystal shards sprayed into the office beyond.

He crooked his elbow and knocked out some remaining pieces of glass, then reached through and slipped the lock.

'Come on,' he said, clambering in.

It was pitch black inside the room and, as Thompson stumbled around, he was sure he could hear breathing.

He realized it must be his own or that of Donna and Brown, who were also now hauling themselves into the office.

When the lights exploded into life, he raised a hand to shield his eyes from the brilliance.

Just as he did he saw other figures in the room.

Old people – their faces set in furious expressions.

He noticed that one was holding a clawhammer.

Another gripped what looked like a baseball bat.

A third, a short plank of wood as thick as those that covered the other windows outside.

Thompson turned to look at Donna and Brown.

He was ready to shout that there was nothing to fear. That these old bastards were no problem.

He saw Donna struck with the plank of wood; saw her hit the ground with blood running from a gash on her head.

Thompson opened his mouth to shout a warning to Brown. To tell him that there was another of the fuckers behind him.

The younger lad turned straight into the powerful swing. Brown raised his arms to protect his head from the blow of the batlike object. The wood cracked against forearms and he shouted in pain. He thought his arm had gone numb so great was the agony.

The second frenzied stroke caught him in the stomach, knocking the wind from him. As he dropped to his knees, another thunderous strike drove his head down towards the floor.

Thompson prepared to fight back.

'You cunts!' he roared.

Then, there was a shattering impact against the back of his skull.

For fleeting seconds, the world first turned brilliant white.

Then blacker than he'd ever known.

86

He heard the crash of breaking glass.

Gordon Faulkner paused momentarily as the sound echoed through the stillness of the night. Then, stealthily, he continued to move across the driveway, all too aware of the loud noise he was making on the gravel.

The movement in the bushes had stopped, but Faulkner was certain the trespassers had merely retreated further.

A number of lights were switched off inside Shelby House, deepening the already cloying darkness around him.

He felt dangerously exposed.

The need for a weapon seemed more pressing than it had when he'd first ventured out of the building.

There was a length of tree branch about a foot long and an inch thick lying nearby. He stooped and picked up the damp wood, hefting it like a club as he continued to advance.

What if he was wrong? What if there was no one out here?

Then get back inside as quickly as possible. Find out what's been broken.

Or what if Donald Tanner was right? What if there were more of the trespassers than he'd thought?

Then turn and run. Get back inside and phone the police. You should have stayed inside to begin with.

Thoughts tumbled through his mind as he pushed his way into the wet bushes.

With Ronni gone, he was the only one to care for the residents of Shelby House. What if this was all some elaborate ploy to lure him outside? To expose the residents to the full fury of the intruders.

Yeah, very good tactics. Leave the people you're supposed to be protecting unguarded.

He gripped the piece of damp branch more tightly and moved on.

There was a loud crack to his right.

Like someone stepping on a piece of wood.

He spun round.

In the shadows, something moved.

Deeper into the bushes.

Further away from Shelby House.

Further away from the light.

Were they tempting him away from the safety of the building?

He swallowed hard and looked around.

More movement.

No going back now. Find them. Catch them.

He heard low whispering.

Or was it just leaves brushed by the wind?

And where the hell was the sound coming from now?

Left? Right?

It seemed to be all around him.

'*What if there's more than one of them?*'

He gritted his teeth as he remembered Tanner's words.

The ground was slippery beneath his feet. He almost overbalanced. The drizzle sheathed his face and he wiped it away from his eyes.

Go back inside now. Before it's too late.

His heart was thumping hard.

Get a grip. They're only kids.

More movement ahead of him.

The same kids that trashed your car and used battery acid on it?

Something struck him hard on the right cheek.

The stone split his skin and he slapped one hand to the cut angrily. The blood looked black in the darkness.

Another followed.

It cracked against his collar bone and bounced off his shoulder.

He heard footfalls on the gravel drive now and rushed through the bushes, anxious to reach the open. If they were running, he would catch them. Outpace them and grab them.

As he reached the drive he saw two of them.

Small figures. Both boys.

'Come here, you little bastards!' he roared and set off after them.

They were close. He was gaining on them.

He heard a loud crack.

There was sudden pain in his right leg.

He stumbled and almost fell.

Ahead of him, the two boys were slowing down.

Another loud crack from away to his right.

The second airgun pellet hit him in the arm and drew blood.

The first of the boys had stopped running and turned to face him.

Faulkner saw him reaching into his jacket.

The knife came free and the boy waved it before him.

This is insane.

Faulkner made a grab for the boy's arm, but missed. The blade slashed across his palm and he stepped back, blood dripping from the wound.

'I'll kill you,' snarled Liam Harper.

Faulkner gritted his teeth, anger now replacing his initial shock. He lunged at the boy, diving full length and crashing into him.

The knife spun away.

He punched Harper hard in the face and heard him whimper.

Go on. Beat the little fucker to a pulp. This isn't a normal kid. This is a fucking monster.

Terry Mackenzie kicked at Faulkner, then dashed to find the knife. He scooped it into his small fist and ran back towards the older man.

Faulkner rolled over to avoid the thrust and was forced to release Harper.

The youth, his face streaming blood, scrambled away, turning once to drive a foot into Faulkner's face.

'Fucking cunt!' he roared.

The kick loosened two of the older man's front teeth.

He saw the knife sweeping down again, aimed at his stomach.

Again he rolled, kicking out and knocking Mackenzie's legs from under him.

This time both boys ran for the end of the driveway.

As he struggled to his feet, Faulkner saw a third figure join them from the bushes to his right.

Tina Craven was still carrying the air rifle.

She turned and pointed it at Faulkner, who threw himself down. He heard the pellet slice through the air close to his face.

When he looked up, the driveway was empty.

'Bastards,' he snarled, his breath coming in gasps.

There was a coppery taste of blood in his mouth. The gash on his cheek hurt like hell; so did the pellet wounds in his arm and leg.

He touched a finger to his mouth, spat blood, then set about looking for the knife.

87

Carl Thompson was blind.

The thought caused him a moment of almost uncontrollable panic, then he realized why.

Understood why the darkness was so total.

Why, when he tried to open his eyes, he couldn't.

They were covered by tape.

Several layers of it had been wrapped around his eyes and mouth. He could only breathe raggedly from his nose and, every time he inhaled, there was a peculiar combination of smells.

The cloying scent of blood. The more acrid stench of perspiration. And a smell like freshly washed clothes.

He tried to sit up.

He realized his hands and feet were bound.

Whoever had tied the rope was an expert. He could barely move his fingers. They were tingling and he wondered if the bonds that held him had been pulled so tight as to cut off his circulation.

He was lying on a cold stone floor and his head was throbbing madly. It felt as if his skull was expanding and contracting with each beat of his heart.

The back of his head was particularly painful and he remembered that was where he'd been hit. Blood had matted in his hair and trickled down his back.

He writhed around on the floor like some kind of spastic snake, then finally gave up and lay still.

Thompson tried to roll over and, as he did, he heard a sound close to him.

It was low, rasping breathing.

Nasal. Thick and mucoid. As if whoever was inhaling and exhaling was doing it through fluid.

He moved towards the sound as best he could, shuffling along in that reptillian way.

His cheek was against a stone floor, that much he knew. As for the rest of his surroundings, he had no clue.

The smells told him nothing.

The tape had been wrapped so tightly and thickly around his eyes he wouldn't have been able to see through it even if he *had* been able to open his lids.

The mucoid breathing continued.

So too did another sound close to him.

A muted sobbing.

Disorientated by his blindness and pain, he struggled to locate its source.

The room he was in was silent but for these sounds. He could hear nothing else but the blood rushing in his own ears and the thumping of his own heart.

He tried to wriggle free of the rope, but the hemp just bit more deeply into the flesh of his wrists.

Thompson wondered how long he'd been here

(*wherever the fuck he was*)

and who had gagged and trussed him so expertly.

He stopped moving when the pain became too great. Besides, the effort of slithering around on the cold floor was making him tired. He had cramp in his shoulders and the pain just seemed to increase the throbbing in his head.

He lay still, sucking in breaths through his nose.

There was a sound away to his right

(*his left? Behind him? There was no way of telling in this void*)

and he heard footsteps moving slowly towards him.

Another smell reached his nostrils.

He felt a hand sliding up the sleeve of his sweatshirt.

Felt something cold and sharp being pushed into his flesh.

He tried to cry out in pain, but the tape that had been used to seal his eyes had also been used to seal his mouth.

The needle was driven into a vein.

Within seconds, he began to lose consciousness.

88

Ronni checked her watch against the clock on the wall of her father's room.

It felt as if she'd been at the hospital for an eternity.

Twice already, a nurse had advised her to go home. That her father's condition had stabilized. That there was nothing she could do.

Twice Ronni had politely refused the offer.

The doctors still didn't know what had caused the sudden fluctuation in blood pressure. It was still high, but at least it had stopped rising. The danger, at least for the time being, appeared to have passed. However, she had been told that her father was still in danger. An operation to remove a steadily growing blood clot now seemed inevitable. And within the next twenty-four hours.

She hadn't rung Andy to tell him what had happened.

What was the point?

What could he do?

She wondered if she should ring Shelby House, then decided against it.

Ronni reached out and touched her father's hand. 'I'm still here, Dad,' she whispered, her voice cracking. 'I won't leave you.'

She bowed her head, eyes closed, just the sound of the ventilator and the ever-present oscilloscope filling the room.

'Dad,' she murmured, looking at him again.

She barely suppressed the scream.

The face of Janice Holland was staring back at her.

Ronni tried to pull her hand away, but Janice gripped it like a vice.

Dead fingers held her tightly.

And, all the time, eyes like those of a fish on a slab fixed her in an unblinking gaze.

The blue-tinged lips moved. Formed words.

But Ronni heard them only inside her head.

'Let him go.'

She closed her eyes again.

When she opened them the vision of Janice Holland was gone.

Her father's motionless body lay where it had always been.

Ronni pulled her hand away quickly, massaging her fingers. She thought she could still feel the touch of cold flesh on them.

Her breath was coming in gasps.

She sat for what seemed a long time staring at her father, as if waiting for his features to transform again into those of Janice Holland.

Wondering if those lifeless lips were going to mouth more words.

Was this what Harry Holland had felt like when he'd watched Janice die?

Was this what she herself had to look forward to?

Ronni swallowed hard and sat back in her chair, not taking her eyes from her father's face.

It was another hour before she left.

Gordon Faulkner banged on the main doors of Shelby House and waited.

Every now and then he dabbed at his cut cheek with his handkerchief. His arm and leg were sore where the pellets had hit him and his mouth felt numb from the kick he'd sustained.

Little bastards.

He had found the knife with relative ease: a nine-inch, wickedly sharp sheath knife with a double-edge.

He looked down at the blade as he continued to bang on the doors. Faulkner had no doubt they would have used the weapon on him if they'd got the chance.

The thought both angered and worried him.

'Donald,' he called. 'It's me. Open up.'

Faulkner had no spare keys with him. When he'd ventured out into the driveway in pursuit of the trespassers, he'd thought it best to leave them all with the older man.

No need to make it easy for them and let them just walk in.

Now he stood, leaning against the door, wondering if the intruders had indeed left the grounds. He'd chased off those three. But there may be more.

Faulkner had decided that it would be safer *inside* than out.

Besides, he needed to get some plasters on these cuts and bruises and swill the blood from his mouth.

He was about to shout again when he heard the key being turned on the other side of the door.

He practically fell into the hallway, almost colliding with Colin Glazer and Donald Tanner.

'Lock it,' Faulkner said breathlessly.

Tanner complied.

Glazer looked at his face. 'What happened?' he wanted to know.

'I had a run-in with the bastards who've been doing this,' Faulkner snapped. He held up the knife as if to reinforce his words. 'Is everyone all right? I thought I heard a window being broken while I was out there.'

'They threw a stone,' Glazer told him. 'They ran off after that.'

George Errington appeared from the day room and peered at Faulkner over the top of his glasses.

Eva Cole joined him and they both gazed on apparently unperturbed by Faulkner's dishevelled and bloodied appearance.

'I'm going to call the police,' Faulkner said.

'What's the point?' Tanner asked. 'They won't do anything anyway.'

'I've got *this*,' Faulkner announced, brandishing the knife. 'It's evidence.'

'Of what?' Glazer said challengingly.

'They tried to kill me. It'll have fingerprints on it.'

'If I was you, I'd let me have a look at those cuts.' The voice came from the stairs.

Jack Fuller advanced towards Faulkner and put a comforting arm around his shoulder.

'It's *me* who's supposed to be looking after *you*.' Faulkner smiled. 'You were a medical orderly in the army. You're not now.'

'Come on,' Fuller insisted.

'It'd be best if we wait until Ronni gets back,' Eva Cole offered.

Glazer put out his hand. 'I'll take the knife, Gordon,' he said flatly.

Faulkner hesitated a moment, then handed it to the older man. 'Which window did they break?' he asked.

'The downstairs office,' Fuller said. 'We'll board it up with some plywood for the time being.'

Faulkner nodded and allowed himself to be led along the corridor by Fuller.

'You need to rest,' Glazer said. 'We'll be fine until Ronni gets back.'

'I hope you're right, Colin,' Faulkner intoned.

Glazer merely smiled.

89

FOR A MOMENT, the taxi driver wondered if she was going to get out. He glanced around at Ronni who sat gazing blankly ahead. 'Nine-fifty, please,' he said.

Ronni nodded and pushed a ten pound note into his hand.

Only then did she reach for the handle and open the door.

She could see lights on inside Shelby House.

'Your change,' said the driver, offering some coins.

'Keep it.'

'Thanks,' he muttered unenthusiastically.

Ronni stepped out into the drive and made her way to the main doors. Behind her, she could hear the tyres crunching gravel.

She hoped he didn't wake any of the residents.

As she unlocked the main doors and walked in, she saw her concerns were unwarranted.

George Errington and Colin Glazer emerged from the day room and smiled at her.

She smiled back as warmly as she could. 'Everything all right, George?' she asked.

He nodded. 'Mr Faulkner's asleep upstairs,' he told her.

'They came again while you were gone,' Glazer added.

'Who?'

'Those kids. They tried to break in.'

'Oh God, no. What happened?'

They ushered her towards the day room and Ronni was

surprised to find all the residents sitting in there despite the lateness of the hour.

Helen Kennedy sat her down.

Barbara Eustace offered a consoling smile and tapped her arm.

'Was anyone hurt?' Ronni asked.

'Gordon got a few cuts and bruises, but that was it,' Jack Fuller informed her.

Ronni ran a hand through her hair. 'When is this going to end?' she murmured and Helen saw tears in her eyes.

'How's your father, Ronni?' she asked.

The younger woman could only shake her head. 'He's hanging on,' she muttered, dabbing at her eyes with a tissue. 'They're not sure . . .'

She looked across at Harry Holland, who was smiling at her understandingly.

'I know how you feel,' he told her.

'I know that, Harry, and I appreciate it.' She sucked in a deep breath. 'Did Gordon call the police?'

'We told him there was no point,' Errington said.

'Perhaps I'd better call them.'

'Why?' Jack Fuller asked. 'They'll do nothing, you know that. Besides, what can you tell them? You weren't even here when it happened.'

Ronni looked at him, wondering if that was an accusatory edge to his voice.

She decided it wasn't.

'Go to bed, Veronica,' Barbara Eustace said. 'Rest.'

'I can't. I should speak to Gordon. Find out—'

'Go to bed,' Fuller said, sharply.

'He's right,' Eva Cole added.

'Go now,' Donald Tanner insisted.

'There's nothing you can do tonight,' Harry Holland told her.

Ronni regarded the row of faces opposite.

'Go to bed,' Fuller repeated.

Ronni nodded and got to her feet. When she reached the door

of the day room she paused and turned to look at the residents once again.

'We'll be fine,' Errington insisted, answering her unspoken words.

She trudged up the stairs, passing the room where Gordon Faulkner was snoring contentedly.

She closed her door, then undressed wearily and sat on the edge of the bed. Through the thick walls, she could no longer hear Faulkner's snoring.

There was a tap on the door.

'Yes?' Ronni said, clearing her throat.

Helen Kennedy entered carrying a mug of steaming liquid. She set it down on the bedside table without speaking, gently squeezed Ronni's arm, then retreated from the room.

'Thanks, Helen,' Ronni said and took a sip of the warm milk.

Helen made her way back downstairs to the day room where her companions waited.

'How much did you give her?' Fuller asked.

'Forty milligrams, like you said,' Helen answered. 'The same as I gave Gordon.'

'They'll sleep until morning,' he said flatly. 'We won't be disturbed.'

90

THE PAIN WAS agonizing.

Carl Thompson howled, but the sound was muffled by the gaffer tape wound tightly around his mouth.

The piece that was ripped from his eyes tore away a small portion of his eyebrow and dozens of eyelashes. For a moment, he thought the left lid itself had torn, so intense was the pain.

Light flooded in from all directions and he squinted as the fluorescent glow assaulted his eyes.

There was still a dull ache at the back of his head, but that had subsided somewhat. Now he began to look around, trying to take in every detail of what was before him.

As far as he could tell, he was in a room about twenty feet square. It was without carpets or furniture, although there were a couple of old filing cabinets in one corner. The only things in the room were several mattresses for both single and double beds and stacks of brilliant white sheets, all covered with thick polythene.

To the rear of the room there were two industrial-size washing machines.

A flight of stone steps led up towards a white door.

The walls of the room itself were also white.

Everything was white it seemed to him.

Even the one small window high up in the wall. It looked as if the glass and the latch had been painted over.

Ceiling. Walls. Doors. And, of course, the sheets.

At last he could identify that smell he'd detected when he'd first woken.

It was freshly laundered linen.

To his right, sitting on the floor, arms and legs bound, was Donna Freeman.

The thick tape was still around her eyes and mouth.

To his left – also on the floor, but lying on it immobile – was Graham Brown. He had a bad cut on his head and blood had dripped from the wound onto the stone floor to form a congealed pool.

He didn't recognize the old man who stood before him holding the piece of gaffer tape.

There were two other old men there as well, one of them peering over the top of his glasses, looking down disdainfully at Thompson.

He also saw an old woman. White hair. Short. She was staring at him as if he was an exhibit in a zoo. Her expression was a combination of distaste and curiosity.

Thompson studied all the faces.

Fucking old bastards.

'Not so tough now, are you, lad?' said Jack Fuller. 'You *or* your friends.'

You let me go and I'll show you fucking tough, you old cunt.

Harry Holland stepped forward and pulled something from his trouser pocket. He thrust it towards Thompson.

It was a photo of Janice Holland.

'You killed my wife,' Holland told him. 'Look at her face. I look at that face every night and realize I'll never see her again. And it's because of you and these – ' he nodded towards Donna and Brown ' – these like you.' Holland stepped back.

George Errington moved towards him, still peering over his thick glasses. He ran appraising eyes over Thompson, then nodded towards the motionless body of Brown.

'That's how you would have left *us*, isn't it?' said Errington.

Thompson held his gaze.

'He might die,' the older man continued. 'It looks as if his skull could be fractured. If you hadn't come in here, it wouldn't have happened, would it? *You're* to blame if anything happens to him. You were trespassing. We were defending ourselves. Remember that.' Errington stepped back.

'Did you make her come with you?'

The next voice belonged to Eva Cole.

She was pointing towards Donna.

Thompson shook his head, but that act caused a resumption of the pain in his skull. He winced.

'Ah,' Eva chided. 'Does it hurt?'

Thompson sucked in air through his nose. When he exhaled a bubble of mucus swelled from his right nostril.

'Is she your girlfriend?' Eva persisted, again nodding towards Donna, who had turned her head in the direction of the voices.

Thompson didn't move. He merely stared deeply into the milky blue eyes of the old woman before him.

When I get out I'm going to fucking kill you, you old cunt.

'Or is *he* your boyfriend?' Eva grinned.

Thompson lunged forward, his eyes blazing. But he could get no closer to the white-haired woman and she merely moved backwards, the smile still on her thin lips.

'We need to talk.'

The voice came from Jack Fuller.

Thompson saw him step forward.

He saw the syringe in his hand; saw him lift it into the air and work the plunger, expelling any air bubbles present. A stream of clear fluid spurted from the tip of the needle.

Thompson felt a sudden twinge of fear. He swallowed hard and tried not to show his concern to the old people watching him.

Fuller moved towards Brown first. He ran the needle into his arm and pressed down on the plunger, then refilled the syringe from a bottle he took from his pocket.

The older man pushed up the sleeve of Donna's jacket. She

began to struggle as he did, but he ignored her vain attempts to scramble away.

He regarded the crook of her arm: the bruises. The track marks.

He shook his head contemptuously. 'No need to make a new hole,' he murmured.

As Donna tried to squeal through the gaffer tape, Fuller took the nail of his index finger and worked it beneath one of the scabs on her arm. The flap of dried skin lifted and he peeled it away, exposing reddish-pink flesh beneath. He ran the needle into the hole he had exposed. Into the pulsing vein.

Donna's squeals of anger turned to muted sobs.

Fuller refilled the hypodermic a third time.

Thompson glared at him.

Without breaking the stare, Fuller drove the needle into Thompson's thigh, pressing down on the plunger.

'We'll talk soon,' the older man said.

Thompson strained against his bonds for a moment. His entire body went rigid, then the images before him began to swim sickeningly. Blurred and distorted.

The darkness returned.

91

THE DRUG CALLED phenobarbital sodium, when administered in soluble form – usually in divided doses from 30mg to 125mg daily – can sedate a patient for up to eighteen hours.

It is tasteless. Especially when mixed with a suspension or with ordinary milk. If crushed to powder, it will dissolve easily in liquid of any kind.

Veronica Porter slept the sleep of the dead.

The clock beside her showed 2.44 a.m.

92

'WE'LL DO WHAT we said we'd do.' Jack Fuller looked around at the expectant faces of those gathered in the day room. 'Has anyone got anything to say?' he continued.

'Are we *sure* they're the ones?' Harry Holland wanted to know.

'We caught them breaking in tonight, didn't we? That seems fairly conclusive.'

'We'll find out once we talk to them,' George Errington added.

'What about the others who were with them?' Helen Kennedy asked. 'What if they come back?'

'Then we'll deal with them too.'

'What if they go to the police?' Colin Glazer offered.

'And tell them what?' Fuller challenged. 'That they were breaking in somewhere and they're worried about three of their friends.' He raised an eyebrow.

'They'll be missed,' Eva Cole said.

'You know the kind of families *that* sort come from,' Errington sneered. 'They don't know where their kids *are* half the time and even if they do they don't care.'

'Even if they *are* missed, who's going to think of looking here?' Barbara Eustace intoned.

'We can't rely on the police, we know that,' Fuller continued.

'I agree,' Donald Tanner added. 'I don't see that we have any choice. They're criminals, after all. It doesn't matter how old they are.'

'They killed Janice,' Harry Holland murmured. 'They should pay.'

'What about Veronica or Mr Faulkner?' Barbara wanted to know. 'What if they find them?'

'We'll have to take them out of the basement,' Fuller answered. 'We won't be able to hide them in there for long.'

'So where do we put them?' Errington asked.

'We'll put them in the room Janice and I had,' Holland said. 'I'll tell Ronni I want to keep some of Janice's things in there, that I don't want it disturbed. I'll tell her I'll clean it. I'll just let the staff take care of the single I'm in now. There'll be no *reason* for them to go into our old room.' He lowered his voice slightly. 'Janice used to do most of the cleaning in there anyway.'

Fuller nodded. 'There's no reason why they should be found,' he said. 'We'll keep them bound and gagged. We'll drug Faulkner and Ronni like we did tonight. It was easy enough getting the phenobarbital from the pharmacy.'

'How long are we going to keep those kids here?' Tanner asked.

All eyes turned towards Fuller.

'Until we have all the information we need,' he said.

'But if we let them go they'll come back. It could be worse the next time,' Barbara Eustace said.

'We can't keep them here for ever,' Colin Glazer interjected. 'They'll be found eventually.'

'We'll keep them here for as long as we have to,' Fuller said sharply. 'The important thing is that we're all agreed on this. We've got to stick together. If any of you start having second thoughts, just remember what they've put us through for the past couple of weeks. Remember it's their fault Janice is gone. Remember what they did to Barbara's dog. They have to be stopped. They have to be dealt with.' He looked around the room; expressions of agreement and nodding heads greeted him. 'It's all gone too far now anyway,' Fuller continued. 'There's no going back for any of us. But we must be strong. And we must do what we said we'd do.'

Again he looked around at the others. 'All those in agreement, raise your hands.'

As if the movement had been rehearsed, eight hands rose simultaneously into the air.

Only Colin Glazer looked a little hesitant. 'What if one of the staff *do* find them?' he wanted to know.

Fuller smiled. 'They won't,' he said, a note of unwavering conviction in his voice.

'Jack's right,' Errington added. 'We've got to stick together. We can't weaken now. We planned this too carefully.'

'They must be punished,' Barbara Eustace added.

'Is that what this is about?' Glazer said. 'Revenge?'

'It's about *justice*, Colin,' Fuller told him. 'They've put us through hell. They would have carried on if we hadn't stopped them.'

'I know you're right.' Glazer sighed. 'It's just that it seems as if we're turning into a bunch of Nazi torturers or something ridiculous like that. One day we're living out our days peacefully here, the next we're vigilantes. It's insane.'

'You can walk away now if you want to, Colin,' Fuller said, looking around the room. 'Any of you can.'

'I'm just trying to consider all the issues,' Glazer insisted.

'There's only *one* issue,' Errington hissed. 'Our safety. I won't live in fear of little bastards like them.'

A murmur of approval rippled around the room.

Even Glazer nodded.

'Any more questions?' Fuller asked.

There were none.

'So, we carry on as we planned,' he said flatly. Fuller looked at his watch, then murmured quietly, 'We'd better get started.'

93

THE COLD WOKE HER.

Donna Freeman shuddered, every inch of her skin puckered into gooseflesh by the chill. It took her a second or two to realize she was naked but for her bra and knickers.

As she turned her head slowly from left to right she saw that Carl Thompson and Graham Brown had also been stripped. They wore just their underwear.

All three were sitting on chairs, secured there firmly by lengths of electrical flex that had been wound around their ankles and wrists.

The tape had been removed from their eyes, but not from their mouths.

Donna coughed, the action causing her body to jerk wildly.

She glanced around at the faces of those who stared at her and her two companions.

One of the old men

(*the tall one with the glasses*)

was smiling crookedly, she was sure, as he surveyed her helplessness.

Her headache had gone. For that she was grateful.

There were bruises on her arms. She saw more on the arms and chest of Brown. Large purple welts that overlapped in places.

Her bare feet were cold on the stone floor. She screwed up her toes as if that action would prevent the feeling, but all she could do was sit and shiver.

'We need to talk to you.'

Donna heard the words and they seemed to echo inside her head for a moment.

She saw who had spoken them and one of the old men stepped towards her.

'When I take this off,' Jack Fuller said slowly, tapping the tape gag over her mouth, 'you can scream if you want to. But the only people who'll hear you will be the ones in this room. No one will come to help you and if you carry on screaming, then I'll gag you again. It's your choice.' He took hold of the gaffer tape and ripped it away.

Donna hissed in pain and glared at Fuller. 'Fuck,' she snarled, her cheeks and lips stinging. She sucked in a few deep breaths, then sat back slightly.

'The first word you speak is an obscenity,' Fuller said, shaking his head.

'Fuck off, grandad,' she rasped.

Fuller stepped back a pace.

'I want my clothes back,' she continued. 'Is that what happens when you can't get it up anymore? When you're too old? Do you just look? Why didn't you take *all* my clothes? If you want to look at my tits and my fanny, then fucking do it.'

'You're disgusting,' Fuller told her, his face set in hard lines.

She held his gaze defiantly.

He turned and moved towards the clothes Donna had been wearing. One by one he held the items up. 'Your clothes,' he said. 'I expect they were stolen or paid for with someone else's money.'

He upended the jeans and shook them. Some loose change flew out and rolled across the floor.

'Was that stolen too?' Fuller asked.

'Leave my clothes alone,' Donna hissed. 'You've got no right—'

'No what?' snarled Fuller. 'No *right*? What do *you* know about *rights*?' He threw the jeans aside.

As she watched, he went through the pockets of her jacket

and found a packet of Silk Cut, some Juicy Fruit and a little more loose change.

'Do you use the money to pay for *those* things?' Errington asked, stepping forward. He pointed first at the stud in her navel, then at her earrings and finally at the nose ring.

'I'm getting another one too,' Donna hissed. 'If you pull my knickers off, I'll show you where it's going to go, you fucking old perv.'

Errington peered at her over his glasses, then leaned close.

Donna tried to pull back.

She swallowed hard then relaxed as he moved away.

'Scum,' Fuller murmured.

'What's your name?' Errington asked.

'Lady Di.' She grinned.

He hit her.

Donna was amazed both at the power in the blow and also at its speed.

The flat of Errington's hand caught her across the cheek. The loud crack as it connected reverberated inside the basement.

Donna gritted her teeth, her cheek stinging.

Errington moved away.

'What's your name?'

It was Harry Holland who asked this time.

'Madonna,' she sneered.

Holland struck her across the same cheek.

She rocked back in the chair, almost overbalancing.

Helen Kennedy stepped forward.

'What's your name?' she said softly.

Donna eyed her warily for a moment. 'Mind your own business,' she said, some of the bravado missing from her tone.

Helen hit her across the other cheek.

'What's your name?' Donald Tanner wanted to know.

Donna hesitated, her eyes flicking from one face to the other. She looked around at Thompson and saw that he was glaring at her.

'Never mind him,' Tanner said, seeing her concern. 'He's next. Now, what's your name?'

Her heart was beating more rapidly now. 'You can't do this,' she protested.

Tanner grinned and struck her so hard he split her bottom lip. Donna licked at it with her tongue and tasted blood.

'What's your name?' Colin Glazer enquired, his voice as even as those before him.

Donna saw no emotion on his face.

She opened her mouth as if to speak.

Glazer struck her before she could.

He caught her with a back-hand blow so hard it almost knocked her over.

Tears began to well up in her eyes.

'What's your name?' Jack Fuller said.

He hit before she even had the chance to speak.

'Donna,' she blurted, tears now coursing down her cheeks. 'Donna Freeman.'

Fuller nodded and turned towards Graham Brown.

94

'IF YOU TOUCH me, I'll fucking kill you,' Brown snarled as the gag was torn free.

'You're not in a position to threaten anyone now,' Fuller reminded him. 'What's *your* name?'

Brown hawked and spat at the older man, the glob of mucus missing him by inches.

'What kind of people are you?' Fuller said, eyeing Brown and the other two with thinly disguised disgust. 'Thieves. Vandals. Murderers.'

'We never killed anyone,' Donna interjected.

'You killed my wife,' Harry Holland rasped.

'We never touched your fucking wife,' Brown sneered.

Fuller struck him hard across the face. 'Name?' he said flatly.

'Fuck you.'

Fuller hit him again. 'What's your name?'

Brown felt the pain building inside his skull once again.

'What is your name?' Fuller continued.

Brown tried to shake his head just as Fuller caught him across the temple with a powerful blow.

'Graham Brown, you old cunt. My fucking name is Graham Brown, right?' the boy blurted.

Fuller nodded and wiped his hand on his handkerchief.

'You butchered a dog that belonged to one of the residents here,' George Errington added.

Brown winced.

Donna said nothing.

'Didn't you?' Errington persisted. 'You killed that dog, didn't you? Then you broke in here and hung it in the wardrobe. Didn't you?'

'Why did you do it?' Fuller added.

Brown swallowed hard.

'Why did you kill the dog?' Helen Kennedy wanted to know.

'And spray graffiti on the walls?' Fuller said.

'And smash our windows?' Errington reminded them.

'Or send those letters?' Tanner offered.

Brown felt as if his head was spinning. The questions were coming from every direction, spoken with the same even-voiced tone, but he knew that it barely hid the anger behind it.

'Why?' Fuller snapped, glaring at Brown.

'Why did you break in?' Errington demanded. 'What did you want here?'

'Why did you kill my wife?' Holland added, stepping forward.

'We didn't . . .' Brown protested weakly.

Holland hit him hard with the back of his hand. 'Why did you kill her?'

'Why did you attack our home?' Eva Cole rasped.

Colin Glazer slapped Brown across the back of the head close to the place where his skull had been cracked. The pain was agonizing and for precious seconds he thought he was going to pass out.

When Glazer looked at his palm there was blood on it.

He crossed to the three piles of clothing on the other side of the room and wiped his hand on Brown's sweatshirt.

'Why did you break in?' Tanner snapped. 'What did you expect to find?'

Brown was now fighting back tears too. The pain inside his head was almost intolerable.

'What did you expect to find?' Tanner repeated. He hit Brown hard across the face and this time the boy began to sob.

'Fuck off,' he whimpered.

Tanner hit him again.

'We thought you had money here,' blurted Donna, twisting against the bonds that held her so tightly.

Carl Thompson roared madly through his gag and all eyes turned towards him.

'Do you want to add something to this discussion?' Fuller asked, taking a step towards the youth. He ripped the tape off. 'What do you want to say?'

Thompson opened his mouth wide, as if to force away the stiffness in his jaw.

'You're the leader, aren't you? You were behind all this?'

Thompson merely held Fuller's gaze.

'Were you the one who told them there was money here?'

No answer.

Fuller struck him across the face. 'Did you think we all had our savings in shoe boxes under our beds?'

Silence.

Fuller clenched his fist and struck the youth.

Blood began to run from his bottom lip.

'Did you think you were going to go from room to room and steal everything we had?'

Thompson barely blinked.

'The tough one, eh?' murmured Fuller, leaning close to his ear. 'I've seen your kind before. I know about people like you.' The older man stepped back.

'You'll have to let us go,' Brown said. 'People are looking for us.'

'No they're not,' Errington told him.

'The fucking police will arrest you,' Brown rasped.

'Shall I call them?' Harry Holland offered. 'You can tell them how you killed my wife.'

'We didn't kill your fucking wife!' wailed Brown.

Holland smashed his hand across the younger boy's face with incredible power.

Blood and mucus spattered the floor.

Brown coughed, his head lolling onto his chest.

Donna looked at Thompson, who ignored her.

'Are you going to call the police?' she asked.

'What's the point?' Fuller mumured.

'You can't keep us here. Someone'll come to find us,' Donna insisted.

Fuller reached for a fresh piece of tape and wound it swiftly around Donna's mouth.

'I need a piss,' Brown said imploringly.

Fuller pulled off a length of tape to seal Brown's mouth.

'I said I need a piss,' the boy repeated.

Fuller pressed the tape into place.

Brown looked up into his eyes.

Fuller reached down swiftly and prodded the boy's lower abdomen hard with his fingers.

Brown groaned as a dark stain began to spread across his pants. The acrid smell of urine filled the air.

Fuller turned away from him. For long moments he stood looking at Thompson, who met his gaze defiantly.

'We'll speak tomorrow,' Fuller muttered.

As he reached forward to stick the gaffer tape in place, Thompson began to jerk his head backwards and forwards.

Harry Holland stepped behind him, clamped his head between his hands and held him still long enough for Fuller to wind the tape around his mouth.

The other occupants of the basement moved towards the staircase.

George Errington accepted a helping hand from Donald Tanner as they climbed.

At the top of the steps Fuller paused, then switched off the lights. The basement was plunged into almost palpable darkness.

Fuller heard the sound of muted sobbing from the subterranean room.

He stepped into the light, then turned and locked the door.

95

RONNI COULD BARELY open her eyes.

She rolled over in bed and groaned.

Sunlight was streaming through the window of the room and she waved one hand at it as if to force it away.

She lay on her stomach, face buried in the pillow, wondering why the alarm wasn't still sending out its electronic signal.

It took her a moment or two to realize the alarm hadn't woken her.

She blinked myopically and reached for the clock.

The hands of the timepiece swam before her. She had trouble conentrating on them.

When she finally managed to bring them into focus she thought she was imagining what she saw: 11.05 a.m.

It was impossible.

The clock must have stopped during the night.

She shook it.

'Oh God,' she murmured and hauled herself out of bed.

Why hadn't Faulkner woken her?

Had she been that tired she hadn't heard the alarm? Or had she merely forgotten to set it the previous night?

Questions tumbled through her mind as she hurried to get dressed.

Why hadn't one of the residents woken her or at least come to check on her?

Who'd given them their breakfast?

Who? Why? What? When?

Faulkner should have woken her. She appreciated his concern that she needed to sleep, but this was not the place to do it. She was supposed to be in charge. It was hardly the kind of example to set.

Ronni splashed her face with water from the sink in the room and swiftly brushed her teeth, then she ran fingers through her hair and hurried out into the corridor.

As she moved down the corridor towards the stairs she heard a sound from Faulkner's room.

The door was open slightly and she paused.

The sound was unmistakable.

It was the low, rasping sound of guttural breathing.

'Gordon,' she called.

There was no answer.

Ronni pushed the door slightly and repeated his name.

Still no answer. Just the rattling breaths.

'Gordon.'

She stepped into the room.

Faulkner was lying on his side, eyes closed, one arm dangling over the edge of the bed.

What the hell was going on here?

She walked across and shook him gently. 'Gordon. Wake up,' she said, more urgently.

He grunted, then opened his eyes. He looked at her, but there was no recognition there.

She spoke his name once more.

'What's going on?' he said, clearing his throat.

'Look at the time,' she urged, pointing towards his watch.

'Oh shit,' he mumbled.

As he sat up he touched a hand to his forehead. 'My head's killing me,' he announced.

'Then take a tablet. I'm going to check on the residents.' She turned towards the door.

'Wait a minute,' he said. 'Have you just woken up too?'

Ronni nodded. 'We must have overslept,' she told him.

'Both of us? Shit.'

Ronni hurried down the stairs in the direction of the day room. As she walked in she saw Colin Glazer sitting reading.

The television was on, but the sound was turned down.

'Morning, Ronni,' he said cheerfully before returning to his book.

Eva Cole was engaged in some embroidery.

Ronni looked at both of them almost in bewilderment. 'Where's everyone else?' she wanted to know.

'Mr Errington's in his room, I think,' Eva announced without looking up. 'Helen and Barbara went for a walk in the grounds as the weather's so nice. I think Mr Tanner went into town.'

'Jack and Harry are out in the garden doing something or other,' Glazer added.

'What did you do about breakfast?'

'Helen and I cooked it,' Eva informed her. 'That was all right, wasn't it? We didn't want to disturb you.'

Ronni sucked in a deep breath. 'Look, I'm sorry this has happened, it—'

Eva cut her short. 'Don't apologize, Ronni,' she said. 'We all know you've got a lot on your mind and we had things to do anyway. No harm's been done.'

Ronni managed a smile. She hesitated a moment, then headed out into the corridor.

Faulkner was hurrying down the stairs. 'Is everyone OK?' he asked.

'Fine. I don't even think they missed us.'

'I've never slept like that before,' Faulkner confessed.

'Me neither. You'd think we'd been drugged.'

They both laughed.

96

THE SUNSHINE DID little to help Ronni's feelings of sluggishness.

As the day wore on and the heat from the blazing orb grew more intense, she found herself feeling uncomfortably drowsy.

Faulkner too complained of similar feelings and, despite several cups of coffee, the malaise continued.

Halfway through the afternoon, Faulkner even took a walk to a nearby shop and returned with two large bottles of Coke and four cans of Red Bull. The result of drinking this amount of caffeine-laden fluid only led to frequent trips to the toilet, not the rush of energy Ronni had hoped for.

The residents, she noticed, all seemed remarkably high-spirited considering the events of the last few days. Whether it was merely a collective mask she didn't know, but even Harry Holland seemed happy enough.

Ronni cleaned rooms

(*all except the double room that had belonged to Harry and Janice Holland – Harry had asked her to allow him to do it and she'd readily agreed*)

and Faulkner used the buffing machine on the hall and the corridors.

Shelby House and its residents enjoyed a day like any other. Indistinguishable from so many before and, Ronni expected, more to come.

It was almost five in the afternoon by the time she rang the hospital.

Putting off the inevitable?

She discovered that her father was still stable, but there had been no improvement. An operation to remove the blood clot seemed inevitable.

When she put the phone down, the weariness she'd felt all day seemed to intensify.

Ronni sat at the desk in the lower office for a moment, gazing at the piece of plywood that had been put over the broken pane.

She wondered if there'd be any more trouble tonight.

As she stared, motes of dust turned lazily in the rays of sunlight. The sound of the clock in the room seemed thunderous, the ticking reverberating inside her head.

She yawned and got to her feet, preparing to make her way outside once more.

The sun was on the wane. The air would start to grow cooler soon.

Perhaps then she could shake off this maddening lethargy.

Perhaps.

All day long they heard movement above them.

Footsteps mostly.

In the late afternoon they heard a low rumbling sound, but could only guess what it was.

Blind in the darkness of the basement and sightless again inside their tape blindfolds, they sat and listened to the sounds.

It was difficult to make out individual voices. Sometimes sound was amplified by the cavernous subterranean room. Sometimes it was simply swallowed by the empty air.

Like Brown before her, Donna had been forced to wet herself and she now sat uncomfortably in sodden knickers, still firmly anchored to the chair.

Brown himself cried softly more than once, his moods alternating between fury and helplessness.

Twice he even attempted to bang the chair legs on the floor, tipping himself back a little, then crashing forward. But he realized that if he toppled backwards he'd more than likely smash his head in on the stone floor and gave up that idea.

Donna flexed her toes and her fingers, trying to loosen the ropes, trying to slip free, but it was useless.

She was aware of her two companions in the blackness but – gagged as they all were – they had no way of communicating.

Thompson sat as still as he could. Thinking.

Thinking of a way out of this place.

Thinking what he would do to the old fuckers when he finally got free.

He'd kill them. Gut them like he'd gutted that dog.

Take his air rifle and press it into their mouths or eyes. Watch the terror on their wrinkled faces as he pulled the trigger.

Use his knife to castrate the old men. Hack the old balls from beneath their wizened, useless cocks.

He might stuff one of the severed bollocks into the mouth of the old woman with the white hair.

He had no idea what time it was when he, too, finally succumbed to the demands of his own bulging bladder. The warm urine spilling over his thighs was momentarily pleasant in the cold basement. However, when the fluid began to cool and the soaking cotton clung to him he felt his anger growing.

The pleasant smell of freshly laundered linen was replaced by that of stale piss.

Thompson wondered who would be the first to shit themselves.

It was only a matter of time.

The three of them sat helplessly in the basement.

Waiting.

97

'TELL US WHAT his name is.'

Jack Fuller stood a foot or so from Graham Brown and pointed in the direction of Thompson.

Brown shook his head.

'His name,' Fuller repeated.

'I'm not telling you.'

'Why? Why are you protecting him? We know *your* name. We know *her* name.' He nodded towards Donna. 'Why not tell us *his*?'

'Do you think he'd protect *you*?' Harry Holland asked, then shook his head slowly.

'If we tell you, will you let us go?' Donna interjected.

'You keep your fucking mouths shut, both of you,' snarled Thompson.

'So, you *can* speak?' Fuller smiled, moving nearer to Thompson. 'Why don't *you* tell us your name?'

'I'm not saying a fucking thing to you.'

Fuller moved closer, careful to avoid the puddle of urine around the base of the chair. 'You'll stay here until you do,' he told him.

'Fuck off. *You're* the ones who'll be in trouble with the police when they find us. This is kidnapping.'

A chorus of chuckles greeted the remark.

'Three fit, able youngsters break into a home for the elderly.' Fuller grinned. 'For the second time. The first time, they hang a dead dog in a wardrobe and cause one of the residents to die of a heart attack. Before that they smash windows, send threatening and abusive letters and spray graffiti on the walls. In order to protect themselves, the old people are forced to fight back. They do this by capturing the youngsters who've been terrorizing them. How is that story going to sound to the police? Who are they going to sympathize with?'

Thompson glared at the older man.

'But we don't need to involve the police in this, do we?' Fuller said softly.

'What are you going to do, then?' Thompson said defiantly.

'Well, even if the police come and we tell them that story and your names and they take away all the evidence, they'll still do nothing.' Fuller turned and walked back to his watching companions.

'We wouldn't do it again,' Brown blurted. 'If you let us go, we'll never bother you again.'

'Shut up,' hissed Thompson.

'No, *you* shut up, Carl. I've had enough of this.'

Colin Glazer smiled. 'Carl,' he said quietly.

'Hello, Carl,' Fuller said, looking straight at Thompson. 'So, we're halfway there. What's your second name?'

'You fucking arsehole,' Thompson yelled at Brown.

'Disgusting,' Helen Kennedy murmured.

'Do you want to go?' George Errington said to Brown. 'Do you want us to let you go?'

Brown looked at the older man warily, then at Donna and Thompson.

Finally he nodded.

'Tell us his last name,' Errington continued.

'You tell them and you're fucking dead,' Thompson rasped.

'What is it?'

'I'm warning you. I'll fucking kill you.'

'Don't listen to him, Graham,' said Donald Tanner. 'He can't hurt you. Look at him: he's helpless.'

'What's his second name?' Errington persisted.

Brown tried to swallow, but his throat was bone dry.

'He can't hurt you,' Eva Cole added soothingly.

'Tell us,' Glazer intoned.

'Tell us now,' Fuller added.

Donna could only look helplessly back and forth at the two youths.

'What's his name, Graham?' Errington said again. 'Tell us and we'll let you go. We know you were just doing what he told you to do.'

'They're lying,' Thompson shouted. 'They won't let you go.'

'He threatened to kill you, Graham,' Fuller reminded the younger boy. 'Are you going to listen to him?'

'Tell us his name,' Harry Holland said.

Brown sniffed back tears. 'It—' he stammered.

'Shut up!' Thompson roared.

'Tell us.'

'His name—'

'Shut your fucking mouth!'

'Tell us his name.'

'I fucking mean it. I'll kill you.'

Brown was almost at breaking point.

'You need treatment for that wound on your head,' Fuller reminded him. 'The quicker you tell us, the quicker we can help you.'

Tears began to roll down Brown's cheeks.

'Tell us.'

The voices seemed to thunder inside his skull.

'Tell us his name.'

Brown's body began to shudder uncontrollably.

'Carl Thompson,' he wailed. 'His name's Carl Thompson. Now please let me go.'

Fuller looked at Thompson and smiled.

'I'm sorry, Carl,' sobbed Brown. He looked at his companion through a mist of tears, but saw only fury in his expression. 'Will you let me go now?' the younger boy persisted, looking at the row of faces before him.

'Graham Brown, Donna Freeman and Carl Thompson,' murmured Errington.

'You said you'd let me go,' Brown gasped, sniffing loudly.

Fuller ignored his entreaties. He walked towards the youngest boy and brandished a strip of gaffer tape before him.

'You said you'd let me go!' cried Brown.

Fuller slapped the tape in place.

The cries trailed away into muted sobs. Mucus, running from both nostrils, trickled over the tape, mingling with the tears still pouring down the boy's cheeks.

'What about *you*, Donna?' Fuller asked. 'Do you want us to let *you* go?'

'But you won't, will you?'

'Do you think you deserve it?'

She licked her cracked, dry lips and lowered her gaze. 'What do you want me to do?' she asked, her voice little more than a whisper.

'You've done enough already.'

Fuller sealed her mouth once again.

'You won't get away with this,' Thompson snarled, but for the first time some of the venom had left his voice.

'Get away with what?' Fuller asked. 'You don't even know what we're going to do.'

Thompson strained against his bonds, but the rope only cut more deeply into his wrists and ankles. 'Our parents will come looking for us,' he said, attempting to inject as much menace into his tone as possible.

'How can they?' Errington wanted to know. 'They don't know where you are. No one does.'

'They certainly wouldn't think to look for you here,' Tanner echoed.

'They'll find us,' Thompson insisted none too convincingly.

'We'll see,' Fuller murmured. 'But not before we've finished.'

'Finished? What the fuck are you talking about?'

Fuller advanced with another piece of thick gaffer tape.

'What are you going to do?' Thompson shouted.

Fuller stuck the tape in place and stepped back.

The three captive youths looked on silently.

Brown was still crying softly.

Donna stared almost imploringly at the faces before her.

Thompson strained once more against his restraints.

'When you break the law you have to pay,' Fuller told them. 'There are lessons to be learned. Things that have to be done. The police won't do them. They won't punish you. So *we* have to. The people you wronged to begin with. You have to learn. There's a price to pay for what you've done.'

As he spoke he reached inside his jacket.

When Thompson saw what he was holding, he began to shudder uncontrollably.

98

THE GUN LOOKED large in Fuller's fist, but he gripped it with assurance as he moved towards the captive youths.

The fluorescents in the ceiling reflected off the polished metal and Thompson could smell the distinctive odour of gun oil.

The weapon was old, but had obviously been well cared for.

Fuller hefted it before him, allowing the terrified trio a good look.

'Smith and Wesson .38 calibre revolver,' Fuller told them calmly. 'I took it from a dead Japanese officer the day we were liberated. He'd stolen it from a British paratrooper when they captured him. Airborne troops and commandos carried these pistols. I took it because it didn't belong to that Jap. And I took it to remind me of what I'd been through. Every day of my life I've cleaned this gun. And every time I clean it, I thank God I'm alive. That I lived through the camp. We all suffered during the war. We've all suffered since. When we came here we thought we'd all live out our years in peace.' He considered each of the faces before him. 'But I don't suppose that means anything to you, does it? You don't care what we went through then and you don't care what *you've* put us through either,' he continued conversationally.

He ran one index finger along the barrel of the weapon.

'It holds six rounds. One in each chamber. The bullet travels at roughly eight hundred feet a second. That means that if I pressed it against your head and pulled the trigger, it would blow away most of the back of your skull. Spread your brains across that wall. Perhaps even put some on the ceiling.'

He gestured skyward with the revolver.

Brown began to cry again.

Thompson attempted to swallow, but his mouth, already parched, felt as if it had been filled with chalk.

Donna closed her eyes so tightly that white stars swam behind the lids.

Fuller pushed the cylinder-eject catch and flipped it free of the frame, then he upended the weapon and six brass-jacketed cartridges fell into his palm.

As Thompson watched, he pushed one back into the cylinder, spun it, then snapped it shut.

'When you started causing trouble here, the police said that whoever was responsible was treating it like a game. Well, now it's time for *us* to play.'

He pressed the barrel against Thompson's forehead and thumbed back the hammer.

Thompson's eyes bulged in the sockets.

'A one in six chance,' Fuller murmured.

Thompson tried to pull his head away, his breathing frantic inside the gag.

His stomach contracted.

The barrel of the gun felt cold against his forehead.

Fuller squeezed the trigger.

The hammer slammed down on an empty chamber.

The sound reverberated around the basement.

Thompson began shaking even more violently.

Fuller spun the cylinder again, then snapped it back into position.

He held the gun by its barrel and handed it to George Errington.

The older man took the .38 and pressed it against Donna's forehead, just above her right eyebrow.

She squeezed her eyelids together even more tightly. Deep in her throat she made a sound that reminded Errington of a noise he'd once heard on a farm in his youth. That of a pig about to be butchered. A high-pitched squeal of total despair.

He pulled the trigger.

There was a loud metallic snap as the hammer again found an empty chamber.

Donna kept her eyes closed, her entire body now rigid.

Errington performed the same ritual as Fuller before him, then passed the weapon to Harry Holland, who took it eagerly and jammed it into the left nostril of Graham Brown.

'This is what my wife must have felt like before she died,' he said evenly.

Brown began to sob.

'Before *you* killed her,' Holland breathed, a tear now trickling down his own cheek. He thumbed back the hammer.

'I hope she's watching this,' he whispered, now pushing the barrel hard against the bridge of Brown's nose.

He gently squeezed the trigger.

The only sound was the gush of excrement that burst from Brown's bowels.

He sat motionless in his own faeces for brief seconds, then passed out.

Holland stepped back, wrinkling his nose at the stench.

He handed the gun back to Fuller, who carefully cocked it, then allowed Eva Cole to take it from him.

'Use both hands to hold it, Eva,' he told her helpfully.

She banged it against Thompson's head, steadied the weapon, then looked into his eyes and squeezed the trigger.

Silence but for the crack of firing pin against cylinder.

Colin Glazer took his turn. He looked indifferently down at Donna and saw how pale her face was, as if all the blood had been drained from her.

'Look at me,' he said.

She didn't open her eyes.

He pressed the barrel against her left eye.

Pulled the trigger.

Nothing.

Donald Tanner didn't wait for Brown to regain consciousness. He pulled the trigger anyway when it was his turn.

Silence.

As Helen Kennedy stepped forward to take her turn, Fuller looked at his watch.

1.49 a.m.

It was almost time.

99

At first she thought she was dreaming.

The hands that clutched at her belonged to phantoms.

The voices that whispered in her ear came from spectres.

Ronni tried to open her eyes, hoping that these intruders would vanish.

She groaned and rolled over.

The only light in the room was from the bedside lamp, but it felt as if someone had pointed a searchlight into her face.

She blinked hard, shielding her eyes despite the fact that the bulb was only a sixty watt.

Images swam before her, blurred and indistinct until they gradually cleared.

She heard her name being whispered.

Again she felt insistent hands on her shoulder, trying to rouse her more fully.

She sat up and looked around her.

On one side of the bed stood Helen Kennedy. On the other, Eva Cole, her white hair looking almost luminescent in the gloom.

'What's wrong?' Ronni said, but the words seemed to catch in her throat. She coughed, then repeated herself.

'You must come with us, Ronni,' Helen said.

Ronni rubbed her eyes and glanced at the clock: 2.11 a.m.

It felt as if someone had stuffed her head full of cotton wool.

'What's wrong?' Ronni repeated. She swung her feet from beneath the covers and shivered.

The sudden cold seemed to accelerate her waking.

Thoughts began to form inside her head.

'Quickly,' Eva insisted.

Ronni reached for her housecoat and pulled it on over the long T-shirt she wore.

Helen was already standing at the door, ushering her through.

'Tell me what's going on,' Ronni said. 'Is everyone all right?'

'Come with us,' Eva urged.

Ronni moved with as much speed as she could, her brain still fuzzy.

As she passed Faulkner's door she heard his snoring.

Perhaps she should wake him too.

The floor felt cold beneath her bare feet.

'Is someone ill?' she wanted to know.

The two women didn't speak. They merely guided her down the stairs to the ground floor, supporting her when she looked as if she might stumble.

Barbara Eustace was waiting at the foot of the stairs, seated in her wheelchair, eyes fixed on Ronni.

'Have those kids come back?' Ronni said, suddenly afraid.

At the bottom of the stairs they guided her along the corridor, past the day room.

Towards the basement.

'What's happening?' Ronni asked, her head clearing somewhat.

'There's something you have to see,' Eva said.

'Tell me what it is.'

'It's simpler if you just look,' Helen assured her.

Eva stepped in front of her and opened the basement door.

As Ronni stepped inside, the stench hit her immediately. She recoiled, shielding her eyes from the glare of the fluorescents. 'What's going on?' she protested.

Then she looked down the flight of stone steps.

What she saw drove away the last vestiges of drowsiness as surely as if someone had stuck her with a cattle prod.

'Oh my God,' she murmured.

100

FOR FLEETING SECONDS, Ronni wondered if, indeed, she was still immersed in a nightmare.

The three nearly naked figures tied to chairs, surrounded by pools of their own excreta.

The blood.

The looks of uncontrollable terror in the eyes of the trio.

The awful pallor of their skin.

The tape wound so tightly around their mouths.

The rope that cut into their wrists and ankles.

Surely, what she was looking at could only belong in the darkest recesses of her mind.

The stench made her realize that wasn't so.

She took a step forward and the basement door was closed behind her.

'Come in,' called Jack Fuller. 'We wanted you to see this.'

She swallowed hard and advanced, the smell growing stronger in her nostrils.

'To see *them*,' Harry Holland added.

Ronni saw Donna turn to face her, tears rolling down her cheeks. She saw a glimmer of recognition in the girl's eyes.

Brown's head was slumped on his chest, but his body was shuddering as he sobbed.

Thompson looked at her blankly, his dead-eyed stare no different from when he defiantly stood before Andy's car.

Ronni wanted to ask what was happening. What were these

314

kids doing here, tied up like this? She wanted to know why they bore cuts and bruises. Why were they soaked with sweat and blood?

Why was there so much excrement around?

She wanted to ask so much, but all she could do was stare at the three captives, her mouth slightly open in a combination of bewilderment and revulsion.

'They were the ones who broke in,' George Errington told her as she reached the bottom of the stairs.

'The ones who sent the letters,' Donald Tanner offered.

'The ones who sprayed graffiti on the walls,' Colin Glazer told her. 'And smashed the windows.'

'They killed Janice,' said Harry Holland.

'And Barbara's dog,' Helen Kennedy muttered.

'They're responsible for everything that's been happening to us,' Eva Cole confirmed.

Ronni stood motionless on the stone floor of the basement, barely noticing the cold beneath her feet.

She couldn't take her eyes from the three youngsters tied to the chairs.

For interminable moments she remained transfixed. Finally, she raised a hand to her face in an effort to blot out the foul smell emanating from the three captives.

She wished that by closing her eyes she could blot out their image too.

Fuller walked behind them and pointed to each one in turn. 'Carl Thompson, Donna Freeman and Graham Brown,' he announced. 'We broke them. They'll tell us anything we want.'

Ronni ran a hand through her hair and wondered, for fleeting seconds, if she was hallucinating.

'Look at them, Ronni,' Errington urged.

She could do little else.

'Who did this to them?' When she spoke, the words sounded as if they were coming from the other side of the room. As if someone else had said them.

'*We* did,' Fuller announced.

'All of us,' Holland added.

'They had to be stopped,' Glazer insisted.

'What they were doing was wrong,' Helen said softly.

'They had to learn,' Eva offered.

Ronni inhaled, her breath shaking. 'How long have they been here?' she wanted to know, still unable to tear her eyes from the youths.

'Nearly two days,' Fuller told her.

'We knew we couldn't keep it from you for ever,' Holland said. 'It seemed the right thing to do, to let you know what was happening.'

'To let you see them,' Errington added.

She looked at each of the pale, tear-stained faces in turn.

'You know yourself the police wouldn't have done anything to them, even if they'd been caught,' Fuller said.

'They killed Janice,' Holland reminded her.

Ronni felt light-headed, and wondered if she was going to faint. She stumbled backwards and Helen Kennedy put out an arm to steady her.

The feeling passed.

'How long did you plan to keep them here?' she said hoarsely.

'Until they'd been punished,' Fuller told her.

'You've got to let them go.'

'Why? So they can come back and start all over again?'

'What you're doing is wrong.'

Fuller laughed. 'What *we're* doing?' he hissed. 'We're simply giving them a taste of their own medicine. Showing them what it's like to live in fear.'

'Whose side are you on, Ronni?' Holland wanted to know.

'It's not a matter of sides.' She waved a hand in the direction of the youths. 'This is . . .'

She couldn't find the words.

'Wrong?' Fuller said challengingly. 'Is that what you think, Ronni? What did you expect us to do? Sit around waiting until they killed *us*?'

'Jack, you've got to let them go,' she said quietly.

Fuller brought the gun into view. He pressed it against the back of Thompson's head.

Ronni took a step forward. 'Jack, for God's sake, don't—'

Fuller thumbed back the hammer.

'You can't kill him,' Ronni protested frantically.

'Can't I? I learned a long time ago that life's cheap.'

'Please, put the gun down. Please.'

Thompson looked imploringly at her, his eyes filled with tears. Fuller had hold of his hair and was tugging gently on it.

'Show her, Don,' Fuller said.

Tanner crossed to the pile of clothes taken from the youngsters and retrieved something. He wandered across to Ronni and reached for her hand, pushing something into her palm.

'Look at it,' Fuller instructed.

Ronni opened her hand.

Lying there was a gold wedding ring. A thick band. It bore an inscription on the inside.

She felt her stomach contract.

'That *is* your father's, isn't it?' Fuller said quietly.

101

'Isn't it?

Fuller's voice echoed around the basement.

Inside her head.

Ronni looked dumbly at the ring.

'That wedding ring belongs to your father, doesn't it, Ronni?' he asserted.

She felt the tears welling in her eyes.

'Your father, who's lying in a hospital waiting to die.'

She nodded. 'Where did you get it?'

'From him.' Fuller pointed at Thompson.

'It was in his pocket,' Holland added.

'He stole it from your father,' said Fuller.

'Took it from him, then tried to kill him,' Holland insisted.

Ronni glared at Thompson. 'Where did you get this?' she said, quietly.

Thompson looked at her.

Fuller suddenly reached round and tore off the tape gag. 'Tell the lady where you got it,' he said evenly.

Thompson sucked in a deep breath.

'Did you get it from my father?' Ronni wanted to know.

'I don't know your old man,' Thompson informed her.

'*How* did you get it?' Ronni snapped.

'Tell her,' insisted Fuller.

Thompson hesitated.

'Tell her,' Glazer snarled.

Fuller pressed the .38 to the back of the youngster's head and thumbed back the hammer.

'We broke into a house,' Thompson said breathlessly.

'Who?'

'The three of us.' He nodded towards his two captive companions. 'There was nothing worth taking,' he continued.

'How did you get the ring?' Ronni whispered.

'The old bastard in the house attacked us. He went mental. We were defending ourselves.'

Ronni took a step towards him.

'He hit us with a cricket bat,' Thompson told her.

The knot of muscles at the side of Ronni's jaw throbbed angrily. She forgot the stench of excrement and stood only inches from Thompson. 'What did the man look like?' she demanded.

'I can't remember,' Thompson gasped.

'But you took this ring from him?'

Thompson nodded.

'And you beat him up?'

Again he nodded.

Ronni looked down at the gold circlet in her hand, then at Thompson.

'We were defending ourselves,' he said. 'He started it. If he'd have kept out of the way—'

Ronni struck him hard across the face, one of her nails tearing the flesh close to his right eye. Blood trickled from the cut.

'Bastard!' she roared, clutching the ring in her free hand.

She stepped towards Donna. 'Were *you* there too?' Ronni demanded.

Donna nodded.

'And you?'

Brown sniffed back tears and moved his head almost imperceptibly.

'They're all guilty, Ronni,' Fuller said flatly. He slowly pushed the .38 towards her.

Ronni shook her head.

'They stole the ring while your father was dying,' Fuller said.

'We didn't *mean* to kill him,' Thompson said. 'He should have kept out of the way.'

Ronni hit him again.

'Take the gun,' Fuller persisted, pushing the butt towards her. 'Think about your father and take it.'

She snatched it from the older man and felt its weight in her fist.

'This is the only justice you'll ever get, Ronni,' Holland insisted.

'Use it,' Errington urged.

Ronni raised the weapon.

'Please don't,' begged Thompson.

She pressed the revolver to his forehead.

Do it.

Her hand was shaking.

Blow his fucking head off. This is the kid that put your father in a coma.

'He doesn't deserve to live,' Holland chided.

'None of them do,' added Tanner.

Ronni tried to grip the .38 in both hands then realized she was still holding her father's ring.

Look at it. All you'll have left of him.

She gritted her teeth.

Go on. Do it. Just a little more pressure on the trigger. These little bastards have torn your life apart for the sake of some sick game. They're at your mercy. You decide whether they live or die. Feels good doesn't it?

'Pull the trigger, Ronni,' Fuller said.

You heard him. These scumbags beat your father into a coma. Doesn't he deserve some justice?

'Sorry,' gasped Thompson, his eyes screwed shut.

Sorry. Is that it? Was that the sum total of his redemption? He's scared. The same as your father was scared when they attacked him.

She pushed the barrel harder against Thompson's head.

'Finish it, Ronni,' Holland whispered.
'They killed your father,' Fuller reminded her.
Justice.
She squeezed the trigger.

102

RONNI WASN'T SURE who screamed the loudest.

Her own yell of rage and frustration was matched by Thompson's caterwaul of terror.

The two sounds melted into one for fleeting seconds, reverberating off the walls of the basement.

She wondered where the roar of the gun was.

Wondered why most of Thompson's head wasn't splattered across the back wall.

She dropped the gun.

It fell to the floor and was hastily retrieved by Fuller.

Ronni stared at the weapon as if it was a venomous serpent.

She stepped back, as if emerging from some monstrous nightmare into the light of reason.

You would have killed that kid.

Fuller was looking at her.

She was aware of the other eyes pinning her in unblinking stares.

You would have killed him.

She began to tremble uncontrollably.

'You see how easy it is?' Fuller said.

'Why didn't the gun go off?' she demanded.

'Because it's empty.' He flipped out the cylinder and spun it. 'It's been empty from the beginning. The bullet I put back in has no primer. It can't be fired. Only three of these bullets are live.' He held them up on the palm of his hand.

'So none of *us* could have killed them?' Holland enquired.

Fuller shook his head. 'It was a game,' he said sardonically, tugging at Thompson's hair. 'Like the games *they* were playing with us.'

'And now it's over, Jack,' Ronni said. 'We've got to call the police.'

'Thirty seconds ago you were prepared to kill one of them. Now you want to save them?'

'This has gone too far.'

'You didn't know that bullet was a dud when you pulled the trigger, Ronni. You would have killed him.'

'Well, I'm glad I didn't. I'm going to call the police. We've got their names. We've heard them confess. The police will be able to do something now.'

'They'll do nothing.'

'They've got to be told.' Ronni turned towards the stairs, but Harry Holland blocked her path. 'Harry,' she murmured. 'Let me pass.'

'What are the police going to say when they arrive, Ronni?' Fuller wanted to know. 'What are they going to say when they find out you held a gun to this boy's head and pulled the trigger?'

Ronni looked at the older man incredulously. 'What are you saying?' she demanded.

'That *your* fingerprints are on the gun too, just like the rest of us.'

'Are you threatening me, Jack?'

'Just pointing out the facts as the police will see them. These kids have been in this basement for nearly two days. Do you think the police are going to believe you knew nothing *about* that? You're in charge here.'

Ronni looked at the other residents.

'Jack's right,' said Donald Tanner.

'What happens if I *do* call the police? Are you going to kill *me*? Where are you going to stop?'

'Call the police and see what happens,' Fuller said challengingly.

Again Ronni regarded the other faces. 'Do you all think the same way as Jack?'

'Yes,' Errington told her.

'They have to be punished,' Helen Kennedy mused.

'What they've done is wrong,' said Eva Cole. 'Not just to us, but to your father too, Ronni.'

'Do you think so little of him that you'd let these bastards walk free?' Errington snapped, jabbing an accusatory finger in the direction of the three captives.

'*They* wouldn't be the ones the police punished,' Harry Holland reminded her. 'You said that yourself. It would be *us*.'

'And you, Ronni,' Fuller reminded her. 'You held the gun. You were prepared to use it. You knew we had them prisoner down here. That makes you an accessory. There are seven of us prepared to testify to that if we have to.'

'This is insane,' she said quietly. 'What do you expect me to do?'

'Help us,' Fuller said.

'To do what? Torture and kill three kids?'

'The kids who attacked your father,' snarled Holland. 'The kids who murdered my Janice. Who made our lives hell.'

'And what do you think Gordon will do when he finds out they're down here?'

'It's up to you to make sure he *doesn't*,' Fuller told her.

Ronni shook her head almost imperceptibly. 'You're no better than them.' She sighed, gesturing towards the captive youths.

'Neither are you, Ronni. You would have killed them all if you could,' said Fuller. 'And you know it. Now you help us. If the police find them here, then we'll all be arrested, but I promise you, we'll take *you* with us.'

She looked into his eyes and saw the anger there.

103

'Go home, Gordon.'

Faulkner looked at Ronni and ran a hand through his hair. 'I said I was tired, I didn't say I wanted to go home,' he told her.

'I know that. I'm telling you to go.'

'Why?'

'Because you're in no fit state to do a day's work.'

'I don't know what the hell is wrong with me. These last two nights . . .' The sentence trailed off.

'Gordon, I'm not angry. I'm telling you to go home for your own sake *and* for mine. You're no good to me the state you're in. I might as *well* be alone here.'

'What about the nights?'

'Everything'll be OK.'

'How can you be sure?'

Because the kids who were terrorizing the place are tied up in the basement.

'We haven't had any trouble for a while, have we?'

Faulkner sipped his coffee and watched the steam rising. 'You look like shit,' he told Ronni, smiling.

'Thanks.'

'You look tired.'

'I didn't sleep very well last night.'

I was down in the basement holding a gun to the head of one of the kids who put my father in a coma.

'I slept like a log again. I needed a Vitamin B shot to wake me up, not an alarm clock.' He grinned.

Ronni attempted a smile, but it was hard work.

Keep up the façade. As you were told.

'I'll be back first thing in the morning, I promise you,' Faulkner said.

She shook her head. 'I'll call you when I need you, Gordon,' Ronni told him. 'How much looking after do the residents need anyway?'

They're capable of capturing and torturing three kids, aren't they?

He regarded her over the rim of his mug and nodded. 'If you're sure,' he murmured.

'I'm *sure*.'

He finished his coffee, got to his feet and left.

Ronni listened to his footsteps echoing away down the corridor.

She reached into the pocket of her jeans and pulled out her father's wedding ring.

The one that had been ripped from his finger after he'd been beaten senseless.

For interminable seconds she gazed at it. She studied every scratch, every subtle change of colour the gold displayed. It was more shiny in some parts than others.

She remembered how her father used to turn it on his finger.

Before he was put in a coma.

Thoughts and images tumbled through her mind.

The captive kids.

Her father lying in that sterile hospital room.

The marks on the kids' bodies.

The gun.

Even thinking about it made her shudder.

Gun.

How the hell had Jack Fuller kept it so well hidden for all these years?

326

She remembered how it had felt in her grip. How much she'd wanted to pull the trigger.

Don't like those thoughts, do you?

How easy it would have been to end the life of the one responsible for putting her father in hospital.

She closed her eyes.

Tried to push those thoughts aside.

They didn't belong. Or did they?

She slipped the ring back into her pocket and got to her feet.

There was something she had to do.

104

THE BASEMENT WAS in darkness.

Despite the fact that it was only late afternoon, the subterranean room had no natural light to brighten it, its one small window having been painted over.

Ronni stood at the top of the stairs, her hand poised over the bank of light switches.

She could hear low breathing.

The stench was there too; fetid and even stronger than the previous night.

She glanced behind her, checking that none of the residents were around, then hurriedly closed the door and slapped on the lights. The fluorescents buzzed into life and Ronni began to descend.

The three youngsters were in virtually the same positions as she'd last seen them.

What did you expect?

Thompson's head was lolling on his chest and his eyes were closed.

So too were Brown's.

Ronni wondered if they were asleep; exhausted by their ordeal and seeking oblivion as their only escape.

Only Donna looked up and Ronni saw the fear in her red-rimmed eyes. She bore little resemblance to the young girl she'd seen in the pub toilet that night; then, she'd smelled of expensive perfume. Now she stank of something else altogether.

Ronni studied the cuts and bruises on her body. The worst were around her wrists and ankles where the rope had first chafed, then chewed into the flesh.

As she moved closer, she heard a low rumbling and realized it was Donna's stomach.

As far as she knew, the trio of youngsters had been given neither food nor drink during their captivity.

Let them starve.

She looked at them, surprised at the vehemence of her thoughts.

Why surprised? They did almost kill your father.

Ronni moved towards Donna and gently eased the tape away from her mouth.

'I'm not going to hurt you,' she said quietly.

Donna tried to swallow but couldn't. Ronni could see how cracked and dry her lips were.

'What do you want?' Donna asked.

'I want to know what's been happening.'

'What does it look like? You heard them last night. They're going to kill us, aren't they?'

'Perhaps they should. Perhaps that's what you deserve. Do you think my father deserved to be beaten almost to death?'

'We didn't know he was your father.'

'It doesn't matter *whose* father it was. You broke into an old man's house, tried to rob him, then attacked him.'

'It was Carl's idea.' She inclined her head towards Thompson.

'You still *did* it though, didn't you? You didn't have to go along with him. You didn't have to join in.'

Donna regarded her balefully. 'What are you going to do?' she asked.

Ronni sucked in a sour breath.

'Are you going to let them kill us?' Donna persisted.

'Would you blame me if I did?'

Brown raised his head and glanced across at her.

Most of the lower half of his body was spattered with his own excrement. He was sitting in it, and there was more beneath the chair.

The stench was vile. He looked utterly degraded; little more than an animal.

One of the cuts on his ankle had already begun to turn septic. The steady dribble of urine down his leg had infected the wound.

Ronni leant across and removed his gag.

He licked his lips and sucked in several deep, racking breaths. He coughed, the spasms almost causing him to overbalance. Finally he hawked loudly and spat some dark-coloured phlegm onto the floor.

Ronni could hear the breath rasping in his lungs.

'Please, can I have a drink?' he said weakly.

'Later,' she told him. 'After we've talked.'

She reached over and pulled the tape from Thompson's mouth too.

The stinging pain stirred him from his stupor.

He jerked his head around and glared at Ronni.

'They'll kill you too if you don't help them,' Donna said.

'No they won't,' Ronni informed her.

Are you sure?

'If they're going to kill *us* they won't want you around as a witness, will they?' Donna continued.

'They're not going to kill you.'

'And you're going to stop them?' Thompson said disdainfully. 'They've got a gun in case you've forgotten.'

'I'd noticed.'

'If you let us go, we'll never come back here again,' Brown told her.

Ronni smiled, bitterly.

'If you won't let us go, then just call the police,' Donna said. 'I'd rather be arrested than kept here.'

'She can't call the police,' Thompson said quietly, his eyes never leaving Ronni. 'Like that old cunt said last night, she's an accessory now. Aren't you?'

Ronni met his gaze and held it.

There was defiance in those bloodshot eyes.

Perhaps you should *have blown the little bastard's head off.*

Ronni pulled her father's wedding ring from her pocket and held it before Thompson.

'Why did you take it?' she wanted to know.

'There was nothing else worth having.'

'Why did you keep it?'

'I don't know. I just put it in my pocket and forgot about it.'

'What were you going to do with it?'

'Sell it. I might have got a few quid for it.'

'I should *let* them kill you. All of you.'

'No, please,' Donna blurted.

'Why not? Who's going to know? Who'd think of looking for you here?'

'Someone'll come for us,' Thompson said flatly. 'Our friends know we're here.'

'You've been here for nearly three days. Don't you think they'd have come by now?' She shook her head. 'You'll never get out. Not without *my* help.'

From the top of the stairs behind her, Ronni heard footsteps. She turned slowly.

Jack Fuller stood there impassively.

105

'Why do you want to help them, Ronni?'

His voice echoed through the basement.

He slowly descended the stairs, Harry Holland and Helen Kennedy close behind him.

'Helen saw you come down here,' Fuller informed her. 'What did you want?'

'I wanted to speak to them myself,' Ronni explained.

'You already know all there is to know,' said Fuller. 'You know what they've done here. You know what they did to your father. What did you expect them to tell you?'

At the top of the stairs, Holland shut the door and stood sentinel there.

'It would have just been more lies, Ronni,' Helen insisted.

Fuller crossed to each of the youngsters in turn and pressed the tape back into place across their mouths.

Helen took Ronni's arm and pulled her gently towards the stairs. 'Come on,' she said quietly.

'The others are waiting,' Fuller told her. He followed them up the stairs, then snapped off the lights.

Behind her, Ronni could hear the sounds of muted weeping.

Harry Holland closed the basement door and locked it.

Ronni pulled away from Helen's surprisingly firm grip and stood before the three residents. 'This has got to end,' she said angrily.

'It will,' Fuller said. 'When they've been punished.'

'Then for Christ's sake get it over with,' snapped Ronni. 'Kill them and have done with it. That's what you want, isn't it?'

'And what do *you* want, Ronni?' Holland asked. 'To let them go? They'd be back here in a day or two and it would all begin again. We've got the chance to stop them once and for all.'

'Harry's right,' Helen added.

'They killed my Janice,' Holland insisted. 'They took the only thing in the world that I cared about from me. *I* won't let you help them.'

'I thought you were on *our* side, Ronni,' Fuller said.

'It isn't a question of sides,' she snapped.

'No, you're right. It's about justice,' Holland told her. 'Justice for my Janice, for *your* father, for all of *us*.'

'Whatever you're going to do to them, I want no part of it,' Ronni said.

'You've got no choice,' Fuller muttered threateningly. 'And you're not walking away from here. I told you before, you're as much a part of this as we are. You'll stay here until it's over.'

Ronni held his gaze.

'If we have to Ronni, we'll treat you like *them*,' Fuller snapped. 'You'll be locked in. Tied up if necessary. Drugged if it's unavoidable.'

Ronni shook her head. 'Jack, what's happened to you?' she whispered. 'And you, Helen? Harry? All of you?'

George Errington stepped from the day room. 'You're either with us or against us, Ronni,' he said, peering over the top of his glasses.

'They deserve everything they get, Veronica,' Barbara Eustace added.

'And when you've finished with *them*,' Ronni murmured. 'Am I next? If I won't help you, will you kill *me*?'

The silence was deafening.

106

IT WAS RINGING, but there was no answer.

Andy Porter waited a moment, then pressed down the cradle and jabbed REDIAL.

As he waited for the phone to be picked up he wedged the receiver between his ear and shoulder and checked he'd got the right number.

He had.

There was no mistake.

SHELBY HOUSE was written on the Post-it note in Ronni's unmistakable hand and, beside it, the number.

It continued to ring.

The number was stuck beside the phone with another list of numbers.

Her father's home.

Not much need for that one at the moment.

The local surgery.

Alison Dean's number.

Gordon Faulkner's too.

And a number of others ranging from an emergency dentist to the local plumber.

The phone was still ringing.

'Come on,' Andy murmured irritably.

'Hello?' said a voice finally.

He didn't recognize it.

'Is that Shelby House?' he said, glancing at the number again.

'Yes.'

'I'd like to speak to Ron— Veronica Porter, please.'

'Who is this?'

'I'm her husband.'

There was a moment's silence at the other end, then he heard a voice he knew.

'Hello, Andy.'

'Ronni, are you all right?' he said.

'Why shouldn't I be?'

'You haven't rung for two nights.'

'You know where I *am*.'

He was puzzled by the acidity of her tone.

'Is everything all right?' he wanted to know.

'What do you mean?'

'Has there been any more bother there? You know, with—'

'I said everything's all right.'

Again that sharpness.

There was an awkward silence, finally broken by Andy.

'How's your dad?'

'There's no change.'

'Have you been to see him?'

'I rang the hospital.'

'I was thinking of going to see him.'

'You don't have to do that.'

'I know I don't *have* to,' he snapped.

'Look, Andy, do you want something? I'm busy.'

'I was checking you were all right,' he hissed, irritated by her manner. 'I don't know why I fucking bothered. When are you coming home?'

'I don't know. When all this is over.'

'Ronni—'

'Don't ring here again, Andy. It disturbs the residents.'

She hung up.

*

Ronni kept her hand on the receiver for a moment, then turned slowly in her chair.

Colin Glazer, Donald Tanner and Harry Holland stood gazing intently at her.

'Well done, Ronni,' Glazer said.

'And now what?' she said challengingly. 'Are you going to take me back to my room and lock me in?'

'If you co-operate there'll be no need for that,' Holland told her.

She regarded each of them in turn.

'Could you come to the day room with us, please?' said Tanner. 'We've been discussing this matter and we've reached a decision.'

107

THE DAY ROOM was unusually silent, Ronni thought as she seated herself. The television was nothing more than a blank eye in one corner; she could see herself reflected in its polished glass.

The residents watched her with the kind of detached indifference a cat reserves for a cornered mouse.

How appropriate.

'I understand you've been discussing things,' she said finally.

Eight pairs of eyes looked on coldly.

'What kind of things?' Ronni persisted. 'How to dispose of the bodies? What to do with me?'

She looked at the eight residents before her and thoughts tumbled through her mind.

If she made a run for it now, she'd reach the main doors. That wasn't a problem.

But *they* had the key.

She glanced at the windows.

She could reach them easily, break them too, but they were still secured by the makeshift bars erected days earlier.

And even if she got out . . . what then? Find the nearest phone? Call the police?

Ronni sucked in a weary breath.

'We think you're right,' Jack Fuller began. 'Those kids have been here long enough.'

Ronni almost managed a smile. 'Are you going to let them go?'

'You know what will happen if we do, Ronni. That's something *else* we've discussed.'

'So what's the point of this meeting, then?' She gestured around her at the residents.

'We've decided to carry out their punishments tonight,' Fuller said flatly. 'Then they'll be released.'

Ronni frowned. 'What kind of punishments?' she asked warily.

'Ones to fit their crimes,' George Errington told her, looking over the top of his glasses.

'What are you planning to do to them?'

'If you don't want to be a part of it, you don't have to,' Fuller said. 'It might be best if you weren't.'

'As soon as you let them go they'll bring the police back here. Or worse,' she protested.

'No they won't,' Harry Holland told her.

'How can you be so sure?'

'They won't be back, Ronni,' Fuller told her. 'Not after tonight.'

'Punishments to fit their crimes, Veronica,' Barbara Eustace echoed.

'And who's going to do it?' Ronni demanded. 'Whatever it is you're planning. Who's going to carry out this ... punishment you've decided on? You, Harry? You, Eva?'

'All of us,' Fuller informed her. 'They wronged us *all*. We'll *all* make them pay.'

She ran a hand through her hair. 'You're no better than a lynch-mob,' she murmured, shaking her head. 'You can't take the law into your own hands like this.'

'By the end of the night it'll be over,' Fuller assured her.

'We can go back to living our lives.'

'With three deaths on your conscience?'

'No one said anything about killing them, Ronni. Though, God knows, they deserve it.'

'Tell me what you're going to do,' she demanded.

Silence.

'Tell me.'

Motes of dust turned lazily in the shafts of watery sunlight poking into the day room.

Nothing else moved.

108

Do something.

But what?

Think.

There must be something you can do.

Ronni paced the locked room again and gazed in the direction of the window.

Think.

She slid the sash open and peered out.

How far to the ground? Fifteen feet? Twenty? Far enough to break both legs if you land badly.

There wasn't even anything beneath the window to break her fall. No bushes. No handy tree she could scramble into the branches of and shin down.

No, that only worked in films, didn't it?

No passing man walking his dog to shout at.

That was one from the movies too. Or the old one about throwing the crumpled note from the window and a passer-by finding it.

It didn't work in real life.

Ronni looked up at the guttering that overhung the window.

Don't even think about it.

Even if it would support her meagre weight

(*which she doubted*)

and supposing she managed to haul herself up onto the roof . . .

What then?

Sit there like some prisoner on protest, lobbing slates off until someone came?

But no one *would* come, would they?

Shelby House, set within its own grounds, was invisible from the road. No one was going to pass by. No one was going to see some crazy woman up on the roof signalling for help.

On the far side of the room, the telephone cable had been cut clean through with a Stanley knife.

No way of reconnecting that.

Even if someone *did* come, what was she going to tell them?

There are three missing kids in the basement who are all due to be punished tonight by the residents. These frail, harmless old people who live here? That's right.

They've kept the kids prisoner for three days. Starved them, beaten them, threatened them with a gun and tonight they're going to do something awful to them. No, I don't know what it is, but I'm sure it's bad.

Why are they doing it? Oh, the kids had been terrorizing them for over a week and the police can't do anything about it. One of the residents had her dog butchered by them and another died of shock when she found the dead animal.

What? Yes, they're the same kids who beat my father so badly he's in a coma. Look, I've got the wedding ring they stole from him. See?

Can you help me get them out?

Why do I want to help them? Well, I'm not really sure . . .

Ronni stopped pacing and sat on the edge of the bed.

The sultry afternoon had given way to an overcast evening. She saw the banks of dark cloud gathering like premonitory warnings.

She hadn't struggled when Harry Holland and Helen Kennedy had escorted her upstairs to her room and locked her in.

What was she supposed to do? Knock them out and make a run for it?

She had even accepted the cup of tea that Helen had made for her.

Quite civilized, really. Most people who kept you prisoner, so she'd read, usually cut your ears off or beat you.

Ronni might have laughed if the situation hadn't been so ludicrous.

For one fleeting second, she wondered what the residents were going to do to the three captives.

What kind of punishment was fitting?

Again she looked out of the window, gazing out across the grounds.

She glanced at her watch: 6.35 p.m.

An hour earlier, Eva Cole had tapped lightly on the door and asked if Ronni had wanted anything to eat.

She hadn't.

Another hour passed before she heard movement outside the door again.

Night had flooded the sky.

She crossed to the door and listened to the sounds of many feet in the corridor.

She heard a key being turned in the lock of the room opposite.

She thought she heard soft whimpering.

Then the door opposite slammed shut.

It opened briefly about ten minutes later and she heard more footsteps.

Slow and deliberate. They disappeared down the stairs, then returned a moment or two later.

Ronni turned the handle of her room as if expecting that the door would have magically unlocked itself.

Needless to say, it hadn't.

She pressed her ear to the wood and listened.

'Ronni.'

The voice startled her, but she didn't answer.

Perhaps whoever was outside would come in. You could overpower them and get out.

'Ronni.'

She recognized the voice of Jack Fuller.

She didn't answer but instead tried to control her breathing.

He didn't twist the handle.

The key didn't turn in the lock.

Ronni heard the door of the room opposite open, then slam shut once more.

Within ten minutes, she heard the first scream.

109

Donna Freeman didn't know their names.

She didn't really care.

All that mattered to her was getting out.

She thought that if she co-operated then they might treat her better. That was why she hadn't struggled when two of the old men had come down into the basement and untied her.

They had left the tape around her mouth, but at last they had released her from the ropes that had cut so deeply into her ankles and wrists for so long.

When she'd first stood up, she'd needed their arms to support her. Her body felt numb from the waist downwards. The joints of her knees, ankles and hips – held in virtually the same position for three days – felt as if they'd locked. Donna pressed her bare feet down hard on the stone floor as if trying to restore the circulation.

After a moment or two, she felt able to walk on her own and allowed herself to be guided towards the stairs.

She glanced behind her at the still-bound forms of Carl Thompson and Graham Brown.

Donna was halfway up the stairs when a thought struck her.

Why had they untied her?

She wanted to ask. She grunted into the tape, but Colin Glazer merely coaxed her gently up the remaining steps, then slapped off the lights behind him, plunging the basement back into darkness.

Donna was shivering; a combination of hunger, cold and fear.

The lights in the corridor made her wince.

Her soiled knickers stuck to her buttocks as she walked.

Another set of steps.

Up to the first floor of the building.

And now she saw the other old people emerging from another room to her right.

They followed her and the two old men with her like some kind of procession.

What the fuck was going on?

If only they'd take off the tape. She could tell them how sorry she was. How it was the other two, down in the basement, who'd been responsible.

She slowed her pace slightly, but Donald Tanner pulled at her arm and forced her onwards.

They reached the landing and Colin Glazer moved ahead to unlock a door.

The other old people followed, their eyes fixed on her.

Donna was shuddering more violently now, despite the fact that there was a radiator on her left. She could feel the heat, but it did little to stop the quivering.

Glazer stood back and ushered the little procession into the room.

Donna allowed herself to be pushed gently across the threshold.

The room was in darkness but for two bedside lights burning on cabinets on either side of the single bed.

The bed itself had been stripped down to the bare mattress.

More and more of the old people crowded into the room, pushing her towards the bed.

The straps were hanging down at the sides, top and bottom.

Thick, leather straps that would be fastened with heavy buckles.

Donna hesitated.

Was she merely going from one place of captivity to another?

She looked at each face in turn and saw only indifference.

Jack Fuller pointed towards the bed.

Donna knelt on it, then lay down on her back.

The straps were fastened quickly and expertly.

One tightly across her chest, forcing the breath from her.

Another across her stomach.

Helen Kennedy wound one around her left wrist and pulled, so that Donna's arm was stretched towards the bedhead.

Eva Cole imitated the action with her right.

Harry Holland gripped her right ankle while Colin Glazer took her left. They fastened the two straps, pulling hard so that her legs were apart.

Donna's heart was thudding against her ribs. Her eyes moved frantically back and forth.

As she looked to her left, she caught sight of a low table beside the bed that she'd not seen until now.

It was little more than a coffee table.

Donna's eyes bulged in the sockets and she began to buck madly against the straps. She tried to scream and felt tears welling up in her eyes once more, trickling hotly down her cheeks.

For long moments, she twisted against the straps, then finally flopped uselessly back onto the bare mattress, sweat beading on her forehead and top lip.

Helen Kennedy took a step forward.

Donna shook her head imploringly.

She continued to stare at what lay on the table.

110

RONNI COULD CONTAIN herself no longer.

She gripped the door handle and twisted it hard.

Nothing happened.

'Open the door,' she called.

No one came.

She banged hard on the wood with the flat of her hand, slamming it repeatedly until her palm throbbed.

They must be able to hear her – they were only across the corridor.

They can *hear you. They're ignoring you. They've got other things on their minds.*

Ronni kicked the bottom of the door angrily, leaving a scuff mark on the paint.

What the hell were they doing in that room?

She tried to swallow, but her throat was dry.

She could hear the blood pounding in her ears, her heart thumping against her ribs.

Again she hammered on the door, using both fists this time.

It was useless.

Ronni took a couple of steps back and looked around the room for something heavy.

Perhaps if she could smash the lock . . .

She could see nothing weighty enough.

A chair?

No good.

She needed something she could grip. Something she could use to batter away at the lock until it splintered and buckled.

There was nothing.

She stepped towards the partition once again and began hammering frantically on the wood with her fists.

They would have to come eventually.

Eva Cole paused for a moment when she heard the thudding of flesh against wood. She looked in the direction of the noise, then at Jack Fuller, who merely nodded. Helen understood.

She crossed to the small, low table and regarded the objects that lay upon it.

A large pair of scissors.

Several needles.

Some black thread.

(which she herself had provided)

Two Stanley knives.

One clawhammer.

A bolt-cutter.

Three pairs of pliers and an assortment of screwdrivers and chisels.

(courtesy of Jack Fuller's toolbox)

Some secateurs.

(from George Errington)

Two fishing hooks.

(brought in by Donald Tanner)

A bottle of iodine, some gauze and bandages.

(taken from the pharmacy by Harry Holland)

Three small handtowels, neatly folded.

Donna was weeping quietly, the sound muffled by the tape across her mouth.

The residents moved closer.

Ronni stood against the door, her fists red. Her arms ached and her head was beginning to throb.

Why hadn't they come? Even if it was only to shut her up.

She raised one hand and struck weakly at the door. Then she backed off and sat on the edge of the bed, staring at the handle as if that would cause it to turn.

What were they doing in that room across the corridor?

Again she looked at the severed telephone cable on the other side of the room.

And if it was connected, who would you ring?

Desperation. Anxiety. Anger.

Emotions whirled around inside her head until she felt her skull would explode.

And, strongest of all, was the crushing feeling of helplessness.

Ronni ran a hand through her hair and approached the door once more.

If you pound away long enough, they've got to come.

She began hammering on the door again.

111

DONNA FREEMAN FELT the pliers being slipped over her index finger and manoeuvred as far as the second knuckle. She sensed the pressure on the bone increasing and, with horror, realized what Errington was about to do.

The jaws of the pliers tightened.

Donna tried to scream through the gag and fresh tears began to drench her cheeks.

She tried desperately to pull her hands free, but her wrists were gripped too tightly.

'I–I'm not sure about this,' Glazer murmured. 'Look at her. Look at what we're *doing*.'

'Just keep your fucking mouth shut and do what you're told,' Fuller rasped, drawing glances from the other residents before returning their gaze to the girl squirming on the mattress. 'I won't have anybody go weak on me now.'

Glazer gulped and nodded.

Errington adjusted his grip on the twin handles of the pliers and prepared to put all his weight into the cut.

It shouldn't be too difficult.

The jaws were sharp and the girl's fingers were slim.

The bone wouldn't be too thick.

He pushed his glasses back on his nose with one finger, then used both hands on the pliers, increasing the pressure.

A thin trickle of blood dribbled from the split skin.

Donna continued to shriek in agony; it sounded like someone bellowing through a pillow.

Errington pressed down, his teeth gritted with the effort. He heard the crack of bone, then the jaws of the pliers cut almost effortlessly through the digit.

The severed end fell to the floor.

Errington completed his task, the middle fingers severed with similar speed, and was surprised at how much blood there was. They had come off with relative ease. Donna had blacked out by the time he had got to the third finger.

Blood jetted from the stump of the little finger and he moved back slightly as the crimson spurts almost splashed his trousers. The radial arteries spouted uncontrollably from the mutilated hands, some soaking into the mattress.

There was more on the floor on either side of the bed.

Helen Kennedy gathered the severed fingers and wrapped them in a towel.

Donna's body was quivering slightly. Fuller thought it must be an unconscious state of shock.

He took the pliers from Errington and wiped them on the mattress, then reached for the gag that covered Donna's mouth. 'We'll do this while she's out. It'll be easier,' he said. 'We'd better sit her up.'

He tore the tape free while Donald Tanner and Eva Cole undid the straps that held Donna so securely to the bed.

Tanner slid his hands beneath her armpits and dragged her upright, her head lolling forward onto her chest, her dishwater-blonde hair spilling across her shoulders.

'Hold her head, Harry,' Fuller said.

Holland crouched beside the bed and did as he was instructed.

There was a thin ribbon of mucus trickling from one corner of Donna's mouth, but Holland ignored it and prised open her mouth.

He gripped her hair tightly, holding her head immobile, then he used his thumb and index finger to reach into her mouth and pull her tongue into view.

Fuller nodded.

Eva Cole handed him the secateurs.

Ronni raised the chair above her head, then hurled it at the door with a furious grunt.

The wooden structure simply disintegrated under the impact.

Two of the legs came away, the seat splintered and the back broke up into half a dozen pieces of varying lengths and thicknesses.

Ronni surveyed the destruction, then picked up one of the chair legs, hefting it before her like a club. She began whacking the door handle with as much force as she could muster.

Perspiration beaded on her forehead and she could feel her blouse sticking to her back as she continued with her furious assault.

The handle bent under the sustained attack.

Inspired by her moment of triumph, Ronni redoubled her efforts.

Paint began to flake away as she battered the door, dents appearing in the partition as stray blows missed their target.

She couldn't be sure how long she'd been smashing away at the handle when she heard someone in the corridor outside call her name.

Ronni struck the door two or three more times, then backed off, her breath coming in gasps.

'Open the door!' she shouted defiantly.

Silence.

'Let me out!' Ronni persisted.

She heard the unmistakable sound of the key turning in the lock and, a second later, the door opened.

Colin Glazer stood there, looking first at Ronni's sweat-sheathed face, then at the lump of wood she held.

Donald Tanner was behind him.

'What are you going to do with that?' Glazer asked, nodding towards the chair leg.

Ronni sucked in a deep breath and dropped the wood. 'What's going on?' she demanded. 'Who's in that room?' She pointed past the two men towards the door opposite.

'The girl,' Tanner told her.

Ronni took a step towards the two men and was surprised when they both allowed her to pass.

'You *should* see, Ronni,' Tanner said flatly.

'What have you done to her?'

'What she deserved,' Glazer said softly, as if convincing himself.

'A punishment to fit her crimes,' Tanner added.

Ronni moved towards the door, listening for any sounds from within.

There were none.

Had they killed her?

One part of her wanted to rush into the room. The other was afraid to.

'Go in,' Tanner instructed. He pushed open the door and it swung lazily back on its hinges.

Ronni paused at the threshold. She could see Harry Holland, Helen Kennedy and George Errington standing in the dimly lit room peering in the direction of the bed.

'Come in, Ronni,' Jack Fuller called.

As she stepped inside she was aware of a powerful coppery odour.

There was something repulsively familiar about the stench.

As she moved into the room, she realized what it was.

She looked in the direction of the bed.

Then wished she hadn't.

112

RONNI DIDN'T KNOW whether to scream or vomit.

She did neither.

She merely dropped to her knees, her eyes bulging madly in the sockets, transfixed by the sight before her.

At first she wondered if what she was staring at was some kind of bizarre joke.

The figure that was propped up on the bed didn't look like a human being. It bore more resemblance to a blood-drenched mannequin.

The crimson fluid was smeared all over it.

The lank, dishwater-blonde hair was matted with it.

The bare mattress was sodden.

The pale flesh was spattered too.

The hands looked as if they'd been dipped in red paint.

When Ronni saw that the fingers and thumbs had been cut off she felt her stomach somersault.

The girl's bra was soaked in blood, most of which seemed to have come from her face and head.

As her head lolled back against the wall, Ronni saw why.

Her mouth was open, but it resembled little more than an open wound, filled with dark clots of blood. Through the tumescent lumps, Ronni could see several cracked teeth. There was also a small cut on the bottom lip that was pumping out fresh crimson fluid.

The whites of Donna's eyes were now pure red, gleaming in the half-light like some creature from a nightmare.

'What have you done to her eyes?' she gasped, barely able to force the words out.

There was blood and clear liquid running down Donna's cheeks.

'What have you done?' Ronni repeated, her voice little more than a whisper.

'Punished her,' said Fuller flatly.

'She desecrated her *own* body,' Donald Tanner said. 'Abused it. Look at those marks on her arms – she injected filth into her veins regularly.'

He indicated the track marks in the crook of her arms. 'Now she's got some *other* piercings,' Tanner hissed.

'Oh my God,' Ronni murmured.

'You were right, Ronni,' Fuller admitted. 'If we'd released her she would have told the police what went on here. They *all* would. *We'd* have been the ones in trouble and that isn't right.'

'Now she *can't* tell anyone what happened,' George Errington added.

'You've killed her,' Ronni said, staring hypnotically at Donna's ravaged body.

'She's not dead,' Fuller assured her. 'We'll release her soon. *And* the others when we've punished them too.'

'The police will come,' Ronni insisted.

'Why should they?' Fuller challenged. 'Why should they suspect *us*? And, as I said, no one will be able to say what happened here.'

Ronni felt a wave of nausea sweep over her and she took a step back. Helen Kennedy put out a hand to steady her.

'We cut off her fingers so she couldn't write down who had done this to her,' Fuller began. 'We cut out her tongue so she couldn't *tell* anyone. We blinded her so she couldn't find her way back here and identify us.'

Ronni finally managed to tear her horrified gaze from Donna's immobile form. She put a hand over her mouth.

'We'll do the same to the others,' Fuller continued.

'This is madness,' Ronni said, shaking her head. 'You're all insane.'

The coppery stench of blood filled her nostrils and she gritted her teeth as she fought back the urge to vomit.

'We've finished with her now,' Fuller insisted, nodding towards the bed and its reeking, bloodied occupant.

Colin Glazer and Harry Holland crossed to Donna. One slid his hands beneath her armpits, the other grabbed her ankles and they carried her out of the room.

Ronni saw some drops of blood dripping onto the polished floor of the corridor.

'She'll die,' snapped Ronni.

'No she won't,' Fuller said with an air of certainty. 'Her wounds have been treated correctly. She's lost some blood, but not enough to kill her.'

'And you'd know, wouldn't you, Jack?'

'I *was* a medical orderly, Ronni.'

'You're a butcher,' Ronni snarled angrily.

'If you don't want to watch, I suggest you go back to your room,' Fuller told her.

'Who's next?' she wanted to know.

'Brown. The youngest.'

'And you're going to mutilate him the same way?'

'We're going to punish him, yes.'

Ronni slumped back against the wall, her head spinning.

From below, she heard footsteps ascending.

113

ANDY PORTER GAZED at the television screen, but little of what he saw registered.

He reached for the mug of tea on the table beside him and took a sip.

Cold.

He winced.

He thought about making himself a hot one, but once he wandered out into the kitchen the idea didn't seem so enticing.

Andy glanced across at the phone on the wall.

The list of numbers pinned next to it.

The doctor.

The emergency dentist.

The hospital.

Various friends.

Shelby House.

'Don't ring here again, it disturbs the residents.'

Ronni's words still echoed in his ears.

Andy crossed to the phone and ran his gaze down the list of numbers.

He paused when he reached that belonging to Alison Dean.

He picked up the receiver.

What are you doing? Why are you calling her?

He pressed down on the cradle.

Gordon Faulkner.

What's the point in ringing him? He works with Ronni.

357

Andy had met him once or twice. He seemed a decent enough bloke.

He should be doing night shifts at Shelby House, not Ronni. Especially with what had been going on there lately. A woman shouldn't be left alone there at night. Especially not his own wife.

He looked at Alison's number again.

She and Ronni had been friends for years. Perhaps she'd know what was going on. Why Ronni hadn't been home for two nights.

Again he pressed the handset to his ear and, this time, he jabbed the first three digits of the number. He hesitated a moment, then pressed the others.

At the other end it was ringing.

And ringing.

'Come on,' Andy murmured.

There was a connection.

He heard a voice.

Fuck it. Answering machine.

He put down the phone and turned away irritably.

As he did, the phone rang. Andy snatched it up.

'Hello?' he said, wondering if it might actually be Ronni.

He didn't recognize the voice.

'Could I speak to Mrs Veronica Porter, please?' it said.

'This is her husband. Can I take a message?'

'Yes. We've been trying to contact your wife—'

'Who *is* this?' Andy asked, cutting the caller short.

'Doctor Greenwood. We met at the hospital when your father-in-law was admitted.'

'Right, sorry. Is he all right?'

'Yes, Mr Porter, I'm delighted to say he's woken from his coma. Obviously it's still early days, but there seems to be definite progress.'

'And my wife doesn't know that?'

'She asked me to call her at work if there were any developments, but I haven't been able to reach her.'

'How long ago did you try?'

'I've tried several times in the last two hours, but there's no answer.'

Andy frowned and glanced at his watch. 11.26 p.m.

'Mr Porter?'

'Sorry. *I'll* call her, Doctor, and thanks for ringing.'

He hung up.

Andy dialled the number of Shelby House and waited.

He gave it ten rings. He actually counted them. Then he hung up and tried again.

This time he waited even longer.

Nothing.

'Fuck this,' he rasped, hanging up.

He wandered through the living room and into the hall where he pulled on his leather jacket.

From his pocket he took his car keys.

114

Ronni stood motionless as Graham Brown was led into the room.

Colin Glazer held one of his arms, Donald Tanner the other.

He was doing little to resist and, to Ronni, it looked as if the two older men were merely dragging him.

His head was bowed and Ronni thought she heard him whimpering quietly.

She wrinkled her nose slightly as she smelled the stench of excrement. His underpants were smeared with it.

As he looked up, Brown saw the blood on the mattress and began to shudder. He strained against the strong hands that gripped him, then seemed to give up and allowed himself to be pushed towards the bed.

Ronni could hear him murmuring something under his breath.

It took her a moment or two to work out what it was.

'I'm sorry,' Brown whispered. The constant intonation sounding like a litany.

She saw him lay back on the bed.

Saw Harry Holland reach for one of the leather straps.

Saw the tears in Brown's eyes.

'Please don't do this,' Ronni said, looking at Jack Fuller. 'Call the police.'

Fuller looked straight through her. 'What's the point?' he said flatly.

'I'm sorry,' Brown continued, looking around at the determined faces glaring at him.

He found he was sitting in a puddle of congealing blood.

There were small fragments of bone on one edge of the mattress.

He began to shudder even more uncontrollably.

George Errington reached for another of the straps.

'For God's sake,' Ronni gasped.

Brown was sitting with his knees drawn up, his head resting on them. He glanced to his left and saw the low table and its selection of bloodied implements.

Fuller nodded and George Errington reached for one of the boy's arms.

'Please don't hurt me,' Brown groaned.

Errington prepared to fasten the strap in position.

'Don't do this,' Ronni said breathlessly.

Fuller reached for a pair of the pliers. 'Strap him down,' the former medical orderly said.

Brown lashed out with a suddeness that caught everyone by surprise. He caught George Errington across the face with a blow that sent him reeling. One of the lenses was driven from the frames of his glasses. As he stepped back, the glass crunched beneath his foot.

Brown snatched up the secateurs and gripped them in one defiant fist. He struck out with the heavy blades and caught Donald Tanner across the back of one hand.

'You fucking cunts,' he snarled and sprung off the bed.

Ronni saw him lunge past Colin Glazer towards the door.

Helen Kennedy tried to grab him, but he pushed her aside with ease and a strength born of desperation. The older woman fell heavily against the door and Brown vaulted her body.

He was into the corridor now.

'Stop him!' shouted Fuller, hurrying out in pursuit.

Brown hurled the secateurs and they slammed into the wall close to Ronni's head.

She saw him standing motionless in the corridor for long seconds, unsure of where to run.

Unsure of how to escape.

The stairs were blocked by Fuller and Harry Holland.

Brown hurtled down the corridor towards the window at the far end.

Eva Cole was helping Helen Kennedy to her feet, the other residents were pursuing Brown.

Fuller still clutched a pair of pliers.

Tanner had snatched up the clawhammer.

Errington, squinting through his one remaining lens, bent to retrieve the secateurs.

Holland was holding the boltcutter.

Ronni saw Brown tug at several doors along the corridor.

They were all locked.

He looked back at the steadily advancing residents, then turned and glanced at the sash window again.

The fury and bravado on his face had been replaced by fear and desperation.

He struggled with the lock on the window, but it wouldn't budge.

The residents were close now.

Less than ten yards from him.

Ronni saw the realization in his eyes.

There was only one hope and he knew it.

115

BROWN DIDN'T HESITATE. He drove his fist through the glass and the entire pane disintegrated.

Huge shards of crystal exploded into the night. Some of the lethal points cut his arm and hand. Blood spurted onto the white frame of the window.

The youth hauled himself through the window, fragments of glass gouging the flesh of his back and legs.

He struggled onto the outside sill and balanced precariously there before reaching up towards the guttering.

'*No!*' screamed Ronni.

Brown dug his fingers into the plastic piping and began to haul himself upwards, towards the roof.

Harry Holland prepared to grab the boy, but Fuller held him back.

Brown felt searing pain in both shoulders as he tried to support his weight on his arms.

Ronni saw him trying to get a foothold on the brickwork.

There was an ominous creak from above him and the guttering snapped under his grip.

Brown tried to climb more quickly.

He could feel the slates of the roof against his fingertips.

If only he could pull himself up . . .

A portion of the guttering came free and fell to the ground twenty feet below.

Brown shouted in fear, but clung on.

'Pull him back in,' Ronni shouted frantically. 'He's going to fall.'

'Leave him,' snarled Fuller.

Brown felt the cold wind whipping around him.

Felt his grip loosening.

Felt the guttering split once again.

Had he been stronger he may have been able to hold on, but Ronni doubted it.

The guttering came away with a loud crack.

Brown was still clutching it when he fell.

He had time for one short scream, then he hit the ground with a sickening thud.

Ronni pushed past Harry Holland and gazed down at the boy's prone body. A steadily widening pool of blood was spreading around his head.

For interminable seconds no one moved; then Fuller touched Colin Glazer on the shoulder.

'Bring him back inside,' he said and Glazer hurried towards the stairs, accompanied by Donald Tanner.

'He's dead, Jack,' Ronni snarled. 'Satisfied?'

Fuller gazed down at the boy.

116

THEY DIDN'T BOTHER trying to carry the body.

They merely took a leg each and pulled.

Colin Glazer and Donald Tanner dragged Graham Brown's corpse across the wet grass towards the stone steps leading up to the main entrance of Shelby House.

What was left of the head bumped against each of the stairs. Portions of shattered skull stuck on the stone. They left a trail of blood across the porch.

Glazer thought that it would have to be cleaned up.

There was lots of it.

They pulled the dead youth into the corridor, careful not to step in the crimson fluid still pouring out from his pulverized cranium.

Tanner locked the main door once again, then looked questioningly at his companion.

They both heard footsteps on the stairs.

'Put him in the basement with the others,' Jack Fuller called.

'And what then, Jack?' Ronni demanded, watching as Brown's body was dragged along the polished floor, the familiar crimson trail marking its passage.

'We'll bury him later,' Fuller said. 'In the grounds.'

Barbara Eustace appeared in the doorway of the day room. She manoeuvred her wheelchair so that she was close to Ronni, one of her tyres leaving a pattern on the floor as it rolled through the wide streak of blood. The older woman barely blinked as she watched Brown being hauled away in the direction of the basement. 'What about the other one?' she asked.

'We'll deal with him next,' said Fuller. 'It'll be all over then.'

'All over?' Ronni rasped. 'It's only just starting. You've killed someone. That boy is dead.' She jabbed a finger in the direction of Brown's corpse.

'He died while trying to break in,' Fuller said, flatly.

'Is that your story? Have you had it prepared from the beginning? Just in case?' She looked at the other faces too.

'No one will know any different,' Harry Holland offered.

'There's no reason why he should ever be found,' George Errington added, squinting through the one remaining lens of his spectacles.

Ronni ran a hand through her hair. She felt like tearing the brown strands from her scalp in frustration.

'Take the tools into the basement,' Fuller said, turning to his companions. 'We'll finish it there.'

Harry Holland and Donald Tanner hurried upstairs to recover the items they needed.

Fuller himself moved off towards his room and disappeared inside.

Ronni looked around her helplessly.

Colin Glazer nudged open the door of the basement and slapped on the lights, then he stepped inside and hauled Brown's body in behind him. He pushed the dead youth and watched as the body tumbled down the stairs, landing heavily at the bottom.

Carl Thompson looked up, his eyes wide.

Beside him, tied to a chair once more, Donna Freeman was unconscious.

Blood was still dribbling from her mouth and dripping from the stumps of her fingers.

Ronni glanced down the corridor towards the main doors.

The keys were still in the lock.

If she could reach them she could slip out.

As easy as that. Just run. Let yourself out, then lock the door from the outside. Go on. Do it.

She ran as fast as her legs would carry her, avoiding the trail of blood that slicked the shining floor.

Eva Cole shot out a hand to grab her, but missed.

Ronni was already half-way down the corridor.

She didn't look back.

She had her hand on the key.

Just a quick turn and you're free. Out of this madhouse.

'Get away from the door.'

She recognized Jack Fuller's voice.

Ronni turned the key.

'Get away from there or I swear to God I'll kill you,' he bellowed.

Ronni glanced back in the direction of the shout.

Fuller had the Smith & Wesson .38 gripped in his fist.

The weapon was aimed at Ronni.

117

'LOCK THE DOOR and step away from it.'

Ronni looked first at the yawning barrel of the pistol, then at Fuller's face.

She thought about telling him that he was bluffing. That he wouldn't shoot her.

She remained motionless, her hand on the key.

'Lock it,' Fuller shouted.

Still Ronni hesitated.

Fuller raised the weapon so that it was pointed at her head.

Ronni could feel her heart thudding madly against her ribs.

She held his gaze, her hand still on the key.

Fuller thumbed back the hammer. 'I won't let you stop us *now*, Ronni,' he said quietly.

She removed her hand slowly.

'What would you have done if you'd got out?' he enquired. 'Gone to the police? Told them what had happened here? I suppose you'd have said we were to blame. That you were no part of it. Do you think they'd have believed you? I told you before, you're as guilty as *we* are in the eyes of the law.'

Ronni stood gazing at the .38. She didn't doubt for one second that, if he was forced to, Jack Fuller would use the gun.

'Bring me the key,' he demanded and she took it from the lock without a second thought.

Fuller accepted it and dropped it into his pocket.

He pressed the gun against Ronni's temple.

As she felt the cold metal she almost screamed.

'You could have made it so easy,' Fuller snarled.

Ronni closed her eyes, her body shuddering. 'Jack, please—'

He cut her short. 'Don't beg like one of *those* little bastards,' he hissed, pushing the barrel harder against her head.

She felt his hand on her shoulder, pushing her towards the basement.

Apart from Barbara Eustace, the other residents were already gathered in the subterranean room.

Waiting.

'I thought you would have helped us, Veronica,' said Barbara, a note of disappointment in her voice.

Ronni allowed herself to be shoved through the basement door.

There was blood on the door frame and the stairs and as she looked down she could see Graham Brown's body lying spread-eagled on the stone floor.

'You'll never get away with this, Jack,' Ronni said. 'Please stop now.'

'Why?' Fuller wanted to know.

She had no answer.

As they reached the top of the stairs she turned to face him.

It was then that Fuller pushed her.

Ronni clutched at empty air for a second, then fell. She screamed briefly before the sound subsided into a moan of pain as she tumbled down the stairs, her head connecting sharply with the steps, her shoes flying loose.

She bounced off the last step and cracked her head hard against the stone floor, blacking out for several seconds.

She was aware of something warm and wet running down the side of her face and she realized she'd cut her head open.

As she tried to rise, she saw Brown's battered face only inches from her.

His eyes were still open, fixing her in a sightless stare.

Again she tried to drag herself upright.

She saw Fuller descending the stairs, the gun still in his hand.
Several of the other residents were advancing towards her.
Her head throbbed.
She couldn't focus.
Nausea gripped her and she knew she was going to pass out.
The floor felt cold beneath her.
She hoped it might keep her conscious.
It didn't.

118

WHY THE HELL were the lights out?

Andy Porter peered through the Peugeot's windscreen and wondered why Shelby House was in darkness.

The tyres crunched gravel as he guided the car slowly up the long driveway towards the building, his headlights cutting through the blackness.

It was late, but not *one* light anywhere, inside *or* out?

Was something wrong?

He glanced to his left and right, looking for any signs of movement in the tall bushes that flanked the driveway.

If those kids had come back, there was no telling what had happened.

Surely there should be some kind of security lighting.

A room light or . . .

As he followed the gentle curve of the drive he finally spotted some lights inside the building.

He assumed they were in residents' rooms.

One on the ground floor. One on the first floor.

But that was it.

Andy brought the car to a halt and switched off the engine. He swung himself out of the vehicle, struck immediately by the solitude.

The building was further back from the road than he'd realized. What little traffic noise there was barely registered.

Andy stood beside the car for a moment and lit a cigarette. He took a deep drag on it, then set off for the main doors of Shelby House.

He saw the blood as he reached the steps.

Lots of it.

Was it blood?

He knelt and slowly pushed one index finger into the crimson fluid.

He rolled it between his fingertips. Sniffed it.

It was blood. No mistake. No joke.

Some had begun to congeal, but most of it was still glistening wetly.

Andy could see the trail led right up to the doors.

He wiped his fingertips on his jeans and glanced in the direction from which the trail had come.

He saw more blood on the grass nearby.

His heart began to thump a little quicker as he followed the crimson slick past several ground-floor windows.

Past the makeshift bars that guarded them.

Just what the hell had *been going on here?*

There was a large puddle of fluid just ahead of him. It had sprayed out several feet in all directions and he could see splashes on the walls of the building.

He heard a noise behind him.

Andy spun round, his breath clouding in the air.

Was someone watching him from the bushes?

He squinted into the blackness, but could see nothing.

There was a torch in the car. If only he'd brought it with him.

He hurried back around to the front of the building, following the trail of blood onto the porch.

Again he looked across the well-manicured lawns towards bushes and trees, but saw nothing.

He took a final drag on his cigarette, then tossed the butt away.

For fleeting seconds, he wondered if he should just get in his car and drive to the nearest phonebox. Get the police now.

Show them what he'd found.

Tell them he could get no answer from the phones at Shelby House.

No. It could wait.

He ran a hand through his hair and prepared to knock on the main doors.

119

RONNI COULDN'T MOVE.

At first she thought that the fall had paralysed her.

That the bang on the head had affected the feeling in her arms and legs.

She blinked hard, trying to clear her vision.

Images swam into sharp focus, then drifted out again.

Her head was throbbing, but when she flexed her fingers she realized that there was no paralysis in her limbs.

She was tied to a chair.

The body of Graham Brown had been wrapped in some sheets and rolled to one side of the basement.

Ronni could see the blood soaking through the linen around his head. Towels had also been wound around the pulped skull, but they too were heavily stained with crimson.

To her right, Donna Freeman was also bound securely to a chair, her head lolling onto her chest.

Ronni wasn't sure whether the girl was still unconscious or dead.

Carl Thompson was seated opposite her.

There was still tape across his mouth, muffling his grunts of anger and fear.

Every now and then he would lurch violently against the rope that held him so firmly.

Ronni watched him impassively.

George Errington was standing behind him holding a pair of pliers.

So too was Harry Holland.

Jack Fuller gripped the .38 in his left hand and one of the chisels in his right hand.

'All you needed to do was keep out of the way,' Fuller told her.

Ronni looked briefly at him, then across at Thompson.

'Well, now you can watch,' Fuller continued.

He nodded towards Thompson and George Errington slipped the pliers over his index finger as far as the second knuckle.

Ronni shook her head.

Errington pressed down on the pliers and severed the finger with ease.

Ronni screamed.

Thompson roared his agony into the gag.

Harry Holland repeated the process with the youth's other hand and two digits lay like bloated, bloodied worms on the stone floor beside him.

Thompson strained against the ropes like a man in an electric chair. His eyes were bulging insanely in the sockets. The veins in his neck and temple throbbed so powerfully they threatened to burst.

Ronni tried to turn her head, but Fuller gripped her hair and forced her to watch.

'You should be thanking us, Ronni,' he hissed. 'Remember who he is.' He nodded towards Thompson. 'Remember who they all are. The ones who killed your father. Thank us.'

Two more of Thompson's fingers were cut off.

Ronni wanted to scream, but all she could manage was a low whimper.

Tears were coursing down her cheeks.

'Why don't you just kill him?' she shouted.

'That's not what we intended. I explained that.'

Holland and Errington moved with disconcerting speed and efficiency.

Just the little fingers and the thumbs now remained on Thompson's hands. His struggles had become less frantic. It was as if the pain had sapped his strength. He only moved sporadically now, driven by the pain rather than anything else.

His thumbs were cut off and Ronni saw the blood spurt furiously from the stumps.

Thompson slumped backwards, seconds from oblivion.

Harry Holland struck him hard across the face, shocking him back to consciousness.

Thompson's eyes rolled in the sockets, but Holland hit him again.

'Don't pass out, you bastard,' the older man snarled.

Donald Tanner stepped forward and, at first, Ronni couldn't see what he held in his hand.

Only when he lifted it before him did she realize it was an open razor. The fluorescents glinted coldly on the polished steel.

'Blind him,' said Fuller quietly.

Again Ronni screamed.

Tanner raised the sharpened metal and moved closer to Thompson, who was frantically trying to jerk his head left and right.

George Errington grabbed him and held him still.

Tanner had the blade inches from the youth's left eye.

He rested the cutting edge against Thompson's cheek.

A single tear ran down his face and puddled on the blade.

Tanner moved it closer to his eye.

From somewhere above them, there was a hammering sound.

It grew louder.

120

ANDY BANGED HARD on the main doors of Shelby House.

When no one came, he banged harder.

The sound reverberated through the building.

If he banged long enough and hard enough then someone, he reasoned, would answer.

Another twenty seconds and he stopped.

There was no sound from the other side of the door.

No footsteps.

No key turning in the lock.

There was a security camera above the door and Andy stepped back to ensure he was visible to whoever might be looking out.

He hoped it was Ronni.

He banged again and waited.

Still nothing.

'Hello?' he called, pressing his face against the doors.

Silence.

'Ronni?'

If she heard him she didn't answer.

He stepped back again and almost slipped in the blood.

The blood. You've got to get inside. Find out what the hell is going on. The old people might need help.

He banged again.

In the basement, no one moved.

It reminded Ronni of some kind of bizarre waxwork tableau.

Different expressions etched onto each face.

She couldn't see her watch, but she guessed it must be well past one in the morning.

She, like the residents, wondered who was knocking at such an hour.

The police?

Why should they be?

A parent of one of the missing kids?

Why would they come *here* to search for their offspring?

Then who?

Tanner kept the open razor inches from Thompson's eye.

Errington retained his grip on the youth's head, peering at Ronni through the one remaining lens of his spectacles.

There was more banging.

Ronni felt something cold thrust against her cheek and realized it was the barrel of the .38.

Simultaneously, Helen Kennedy began to unfasten the ropes that held her so tightly.

Upstairs, the thumping on the main doors continued.

Leave it. Call the police.

Get back in your car and find the nearest phonebox.

Call them.

Something's obviously wrong. Badly wrong.

Andy stepped back and looked first at the doors, then again at the security camera.

He stroked his chin thoughtfully.

Someone would have answered by now.

Wouldn't they?

A member of staff.

One of the residents.

Ronni.

What if they were too afraid to open the door? After everything that had happened, it'd be understandable.

But whoever checked the security monitor inside would

be able to see him. If Ronni was watching it, she'd see it was him.

So why didn't she come?

'Don't call here again, it disturbs the residents.'

Again her words echoed inside his head.

But so too did the words of the doctor who'd rung the house.

'I haven't been able to reach your wife . . . I've tried a number of times . . .'

Andy spun round and prepared to walk to the car.

As he did he heard movement on the other side of the main doors.

121

Ronni turned the key in the main doors of Shelby House and peered out onto the porch.

She managed a smile when she saw Andy.

'What the hell's been going on here?' he wanted to know, wondering why she didn't open the door wider. He could barely see her through the tiny gap between door and frame.

'Why are you here, Andy?' she asked, trying to keep her voice even.

'I was worried about you. The hospital rang and said—'

'Is my dad all right?' she interrupted.

'That's what they rang about. He's out of the coma. He's improving. They tried to contact you, but they said there was no answer.'

She squeezed her eyes tightly together. The colour, drained from her cheeks long ago, seemed to return briefly.

'Let me in,' he said.

'I can't,' she snapped.

'Why not?'

'The residents. You'll wake them.'

He regarded her through the crack in the door. 'What's wrong, Ronni?' he asked.

She looked at the floor.

'Ronni.'

'Nothing. Nothing's wrong,' she said, a little too quickly.

'What about that?' He pointed to the trail of blood, noticing that it continued beyond the door into the building itself.

'There was an accident,' she told him.

'Who got hurt?'

Again she looked at the floor. 'Andy, I—'

She started to push the door shut.

He put his foot against it, like some overenthusiastic doorstep salesman.

'Andy, please, just go,' she said imploringly.

'Tell me what happened here.'

'Just go.'

Again she tried to close the door.

Again he blocked it.

'Ronni, for Christ's sake. If there's been an accident let me call for help. Who got hurt?'

'It's been dealt with.'

They faced each other in silence.

'Why are all the lights out?' he said finally.

'The residents are sleeping. You'd better go before you disturb them.'

'Just tell me what's been happening. Have those fucking kids been back here?'

She swallowed hard.

'Ronni?'

'Go now, Andy,' she urged. 'While you still can.'

He looked puzzled. 'While I still can . . . ?'

The door was suddenly wrenched open.

For fleeting seconds he wondered who the figure was standing behind his wife.

Wondered what he was holding.

Jack Fuller lifted the .38 into view and aimed it at Andy's head.

'Get inside,' the older man snapped.

Andy looked at Ronni and saw the blood on her face and clothes.

'What the fuck *is* this?' he demanded. 'What happened?'

'If you don't do as I say, I'll kill both of you,' rasped Fuller. He pulled back the hammer of the pistol and the metallic click sounded like thunder in the silence.

122

As the door was locked behind him, Andy didn't know what to focus on first:

The trail of blood that led from the entrance all the way down the corridor . . .

The bruised and bloodied features of his wife . . .

Or the gun pointed at his head.

The gun. How fucking stupid did that sound? The gun.

He looked at Jack Fuller.

The gun being held by the resident of Shelby House. The gun being held by this man who was living out his last years in an old people's home.

The gun.

Andy looked at his wife waiting for her to burst out laughing.

Surely, any moment they would both start and let him in on this joke.

Wouldn't they?

There were a couple of fluorescents glowing in the ceiling and, as he walked, Andy could see the blood glistening in their cold light.

The trail led towards another open door at the end of the corridor.

It was towards this that he and Ronni were being forced.

All the other doors on either side of the walkway were firmly closed.

'What's going on?' he asked finally.

'We had some trouble,' Fuller said flatly. 'We've been dealing with it.'

'Who got hurt?' Andy enquired, nodding towards the blood. 'And what happened to your face?' He looked at the cut above her eye, the blood that had congealed on her cheek and chin and the dark bruises that had mottled her flesh.

'A boy was killed,' Ronni told him.

Andy swallowed hard. 'Who killed him?' he wanted to know.

'No one killed him,' snapped Fuller. 'It was an accident.'

'Was it one of the kids who've been causing trouble here?'

'One of them,' Ronni said quietly.

'You know about our problems then, Mr Porter?' Fuller observed.

'Ronni told me.'

'Did she also tell you that the same children were responsible for putting her father in hospital?'

Andy looked at Ronni in bewilderment.

She nodded in affirmation.

'And one of them got inside here?' he persisted.

'Three of them,' Fuller told him. 'Go in.' He nodded towards the basement door. 'Have a look.'

Andy looked at Fuller.

Then the gun.

And finally at Ronni.

At her injuries.

'Who did that to you?' he asked, reaching out to touch her face.

'I fell,' she told him, sniffing back tears.

'Did you do *that* to her?' Andy rasped, turning to look at Fuller. 'If you did, I'll—'

'What, Mr Porter? *What* will you do? Don't threaten me. You're hardly in a position, are you?'

Again he nodded towards the basement door.

Andy glanced at the blood on the frame and the threshold, then stepped through.

He looked down into the subterranean room.

It was like looking at a scene from a nightmare.

'Oh, Jesus Christ,' he whispered.

123

'THEY DIDN'T GIVE us any choice.'

Andy walked slowly down the basement steps, Jack Fuller's words reverberating around him.

'They killed my wife,' Harry Holland added.

'They've been punished for what they did,' George Errington said flatly.

Andy gazed at the body of Graham Brown lying prone on the cold floor, blood still seeping from his shattered skull. Then he glanced at the unconscious figure of Donna Freeman, still tied to the chair, her dishwater-blonde hair matted and tangled, her face and chest splashed with crimson.

Carl Thompson looked at him warily, the tape gag still firmly in place across his mouth.

Andy saw the bruises on the boy's body. The cuts and grazes on his face.

He looked at Ronni as if wanting confirmation that what he saw before him was real and not the product of some fevered dream.

So many questions crowded his mind, but he seemed incapable of giving them voice. Besides, where the hell would he start?

'I tried to stop them,' Ronni said softly.

Fuller grinned. 'That's a lie and you know it, Ronni,' he chided. 'You helped us. How else could we have kept them here for so long?'

'And no one would have blamed you,' Harry Holland offered. 'They're the ones who almost killed your father.'

Again Andy looked at his wife.

She shook her head.

'Why didn't you just call the police?' he wanted to know.

'Because the police wouldn't help,' Fuller snapped. 'We've been through all this.'

'So now what?' Andy asked.

Donald Tanner produced the open razor.

'Watch,' said Fuller.

Tanner lifted the blade so that it was level with Thompson's right eye.

'What the fuck is he doing?' Andy gasped.

Ronni could only shake her head.

Errington gripped Thompson's head to prevent him moving.

Tanner brought the blade closer and prepared to cut; one single horizontal slash that would slice the eyeball cleanly in two.

The blade sparkled under the cold white light.

'This is justice, Mr Porter,' Fuller said flatly.

Tanner steadied himself.

'No!'

The shout came from Andy.

He launched himself at Tanner and crashed into the older man, the impact causing him to drop the razor.

The two of them slammed into Thompson, who fell backwards, smacking his head hard against the floor.

George Errington stumbled away from the tangle of bodies.

Ronni spun round and struck at Fuller's face, the sudden movement catching him unawares. She connected with his lower jaw and saw him stagger backwards.

Andy was on his feet by now, hurtling after her as she ran for the stairs.

'Go!' he roared behind her, aware of the residents moving towards them.

Colin Glazer swiped at him with one of the Stanley knives and Andy felt something cold slice into the skin of his upper arm.

Ronni was halfway up the stairs now.

Andy followed.

He stumbled close to the top, fell to his knees.

Ronni was already into the corridor beyond.

Andy clambered to his feet and prepared to follow her.

The roar of the .38 was deafening in the subterranean room.

Andy felt as if he'd been hit by a red-hot hammer.

The heavy-grain bullet caught him in the back, tore through his lung and exploded from his chest carrying a flux of blood, sputum and pinkish-grey gobbets of lung tissue with it, some of which spattered Ronni.

She spun round and saw him hit the ground.

Saw the look of shock and pain on his face.

Saw the blood pouring from the wound.

He tried to crawl.

She tried to drag him.

The blood was spreading around him like ink soaking into blotting paper.

Every time he tried to breathe, she could hear a wet gurgling noise.

It took her a second to realize it was coming from the wound itself.

A second longer to realize that his riven lung was filling with blood.

He would soon drown in his own life fluid.

She looked beyond him, down into the basement.

Fuller was moving steadily up the steps.

No hurry.

No urgency.

Andy tried to speak, but blood filled his throat and spilled over his lips.

He sounded as if he was gargling.

Then Ronni saw the key.

The basement key.

Still in the lock.

She snatched at it.

Fuller saw it too.

He raised the .38 and prepared to shoot her.

Like a dog.

She slammed the door shut.

Locked it and slid the key into her pocket.

From inside, she heard furious shouts.

Then the first thunderous impact against the door.

She knew she didn't have long.

124

'ANDY.'

She gripped his hand tightly.

His eyes were open, but he didn't seem to see her.

His lips fluttered soundlessly.

Ronni slid her hands beneath his armpits and tried to lift him. The movement made him groan with pain and she thought about leaving him where he lay.

'Get up, Andy,' she begged.

He coughed and bright red blood sprayed in all directions.

He pushed against the slippery floor, desperate to haul himself upright, desperate to help her.

The pounding against the inside of the cellar door grew louder.

She knew it wouldn't hold them for long.

They had a hammer. Chisels. A bolt-cutter.

The door would not present too much of problem for them.

And once they emerged, Jack Fuller still had the gun.

The thought of the weapon seemed to spur her on and she kept hold of Andy, ignoring the blood that stained her blouse and skirt.

She found reserves of strength she didn't know she had and she half-carried, half-dragged him along the corridor, his legs sometimes giving way.

'Get the police,' he gasped thickly.

He slid to the floor and she tried again to pull him, but he shook his head and tried to crawl on all fours, like some stricken animal.

A cow on its way to the slaughterhouse.

He forced himself on, his hands slipping in his own blood.

She was aware of movement to her right.

Barbara Eustace emerged from the day room, the wheels of her chair slipping in the blood.

Ronni looked at the older woman.

Barbara glanced down at Andy. At the blood. At the pallor of his skin.

For precious seconds no one moved or spoke.

They held each other's gaze.

'Don't try to stop me, Barbara,' Ronni hissed.

Andy groaned in pain.

Barbara manoeuvred herself back into the day room and pushed the door shut.

Ronni sprinted off towards the downstairs office.

From behind her there was a shriek of splintering wood.

A panel of the door exploded outwards into the corridor.

Then another.

She saw hands fumbling through the gap, reaching for the lock.

Searching for the key.

Blows began to rain down upon the lock itself.

Andy was still crawling along, head bowed, blood spilling from his nose and mouth.

She dashed into the office and snatched up the receiver.

Jabbed three nines and waited.

In the corridor, Andy groaned and fell forward, his lips quivering, his eyes now barely open.

A voice answered on the other end of the phone. *'Which service do you require?'*

'Police and ambulance! Hurry!' Ronni shouted into the receiver. 'Shelby House Residential Home. Quickly!'

She dropped the receiver and ducked out into the corridor and knelt beside Andy.

Again she squeezed his hand.

'Get out,' he said, his voice barely audible.

'I'm not leaving you,' she told him.

He saw the fire in her eyes.

When he tried to breathe it felt as if someone was sitting on his chest.

It was a terrifying feeling. Like drowning.

He began to shake uncontrollably.

'Hold on,' Ronni said imploringly.

At the far end of the corridor there was another thunderous explosion.

She realized Fuller had shot the lock off.

The basement door opened.

The residents emerged into the corridor.

125

Ronni looked at each of them in turn.

Donald Tanner had retrieved the open razor and now brandished it before him.

Colin Glazer held the clawhammer.

George Errington one of the chisels.

Harry Holland the bolt-cutters.

Even Eva Cole and Helen Kennedy had Stanley knives in their liver-spotted hands.

And, leading them, Jack Fuller walked purposefully along the corridor, the Smith and Wesson .38 revolver gripped in his fist.

'The police are on their way,' Ronni called defiantly. 'I called them.'

'You're lying,' Fuller said challengingly.

'Am I?'

He continued to advance.

'If you're going to kill me you'd better do it now, Jack, before they get here.'

The knot of muscles at the side of Fuller's jaw pulsed.

'You've got one bullet left,' Ronni told him. 'I know that. I remember. You said that only three of them were live. You used one on the basement door. Another to shoot Andy.' She looked down at her husband. He had slipped into unconsciousness. 'That's one left for me, Jack,' she continued. 'Use it now.'

Fuller stood a few feet from her and aimed the pistol at her head. 'I thought you would have understood, Ronni,' he said quietly. 'We *all* did.'

'Understood what, Jack?'

'What we've done. What we *had* to do.'

'We trusted you, Ronni,' Harry Holland added. 'Especially after Janice died and then, with what happened to your own father . . .' He allowed the sentence to trail off.

'They'd made us prisoners here,' Fuller hissed. 'Terrified of every night. Wondering what they were going to do next. And now, when the police come, they'll make us prisoners too. Like you, they won't understand what's happened here.'

'Jack, people have died,' Ronni said, tears trickling down her cheeks.

'Don't you think we know that?' Fuller snarled. 'One of them was one of us. And no one cared. No one *cared* except us. No one helped us so we helped ourselves. And now what have we got to look forward to? Prison?' He shook his head. 'I was a prisoner for four years of my life, Ronni. I won't be a prisoner again. I know you can't understand. No one can unless they've had *their* freedom taken from *them*. It's the most precious thing in the world. I won't lose it twice.'

Ronni closed her eyes.

Waiting for the bang. The explosion from the .38's barrel that would end her life.

It never came.

She opened her eyes again.

Fuller had pushed the barrel of the pistol into his mouth.

There were tears in his eyes.

She screamed his name.

He pulled the trigger and the thunderous blast eclipsed every other sound.

The bullet tore its way through his head, splintering bone and pulping brain with ease.

For fleeting seconds, it looked as though someone had detonated a charge inside his skull. Portions of the cranium rose on a huge gout of blood, propelled by the heavy-grain slug.

Fuller toppled backwards, his own blood mingling with that of Ronni's husband.

The corridor looked like an abbatoir.

As if a spell had been broken, Helen Kennedy dropped the Stanley knife she'd been holding.

So too did Eva Cole.

Helen began to weep softly.

Eva pulled her close.

Ronni looked at the other residents.

At the clawhammer still held by Colin Glazer. The open razor Donald Tanner brandished.

The bolt-cutters.

The chisel.

Glazer dropped the hammer, turned his back and headed off towards the day room.

The others merely stood where they were, looking down at the body of Fuller.

Helen was still crying.

Ronni still gripped Andy's hand.

As she felt for a pulse she heard a far off siren drawing nearer.

126

SHE WATCHED THE blue lights turning silently in the night.

Ronni stood outside Shelby House gazing blankly at the emergency vehicles parked in the drive.

A WPC had draped a blanket around her shoulders about five minutes earlier, but the chill of the night still seemed to penetrate to the bone.

One police car and an ambulance had arrived to begin with.

Four more had since joined them.

Uniformed men and women walked back and forth over the gravel drive from their vehicles carrying things, making notes.

Every now and then, Ronni heard voices from inside Shelby House.

Once, when she turned, she saw flashbulbs exploding just inside the main entrance.

'Mrs Porter.'

The voice startled her and she turned to see Detective Sergeant David Marsh standing there.

'Are you all right?' he asked softly.

She nodded. 'You haven't got a cigarette, have you?'

Marsh dug in his jacket pocket and offered her a Rothmans. She jammed it between her lips and he cupped his hand around the tip as he lit it for her.

She drew hard on the cigarette.

'How's my husband?' she wanted to know.

'The paramedics have been attending to him. They said he'll make it. Are you going with him to the hospital?'

'If I'm allowed to.'

He nodded. 'I'll need to take a statement from you soon,' Marsh said almost apologetically.

'I understand.' She blew out a stream of smoke. 'What about the residents?'

'They're giving statements now.'

Ronni was aware of him looking at her.

'What I've seen in there,' he began. 'It's unbelievable. I've never seen anything like it before.'

'Join the club.' She took another drag on the cigarette, then dropped it to the ground. It hissed on the wet grass. 'What will happen to the residents?'

'That's not for me to say until we know all the facts.'

'And what about me?'

'Don't worry about that now.' He shrugged, turning back towards Shelby House.

'The worst thing is, I understand why they did it,' she said softly.

'If it's any consolation, so do I.' He wandered back up the steps and disappeared inside the building.

Ronni stood motionless for a moment.

When she saw two paramedics emerging from the main entrance pushing a collapsible gurney between them, she rushed across.

Andy was lying beneath a blanket, an oxygen mask over his nose and mouth, a drip attached to his right arm.

His eyes were closed.

'Is he alive?' she asked.

'Yes, but he's lost a lot of blood,' one of them told her, pulling open both rear doors of the nearest ambulance.

'Is he going to die?'

The paramedic shook his head.

She watched as they lifted the gurney into the emergency vehicle, then climbed in after them.

One of the men closed the doors and banged on the side of the cab.

The ambulance moved off up the gravel drive towards the road.

Ronni slid a hand beneath the blanket and gripped Andy's hand.

She sniffed back tears.

One of the paramedics was writing something on a chart. The other was bending over Andy, adjusting one of the leads taped to his chest. His wound had been dressed, but Ronni could still see blood seeping into the gauze that covered it.

The ambulance suddenly lurched to one side and stopped.

'What the hell's going on?' said one of the men and pushed open the rear doors.

He found the driver kneeling beside one of the front tyres.

Ronni also stepped out into the night.

'Bloody tyre's blown,' said the driver angrily. 'No wonder, is it?' He held up a piece of jagged glass he'd pulled from the torn rubber.

There was more of it scattered across the driveway.

'It looks like a broken bottle. How did you miss it when we arrived?' asked one of the paramedics.

'It wasn't *here* when we arrived,' the driver snapped.

Ronni walked past the two men into the street, glancing right and left.

It was in the shadows opposite she saw movement.

Two small shapes.

Both on bikes.

Kids. They couldn't have been more than eleven or twelve.

One of them was drinking from a bottle of Sprite.

As Ronni watched, he drained the last dregs, then they both cycled towards her.

Only when they were four or five yards away did she realize what was happening.

The empty bottle hurtled in her direction, missed by a foot or so and shattered on the pavement.

Ronni moved back, her body quivering, her eyes fixed on the two boys.

'See you around,' shouted Terry Mackenzie.

'Yeah, you *and* those old cunts,' Liam Harper echoed.

They disappeared into the darkness.

Ronni stared after them.

'Little bastards,' rasped the voice of one of the paramedics, appearing beside her. 'Are you all right?'

She continued to stare into the gloom.

'I'll bet they were the ones who put the glass across the drive,' the paramedic muttered. 'What do you *do* with kids like that?'

Ronni didn't answer.

. . . A PENSIONER WAS hounded to death by a gang of children, who waged a terrifying hate campaign against him.

The hate campaign escalated until gangs of youths aged between ten and fifteen gathered outside the house every night.

The man's son said, 'My father would still be alive today if police had taken action earlier.'

Express, 30 March 2000

CARRY ME THROUGH tomorrow, guide me along the way,
If this is the youth of tomorrow,
I'm running the other way . . .

Queensrÿche